Praise for

A *BookPage* Best

"Dazzling." —**Marilyn Stas**

"Terrifically entertaining." —**Adam Woog, *The Seattle Times***

"[Siri] is the most wonderfully human of heroes . . . *I Shot the Buddha* will delight readers with a taste for Siri's mystical side . . . [It] has a chewy heft, in the fine tradition of its 10 siblings: history, geopolitics, chromatic characters, genus loci, the human condition, and the pilgrim's progress—and love."
—***The Christian Science Monitor***

"Filled with magic and quirkiness . . . A madcap and international caper." —***Ellery Queen Mystery Magazine***

"Cotterill spins another quirky, entertaining mystery in his 11th Dr. Siri novel, *I Shot the Buddha* . . . [His] twisty mystery plot will entertain readers while his cast of eccentric characters charms."
—**Shelf Awareness**

"Highly unusual and immensely appealing."
—***Alfred Hitchcock Mystery Magazine***

"Stunning . . . This series offers unfailingly satisfying reading, especially so for the glimpses we get into the still-revolutionary characters of Siri and Madame Daeng, both bursting with caustic wit and adventurous spirit." —***Booklist*, Starred Review**

"Cotterill excels in the portrayal of potentially serious and momentous topics with lighthearted humor, imbuing his characters with grace and empathy in the midst of a particularly difficult chapter of Southeast Asia's history."
—***BookPage*, Top Pick in Mystery**

"Highly entertaining . . . Cotterill's subtle humor, coupled with the charm of his leads, will likely trump any discomfort with scenes with supernatural elements, even for readers who disapprove of such in their whodunits." —***Publishers Weekly*, Starred Review**

I Shot the Buddha

I Shot the Buddha

COLIN COTTERILL

Published by
Soho Press, Inc.
227 W 17th Street
New York, NY 10011

Library of Congress Cataloging-in-Publication Data

Cotterill, Colin.
I shot the Buddha / Colin Cotterill.
1. Paiboun, Siri, Doctor (Fictitious character)—Fiction.
2. Coroners—Fiction. 3. Laos—Fiction. I. Title
PR6053.O778 I4 2016
823'.914—dc23 2016003707

ISBN 978-1-61695-829-9
eISBN 978-1-61695-723-0

Printed in the United States of America

10 9 8 7 6 5 4

For their invaluable help in this venture
I should like to thank the following: Laurie, David,
Ouayporn, Lizzie, Danielle, Leila, Dad, Brother John,
Tony, Rachel, Robert, Bambina, Miki M., Paul N., Elliot,
and for the patience and love of my dear wife, Kyoko.

A mental health warning: Through necessity this edition is heavily spiced with supernatural elements. For those of you who prefer your mysteries dull and earthly, this is not the tome for you. Don't say I didn't warn you.

TABLE OF CONTENTS

1

Goodnight, Ladies

It was midnight to the second with a full moon overhead when three women were being killed in three separate locations. Had this been the script of a film, such a twist of fate would have been the type of cinematic plot device that annoyed Comrades Siri and Civilai immensely. In their book, coincidences came in a close third behind convenient amnesia and the sudden appearance of an identical twin. But this was real life, so there was no argument to be had.

The first woman died. She was elderly, was in bad health, and was an alcoholic. But it wasn't angina or alcohol that killed her. It was a sledgehammer. For much of her life she'd scratched a living repairing clothing on an old French sewing machine. When her hands weren't shaking she didn't do such a bad job of it, and hers was the only functioning sewing machine for a hundred kilometers. There was a time when she'd divide her income: half for food, half for rice whisky. But she figured rice whisky was rice, right? What was the point of paying twice for rice?

She had papayas and bananas growing naturally around her hut, so, although she spent much of her day in the latrine, she decided she got enough nutrition for someone who wasn't expecting to grow. From then on, every kip she made taking up or taking down the hems of *phasin* skirts was spent on drink.

And that night, that cloudless full moon night, she lay pickled on the bamboo bench her father had made with his own hands and she fancied she could see Hanuman's face in the moon. And then a shadow fell across it and for a second she saw the only love of her life, then a smile, then a sledgehammer.

A second woman died. She had bathed from a bucket of rainwater behind her hut and washed her hair with a sachet of the latest Sunsilk shampoo, a free sample from the company. She was still wearing her damp sarong and deciding whether to keep it on and say, "Ooh, you caught me by surprise," or to put on her yellow sundress, the one he'd mentioned made her look sexy in the light of her little wax candle. She'd climbed the bamboo ladder, creaked through the open doorway and across to the wooden potato box where she kept her clothes. She was changing—she'd decided to go for the sundress—when she heard another creak on the balcony. Her dress was only halfway over her head. She struggled to pull it down. Her Vietnamese driver beau had come early, although it was odd she hadn't heard the truck pull off the road.

"Give me a sec," she said. "I'm half naked. You've spoiled the surprise."

The footsteps creaked behind her, and she anticipated the feel of his hand on her suety breast. But she hadn't anticipated the knife. From the tiny naked candle flame she could see the glint of the blade. She watched frozen as the tip entered her belly and the hilt twisted left and right the way the samurai killed themselves in the movies she used to love so much before they closed down the last cinema.

A third woman died. This was obviously a bad night to be a woman. There are illnesses that make you feel like death but are unlikely to dispatch you there. There are illnesses that are unpleasant but not necessarily uncomfortable, yet without the right treatment at the right moment you're gone as quickly as a sparrow in a jet engine. Hepatitis falls into that latter category. You think you've got the flu, a few aches and pains, no energy, so you sleep all day waiting for it to pass. Then you wake up, and you're dead.

But she'd awoken to see the nice old doctor sitting beside her sleeping mat. He'd given her some pills, and she'd thanked him and fallen back asleep. But the next time she woke it was night and a big old moon was smiling through the window. She felt so well she even considered getting up, giving her stiff legs a walk around the hut. Perhaps a little skip or two. But she opted to stay there beneath the mosquito net where she could imagine dancing at the next village fete.

The moon carved out shapes in her little room, grey shades. Boxes full of memories of her eight children, taken every one of them by violence or disease or flashing colored lights in big cities. Of a husband who never really liked her that much, who fathered their eighth child, then stepped on an unexploded bomb that took out half the buffalo and all of him. On the walls hung pictures of ancient royals and an old calendar. And there in a blurry corner at a low table the kindly old doctor sat mixing some more medicinal compounds.

"I'm feeling much better already," she said.

But he didn't respond. She heard the last swizzle of liquid mixing in the glass and the old doctor walked on his knees to the net. He was between her and the moon the whole time so she couldn't see if he was smiling. She recalled he had a nice smile. With his left hand he held out a glass containing a few centimeters of cloudy liquid. It seemed luminous in the rays of the moon. With his right hand he pulled up the netting so he was inside with her. He gently lifted her head just enough that she could drink the medicine. There was a smell of incense about him. She thanked him and the last memory she would ever have was of a kindly old doctor in the robe of a monk.

2

Three Isms (Two Weeks Earlier)

There was the question of appropriateness. Should Dr. Siri Paiboun and his wife, Madam Daeng, have been attending a Party seminar that condemned the pagan rituals of spirit worship? It was particularly inapt given the doctor had become prone to vanishing from time to time and his wife had grown a small but neat tail. She had not yet mastered the art of wagging. It was true that no third party had witnessed these supernatural phenomena so there was always the possibility the couple had become dotty in their dotage and were given to hallucinations. But there was no denying the clunky wooden chair was playing havoc with Madam Daeng's backside or that she would periodically squeeze the hand she held and look to her left to be sure there was still a doctor attached to it. These were odd times in the People's Democratic Republic of Laos, but there were few times that could boast normality.

The seminar, as well as this tale (not tail), came about due to an uncomfortable conflict that had arisen amongst the three *ism*s: Buddhism, animism and Communism. Those who preferred their public forums free of hocus pocus needed not attend. But it was undeniable that even into the fifth year of socialist rule, the *phi*—the spirits of the land and the air and those that resided inside folk—were the only authorities peasants in the countryside could count on with any certainty. The *phi*'s growing influence was a bother to the still fledgling government. In its attempt to do away with the wizardry that had seeped into Buddhist practices, the government had all but wiped out Buddhism completely. By the end of 1979 there were no more than two thousand active monks in the country, down from ten times that number when the reds took over. Temples were being used to store grain or host re-education courses for doubting officials or as long-term accommodation for the homeless. With no organized religion to fall back on, and with uninspiring local cadres representing Vientiane, a good number of rural folk were reanimating pagan gods and seeking advice from spirits. Assuming, that is, that they'd ever really stopped doing so.

According to the Ministry of Culture, this increasing addiction to the occult was unacceptable. Senior Party members were told categorically not to be seen partaking in the rituals of mumbo jumbo. This presented problems as their wives were sometimes spotted sneaking out of the house before dawn to give alms to the monks who had survived the purge. Perhaps the maids of ministers were not discouraged from refreshing the flowers and soft drinks that adorned the spirit houses, or from burning incense at the family altar. In the ill-conceived words of senior Party member Judge Haeng, "A good socialist does not need to believe in the phantoms and freaks of folklore or religion because he has Communism to fulfill every need."

But both the judge and Dr. Siri had other things on

their minds as they sat listening to the Party's bureaucratic attempts at exorcism. The previous evening they
had received a visitor both men had believed, and wished,
to be dead. He had first arrived at the crowded grand re-
opening of Madam Daeng's noodle shop, lurking in the
shadows of the riverbank opposite. Siri's dog, Ugly, had
felt the need to single out the uniformed figure and stand
on the curb, barking in its direction. Odd, that.

In the light from the only firework to be had at the
morning market that day—a Shanghai Golden Shower—
Siri had clearly seen the face. There was no doubt. Nor
was the doctor surprised on the morning of the seminar
to have been approached by the little judge, his acne twin-
kling like festive lights. He dared not look into the doctor's
bright green eyes when he spoke.

"Siri," he'd said, "I was . . . umm . . . visited again last night."

"I expected so," said the doctor. "Me too."

"Well, what . . . I mean, what should we do?"

"We? I'm a retired coroner and noodle shop proprietor.
You're head of the public prosecution department. You're
in a much better position to do something."

"Don't be ridiculous, man. You know we don't have a
protocol to deal with . . . with . . ."

". . . ghosts?"

"Whatever you choose to call it."

This was not the first time they'd discussed the matter.
They'd had a similar conversation a week earlier. At an
interminably long workshop on Marxist economic policy,
out of boredom and devilishness, Siri had nudged Judge
Haeng seated beside him.

"You'll never guess who I woke up next to this morning," said the doctor.

"I hope she was much younger and better looking than your wife," Haeng replied, hoping to be offensive.

"There is no woman better looking than my wife," said Siri. "It was actually Comrade Koomki from Housing."

Siri knew how the judge would detest such a notion. Comrade Koomki from the Department of Housing had been incinerated in the fire that leveled Madam Daeng's original noodle shop. He had been up to no good, of course, and few people felt sorry for him. But he was unquestionably dead.

Siri was used to visits from the other side. "Step overs from limbo," he called them. He saw spirits everywhere he went. It was a curse he bore. But he rarely discussed such matters, particularly not with Party members. One of the numerous things socialists did not understand was the interplay of dimensions. But there was something about retirement that made a seventy-five-year-old doctor deliberately cantankerous. He'd expected the young man to snort through his nose and reprimand him with a motto, but instead, the judge had turned the color of sticky rice.

"Siri," he'd whispered, "I saw him too. I looked out of my window last night, and there he was, clearly visible in the light from the street lamp."

Siri was surprised not that Haeng had seen a spirit, but that he would admit to it. Clearly the judge had been far more traumatized by the visit than the doctor. During the ensuing hushed conversation they'd attempted to piece together why they might have been singled out for such visitations. The chat had brightened an otherwise gloomy afternoon for Siri. It was the first time the two had cooperated with any enthusiasm, but they had not been able to arrive at a common denominator. Neither man had rendered Koomki unconscious. Neither had lit the fire that consumed him. And neither had danced on his grave.

But now, here it was, a second coming, and not a clue as to the apparition's intent. Siri's train of thought was shunted into a siding by his wife.

"How long do we have to stay here?" she asked, not bothering to whisper.

"You said you wanted to come," he reminded her.

"It was a mistake. I suppose I was hoping for something more . . ."

"Interesting?"

"Rational."

"Well, that's a good one. A rational argument at a Party seminar. Next you'll be expecting cold beer and popcorn during the interval."

"You know what I mean. They advertised it as an appraisal of the coming together of politics, religion and the occult in modern society. But all they're doing up there is belittling the worship of anything that doesn't have a hammer and sickle stuck on it. Do you see any monks or shamans on the stage? No. Is there—?"

Madam Daeng was interrupted by a spindly man in a rumpled denim shirt who turned around in his seat and said, "Some of us have come here to listen to the learned senior comrades."

He turned back as if that were enough said. Daeng leaned forward and flicked his ear. It was a large ear and a powerful flick, so the sound echoed around the auditorium. Some other nearby seat-fidgeters could not resist a chuckle. The kerfuffle temporarily disturbed the speaker at the podium, who lost his place in the script and read the same sentence twice. It was unquestionably the high point of the afternoon.

The big-eared man leapt to his feet, leaned over his chair and took a swing at Madam Daeng. Even in her sixties, Daeng, an ex-freedom fighter, had remarkable reflexes. She ducked beneath the blow and the man was thrown off balance. He fell over the back of the chair and landed on his nose at Siri's feet. The result was a most bloody triumph for the old folk. To his credit, Siri did offer the man his handkerchief to stem the bleeding.

"I would have had him with an uppercut to the throat if he hadn't lost his balance," said Daeng.

It was late at night, and the gang was sitting around the tables in her noodle shop. The curfew was currently nine o'clock, but the two officials who patrolled Fah Ngam Avenue were sitting on the riverbank opposite enjoying a bottle of Siri's rice whisky. But even without the incentive it was unlikely they'd have filed a complaint about this gathering. A quick reckoning with an abacus would have put the accumulated years of Communist Party membership in that room at over a hundred. Inside Madam Daeng's open-fronted noodle establishment sat senior police inspector Phosy; his wife, Nurse Dtui, cradling their daughter, Malee; ex-politburo member Civilai Songsawat and his best friend, Dr. Siri; and, finally but not least, retired morgue assistant, Mr. Geung.

Nurse Dtui repositioned Malee on her ample lap and raised her drink in support of Madam Daeng's boast. Mr. Geung, who often caused them to forget that Down syndrome was a disadvantage, laughed and raised his own glass of deathly sweet undiluted orange cordial. He called it the hard stuff.

"I would have had him with a karate chop first." Siri huffed. "Who's to say I wouldn't have saved your life? Without my background in martial arts, who knows what damage he might have done you?"

"I hardly think sitting through a dozen Bruce Lee films would be considered martial arts training," said the old politburo man. "If skills were that easily transferred, I'd be dancing like Fred Astaire by now."

Siri and Civilai shared a world of references that meant nothing to their Lao family and friends. A world of European culture nurtured in their study years in Paris. An addiction to cinema and literature and music that recognized no ideological borders. A knowledge of art and philosophy that often had them volleying jokes back and forth like tennis players in a stadium full of bemused professional wrestling fans.

It was Saturday night and there was nothing more enjoyable than an after-hour's get-together at Madam Daeng's. In fact there was little else to do in Vientiane, even on a Saturday. The city was shuttered and dusty, and the only sounds at night were the burping of frogs and the occasional crashing of hopes. The few foreign diplomats and aid workers and experts had their favorite haunts, but they were beyond the budget of common Lao folk. And not even rubles or dollars or dong could keep a place open beyond curfew. These were the years when housebound family members got to know each other very, very well. But even if there had been cinemas or television or late-night concerts, Madam Daeng's noodle shop still would have been the location of choice for these old friends.

"If I'd been there I would have arrested you," said Inspector Phosy, already pink of cheek and slurring.

"For what crime?" asked Siri.

"Annoyance," said Phosy. "There were you two yakking away behind some poor comrade who was just trying to enjoy the seminar."

"Well, there's grounds for arrest right there," said Siri. "Enjoying a seminar? The man couldn't have been in his right mind. He's the one who needs locking up."

"As I see it," said Civilai, a pork spring roll protruding cigar-like between his teeth, "you and Daeng were attending the meeting voluntarily. What does that say about your sanity?"

"I was there under duress," said Siri.

"He was not," said Daeng. "Since he retired, he's been so desperate for entertainment he forces me to the most obscure public gatherings. No topic is too dull for him. He scours the cremation schedules for ceremonies to attend."

"Only people I knew," said Siri.

"He rides his bicycle around the streets hoping to encounter a skirmish," she continued. "To rescue a cat from a tree. To step in on a domestic tiff. You're bored, Siri."

"You're boh . . . boh . . . bored, Comrade Doctor," Mr. Geung agreed.

Siri looked at him in dismay. "How can you say such a thing?" he asked. "Am I not your foreman? Do I not supervise your daily activities here at the restaurant? Do I not negotiate a fair salary for you from your employer?"

"Perhaps Madam Daeng could do without a shop steward stirring up her employees," said Nurse Dtui.

The look between the two women told Siri they'd been discussing his role in the new restaurant behind his back. He'd reluctantly convinced himself he could be of service there. But if he were to be honest he had no love for the place. He had no skill for producing noodles, so it was just as well his wife was a genius in the kitchen. He had no patience with accounting, no creativity in marketing, no tolerance for spending long hours in one spot. After a lifetime of travel and excitement and near-death experiences, a noodle shop was heaven's waiting room for someone like Siri. And everyone there knew it.

Ever diplomatic at the domestic level, Civilai changed the subject.

"What news of your zoo?" he asked.

"The Zoo" was the latest nickname for Siri's official government residence, which he had illegally stacked with homeless people. As a government official, Siri had been forced to accept the cement box home out past the That Luang monument. As he was cohabiting with his wife above the restaurant he'd opted to fill his official residence with the needy. It was this blatant disregard of Party guidelines that had first introduced Siri to Comrade Koomki of Housing, the same Comrade Koomki currently haunting Judge Haeng and himself for no apparent reason. Even in such a claustrophobic bureaucracy it was unlikely a second-grade clerk would pursue revenge for regulation infringement from the grave.

"A bit of excitement from Noo," said Siri.

"He's the monk, right?" said Phosy.

"A Thai forest monk to be exact," said Siri. "On the run from the Thai military."

"What exactly did he do?" Dtui asked.

"A general decided he liked the look of a tract of land and felt it would make a pleasant holiday resort. Problem was, right up until the day the bulldozers arrived it had legally been national parkland. Overnight the paperwork rewrote itself, and General Disorder was the legal owner of said land. Enter Noo: Itinerant monk. The Lone Ranger. Sworn to protect virgin jungles. He riles up the locals, blesses a couple of two-thousand-year-old trees, wraps them in saffron, declares the area a holy ground and buries himself up to his neck in front of a backhoe. Impressive front-page news photo."

"And, of course, the general's arrested, the land reverts to national park and Noo gets the Magsaysay Award for community service," said Civilai.

"Almost," said Siri. "Most of the annoying trees had already been cleared to make log cabins, and the resort opened three months later. Up-and-coming teenage idol Pueng Duangjan cut the ribbon. The provincial governor gave a thank-you speech. Then Noo was arrested and charged with treason as a Communist insurgent."

"And he's not?" asked Phosy.

"A Communist? Yes. Of course he is. But nobody ever asked him. And none of his actions were politically motivated. But the timing was bad. They'd just started their mop-up operation of Thai Communists living in the northern jungles along the border. Since they lost Khmer Rouge support, the reds were surrendering in hordes. Big propaganda program in the media. Military telling everyone the evil Commies will sneak into their bedrooms at night and eat their children and stamp on their puppies." Ugly the dog snarled from beneath Siri's table. "Nobody's safe until the bad guys are eliminated. That sort of thing. You just have to hint someone is a Communist and public opinion hones the guillotine."

The two curfew officers had arrived and were waiting politely for a natural break in the conversation.

"What is it?" said the inspector.

"We'll be off now," said one, swaying gently at the open shutter.

"We'll be back in an hour," said the other. "And we'll expect you to observe the curfew regulations." He hiccupped. "Or there'll be trouble."

"Right," said Madam Daeng. "Are you boys sure you'll be all right on that motor scooter?"

"Yes, thank you, Auntie," said the first. And the two walked across the street arm in arm in search of their vehicle.

"So," said Dtui, "how did forest monk Noo escape?"

"They locked him up in the provincial jail instead of the military stockade," said Daeng, who loved nothing more than hijacking her husband's stories. "In Nan Province he was something of a folk hero. So security wasn't that strict. They even let him go to collect alms in the mornings. Made him promise he'd return."

"And not surprisingly one morning he didn't come back," said Siri, "reminding them all that monks are just men with very short haircuts."

"And here he was on your doorstep," said Civilai. "Giving free illegal sermons in your backyard."

"How did he know where to come?" asked Phosy.

"Troublemakers have a sort of homing device," Civilai told him.

"So what's the excitement at the Zoo?" asked Dtui, her baby shifting happily in her sleep like a piglet scratching its back on short grass.

"I don't really know what's happened," said Siri. "One of the housemates delivered this note today."

He pulled a neatly folded paper from his top pocket.

"Dear Brother Siri," he read, "I have been entrusted with a top-secret mission that I feel is safer not to discuss in this note. Should anything go wrong you can find further information in the place Imelda Marcos keeps her favorite shoes."

"A bit melodramatic," said Civilai.

"Shoes," said Mr. Geung, laughing on a sugar high.

"Who's Imelda Marcos?" asked Phosy.

"I haven't got a clue," said Siri.

3

The Sedentary Nomad

Siri didn't know whether Noo's failure to return home that night constituted something *going wrong*. It was the first time the forest monk had failed to unroll his sleeping mat on the back porch of the house. But as he was supposed to be an itinerant monk, perhaps that was nothing to worry about. Siri had mentioned often that, for a nomad, Noo was somewhat sedentary. In fact he hadn't gone anywhere at all since he arrived from Thailand. So perhaps this was just a reaction. A coincidence admittedly that it should occur right after the note, but either way Siri chose to ignore the first night's absence and wait to see what transpired.

It had been harder for Siri to ignore the memoranda from Judge Haeng's office. There had been three all before coffee time. He rode his bicycle along an empty Samsenthai Boulevard with Ugly trotting along beside him. The doctor had grown up in the East and left for France in his teens. Upon his return he'd spent all his time as a field surgeon in the provinces. He'd first arrived in the capital with the revolutionary forces in '75. Much of

the population had fled, and the businesses closed down.
He'd only ever seen downtown as a ghostly, empty place.
He couldn't imagine the heady days of clubs and drugs
and prostitution, of American dollars and tourists and
shops with interesting items for sale. He turned onto Lan
Xang. It was midmorning and he and Ugly were alone on
the Champs-Élysées de Laos.

He found the judge cowering in the corner of his office
at the Ministry of Justice. When Siri threw open the door
Haeng squealed and dropped the file he'd been pretending to read.

"Siri," he said, "what kept you?"

"Lack of interest," said the doctor.

The judge rose stiffly from the bathroom stool. He
walked like an elderly gentleman to his desk and collapsed
onto his padded vinyl chair.

"Do not make light of this," he said. "I haven't slept for
two nights. I'm considering visiting a psychologist I know
in Hanoi."

"That's a long way to go to be told you're a nutcase."

"Am I, Siri? Am I mad?"

"Without question."

"But you've seen him too."

"And you think I'm sane?"

Siri looked at the young man and against his better
judgment felt a little sorry for him. His crinkled white shirt
was stained with sweat at the armpits. His black plastic belt
had skipped one or two loops. He looked even more ratty
than usual.

"I heard the rumors, Siri," he said. "Your dealings with
the afterlife. Of course I believed none of it."

"Very wise."

"But here . . . here I am seeing a man who is without question deceased."

"What if it's someone pretending to be Comrade Koomki?" said Siri. "Someone dressed up like him, made up?"

"So I first thought, Siri. That's what I desperately wanted to believe."

Siri sat on the edge of the judge's desk waiting for a "but."

"But he changes size, Siri," said the judge. "Sometimes he's a midget. As you remember that was his normal stature. Then next minute he's as huge as a weather balloon. Then he fits in a toothbrush mug."

"You appear to be seeing a lot of him."

"He's everywhere, Siri. Everywhere I go. What does he want? Why me?"

Siri could see the judge was in need of mystic logic.

"Very well," he said. "I have learned from experience that there are two major reasons for a haunting. One is revenge. The other is unfinished business. Now, unless there's something you haven't told me about your relationship with Comrade Koomki, I don't see he'd have reason to terrorize you."

"I did think poorly of his height."

"I don't think that's enough. In fact, if revenge is what he's about, he'd have far more cause to make my life miserable than yours. But all I get is the occasional sighting."

"So it's not revenge?" said the judge, somewhat relieved. "Then you think there might be something he had no time to complete before . . ."

"It's possible."

"And how would we know what that is?"

Siri's first reaction to that question should have been, "I'll ask him." But the doctor still lacked a number of fundamental shamanic skills. Basic communication with the afterlife was one of them.

"You handled his paperwork," said the doctor, "and his personal effects. Nurse Dtui did the autopsy on what was left of him. Phosy wrote the crime sheet. I suggest we go through all the notes to see whether we did anything wrong. Whether we missed anything important. Something's disturbing our Comrade Koomki. I get the feeling he won't be able to move along until we discover what that was."

◙   ◙   ◙

"What did you put for question five hundred and forty-one?" Civilai asked.

"Elvis Presley," said Siri.

The old boys had finished their canned pilchard baguettes and were kneeling on the grass using their log as a desk. There were over six hundred questions in the Department of Religious Affairs' affiliations questionnaire. As that was hard work, they'd decided to answer only the prime numbers.

"Do you think anyone's going to answer this thing honestly?" Siri asked.

"No. It's probably a trap. I mean, page one: 'your religious convictions.' Who's going to answer that truthfully? The Party line is that everyone's free to worship whoever or whatever they like. But there they are re-educating the novices to preach Marxist Buddhist theory: the Lord Buddha as a pioneer of socialist ideology. No religion in the elementary school curriculum. All mention of Buddha removed from the national anthem. Monks are told to teach the masses how to economize and increase productivity. They've become morals police, telling common folk to live virtuously within the system. In every other country the monks are chastised for engaging in politics. Here they give out gold stars for it. People have forgotten what Buddhism's all about. And nobody's sure whether to admit to being a believer."

"What did you answer for that one?" Siri asked.

"Agnostic," said Civilai. "What? Don't look at me like that. I am."

"I believe you," said Siri.

"I don't . . ."

"I know."

"You are too."

"That's true."

"Then stop making that lemony face," Civilai said. "Your childhood in a temple. Your Christian college education. Your reawakening as the descendant of a shaman—a bone reader. All that but it's still brought you to the same conclusion. There is nothing you can worship with any certainty. Nothing you can honestly believe in."

Siri put his hand to his chest where the white amulet hung from his neck. It was nothing elaborate: a lump of roughly chiseled stone. But there was no question that, without it, he would have been long dead. Without the blessings and shamanistic hogwash that had somehow been sucked into it, the malevolent spirits of the forest, the *phibob*, would have tricked him out of his life. They had the power. Hollywood was misinformed about evil spirits. A ghost cannot attack a human being. It cannot hurl rocks or strangle a virgin in her sleep or reach into a man's chest and pull out his heart. But, through trickery, it can convince a man his heart is being crushed by a giant naga, that he can jump from a tall building and swim through the clouds, that a cocktail of bleach and toilet cleanser tastes every bit as good as whisky soda with a pinch of lemon. That's how real spirits operate, by taking over the mind. And of all the Lao and Thai demons that did mischief on a daily basis, none were as spiteful as the *phibob*. And for some reason probably tied to the deeds of Siri's ancestor, Yeh Ming, the doctor was on their Most Wanted list.

"What did you answer for that one?" Civilai asked.

"Tree worship."

"That's the spirit."

They had no intention of submitting their questionnaires. The exercise was just another way for two retirees to kill an afternoon in Vientiane. They'd be fined, of course. Their names would be submitted to the disciplinary council—again—but they'd had a couple of hours of fun. For two active minds rapidly going to seed, stimulation was vital. Siri was envious of his friend's contacts in high places who sent the old man on missions. Siri was such a troublemaker nobody sent him anywhere. He'd never have been offered the post of ambassador to Kampuchea, as Civilai had. Siri wouldn't have been sent to the Chinese border to avert an invasion, although he went anyway. As he often said, "Diplomacy, like Catherine Deneuve, has never found its way into my bed." Civilai, although riddled with prejudice and racism, was a natural peacemaker. Siri could start a riot in an aquarium.

They folded their questionnaires into the shape of

boats, stood shin deep in the coffee-esque Mekhong and launched them on their way to the Khong Falls. The water was cool, and the mud oozed delightfully between their toes.

"Are you really going tomorrow?" Siri asked.

"Absolutely," said Civilai.

"You don't think it's a bit . . . ridiculous?"

"Not at all. It fits. This is Buddhism theme week: you and your seminar, a lost monk, a religious affiliation questionnaire. It's karma. I can't believe there's so much cosmic energy around."

"But . . . ?"

"I know. Very silly, but it's all expenses paid, and I can take Madam Nong for a change. And we have to ride this 'be nice to Thailand' wagon while it's in the depot. We agreed to follow up on the claim. We haven't been to Pak Xan for a while. And it's not a big deal. Evidently, the Buddhist council in Bangkok investigates a dozen claims a month. They have a budget for it. Are you sure you don't want to come? You could be my caddy."

"Positive."

"But what if it's really Him? How exciting would that be? One of those classic 'I was there when . . .' moments."

"So did this fellow actually write in to say he was the next Buddha?"

"No, evidently it was just 'known' instinctively. A bit like Jesus in the stable. Except this is a Buddha in a mechanic's yard."

"Will you be taking any precious metals as a gift?"

"No, but we'll take a couple of nice bottles of red. They have spectacular river clams down there."

"Why are they sending you?"

"All part of the recent Thai delegation's cross border détente bill of fare. They're doing favors for us. We're doing favors for them. Our politburo doesn't want to be seen supporting a Buddhist mission, but they want to keep the Thais happy. They don't want Siamese wandering around the countryside of Laos, but they do not want to send a senior Lao official either, so they had to find someone decommissioned and neutral."

"And you're neutral?"

"I have splinters from all the fence sitting I do."

"And you think two days will be enough to assess the veracity of the claim? In fairness, I don't see you as even remotely qualified to decide."

"Who is? It's a once-in-two-thousand-years appointment. I imagine it'll have to be a sort of gut reaction. You remember, little brother, that buzz we got standing beside Castro?"

"That was a celebrity thing. Fan worship."

"Well, magnify that by a trillion. That's how it'll be. Were I to wear socks, if he turned out to be the next Buddha he would knock them off."

"Wait, two thousand years? Wouldn't that make the previous Buddha a brontosaurus?"

"Now, Siri. Let's not get embroiled in the dubious myth of evolution. What's relevant is that I'm getting a generous per diem and a chauffeur-driven vehicle. It'll be like a second honeymoon, and I know for certain the villagers will go out of their way to entertain us. After all, if they want their boy to be recognized they damned well better butter me up."

◙ ◙ ◙

The national police headquarters moved around a lot. It was currently housed beside the Ministry of Interior at Ban That Foun. The joke going around the city was that the place saved a lot of money on furniture because most of the detectives couldn't find their own offices. Inspector Phosy sat at an old desk with its registration number stenciled on the front. The government discouraged attachments, so everything in his office had belonged to other people before the move. There was nothing new in the airy room, nothing without quirks. The metal cabinet screeched, the chairs wobbled and the desk lamps flickered like stage lightning. Even the framed pictures of the beloved leaders wore the ghosts of goatees and horns half-scrubbed from the glass.

Until the ever-impending arrival of two new recruits, Phosy was the head and sum total of the Political Malfeasance Division, the department that specialized in crimes against, rather than by, government officials. When Siri arrived the policeman was two squares away from solving a Rubik's cube, which, experts would tell you, was the furthest possible point from success.

"If you're busy I'll call back later," said the doctor from the open doorway.

Phosy looked up. "Damn. How did you find me?"

"Your hand-painted name plaque over the door. Very nice. You've all got them, I see."

"Even the secret police department," said Phosy.

"I went there first. There's nobody there."

"Oh, they're there all right. You just wouldn't know where to look. Take a seat."

Siri chose a chair behind one of the empty desks. He looked out the window. The view was the non-rendered brickwork of the ministry building. A large lizard hung on the wall under the delusion she was camouflaged.

"How's Nurse Dtui?" Siri asked.

"Her classes at the nursing college are getting her down."

"A remarkable woman performing unremarkable feats. The teaching of advanced anatomy to buffalo girls. It's enough to drag anyone down."

Phosy poured him a cup of lukewarm tea from his thermos and delivered it to his visitor's desk. It was a routine both had become accustomed to. The old fellow stopped there often in his desperate quest for something to do. But this day he surprised the policeman with his demand.

"I have a case for you," he said.

"I'm not allowed to do requests," said Phosy.

"I know. This would be a sort of . . . hobby. Something to fill in the time before the next ministerial assassination attempt."

"That wouldn't give us very long. What's it about?" Phosy returned to his own desk and instinctively reached for a pad and pen.

"You remember on Saturday I was telling you about our Thai forest monk?"

"Noo?"

"Yes. Well, he's gone. Vanished into thin air."

"He's a wandering monk. Isn't he supposed to . . . wander?"

"Yes, normally I'd agree with you, but Noo isn't the type to just flee without telling anyone. And he's left all of his stuff at the house, some personal things."

"He's an illegal. Immigration might have nabbed him."

"I've considered that. But I don't think so. You heard his note."

"Entrusted on a top secret mission?"

"I think he's got himself into trouble."

Phosy leaned back on two legs but the chair wasn't into it. He dropped back to the floor.

"Hmm. Did you work out the message?"

"Mrs. Marcos is possibly the wife of the President of the Philippines. But as for her shoes . . . No idea. It's not something you can just look up."

"When was the last time anyone saw the monk?" asked Phosy.

"Saturday afternoon. That's when he gave the note to one of the children from the house. He reportedly climbed on the house bicycle and headed east. Mrs. Fah's kids waved him off."

"Was he robed?"

"No. He always said that saffron was like day-neon. Not too many monks on the streets after noon. No, he was in his disguise. Hawaiian shirt, straw hat and shorts. According to the kids, he might have even penciled on some eyebrows."

"Some serious undercover work. Nobody else at the house has any idea where he might have gone?"

"No. They said he'd been spending a fair bit of time with a young monk recently. Nobody knew him. He wasn't introduced. He just arrived out of nowhere a week before."

"So, temple-related intrigue. Interesting."

"You'll help?"

"Yes, Siri. I don't like the idea of good people vanishing without a trace in our city."

For once, Siri kept his mouth shut.

4

At the Whim of a Dead Transvestite

Of course throughout history husbands had been known to disappear, some permanently. But this vanishing trick invariably involved a suitcase and a vehicle. Dr. Siri's dematerializations were sudden and dramatic and most certainly of psychic origins. For the record it would help to note that the doctor hosted the spirit of a thousand-year-old Hmong shaman named Yeh Ming. The old ghost had lain dormant for most of the doctor's life, but over the past five years there had been stirrings. Siri hadn't known his parents, so the reason for this possession remained a mystery. Yet every person with true psychic abilities could sense the presence of the old Hmong. And every passing spirit latched on to the doctor like sticky weed. Although Siri had yet to learn how to communicate directly with them, he now had a collection of dissatisfied spirits loitering in his subconscious. The most annoying of these was certainly Auntie Bpoo, the transvestite fortune-teller. Even when still alive, the seer had haunted Siri with her eerily accurate predictions. Although she claimed to be a lucky amateur, it was clear she could see beyond this dimension. She knew that Siri had been cursed from birth to carry the spirit of the shaman. She knew that he had yet to master the skills necessary to communicate with the spirit world. And, when she had died, she opted to join the frustrated spirits that possessed the old coroner. She had become the shop steward for his disgruntled inhabitants. She was the medium with the most potential to guide Siri. She better than anyone else could have taught him to engage in meaningful dialogue with the other side. But Auntie Bpoo proved to be an awful roommate. She was ornery and sarcastic and uncooperative. Their communication was one-sided and at the whim of the dead transvestite. This was particularly frustrating given that while working as a coroner Siri had been closely aligned to and fascinated by the spirit world and he would have sold his ragged old soul for a sit-down chat with the departed. Instead he was a voyeur, watching the dead perform in his dreams or hearing them as background rhubarb at inopportune moments.

That was the reason he had accepted the potion from the medium in Luang Namtha on his previous trip. She'd promised him it would help him travel to the other side to spend time with the specters and the *phi*. In a two-for-one deal he'd accepted a second potion to treat Madam Daeng's arthritis. The medium had warned that there were likely to be side effects in both cases. Madam Daeng had gladly accepted hers: a tail in return for blissful pain-free days tangoing to and fro between the tables of her

restaurant. But Siri had not been so lucky. His disap-
pearances left him wedged in some dark space like a
man caught between the doors of adjoining hotel rooms.
There was no handle on either and barely enough room
to turn around. He'd tried chanting and feeling for
secret latches and using terms from literature such as
"Open sesame!" all to no avail. He felt certain the other
side was just beyond that second door but had no idea
how to travel there. Auntie Bpoo had been right. Siri
was a most pitiful shaman. But that Auntie Bpoo, she was
something else.

"Good morning, darling."

Siri opened his eyes to find Auntie Bpoo lying beside
him on a luxurious Western bed with pink sheets and soft,
frilly pillows. It was a girly bed, most certainly Bpoo's taste.
She was wearing what they used to call a baby-doll nightie
that contrasted drastically with her rugby forward's build
and military haircut. Thick makeup coagulated around
the bristles on her chin.

"No, don't try to speak, darling," said Bpoo.

Siri couldn't. He was gagged and tied to the bedstead
with black nylon stockings. To his relief, he was fully
dressed. The room was bright. Sunlight was streaming in
through the French windows. A blue and red lizard rode
blissfully on the slow-moving overhead fan.

"You know you only make a fool of yourself when you try
to speak," said Bpoo. "And anyway. I have a poem for you.
I know how you adore my poems."

Siri yanked at the nylon tethers, but he had no choice
but to listen.

Information, she began
The Invasion   Of your privacium
            You'll never see 'em
They hear   and watch ya
Each breath
To the death

            Then they've gotcha.
        Whatever
        Never trust the ghosts.
They have no scruples.

"I hope you can remember it," she said, "because I get the feeling it will be very useful for you sometime in the future or in the past. Whichever comes first. You do know you'll be out of the country, don't you? No, of course you don't. You know so little for such a learned man. Now, my miniscule one, the door's over there. Be on your way."

Siri looked toward the door then back to the transvestite. But she was gone, as were the bindings. He was alone on the bed. He tested his voice, which seemed to work perfectly.

"See? I can speak," he said, but of course there was nobody to hear.

He stood and walked to the door and stepped through it without thinking. When he realized what he'd done it was too late. One door slammed behind him, and he was stuck again in that no-doorknob space between dimensions. He knew when Madam Daeng turned to cuddle him in their actual bed he wouldn't be there. She'd assume he was in the bathroom rather than in the limbo between doors. But this time he had a voice.

"Is there anybody there?" he shouted, and knocked on the second door. His voice echoed clearly in the space but the knock made no sound. He listened. There were mutterings coming from the other side. Domestic. A radio playing. Children laughing. Some kind of machine. Perhaps a vacuum cleaner. Then an eerie silence. Then a deathly scream.

Siri waited but there were no more sounds. He was afraid the connection had been lost.

"Hello," he shouted again. "Can you hear me?"

Then came a man's voice. Not Lao. Thai.

"Who's in there?"

"It's me," shouted the doctor. "Can you hear me?"

The door before him began to open slightly. Light poured in through the crack and dazzled him. A hand dropped onto his shoulder.

"I wouldn't be surprised if they could hear you in Australia," said Madam Daeng.

He lay beside her in their bed.

"Oh, no," said Siri.

"Not pleased to see me?" she asked.

"No . . . I mean, yes, of course." He sat up and looked at the milky moon through the window. "It's just that I was close. I almost crossed over. I'm sure of it. I heard a voice."

Most wives would be woken by their husbands in the middle of the night to hear complaints about belly gas or weak bladders. Madam Daeng was not most wives and she understood perfectly. Her husband had vanished and taken one giant leap for humankind and she was proud of him. Theirs was a relationship made, if not in heaven, then at least some other unearthly place.

◙ ◙ ◙

Government workers in Vientiane were earning some seven dollars a month, so everyone took a second job. This created a sort of zombie population: sleepless people shuffling around with little time for their loved ones or gossip or political issues. If you were lucky enough to have two jobs you did both of them to half of your ability so as not to burn out. Expecting a smile from a public official, therefore, was like asking a cooperative farmer to give up a pig. Yet there was something about Madam Daeng's noodle shop that made everyone forget how depressed they were. For lunch and dinner the place was packed with people going to and from their workplaces. Mr. Geung's funny lines and Daeng's smiles and gourmet noodles at rock-bottom prices put the workers' minds in a happy place. They sat beside strangers but in the twenty minutes between putting in an order to the sound of Chinese spoons scraping bowls, they gave up their life stories and learned half a dozen secrets. It was noisy there, as a good restaurant should be. In Paris, Siri had always been bemused by the lowering of volume as the menu prices increased. He'd never been to a Michelin-rated restaurant but he imagined large rooms as silent as libraries where orders were taken in mime and soup-slurpers were thrown out unceremoniously on their derrieres.

It was so noisy in the noodle shop that Siri had to invite Judge Haeng upstairs so they could hear each other. Siri's illicit library of French classics had been consumed by the fire, so no rooms were out of bounds. The judge did take time to peruse the Thai Mekhong Whisky bikini calendar at the top of the stairs.

"It's Daeng's," said Siri.

He noticed that the judge had applied foundation to hide the dark bags under his eyes. His voice slurred from lack of sleep.

"This is everything," said Haeng, laying a pile of files on the coffee table as he sat on the wooden sofa. "And I've been through it a hundred times. The man lived alone. He had no lover, no friends and no social life as far as I can make out. He lived for his job. He was a star at Housing. He hounded out illegal squatters and had a hundred-percent conviction rate against residents making illegal alterations to their properties. From that you can deduce he was a pedant. A little creep, Siri."

Siri sat on the floor opposite the judge. "What in these files did you handle personally?" he asked.

"I beg your pardon?"

"I mean, I imagine you meted out most of the documentation to your underlings and just signed."

"Well, I . . ."

"Was there anything that you handled yourself? Something that might cause Comrade Koomki to single you out for attention?"

"No, Siri. The minister signed the document that posthumously cut him dishonorably from the list of public servants. Everything else was just general paperwork, except for the home visit."

"Tell me about that."

The judge rolled his eyes. It was a most annoying habit. "Following the police investigation," he said, "an officer of the public prosecution department visits the home of the accused to assess what property needs to be destroyed or redistributed for the good of the republic."

"Isn't that rather a menial task for the head of department?"

"Most of our officials were off with the flu. But I was curious anyway to see if there was anything to connect him to insurgents. The destruction of property is a favorite practice of cross-border terrorists. A good public prosecutor leaves no—"

"Tell me about his place."

"Nothing to tell, really. Basic. Smelled of rats. An old colonial shared house. Three families and seven single officials. Communal bathroom down the hall. Koomki lived in one room that had a tiny scullery at the back with an ancient refrigerator and a single-burner gas range."

"And you didn't take or damage anything?"

"What do you take me for, Siri?"

Siri had an answer for that but he kept it to himself. "So tell me what you did there," he said.

"Is this really necessary?"

"Do you eventually want to get some sleep?"

The judge sighed and wiped a hand over his face. "I walked around," he said. "I had to be certain the police hadn't damaged anything. It's all government housing, you see. I had to sign off on the property checklist. I put the few items that could be considered valuable in the wardrobe and locked it."

"What items?"

"An alarm clock, a transistor radio, a small brass Buddha image . . . It's all here in the invoice. It's policy to prevent robbery as best we can. There are those who prey on the dead, you know?"

"I know. Then what did you do?"

"I completed my list, turned off the light, walked into the hallway and locked the door. I put the two keys in a manila envelope and returned them to my office. Siri, this is not—"

"Describe the room to me."

"I don't see—"

"Please."

"All right. It was spartan. Bedroll against one wall, a little ripped. A towel open flat on the floor beside it. A shelf made out of river driftwood and bricks. About ten books."

"What language?"

"Thai. Mostly building regulations. Some comic books."

"Topic?"

"Childish things. Cartoon animals, little girls' adventures."

"What else?"

"Table. One chair. A box of clothes. That's pretty much all."

"Was everything neat and tidy?"

"There were odds and ends lying around. A shirt slung over the chair. A cup and a spoon on the table. A saucer beneath it on the ground. A saucepan on the range, quite clean. Its lid off and lying beside it. A jacket on a nail behind the door."

Siri closed his eyes to imagine the scene. "So nothing unusual happened during the entire time you were in the room?"

"Nothing at all. When I was walking out I heard one of the inhabitants of another room crying. A woman or a young girl. But that was none of my business."

"Did they match?"

"Did what match?"

"The cup on the table and the saucer on the floor."

"How on earth is that relevant?"

"Indulge an old man."

"I must say I didn't make a note of the design."

"Was the saucer broken?"

"No."

"What was it made of?"

"Some sort of ceramic material I imagine. I don't know. I didn't pick it up. I wasn't about to do the washing up."

The doctor put his hand to his chin like all good detectives in the films were wont to do. Mr. Geung arrived at the top of the stairs with a large steaming bowl of broth and handed it to the judge.

"I don't . . ." Haeng began, but the aroma from the bowl cut his rejection short.

"You will," said Siri. "And I don't suppose you still have those keys in your office, do you?"

◎ ◎ ◎

"We're looking for my uncle," said Nurse Dtui. "We're a little worried about him. He set off on his bicycle three days ago, and we haven't seen him since. He's senile, you know."

It was an untruthful story repeated twenty times. Dtui sat on the rear seat of the police department's lilac Vespa while Phosy played the dumb driver. Citizens were more likely to help a fat woman with a young child than a policeman. Residents would even duck into the neighbors' places to ask around.

"She's lost her uncle," they'd say. "He's quite mad," they'd say. And those days a lot of old and infirm people with nothing to do sat on their front stoops staring gormlessly at the road. So far Phosy and Dtui had three confirmed sightings of Noo the forest monk heading southeast the Saturday before. He'd set off along Nongbon Avenue and made a number of lefts and rights on small dirt lanes before arriving at the Tardeua road. He seemed to be heading away from everything. He was already two kilometers from where he'd set out and showed no signs of flagging. He clearly had an objective even though Phosy's map displayed few landmarks along the quiet road that eventually led to the ferry crossing.

A kilometer from the last sighting, just before the Australian recreation center, Phosy and Dtui struck gold. They'd worked up a thirst from the road dust so they stopped at a bamboo kiosk. The proprietor, a shorter but wider version of Dtui, sat on a stool behind a regiment of cordial bottles. The colors bore no relation to anything to be found in nature, so you tended to order by color rather than flavor. To a blind man the tastes would have been identical.

An untidy banana tree provided the only shade, so Phosy parked beneath it, and there they drank their sugary colors. The woman stared at them.

"From Vientiane, are you?" she said. Making it sound as if the city were a short flight away rather than a twenty-minute ride.

"Resident but not born there," Dtui told her. "Out on a day trip. This is a nice, quiet spot."

The woman continued to stare at them rudely. Dtui was about to tell her the story of their uncle when the woman beat her to it.

"You'd be surprised," she said.

"About what?" asked Dtui.

Malee was already buzzed from the sugar hit, so her

mother pulled the glass away. As the addiction had started to kick in, the child voiced her displeasure. Dtui took a small ice cube and put it into her daughter's mouth. It's hard to whine with a lump of ice on your tongue.

"You'd think out here in the wilds nothing would ever happen," said the woman. "I mean, there can't be more than twenty vehicles a day passing my shop. But you'd be surprised."

"Then surprise us," said Dtui.

"Right there," she said, pointing to a spot beside the road that had nothing remarkable about it. "That's where they nabbed him."

"Who?" said Phosy.

"Some poor little old uncle on a bicycle," she said.

"Straw hat? Flowery shirt?" asked Dtui.

"Yes. Looked like he done no harm to no one in his life. Just pottering along on his bicycle he was. Having a nice ride."

Phosy and Dtui stepped down from the bike and stood on either side of her.

"What happened?" Dtui asked.

The woman smiled for the first time. This was her blockbuster story, and she wanted everyone to know it.

"He was pottering along," she said.

"We know that," said Phosy.

"And the two boys was behind him on a big motorcycle. They was riding really slow, and they bumped him. Bang. No, not really 'bang.' In fact there wasn't no sound. Just their tire bumped his tire, and the old uncle lost his balance and fell off. Probably got a nasty graze from the gravel. They keep saying they're going to put a surface on this road but—"

"What happened to the uncle?" Dtui asked.

"That's just it. The boys got off their bike and went to pick him up. I'm thinking they're saying 'Sorry, Uncle,' you know? Something like that. 'You all right?' But instead they grab him really rough-like. And one of the boys looks over here at my enterprise. At first I thought he might want to buy a glass of red to revive the uncle, but afterward, I got to thinking. What if he was checking for witnesses? You see, I'm a bit short and from the road you can't barely see me behind the bottles. So perhaps they're thinking I'm off on my lunch break. I only thought that after. I've had time to think, you see?"

"But then . . . ?" said Dtui.

"But then, to my shock and horror, they punch him one in the face and drag him to their bike and squash him like in a sandwich. One of them in front, one at the back. And they drive off with him. Just like that."

"Did he put up a fight?" Phosy asked.

"No, went like a baby."

"What direction did they go?"

"Turned round and went right back the way they came."

"Were they in uniform?"

"No. T-shirts and long trousers."

"Short hair?"

"Yeah. Military types. Both of them were quite good-looking to tell you the truth. Wouldn't have minded if they'd come for a drink, if you know what I mean. Unless they were planning to kill me, of course. I wouldn't have liked that at all."

"Where's the bicycle?" asked Dtui.

"What?" Blood leaked into the woman's cheeks.

"The uncle's bicycle," said Dtui. "What happened to it?"

"Don't know," said the woman in a way that made it obvious she did.

Phosy flashed his badge, she shrugged and they all traipsed off to the woman's small hut some thirty meters from the road. The bicycle took pride of place behind a mountain of empty cordial bottles.

As Laos had no coinage, Dtui flipped a bottle top and Phosy had the honor of riding the bicycle back to police headquarters. Dtui drove the Vespa with Malee on her lap. On the way home she considered what she'd heard. Comrade Noo had been snatched in broad daylight. But why and by whom? She had a feeling her husband was about to get himself involved in a very elaborate runaround.

◙ ◙ ◙

Siri's beloved Triumph motorcycle lived under a tarpaulin in the backyard of his government-appointed house. Thanks to a little good fortune that had befallen him and Civilai during a previous case, he had a sum of money put aside. This meant that unlike everyone else he'd be able to fill his tank and go places. But the paper chain of documents needed just to pass the first police post ten kilometers from the city, and the subsequent laissez-passers to enter every town thereafter, really took away a man's urge. He wasn't the type to ride around Vientiane with his nose in the air, so the Triumph went nowhere. He did like to look at it from time to time, though.

"I'll buy it from you," said Inthanet, the old Luang Prabang puppet master.

"With what?" asked Siri.

"My fiancée has a nest egg," he said, proudly.

Siri looked at him and, as usual, could see nothing irresistible: thinning hair hanging on for dear life to a bald patch, beady eyes, a small stack of chins and a weedy frame with no arse. Yet the man was like a magnet to thoroughly passable women of all ages. It could have been explained if he were a multimillionaire, but to make matters worse, he was always broke.

"Is this the fiancée who sings ballads at the Anou Hotel?" Siri asked.

"Ah, Siri, sadly, that didn't work out. My current darling has a cattery. Siamese. Some very valuable. As soon as the Thais reopen the border crossings we have orders queued up."

"Shouldn't be long," said Siri. "Their prime minister was here last week mending fences. He and our fellow issued a joint communiqué about certain past misunderstandings along the border. I'm not sure who's courting whom but I'm sure we can expect to see a lot more Thai rubbish in the market quite soon. Get your kitties out while the coast's clear. It never lasts."

They were joined by Tong, the reformed prostitute who had become the house mother at Siri's home for strays.

"Hello, Granddad," she said, and put her arm around Siri's waist. He could smell an entire garden of passionflower oil on her.

"Isn't it about time to start coating that old motorbike with gold leaf?" she said.

"We aren't worshipping her," said Siri. "We're admiring her lines. Basking in the nostalgia of how fast she used to go."

"I suppose I can relate to that," she said. "Are you here for a house meeting?"

"No. Nothing to talk about. I'm here to see you."

"Ooh, we are honored."

"What do you know about Imelda Marcos?"

"I know she's not having my room," said Tong. "I suppose she could double up with the Vietnamese, but she has strange bathing habits."

"Actually she's the wife of . . ." Siri began.

"I know who she is. I'm just playing with you."

"Do you know where she keeps her favorite shoes?"

"Of course I do. It was in Thai Fanzine a week ago. I read it to everyone in the house."

"Was Noo here?"

"He was eating it up. He loves celebrity gossip."

"And?"

"And what?"

"Where does she keep her favorite shoes?"

The house refrigerator was a Dnepr made in the Soviet Union and barely large enough for a sad Leningrad spinster, let alone a dozen assorted squatters. Yet there was something traditionally Lao about the contents. In a shared house in the West there'd be territories. "Susan's shelf." "William's yogurt. Hands off." But the Lao fridge had no such borders. You'd eat something, and the next time you went to the market you'd buy something similar. Or you cooked for everyone and everyone went food shopping. No reason at all for heart palpitations over a missing radish. But it was a policy that made it difficult to identify anything specifically belonging to Noo.

"Imelda Marcos loves crocodile skin so fresh it almost snaps at her toes," said Tong, still quoting the fanzine article. "But, surprisingly, crocodile skin doesn't like the tropics. It goes bad easy. Smells a bit. So when you're the wife of the President of the Philippines, you probably have twenty refrigerators just for your shoes."

She stood with Siri staring into the fridge, looking for something with personality. But it was a generic food supply depot. No labels. Nothing allergy specific. No personal tastes.

"It all looks so healthy," said Siri.

"We can't afford junk," said Tong. "But Noo did have a sweet tooth."

"Hm," said Siri. "Healthy but sweet. Let's start digging."

They removed the fridge contents one by one, examining each leaf, every spring roll skin for hidden messages. Siri reached the point where he was looking for the meaning behind ingredients that shared a plastic bag or were tied together in a bundle. Then he saw the bamboo. There was one stick of *kow lahm*; sticky rice baked in a narrow bamboo tube and sweetened with red beans. The tube was sealed at each end with a wedge of banana leaf. Even before he opened it, Siri knew where he'd find the hidden message of Comrade Noo.

"There were two notes," said Siri.

He turned on the flashlight to show Daeng the first. He and Daeng had cleaned up after the evening rush and were sitting on bamboo recliners on the riverbank. The Mekhong was scarred with sandbanks that sliced the twinkly reflections from the Thai side. The only lighting Vientiane had to offer was the dim papaya glow of candles in windows here and there. The moon was late to rise. The Lao liked to say that it was probably held up by paperwork.

The first of Noo's notes was written in Thai in beautiful hand on one side of a sheet of lined paper. Siri let Daeng read it silently to herself.

Dear Siri,

This letter is probably unnecessary but in light of the commitments I've made this past week, I considered what a shame it would be if I merely disappeared. I'm sorry to have been so secretive about my past and I apologize deeply that I am sharing this information in writing and not in person. It means a lot to me that you and Daeng never pried into my past. My story is brief and its content not uncommon.

I joined the monkhood because my wife left with our daughter, to live with another man. They moved to Bangkok. My first reaction was to kill them. I followed them to the capital and traced their whereabouts. I procured a gun and lay in wait. That their movements diverted them from a fatal confrontation with me again and again could only have been fate. The endless wait allowed me time to reflect on why karma had been so biased in their favor when I was the wronged party. And one night I awoke and saw my true self as clearly as a cockroach stepping under a kitchen lightbulb. I saw all my faults and failings and I detested myself. I threw the gun into the Chao Praya River and fled to a monastery.

Twenty-five years on I am still in robes and on the road, putting myself in harm's way in an attempt to purge myself of the bastard in me. On the back of this note is an address in Bangkok. It's where my daughter lives with her family. I've had the abbot at her local temple keep me informed of her movements. At first I thought I'd like someone to tell her about the selfishly motivated good deeds I've done. But, actually, I regret that I lacked the courage to tell her I was sorry. Sorry I didn't give her a better start to her life. Sorry that I ignored her. All I want her to know is that I spent almost half my life trying to gain her respect . . . yet was too afraid to beg for it.

Daeng released a puff of air. Somewhere in the middle of the note she'd stopped breathing.

"It wasn't till I read it that I realized I'd known nothing about him," said Siri. "We'd been acquainted for almost a year but we'd never talked about his life."

Daeng took a swig of her nightcap. "So many people are congested with guilt," she said. "Clogged with secrets and unsated hatred and regrets. It's a wonder they don't burst."

"I suppose we all burst in our own ways," said Siri.

"Does it get worse in note two?"

"Not at all. He's got everything off his chest. In note two we arrive at the intrigue."

Dear Siri Part Two,

I suppose whilst in this "if something has happened to me" mode, I may as well attempt to salvage the mission I've obviously failed at. Siri, I have absolutely no right to ask you to do this, but, should insanity once again strike you, here is the plan as it stands. On the morning of the twenty-ninth of this month, at 2 A.M., I was to meet a monk on Donchan Island. Measures would be taken to neutralize the Lao sentries at that point there along the river. A small boat would come from the Thai side and take us across to a spot where a truck would be waiting for us. It would take us to Nong Khai where we'd spend the night and take the first public bus to Udon. There, a Thai delegation would be waiting for us. They would take responsibility for the monk and my task would have been fulfilled. As simple as that. I'm sorry I'm unable to

give you any more details but you have to understand
this is a vital mission. It would mean a great deal to me
if you could take it on. If you do decide to do so, I can't
offer you any reward other than the likelihood that you
will be reincarnated as the next king of Laos if you are
successful.

Daeng looked at Siri while the small flickering lights
could still pick out his smiling eyes.

"Siri," she said.

"Yes, my love?"

"You're considering it, aren't you?"

"Of course not."

"Siri?"

"Perhaps a little bit. Although there are any number of
reasons why I'd not want to come back as the king of Laos."

They sipped on their Vietnamese rum, its edge tem-
pered by a squeeze of sweet plum. In the river they saw the
silhouette of a naked man wading between the sandbanks.
Crazy Rajhid the Indian came into his own after dark,
inhabiting a world only he could see. Siri waved at him
and he froze in position. He still believed he could make
himself invisible by keeping very still.

"We can see you!" shouted Siri.

"I'd have to come too, of course," said Daeng.

"I wouldn't want it any other way," said Siri. "But what
about . . ."

"The shop? You'd be surprised what Mr. Geung has
learned to do with a noodle sieve."

Before parting company, the league of comrades had one
last afternoon meeting in the noodle restaurant. The topic

was the eerie connection: three separate missions all related to Buddhism. Dtui, delighted to be taking a week away from her deathly dull classes, would be managing the restaurant in Daeng's absence. Mr. Geung would produce the noodles. He'd already displayed his prowess that lunchtime. Some were even game to admit there was little difference between the two chefs. As Geung's teacher, Madam Daeng was not in the least offended. Mr. Geung's fiancée, Tukta, would wait tables and provide the glamour. There were still those who looked down on a Down syndrome relationship but Daeng's no-name restaurant didn't want customers like that anyway.

Before they went their separate ways, the team members summarized the status of events. Siri read them only the second note from Noo, and everyone shouted down Inspector Phosy when he pointed out the illegality and danger involved in crossing over to Thailand. He mentioned the latest river guard practice of launching innocuous-looking floating objects attached to mines.

"They put them into the river upstream," he said. "If they don't explode on contact with those illegally fleeing the country, they'll be collected in a net down river, returned and relaunched."

"Can't say I've heard any explosions," said Siri.

"And what does that mean," asked Phosy, "'the Lao sentries will be neutralized'? Eh? What are they planning to do, exactly?"

"They're Buddhists," said Daeng. "First precept: 'I undertake the rule to abstain from killing.' They'll probably just get them drunk like you do."

Phosy was in no position to argue with that.

Civilai spent most of his allotted time describing the

food he'd prepared for the weekend "picnic" he'd be enjoying with his wife. They all made light of the alleged purpose of the trip and looked forward to one hell of a good story when he came back.

The report from Dtui and Phosy was far more serious. They described the cordial seller's account of the kidnapping and the inspector's ongoing attempts to discover where the Thai monk might be held. There was no trace of him in police lockups around the city and the immigration department had categorically denied any involvement in his disappearance. Their officials had even offered to assist the policeman in the search. It occurred to Phosy that in a country nobody wanted to come to, an immigration department must have been somewhat underused.

The final item on the agenda was Ugly. Whenever they'd tried to farm him out to reluctant dog sitters, he'd escaped and caught up with his trusted master. No chain or leather bond or wooden cage had held him.

"You sh-sh-should take him," said Mr. Geung.

"To Thailand?" said Dtui.

"If that's what he wants, why n-not?"

"Because he's a dog," said Civilai. "It's not like the movies where your faithful dog helps you out of scrapes and saves your life. He'll complicate things. We have a dog-proof high fence behind our place. I'll have my housekeeper look after him. It's time to show that dog who his master is."

There came a growl from beneath the table.

5

Mellow Yellow

A lot of couples crossed the rusty metal footbridge to Don-chan Island to watch the sunset and perhaps steal a kiss or two when it was dark enough. The island, just beyond the hairy water tower at kilometer one, was a large chunk of land that had withstood years of torrents and never been washed away. The locals used it as an allotment for fruit and vegetables, so the scent of ripe tomatoes and papaya wafted around the couples on the evening river breezes. For citizens in a landlocked country, Donchan, in some small way, provided the missing awe of being surrounded by water. But Siri and Daeng weren't there to dream of romantic islands or canoodle in the semidarkness. They were there to complete Noo's mission: to meet a mysterious monk and float with him across the river.

They'd arrived before sunset so as not to arouse suspicion in the eyes of the bridge guard. There were a number of rustic homes on the island but the authorities had recently extended the curfew to Donchan. Even the farmers had to leave after dark. Siri and Daeng found a comfortable spot with a view of Thailand and watched patiently as the others left: first the families with children, then the couples, then the sad people with nowhere to go. An hour after sundown, they were alone and invisible on the dark bank of the river.

"So," said Madam Daeng, "we have seven and a half hours to kill. The mosquitoes are armed with Kalashnikov rifles, the water snakes are in search of warm dry grass and the Lao border guards patrol the island every hour after nine and arrest curfew violators. Any suggestions as to how we might fill our time?"

As always, Siri's travel baggage amounted to a small cloth shoulder bag with wool bobbles dangling from it. But everything he needed on a journey could fit comfortably into that bag. This evening it was oddly bulky. He reached into it and produced a bottle of whisky, and not just any whisky: Glenfiddich. Daeng welcomed it into her arms like a mother being handed her newborn for the first time.

"This is your plan?" she said.

"Our plan, my dear," he said, "is that we sip it sparingly. When anyone comes to drag us away he sees a feeble old couple of drunkards. We invite him to join us to celebrate our grandson's graduation from the Communist Leadership Program in Hanoi. We talk of how you were the prime minister's primary school teacher and how I, as a surgeon, saved the leg of Pornlamy Makdaeng, the Lao national center forward who went on to score four goals in the World Cup of Socialist Nations tournament semifinal. We keep talking until he's drunk and unconscious. The monk steps out of the shadows. The boat arrives. Nobody gets hurt."

"Unless, alternatively, he shoots us on sight and runs off with our whisky," said Daeng.

"In which case we should drink it as quickly as we can."

Both plans were fraught with potential disaster, but they had rice cakes and dried fish, and you certainly had to wash those down with something. They had water, but . . . well, water isn't Glenfiddich.

Four hours into the wait they'd already attained a scotch-inspired confidence. They hadn't been bitten or shot and their whispers had risen to a self-assured volume. Their laughter, even stifled behind their palms, was enough to alert the sleepiest of guards.

"We need to keep our wits about us, Siri," said Daeng. "Just in case."

"In case of what?"

"In case we lose sight of our wits." She giggled. "I love this, Siri," she slurred. "Mystery. Intrigue. I mean, noodles are fine but you can't beat a good garroting. There's nothing to compare to castrating a would-be attacker or going into a knife fight with your bare hands."

"You know we're merely escorting a monk to Thailand?"

"So you say. So you say. How do we know? We're already part of a monk-smuggling cartel. Noo's probably being tortured to give up our names. He won't hold out. There could be a helicopter landing here any second. Door-mounted machine gun, *blatblatblatblat*. Us cut to pieces. Ah, the good old days. Don't you feel that thrill of the unknown? How close we are to the edge of the abyss?"

In fact, Siri had accepted the job to overcome the boredom of domesticity. He'd not considered being cut to pieces. He knew his wife's whisky tolerance levels. She'd reach a peak of excitement then sleep like a lump of concrete for half an hour. Euphoria—concrete, euphoria—concrete, until the bottle was gone. She was a woman. She needed a good man by her side who could really drink.

Siri was drooling. He was in a long, flat, dark sleep, but still he could feel his face being slapped. It wasn't an unpleasant experience. It might just as well have been someone else's face. It wasn't the slapping that brought him around; it was the heavy weight on his chest. His eyes were hyphenated and all he could see were lights far off and a dark shape on top of him. One more slap.

"Siri, we have to go."

It was Daeng, straddling him. Slapping him. All too blurry and confusing for him to retaliate. A warm tongue licked his face. Behind the outline of his wife he made out another shape, standing. It could have been a monk . . . or a monkey or a stone statue. Beyond the shape, movement. Somewhere in the distance, a whistle.

"Can you stand up?" Daeng asked.

Although he couldn't coax the words from his mouth, he thought how he'd been standing since he was nine months old. It occurred to him he was drunk as a flock of bridesmaids. He attempted to show how good he was at standing, but he couldn't find the ground beneath him, couldn't feel his legs. Another character was helping Daeng lift him to his feet. They walked him to the water where an uneasy-looking fiberglass rowboat bobbed, no removable parts. They sat Siri on a molded seat and Daeng took up a pivotal role beside him. Scenes blurred in and out. An old monk trotting down the bank. The boatman with ping-pong paddles for oars. Daeng with their two shoulder bags around her neck. And, from nowhere he remembered the French version of "A Life on the Ocean Way." He was only one stanza into it when his wife slapped her hand over his mouth.

And they launched the tiny boat with three table tennis players looking for their balls in the black water. And on top of the water—the head of a dog. And a distant whistle. And a hand patting his back after he'd thrown up overboard. And the close-up of a floating mine on a foam raft with its Russian warning engraved on the casing. And the head of a dog.

And the head of a dog.

And the head of . . .

◙ ◙ ◙

Civilai and his lifelong wife, Madam Nong, arrived at Ban Toop just as the sun was beginning its arc to the horizon. Officially, his mission was to interview a man and test his credentials as a prospective reincarnation of the Buddha. Civilai considered it a foolish notion but a good enough excuse for a short vacation. He would write a brief report and submit it to the politburo. He'd already composed the message in his head. The government jeep had been comfortable, but the road was too unpredictable to build up any speed due to the unending roadwork. Suddenly the dirt surface would open into a gash and send the passengers' teeth into the base of their brains. So the hundred-kilometer journey had taken them the best part of a day.

Ban Toop was another flatland village surrounded by untended paddy fields. The road that ran through its center was more like a dried-up riverbed. The houses on either side seemed to have been erected in a hurry many years before but never renovated. The gardens were unflowered and the dogs unfed. It was a thoroughly disappointing place. Civilai had been expecting flags, at the very least, a street tarpaulin under which village officials had sweated throughout the day in anticipation of the arrival of an ex-politburo man. There was no school band, no jasmine lei on a silver platter, no accidental *nop* from the village headman (the prayer-like gesture had been banned but country folk tended to forget its banishment). He would have settled for a little respect, recognition, interest, anything. But there was nothing.

The jeep pulled up in front of an incongruous French colonial house. It was the only structure with any permanence in the village. Such buildings throughout the country had been claimed by the government and crammed with families who watched as the house deteriorated around them. Yet this place stood proud. The roof tiles were all in place, and none of the shutters hung like broken wings from the windows.

Civilai sent in the driver to ask where they might find the local cadre and the reception committee. He returned with the news that the headman and most of the senior villagers were off at a cockfight in the next village. The woman he'd spoken to had no idea where the guests might stay as there was no guesthouse, and, as far as she knew, nobody had been alerted there would be visitors. She suggested they go back to Pak Xan and spend the night there.

"Well, they obviously don't know we're here," said Civilai in a huff. "They must have got the days mixed up. We'll wait."

Madam Nong squeezed his hand. "Lai, they don't want us here."

"Certainly they do."

"Let's take our picnic to Pak Xan like she says and check in to a nice guesthouse and have a glass of wine to wash the road from our throats."

"I can't start a mission by losing face," he said.

"You're not. Nobody knows you're here. They haven't even seen your face. We can return tomorrow, refreshed, and they'll all be embarrassed about today and your face will be intact."

It annoyed him that his wife was so often correct in her appraisals. Reluctantly, he agreed to head back the way they'd come onto the main road for the trip to the nearest town. Pak Xan, at the confluence of the Mekhong and Xan rivers, was what you might expect from a highway truck stop. It clung to the road like barnacles on a rope. It had no noticeable downtown and no street lamps. The jeep's headlights cleared a path through the darkness to a small shanty of huts down by the Xan River where the driver knew of a guesthouse. It was the only two-story place around. It had no sign and no semblance of activity but after one or two inquiries they discovered it had Thai beer chilling in a tin bathtub of cold water, so they stayed for the night.

◙   ◙   ◙

Siri awoke from a deep Glenfiddich sleep with a surprisingly clear head. So clear, in fact, that it contained few recollections of the previous night. Apart from flashes of a boat trip, his memory had been erased. Now here he was flat on his back on one of three wooden benches in a public gazebo. The sun was low, so the roof overhead did nothing to block its rays. A torn advertisement for a moneylender was nailed to a post. It was in Thai. He was in a foreign country. This was Nong Khai, the little Thai Nirvana where tourists came to eat river fish and drink Mekhong whisky and look across the river at Laos. There was nothing exotic about the scenery on the far bank. No buildings were visible apart from the concrete ferry port, which was closed more often than it was open. But still they'd take photos of themselves dangerously close to an evil Communist country and buy souvenirs that said MADE IN LAOS even though they weren't.

On the next bench, Madam Daeng lay on her side, smiling in her sleep. And opposite lay an elderly monk, so motionless he might have been a corpse. Ugly, the uninvited dog, none the worse for wear from his swim, lay on the wooden boards below Siri.

The doctor eased himself into a sitting position and smiled at the familiar bone joint percussion. He squinted against the dazzling sun to make out the scene across the street. A shirtless coach boy was hosing down an orange bus and scrubbing it with a broom. He sang as he worked: Thai pop, no less off-key than the original.

When Siri stood the boards creaked and Ugly's eyes sprang open. In seconds the mutt was on his feet, his deformed tail wagging, his tongue unfurled. All he ever needed was a morning pat on the head and his day was made. Siri collected his thoughts. Here they were, three Lao with no legal documentation, but, he hoped, enough savvy to get away with it. Thais of his generation often traveled without identification just to maintain their independence. Every country had its stubborn old coots. And no checkpoint police were going to harass an old couple and a monk. The elderly still commanded respect from their juniors. This was the ploy they'd be pursuing.

He stood over his wife; so beautiful. Her hands cupped beneath one cheek like a Botticelli cherub. Her eyelids twitching. He imagined a marvelous film being projected onto them from the inside. He never once failed to admire Daeng of a morning, to take in the glory of her. He was a lucky man.

He shuffled over for a closer look at the monk. The old man lay on his back, sleeping with his palms together like the stone tomb carving of a French knight. His breath was barely perceivable. His expression was blissfully sweet. But beyond the smile, Siri saw something surprising. Civilai had always claimed to have trouble identifying monks. He said with soldiers he had no problems. Even in the same uniforms with the same haircuts they had character. But monks, he said, were like penguins. Once the eyebrows were gone, he couldn't make out one from the next. But Siri didn't have such face blindness because he always looked first into a man's eyes. It was there you could find his true identity. It was in the eyes that all the joys and scars floated like lotus leaves just below the surface of a pond.

But this monk did not need to open his eyes because even in sleep Siri recognized him. He'd seen the face in photographs in the Pasason Lao newsletter. He'd run his fingers over the likeness carved in miniature on good-luck talismans. This was the Sangharaj: the Supreme Patriarch. The head honcho of Lao Buddhists was unconscious at a Thai bus stop and Siri had been charged with his well-being.

"Heaven help you," said the doctor.

◙ ◙ ◙

Inspector Phosy had been handed two uninteresting but complicated cases by his superiors at police headquarters, which made time juggling a little difficult. He had to either pursue inquiries into the disappearance of Noo on his own time or find some way to have the new cases overlap. And that's exactly what happened at the Ministry of the Armed Forces. Phosy had been looking into accusations that an army officer had made lewd advances to the wife of a central committee member. As it turned out, the issue was not the officer making approaches to the wife, but his rejection of impolite suggestions from her. Phosy was at the ministry to see whether the military board would be prepared to issue a mild statement of censure against the officer—one that would not appear on his record but would placate the wife. Phosy had been afraid there might be some posturing by the top brass. But as it turned out they considered the matter so trivial he was allowed to dictate the statement himself. They didn't even ask the typist to use carbon paper. A passing general signed the document, and it was all over.

The military building was by far the most imposing of all the ministries. From the street it looked like a first-class hotel in one of the stuffier Communist countries. Even on official business it was hard to get into. However, once in, nobody stopped you from wandering the corridors. So Phosy wandered and considered his next move. He'd come up blank with the police and immigration departments so the army was the next logical port of call. The question was which of the many doors he should step through to get answers. After ten minutes he settled on one. It was one of the few closed doors and was marked appropriately: ARMY AND POLICE LIAISON DEPARTMENT. He'd had no idea such a relationship existed. His tour of the building had given him time to formulate a plan. He knocked before stepping inside.

The man sitting at the desk looked like a cartoon character. He had a head and face that could have been drawn with nothing but circles and curved lines. The dots of his eyes nestled either side of his nose facing one another. When he said hello, Phosy looked around the room to see whom he was talking to. Those eyes never once settled on the inspector.

"How are you, comrade," said Phosy. "I'm—"

". . . Inspector Phosy Vongvichai of the political malfeasance division," said the man. "Of course you are. I confess you're something of a hero of mine. Excellent job on that business up in Luang Namtha."

It's difficult to remain humble after such an introduction, but there was something uncomfortable about both the speed with which this stranger recognized Phosy and the fact that he knew about his cases. The policeman could imagine the man poring over his photograph, memorizing the details in his file. He wondered whether "liaison" might not be just a synonym for "spying." There was no salute or handshake. Phosy sat on the sofa opposite and studied him. From the dowdy uniform he knew the man was a corporal. He ate too much junk and didn't exercise enough. He hadn't started to shave yet, and he'd removed his boots behind the desk and was working in his socks.

"What can I do for you, Inspector?" he asked.

"You could tell me your name," said Phosy.

"Oh, you're right. Sorry about that. I'm Corporal Suwit. Now . . . ?"

Phosy wondered how far the army spy network reached and decided to tell a lie. If that worked, he'd tell a few more.

"I'm hunting down a witness to a very serious crime," he said.

"I'm fascinated," said the corporal, not looking remotely fascinated. "What was the crime?"

"I'm afraid I'm not at liberty to discuss the case," said Phosy. "The investigation is ongoing. But, let's say it would help us to no end to get a statement from this witness."

"I understand. But why do you think the army can help in this matter?"

"Well, Corporal Suwit, between you and me, my witness was last seen in the company of two junior army officers."

The corporal smiled and the cartoon was complete. He was missing his two front teeth.

"I assume you have their names," he said.

"No. Haven't got that far yet. Still early days in the investigation."

"Then, how do you know they're army?"

"They were recognized."

"By whom?"

"Can't tell you that either, I'm afraid. But not to worry. Once I've learned the names and we've identified their unit I'll be back to liaise heavily."

The gap-toothed grin still hadn't left the corporal's face, but it was humorless. Phosy stood.

"I can't tell you how pleased I am to have discovered this department," he said. "As you know, there are so often misunderstandings between the military and us. I'm delighted that your ministry's aware that we aren't at all stupid."

"I don't . . ."

"And vice versa, of course. The liaison of two very bright groups of people with networks." He stepped up to the desk and put down a small square of paper. "In case you don't have it already, this is my contact number. It might take a while for the telephonist to walk over to my office to get me. You just have to be patient." Phosy smiled and walked to the door. "It's been a real pleasure," he said.

"Of course I'll share whatever information we find," said the corporal.

"Of course."

Phosy showed himself out and smiled as he walked down the concrete staircase to the ground floor. Often, the most valuable information a policeman can gather comes from things unsaid: from questions that were not asked. Phosy had not given or been asked for the identity of his missing witness.

◙ ◙ ◙

There were live chickens in rattan cages on the bus and angry river crabs in buckets, even a pig trussed up and crammed under a seat. So it was surprising the driver should lean back in his seat and shout, "Get that bloody dog off my bus!"

The passengers turned around expecting to see something rabid and flea-bitten, but saw only Ugly sitting politely beside Siri, licking his paw. The last thing the Lao couple wanted was a scene. The whole point was to blend in, so Siri and Daeng kept their mouths shut. The coach boy walked to the back of the bus with a metal crank iron in his hand and raised it to the dog. Most Thai mutts, familiar with cruelty, would have cringed and retreated at that point. But Ugly looked up at the boy and snarled. The boy feigned to strike. Ugly didn't flinch. Siri was poised to pounce on the boy. It wasn't until everyone on the bus had made a personal wager on the success of either the dog or the youth that the Sangharaj stood and whispered something in the boy's ear. The young man looked as if the world had split apart at the equator. He walked to the driver and passed on the message. The driver looked in his rearview, spat out his toothpick, laughed and threw the bus into gear.

The old Sangharaj had opted to sit two seats in front of his bodyguards. None of the other passengers dared sit anywhere near him, so the rear of the bus was occupied by only the Lao invaders. Siri was surprised at how little the man spoke. They were twenty minutes from Udon and the monk hadn't uttered a word or responded to questions. In fact he'd said more to the coach boy than he had to Siri, and he wouldn't even tell them what words of wisdom had saved the dog. Daeng and the doctor attempted to engage him but he merely stared out the window. Daeng said he hadn't uttered a word all morning on their way to Nong Khai, nor in the boat. Siri turned to Daeng and shook his head. "I mean, what good is there in spending a night with a supreme patriarch if he doesn't tell us anything?" he said, loud enough for the old monk to hear him. "At the very least you'd want a philosophical line or two to share with your friends over a drink. 'So the Sangharaj says to me . . .'"

But this was a particularly mellow, absolutely mum monk. Not even the retelling of the best of Civilai's colorful jokes could break through the old man's field of inscrutability. With the motorcycle dealerships of Udon in sight, Siri was about to concede defeat when the Sangharaj turned around in his seat and in a crunchy voice said, "They told me this Dr. Siri was a wise one. But all I see is a drunkard. The fool before me couldn't find a thank you in a glass of ginseng juice."

And with that he returned to his sightseeing. Siri turned to Daeng and raised his eyebrows.

"Well, that certainly put you in your place," she said with a smile. Like Siri, Daeng was no serious believer. She'd seen too many men commit atrocities in the name of their religion to take any of them seriously.

"Was that profound?" Siri asked his wife.

"It was perfectly clear to me," said Daeng.

"Liar," said Siri and he spent the remaining minutes of the journey trying to make sense of the sentence.

After bus trips it was customary in Thailand for all the passengers to rush to one of the public latrines. This was also the first thing on the mind of the monk, who joined the stampede the moment he stepped down from the bus. Siri and Daeng had assorted malfunctioning parts but bladders were not amongst them. They stood in the bus terminal attempting to identify a delegation. They were to be met there at nine. It was nine-fifteen. What exactly would a delegation look like? Once identified, should they ask them to sign some sort of receipt? They'd never been couriers before. In a way, Siri was disappointed the mission had been so uneventful. A little weird, perhaps but not exactly an adventure.

Like Laos, Thailand was currently under the influence of a military government. But while the Pathet Lao made no promises their national status quo would ever come to an end, numerous Thai coup leaders were keen to hand over power to a trustworthy civilian government as soon as it was safe to do so. This process involved the officers resigning from the military, putting on suits and stepping into lucrative ministerial roles. For some reason, the population never seemed to notice or care. In many ways, politics in Thailand had greased the wheels of the Communist takeover in Laos.

"Look over the river," they'd say. "Do you want to live in a system like that?"

Thailand served to remind the Lao of what life was like under the rule of sleazy politicians.

Given the high-profile army presence in the northeast, perhaps it wasn't such a surprise when an armored car drove into the bus station and parked with one wheel on the curb. Three very smart officers in white dress uniforms stepped from the vehicle and straightened their jackets. They were scanning the crowd for somebody.

"I bet they're our boys," said Daeng. "Let's go say hello."

The officers looked right through the old couple when they approached.

Daeng sidled up to the best-looking and most senior officer and, in a stage whisper from behind her palm, said, "Are you fellows here to pick up a parcel from Laos?"

The officer looked down at her. "What if we are?" he said.

"Well, he's taking a leak," she said. "Be with you in a shake or two."

"You're the best thing the Lao could offer up as

bodyguards?" said the second officer. His colleagues laughed rudely.

"We're in disguise," said Siri. "Actually we're twenty-five-year-old academy graduates with black belts."

Ugly was sniffing around the soldiers' shoes, expertly avoiding their kicks.

"And that's Rin Tin Tin," said Siri. "He's got a black belt too."

The officer stiffened when he realized he was being made fun of. "Go and get the monk," he said. "We haven't got all day."

"Well, comrade," said Siri, "you know you can't hurry an eighty-year-old bladder."

The word "comrade" hit the three Thais like mortar fire. It wiped the smiles off their faces and labeled Siri as the enemy. But, of course, he'd known that would be the result. The senior officer nodded to his juniors and they headed off to the latrines. This left the commander, Siri and Daeng in an awkward silence. Daeng decided to fill it.

"Been mild for the time of year," she said to the Thai officer. He ignored her.

"Usually really hot about now," said Siri.

"Don't you think the officer's uniform is spectacularly white?" said Daeng.

"You know I was just thinking the same thing," said her husband. "No, don't tell us."

"I'd hazard a guess the officer uses Rinso," said Daeng. "Only Rinso can give whites that true sunshine sparkle."

"Not very useful as camouflage, I'd have to say," said Siri.

The officer was looking particularly hot in his dress uniform. Ugly lay a meter behind him snarling.

"Unless you're in Finland," said Daeng.

"Right enough. If I were in Finland this is exactly the uniform I'd wear. I might have to powder my nose a bit."

"Most certainly. A sniper would pick out that nose from three hundred meters."

"And I wouldn't want my nose picked out. You can't—"

"Will you two shut up," shouted the officer.

Ugly began to bark. Siri and Daeng stood to attention and saluted. They were still in that position when the two other men returned at a trot.

"He's not there," said the second officer.

"What do you mean he's not there?" said the senior man.

"What do you mean he's not there?" said Siri.

"The toilet cashier woman said some old monk walked straight past her table to the motorcycle taxi rank. He jumped on the back of one and they went off."

"Went off to where?" yelled the elder.

"None of the other riders heard," said the junior. "They headed northwest on Prajak Road."

"Goddamn him," said the elder. "You!" He pointed to the second officer. "You stay here in case he comes back. We'll head after him."

He pointed at Siri and Daeng. "And you two, you're coming with me," he said.

"No we're not," said Siri.

"You'll do as you're told unless you want to be arrested. You know what the old guy looks like."

"Can't help you there," said Daeng.

"Do you really want to be wrestled into an armored car?"

The good thing about the dress uniform was it didn't include a pistol. The soldiers weren't even carrying their swords.

"You should tell him, Daeng," said Siri.

She stepped forward. "Firstly," said Daeng. "If you and your fellow snowmen laid a hand on us you'd come off worse. And secondly, just touching this man would spark a diplomatic disaster for your country. This is Civilai Songsawat, ex-member of the Lao politburo. Go and look it up. With your prime minister trying so hard to mend fences with our government, at the very least you'd lose your rank for abusing a senior Party member. But my guess is they'd be more likely to shoot you as an apology to Laos."

The red of the senior soldier's face contrasted nicely with the white of his damp collar. "You shitty little Commie bastards!" he said.

"Now that in itself is worth a rebuke at the highest levels," said Siri.

"Come!" said the elder to the junior officer, and they ran to the car. "Don't let these two reds go anywhere until we get back."

The vehicle reversed clumsily in the confined spaces of the depot. Siri and Daeng smiled at the poor officer who'd been left behind.

"It's all right, son," said Daeng. "We'll go sit over there on the benches. Our bus doesn't leave for twenty minutes."

Any hope the Lao might have harbored of remaining incognito had by now been extinguished. Everyone in the terminal was looking at them. Most were smiling. Two criminal types even gave up their seats so the old couple could sit down.

"Thank you, young men," said Daeng.

They sat quietly for a while. Siri admired the splendid old clock that was stuck on twenty past three. Daeng jiggled her legs just to enjoy the painless thrill of them. Buses came and went. Aggressive coach boys old and young leaned from the doors to solicit passengers. Resting drivers played checkers with bottle tops and drank syrupy caffeine drinks. Ragged dogs came to sniff Ugly then went on their way.

"Right then," said Siri.

"If this isn't a fine basket of winkles," said Daeng.

"I suppose, technically, we didn't fail," said Siri. "I mean, we did get him here."

"Didn't quite manage the handover though, did we? If only the lily-white soldiers had been here on time they'd have offloaded him from the bus, and we'd be on our way."

A reversing bus ran over a bicycle. Both the driver and the owner of the crumpled wreck laughed away their embarrassment.

"So you think we're still responsible for him?" Siri asked.

"No question about it."

"Damn."

"What do we do now?" asked Daeng.

"We think more deeply about what we're involved in. The Sangharaj sneaks out of Laos early in the morning on a fiberglass boat."

"So this obviously isn't an official state visit. More like an escape."

"But, unlike most of our fleeing countrymen, he isn't arrested and carted off to a refugee camp," said Siri.

"In fact he gets a very official reception committee," said Daeng.

"But they don't want to meet him at the border. Too many of our people up there. Looks too much like a rescue. Too high profile? Too official? So we have to bring him to Udon."

"And once he's here they show him some respect, which suggests someone important is waiting for him. Probably a helicopter in an airfield somewhere. What does that say, Daeng?"

"He's defecting."

"'Supreme Patriarch treated badly in wicked Communist country.' Their propaganda people could dine out on that for a year."

"But I thought the Thais were courting us," said Daeng.

"You know as well as I do how fickle that kind of romance is. You always have to maintain some leverage. Plant the seeds of goodwill, but keep the chainsaw oiled. They're being nice to us because border skirmishes cost money and don't look nice in the international press. They send us some beads and mirrors to keep us docile while they build up their arsenal. A defecting Lao Sangharaj would be a great asset in the hands of the enemy."

"So you think the monk got cold feet?"

"He seemed pretty calm to me."

"Then what happened? Why did he flee the scene?"

They considered that question for a while.

"You know," said Siri, "I wonder if he didn't plan this all along. Go through with the escape but have no intention of going to Bangkok."

"How could he have known the military boys would be late?"

"This is Thailand. Fifteen minutes isn't late."

"If that were true then he'd need somewhere to hide out in Thailand," said Daeng.

"He's a monk," said Siri. "Unless he's planning to slip back into civvies the only place he could fade away is with other monks."

"So he'd be heading for a temple. Well, that narrows things down to no end. There are half a million temples in this country."

"But he wouldn't turn up at just any temple asking for a room," Siri reminded her. "A lot of Thai monks have shady pasts. Temples are great refuges for escaped convicts and disgraced politicians. So he'd have to go to a place where they wouldn't turn him in for the reward money. It would have to be a temple run by a friend. A Thai monk he's had recent contact with. It's almost impossible to send letters out of Laos uncensored, and there's only one overseas phone line."

"And the Sangharaj hasn't been allowed out of the country since the takeover," Daeng added.

"The only way they could have met up in that time was if the Thai monk went to Laos," said Siri.

"So he'd need . . ."

". . . a visa," they said together and shook hands.

They walked over to where the uncomfortable soldier stood sweating. He stood out in the bus terminal like a polar bear in a pig farm.

"We'll be going now, son," said Daeng.

The soldier didn't know what to do or say.

"If your boss asks," said Siri, "you can tell him we know where the Lao monk has gone, and we'll sort it all out for him."

"I don't think they'll blame you for losing us," said Daeng.

The coach boy shouted the imminent departure of number twenty-two: the next service to Nong Khai. His bus was already edging slowly out of its allotted spot. Siri and Daeng had no trouble catching up with it and hopping on board. In fact, Madam Daeng stepped off the running board and jumped back on, just to show off. The officer cast a despondent figure behind them in the bustling terminal.

6

A Disturbing Sexual Disorientation

If it were possible, the second visit of Civilai and Madam Nong to Ban Toop was met with even less fanfare than on the previous day. It was like driving into a deserted nuclear test town in the Nevada desert.

"It's ten o'clock," said Civilai. "Where is everyone?"

"Probably all gathered at the meeting hall awaiting your arrival," said Nong with little conviction.

They drove slowly along the same dusty main street past the same French colonial building. They stopped this time at the headman's house, identifiable from a small hand-painted sign that read, *Headman Noulak*. This time, Civilai himself went to knock on the ill-fitting door. Front doors in Laos rarely remained closed during the day. At first there was no sound from inside. He knocked again and waited. Then . . .

"Just a minute," came a woman's voice.

It was an uncomfortably long minute before a comely woman with prematurely grey hair came to the door.

"If you're here for Lak, he's not back from the cock-fight," she said. "If that really is where he's gone. Not that

I care. Sooner he *rumwong*s with someone else's wife than with me, I say. Wake me up at two in the morning and tell me he's got an itch."

Civilai had no idea how to react but he had an odd feeling that he was being lied to. The woman's words seemed too much like a performance.

"I'm Civilai Songsawat," he said at last. "I was invited here to meet a Comrade Maitreya."

He detected a look of disdain, although he wasn't sure if it was meant for Maitreya or himself. She looked over his shoulder at the jeep.

"Not sure if he'll help you much with that," she said. "He's more into bicycles and motorbikes. But you could try. He'll look at it for you, but I wouldn't put too much faith in him."

"Where can I . . . ?"

"End of the village, left over the little bridge. You'll see the truck tire hanging from a fig tree. That's his yard."

Civilai sat confused in the passenger seat as they crossed the small bamboo bridge. He was on his way to meet the next Buddha and the only comment about him so far was, "I wouldn't put much faith in him." The bare fig tree with its suspended tire leaned out across the track, more like a deterrent than a welcome. Behind it was an untidy mechanic's yard that reached around a small open-fronted house. The building was made of brick rather than local wood, which suggested the mechanic had, at some point, made a reasonable living from his business. But the condition of the rusty parts lying around and the absence of wheel ruts on the sand frontage implied that it was past its heyday.

At the sound of the jeep's engine, a jolly man, shirtless

with a belly like a medicine ball, came running from the house. He had pleasant enough Chinese features, a bubble nose and a poor attempt at a mustache. He was probably in his fifties.

"I can fix it. I can fix it," he shouted.

Even when the passengers alighted, he seemed more interested in the jeep than in them. He spat on a rag and walked over to wipe mud off the side mirror.

"What's wrong with it?" he asked.

Civilai massaged his eyeballs through his eyelids. The mission was caving in all around him. He'd expected this to be a fun wined and dined weekend with a group of yokels attempting to convince him their representative was the Buddha incarnate. It had turned into a disaster. When he opened his eyes the first thing he saw was the sign over the workshop, TASITU ENGINE REPAIR SHOP. *Tusita* was the name of the heaven where the previous Buddha had spent time in transit awaiting his rebirth. They couldn't even spell it right.

"So this is the Tasitu Engine Repair Shop," said Civilai, intending to embarrass, but without luck.

"That's right, Uncle," said the man. "You've found it."

"And you're Comrade Maitreya?" Civilai asked.

"Right again."

"Comrade Maitreya, the next Buddha?"

The man laughed and looked embarrassed. "Yeah, I get that a lot," he said. "Now, what did you say was wrong with your jeep?"

"The carburetor's running a bit slow," said Civilai.

"No it's not," said the driver indignantly. He was from the politburo motor pool, a band of men like the Hell's Angels but more intense. They took their engines very seriously. You didn't insult a politburo motor pool driver's carburetor. But this driver had spent a good deal of time with Civilai, and they had signals. Civilai licked his top lip, which meant, "Play along and I'll explain later." The driver reluctantly played along. He agreed that the carburetor could use some work.

Maitreya was so pleased he ran into the house and reemerged in a shirt with the words LEAD MECHANIC embroidered on the back. "Only for special occasions," he said. He popped the bonnet and salivated over the contents beneath. "Lovely piece of equipment. Lovely. It's been a while since I had any quality mechanism in my yard."

He climbed in the driver's seat and turned over the engine. He listened like a piano tuner to the cords. "Not much wrong with it," he said.

The driver refused to watch, so he went for a cigarette. Madam Nong sat in the shade of the workshop. Civilai joined the mechanic beneath the bonnet. He watched the man expertly manipulate the carburetor.

"Live here alone?" Civilai asked.

"Now I do," said the mechanic. "Dengue took the wife before we could start a family."

"I'm sorry," said Civilai. "Not got around to finding somebody else?"

"No."

"Why not?"

"I'm destined to walk this earth alone."

"So you are the Buddha."

Maitreya laughed again. "It's a pity my parents didn't name me Mohamed," he said. "The Buddha jokes get old really fast."

"But you named your yard Tusita."

"It's Tasitu. It's a kind of joke. I changed it when my dad died. He was the religious one. He's the one who named me. He had high hopes for his only son. He was convinced I'd be the next Buddha."

"Why?"

"Dreams. He used to make my mother insane with his dream interpretations. Even on his way to the pyre he was still going on about it."

"So you don't believe you're the Buddha?"

"Don't be ridiculous," said the mechanic. "Look around. Don't you think if I was the Buddha I'd fix the place up a bit? Splash of paint. A few flowers. I'm just a mechanic."

"The last Buddha was just a millionaire prince. You can never tell what's around the next bend. Somebody believes it's you. I was sent here by the Supreme Sangha Council in Thailand to check you out."

"I'm sorry you've had a wasted journey. Somebody's pulling your leg."

"So it seems."

"And you know what the funniest thing is, Uncle?" said the mechanic.

"Not yet."

"I'm not even Buddhist."

Even the motor pool driver had to admit the engine was running more smoothly than he'd ever heard it.

"That man has some sort of magical touch," he said.

The mechanic had tightened a few nuts and cleaned a couple of tubes and did the familiar "Up to you," when asked how much he wanted for his labor. And perhaps that was a good ploy because Civilai had given him more than the job was worth. And, on the off chance Maitreya turned out to be the next Buddha after all, it wouldn't hurt to have him remember a generous tip back when he was still an unknown.

"Have you concluded your investigation?" asked Madam Nong. They were on their way back to the small but comfortable guesthouse in Pak Xan.

"I'm almost embarrassed to take the Thais' money," Civilai told her. "He shouldn't even have been on their list. But they don't just take anyone's word that they're the Buddha. The claim must have come from a credible source. And I didn't see anyone credible in that place. I doubt they would have taken the word of the dead father. The man was obsessed, fanatical about fathering the next almighty. He must have been devastated the boy turned out to be so ordinary. Good mechanic but light on sanctity."

The jeep pulled up in front of the guesthouse, and Civilai took his wife's hand as they walked up the uneven stone steps. They were looking forward to an evening meal and a beer or two. Since the Bier Lao factory had been taken over by the government, no one bottle of beer tasted like the next. But the locals in Pak Xan ferried Singha over from Thailand on the same rafts that exported refugees. Civilai was not one to enjoy surprises when drinking beer. Singha guaranteed a consistent taste with that consistent chemical hangover.

The evening meal was only available to guests who ordered it in the morning. Few restaurants bothered to keep food on speculation. Civilai and his wife were about to go to their room to freshen up before dinner when a wispy old woman with gaps in her hair came up to them in the small reception area.

"Are you the ones?" she asked.

"We are two of the ones," said Civilai. "Which I suppose would make us a two."

As usual, his attempt at humor fell on deaf ears.

"I heard you're looking for Maitreya," she continued.

"How did you hear that?" Civilai asked.

"Voices."

"Right. And how might you be connected to Comrade Maitreya?"

"I gave birth to him."

"Ah, so you're his mother."

"I didn't say that."

"But . . ."

"He would have told you about his father. Dad did this. Dad did that. Right? It's his favorite topic."

"You didn't get along with your husband?"

It was as if a steel veil dropped over her face.

"I've never had a husband," she said. "I've never had a man."

"If that's the way you prefer to remember it," said Civilai, gesturing to Nong that he'd prefer to be under the shower to standing there.

"It's the way it was," she said. She pulled an ancient roll of paper from her shoulder bag and handed it to Civilai.

"It's from the hospital," she said. "It's in English, but I can help you with that. It says I gave birth to that boy on February fifteenth, 1927. It says the boy was healthy. It says there were complications because in order to birth the child they had to surgically remove my intact hymen. Perhaps you'll have to ask your wife what that means."

◙ ◙ ◙

From Thailand there were two ways to obtain a visa for Laos. The first involved traveling to Bangkok and showing an official invitation from somebody on the Lao side. Even with a sponsor the wait could take weeks before the passport was stamped.

The second method was to go to Nong Khai and see No-Nose Looi. Nobody living in the north could be bothered to travel all the way to smoke city for a visa. It was a predicament begging for a corrupt solution, and Looi was your man. He had what the Lao morals police referred to as "a disturbing sexual disorientation." In other words he was gay and had been in a secret relationship with a junior official at the Interior Ministry. Like drug addicts or misfits with Down syndrome, homosexuals were treated with disdain by the Party. Looi and his lover were the acme of discretion. But the ministry fellow had read a Thai magazine article about an operation that could make a man's nose as cute as a button. There were before and after photographs to prove it worked. He showed the spread to Looi and offered to sponsor a nose job in Thailand where plastic surgery clinics were springing up like toadstools. All of them offered promotional rates but no guarantees of success.

Looi had selected a clinic with the most impressive advertising and returned to Laos a month later without a nose. Not as cute as a button, but certainly the size and shape of one. The nostrils sloped upward, and he had to plug them with wax during rainstorms to avoid drowning. The junior official was appalled at the sight of it, and, rather than offer his love and support, he trumped up a charge to get his lover kicked out of the country and his Lao passport revoked. As the official was a happily married man with two children, nobody suspected ulterior motives.

In revenge, Looi forged himself a Thai identity card, set up an office in Nong Khai, bought used visa stamps from a disreputable officer at the Lao embassy in Bangkok and offered tourists an express Lao visa service. Anyone with money could get one. There was no vetting. It wasn't cheap, but it certainly beat traveling to Bangkok and being humiliated. As there was no obvious difference between the actual and fake visa stamps, all sorts of criminals and ill-intents found their way into Laos. This caused an endless migraine to the ex-lover, whose job it was to monitor arrivals and be accountable for any foreigners misbehaving.

Siri and Daeng left Ugly outside and entered Looi's office just before lunchtime. They found him sitting at a coffee table counting money. He had a fresh white bandage taped over his nose. He looked up and squealed with delight when he saw the couple. Before his exile he'd been one of Madam Daeng's best customers. He adored her noodles and the only real downside of being thrown out of Laos was that he could no longer enjoy Madam Daeng's spicy number 3. He'd even offered to sponsor a branch of her restaurant on the Thai side.

Before they could get down to business, Siri and Daeng had to hear all about Looi's latest operation, where they'd attempted to graft a chunk of ankle bone onto his face.

"When that takes," he said, "they'll be able to start all over again with the nose. It's exciting. I've selected a Marlon Brando from the menu. Of course, I'm having a bit of trouble walking right now, but that's the way it is. Now, what can I do for you both?"

"We're looking for a monk," said Daeng. "Probably an

abbot from the Thai side who could have made one or two trips over the river. Given the religious climate in Laos we're assuming not too many monks are heading north."

"They mostly go as delegates at the invitation of the United Buddhist Council," said Looi. "And because it's a government invite they're obliged to get their visas through the embassy."

"We're imagining this fellow was traveling alone," said Siri. "Maybe staying for a few days. Possibly a week."

"Visiting the Supreme Patriarch?" asked Looi.

Siri's white eyebrows bristled.

"How did you know?" said Daeng. "Yes, sir, that's exactly where he was going."

"Not he," said Looi. "Them. There are three that go over often."

"Together?" asked Siri.

"Not so far," said Looi. "Single monks on pilgrimages, it looks like. Don't forget, my customers don't have to fill out forms, but I'm interested in why people want to go to Laos. So I chat while I'm stamping their travel documents, especially if they're nice-looking. One of them was from the northeast, but I can't say I asked him what town. Another was from Bangkok. Don't know about the third. He wasn't much of a talker. Unsociable type."

"I'm betting on the one from the northeast," said Daeng. "The Sangharaj headed northwest out of the Udon bus terminal."

"So the old fellow finally skipped, did he?" said Looi. "Good luck to him. They treated him like dirt."

"Are you sure you don't remember anything about the local Thai monk?" asked Daeng. "A name perhaps?"

"I don't keep records here. Too incriminating if they

ever come for me. I do remember he said he was in a new-
ish temple about twenty minutes' drive from town, and
he was often there by himself. But he was talking about
his students, so I'm guessing it's a temple that doubles as
a school."

Siri considered where the Lao monk might go. It would
be somewhere low key. Probably deep in the countryside.

"I don't suppose there's a town near here called Nam
Som?" he asked.

"There is," said Looi. "It's about two hours west of
Udon."

Daeng smiled. "You think the Sangharaj was telling you
where he was going?" she said.

"'You couldn't find a thank you in a glass of ginseng
juice,' was what he said on the bus," said Siri. "There's the
word *'pra'*—a monk—in *'koprakoon'*—thank you. And *nam
som* is ginseng juice. And, to tell the truth we haven't got
anything else to go on."

The local bus to Nam Som was the type to make a Lao
doubt the stories about Thai development. It was like
being dragged over rocks on a tin tray. There were
taxis—some of them forty years old—that ferried passengers to the ferry at Tardeua, but even those had
suspension. This country bus was as stiff as a box cart.
No longer able to tolerate the pummeling to her tail,
Madam Daeng had resorted to standing. She held onto
the seat in front and bent her knees like a charioteer.
Siri had one arm around her waist, but he lost her a couple of times when the bus left the ground and landed
nose first on the gravel road. Even Ugly growled in frus-
tration at the quality of service.

It took three punishing hours in all. They'd never been
so delighted to get off a bus. Nam Som had only recently
been upgraded to a district. At first glance it appeared that
the upgrading had been largely on paper. It was a sleepy,
slow-moving place with nothing to distinguish it from the
other small towns they'd passed. Once the knots had been
shaken out of their joints, Siri and Daeng went directly to
the motorcycle *samlor* stand at the bus stop. None of the
three drivers seemed that interested in hustling for passengers or taxing their brains. When Daeng had finished
explaining that they were looking for a comparatively new
temple some twenty kilometers from Nam Som, perhaps
with just the one abbot in residence who taught school,
they all shook their heads. Something about the shaking
suggested they knew of the place but had no intention of
going there.

"My husband only has three days left to live," said
Daeng. "It's his last wish to visit his son at the temple and
beg forgiveness for casting him out of the house when he
was just a child. He's been searching for him for a year.
Please help an old man fulfill his dying wish."

Siri coughed and held his heart.

The drivers exchanged glances.

"I'll take you as close as I dare," said the most ragged of
the three.

There were two short wooden benches behind the
motorcycle with just enough space for Siri and Daeng with
Ugly at their feet. The engine sounded like an ancient
machine gun. They had to shout to be heard.

"Why is it always me who's about to die?" said Siri.

"Look at you," said Daeng. "Who'd ever believe a
woman in my condition only had three days to live?"

"What do you suppose he meant by, 'as close as I dare'?"
"No idea."

They arrived, not exactly in the village, but at a signpost that said SAWAN. It was a metal sign peppered with small-bore bullet holes. The driver told them the road from there on was impassable by vehicle, but the village was only half a kilometer around the bend. They would come to the temple before that. So the three adventurers set off on foot. The dirt road didn't appear to deteriorate at all after they rounded the first bend. In fact, with few ruts and tire tracks, it seemed to improve. They walked along what might one day be a dotted line at the center and enjoyed the cries of the birds and beasts. It was evening, and as they walked the other sounds were drowned beneath the late chorus of cicadas.

"You do realize," said Siri, leaning into his wife's ear, "that we'll probably get to the temple and discover the abbot's never heard of our Sangharaj and he was just visiting Laos for a little female companionship."

"For a man who grew up in a temple, you aren't very respectful, are you, Dr. Siri?" she replied.

"Grew up there?" said Siri. "I was dumped by some mysterious relative who didn't want me."

"But you were a novice. You learned the precepts."

"The way a Catholic learns catechisms. It was rote. It was a school. I was a rebel. I concentrated on the skills that would get me out of the place as soon as possible rather than the ones that would leave me a prisoner there for life. I was a scientist long before I knew what science was. I'd heard that scientists debunked religion, so I wanted to sign up."

Daeng smiled. "If I remember rightly, this is the point where you start talking about lotus flowers and onions," she said.

"Too right I do," said Siri. "In the lycée I charged through anything that could be proven and resented the time I'd wasted in the temple school dancing on lotus flowers. Then I'm in France, and they want me to juggle onions because they were paying the bill. They called it Catholicism, but I recognized it soon enough as their version of lotus dancing. Over in England they were juggling potatoes. The Arabs were jumping camels through hoops. In Israel they were climbing walls with their lips. Everyone had to have a cabaret act. So I'd juggle with my left hand and learn how to sew up bodies with my right. I did my tricks, Daeng, but they never got me in the circus."

Daeng squeezed his hand. "Remind me where my tail and your inner-shaman come in the program of circus events," she said, although she'd listened to his philosophy many times before.

"Now there's a conundrum," he said. "The religions, you see, they let you leave. They don't even put up a fight. So when you realize they're useless you can just move on. But the spirits? They really are annoying. They're the clowns perhaps. The harder you laugh at them and tell them they aren't real, the more times they trip you up and leave you flat on your face. My science can make a fool of any religion, but I can make no sense at all of the power the spirits have over me."

The half-kilometer to the temple turned out to be a lot farther. They'd been walking for forty minutes, and they could see the distant sun quartered and diced as it sank behind the leafless forest ahead. The birds and animals had uttered their last chorus for the day, and, as one, the cicadas fell silent.

"I don't see the road becoming impassable, do you?" said Daeng.

"Just endless," said Siri. "Those Thais. Any excuse to save a liter of benzene."

With night approaching, Siri wondered how much longer they'd have to walk but said nothing. Neither did he mention the reaction of the white talisman that hung from his neck. It had been selected for its sensitivity to the paranormal and blessed to ward off evil spirits. It was nonsensical but had, on occasions, saved his life: the scientist's paradox. And here it was, hot against his chest, alert, vibrating a warning. Ugly, who had spent much of the walk far out in front, now dropped back to be with his master. His ears and his tail were down, and he growled quietly.

"What's wrong with him?" Daeng asked.

"He's a dog," said Siri.

"You don't say? And there I was thinking he's a can of pickles."

"It's a phrase that explains itself," said her husband. "It's like saying, 'That Dr. Siri, he's a man.' You see? And every woman for kilometers around understands the meaning."

Siri was talking for talking's sake. He could feel a nervous tingle in his wife's fingers. He could sense that she too was on alert. Yet neither of them said anything about it.

Ugly stopped dead in his tracks. He refused to walk another step. Siri's amulet was fluttering beneath his shirt like a warm bat. The sun had sunk and left a mauve hangover along the horizon. The road ahead bled into it and disappeared. At their backs the moon had not yet put in an appearance. Daeng stopped and reached into her shoulder bag. She produced a flashlight, flicked the switch and a long wormhole of white light reached off into the distance. And at its farthest point it briefly made out two pink eyes caught in its beam. At that second the light gave out and left them there in a moonless blot.

"Shit," said Daeng, and she rattled the flashlight and turned the switch on and off with no result.

Ugly began to howl the way city dogs howled, collecting other voices one by one, until the neighborhood was awash in one pitiful chorus. But here, Ugly howled alone.

"All we need is a slither of lightning and a burst of thunder, and we'd have a Hammer film," said Siri, his impenetrable funny lines all but exhausted.

"I just put new batteries in this thing in Nong Khai," said Daeng, slapping the flashlight against her thigh. Ugly's howl turned to a bark, and he ran in front of them. Two silent pink lights were coming toward them along the road ahead. Ugly danced left and right, his bark more desperate.

"I don't suppose you remembered to pack the shot-gun?" said Daeng.

"Then I wouldn't have had room for the whisky," said Siri, who did however have a scalpel in his hand. Daeng held a penknife. Neither were much use if they were about to get shot.

◙   ◙   ◙

"They're all raving mad," said Civilai. "A deserted village. A reluctant would-be Buddha who may or may not have been lying about his father. And now the Virgin Mary joins the cast. What's going on here?"

The guesthouse was a block away from the bank of the Xan River, but that's where Civilai and Madam Nong decided to sit. Running water helped them concentrate and relax at the same time. The owner loaned Civilai an ice-cream vendor's bicycle horn to beep whenever they needed another drink or a snack. His wife was glad to run back and forth with a tray.

"I don't see why we can't go home together tomorrow," said Nong. "You write your report that you found no evidence of a reincarnation, and we forget all this nonsense."

"You know why I can't," said Civilai.

"Because you're meddlesome," she said. "You picked it up from Siri."

"I did not. I've always been meddlesome. He's the cantankerous one."

"Tell me, what's so fascinating about this place you'd want to stay another night? Don't tell me you're still miffed that they didn't have a reception for you."

"That's part of it," said Civilai. "There's a system, you see. The ministry contacts the provincial office to say a bigwig is coming to visit. The provincial office passes this on to the regional council. The regional council informs the village and provides a budget. The village prepares for the visit, not because they're excited at the thought of seeing me, but because it's what they are supposed to do."

"I thought you didn't approve of unnecessary pomp and ceremony?"

"I don't. Complete waste of money and manpower. But the protocol exists, and tomorrow I'll go to the regional office to see why it broke down. And, to be honest, in the light of our Mary's story, I think I'd like to have another chat with Comrade Maitreya."

"Surely you didn't believe the word of a seventy-year-old virgin, Lai. Her hospital report was handwritten on a lined page torn from a school exercise book. It was in English, but the birth predated any American hospital aid projects. And if they had been here they would have made a song and dance about an immaculate conception in the third world. They would have sent reports to every medical journal, *The Times*."

"And who would have believed it?"

They reverted to staring at the river. A bicycle ice-cream vendor rode past beeping his horn, and two minutes later the wife of the guesthouse owner arrived breathless with two new beers. Civilai and Nong were only halfway through the first round, but they accepted the fresh bottles and ordered more food.

"And the thing is we still have no idea who contacted the Supreme Sangha Council in Thailand to make this claim," said Civilai. It wasn't the Buddha himself because he isn't the least bit interested. The headman was so luke-warm about it he didn't even bother showing up. But they wouldn't have counted anyway. The Supreme Sangha Council is a bit like the Vatican. The Italians wouldn't rush off into the jungle to see whether Mother Theresa was worthy of a sainthood unless a credible source could vouch for the fact she hadn't spent all her time with her feet up drinking gin and tonic. They're not going to sanctify her because her auntie said she was a good girl. No, whoever contacted Bangkok wielded some influence, and I want to know who it was . . . and why."

"Meddlesome," said his wife.

"Aren't you even a little bit curious?"

"I have to be back for my Women's Union meeting on Tuesday."

"But if you didn't . . . ?"

"Then, no. Not in the least. There are far more important things in life to be curious about."

7

Felonious Monk

Siri and Daeng had slept well in the guesthouse of the temple in Sawan, although the bags under Ugly's eyes suggested he'd been up all night. They'd been met on the road by the Supreme Patriarch and his friend Abbot Rayron carrying mountain salt lamps. The Sangharaj was an entirely different character than the mellow lump of stone they'd traveled with from Nong Khai. Siri had passed the test and was granted access to the man inside the rank. Old Sangharaj was a lad. He was funny and had a keen intellect, and he announced he'd already heard Civilai's jokes—perhaps even the dirtier versions. When asked what it was he'd said to the coach boy on the Udon-bound bus, he confessed that he might have threatened to punch the boy on the nose if he harmed the dog. They'd talked long into the night, although the topic had been mostly Siri and Daeng.

"I knew it," said the Sangharaj. "I knew if I antagonized and tested you a little your curiosity would get the better of you. And here you are. Remarkable. All those stories are indeed true."

"What stories?" asked Daeng.

"Do I really need to retell them?" said the monk. "Daeng, the famous fleur-de-lis of the Free Lao underground movement. Dr. Siri, who saved so many on the battlefront then solved impossible mysteries as the national coroner. And who knows what celestial contacts you two have amassed."

"Wait," said Siri, "haven't you been in the stockade since '75? Where do you hear all these rumors?"

"The legends existed long before I was decommissioned," said the Sangharaj. "Temples have been the grapes on the vine for centuries. It's a worldwide saffron network. We attract all sorts—or used to. Intellectuals who've given up on the material world, old soldiers, frustrated shamans, murderers. Can you imagine the stories we hear around the campfire? It's destiny that you should be here with us now. I can think of no two people more qualified to address the chaos we have in Sawan."

"My husband isn't so big on destiny," said Daeng.

"Then let's call it something else. How about coincidence?"

"That's even worse," said Siri.

"Then let's not call it anything at all. You're here, and you'll help us. And for that we thank you."

"We're here because we agreed to deliver you to the Thais," said Daeng.

"Following your defection," added Siri.

The Sangharaj laughed. "Ah, yes. My defection. What say we discuss that later this morning over breakfast? The Thais are very generous when it comes to alms. Goodness, Abbot Rayron even had a pot of fresh strawberry jam yesterday. Can you believe it? A monk could actually put on weight here."

"All right," said Siri, "if you're sending us to bed early, how about a little story to lull us to sleep?"

"Which one would you like to hear, Brother Siri?"

"The one where the Supreme Patriarch flees Udon bus station on a motorcycle and heads for a temple in the middle of nowhere because there's chaos he presumably knew of long before he got there."

"It's complicated."

"Give us the simple version."

"Very well," said the monk. "At the root of the chaos there is a simple drama. A suspected murder. There sits the accused."

They all turned around to look at the abbot who had posed as a life-sized ornament in the shadows since their arrival. He was slim and sinewy and looked as if he could account for himself in a fist fight. He was very quiet and seemed embarrassed by the sudden attention, but allowed himself a slither of a smile.

"This," said the Sangharaj, "is Abbot Rayron. He has run this temple since it was erected ten years ago. He used to be well respected in the region, but over the last three months, he's murdered three people."

The Sangharaj paused here for effect.

"And, according to one of our village shamans," he continued, "the murderer will kill again before the new week begins. So I suggest you wedge a chair under your doorknob when you go to sleep . . . which will be right now."

"A lapsed Catholic, a thousand-year-old shaman and a homicidal Buddhist monk walk into a bar. And the barman says, 'We only serve spirits in here.' So the Catholic says, 'We have the biggest spirit of all. The Holy Spirit. So I should get a glass of your best scotch . . .'"

It was the beginning of a joke that wouldn't have worked in Lao, so Auntie Bpoo was telling it in French. Siri had no idea she could speak French, and perhaps she couldn't because this was a dream . . . possibly. In dreams, miracles happened. Miracles like when a man's just about to give up attempting to speak on a long distance line, and suddenly the signal's as clear as a bell.

"I've heard it," said Siri, even though he hadn't. He was back in the connecting door space and the gap between the doors was getting narrower.

"What?" said Auntie Bpoo.

"I said I've heard the joke before."

"Alleluia," said Bpoo in whatever language *alleluia* was supposed to be.

"Alleluia, what?" asked Siri.

"Don't you notice anything different?"

"There's a handle on the door behind me," said Siri. "So presumably I can go back to bed anytime I like."

"Old dog, you're so hard to please. Can't you hear we're talking?"

"I've had these two-way dreams before," said Siri. "I've had conversations. I once spent the night wining and dining Audrey Hepburn."

"Siri, you absolute idiot," said Bpoo, "that was you talking to yourself pretending to be someone else. That's not a dialogue. That's a monologue with you doing all the voices. This is real. This is your breakthrough."

A huge sense of relief washed over Siri like a spicy nasal spray. "So I can only speak to spirits in French?" he said.

"I don't know. I can't speak French."

"Then what's this?"

"We don't do languages here."

"Then, what . . . ?"

The signal began to break up. It deteriorated so rapidly Siri was left in the connecting doorway yelling at himself.

"Wait," he said. "I lied. I haven't heard it. What's the end of the joke?"

But he was alone.

He contemplated opening the door behind him and curling up beside his warm wife, but he gave the door ahead one last push.

And it opened.

He was in an unfamiliar room, and it was nighttime. He stepped through the door. The room was lit only by a street lamp outside the window. Flying insects gathered there in such numbers that the lamplight danced around the room. On the glass windowpane a battalion of lizards dined on the insects. As lizards have no self-control they too would be dead by morning. Stuffed to oblivion.

Siri stood in the room, knowing that he was on the other side for the first time. But there was nobody to talk to. Fearing the visit might be a fleeting one he endeavored to take in as many facts as he could. It was an office. A calendar on the wall told him he was in Thailand as he recognized the photograph of the king. The last date marked was February 7th. There was a desk with drawers, but as Siri wasn't actually there he couldn't open them. Nor could he pick up papers or thumb through the books on the shelves. All he could do was observe and remember. There had to be a reason for his being there. On the parquet flooring in front of the desk he noted a large stain the shape of Africa. He memorized the books, mostly academic: history, politics, engineering, science, literature. Most were in Thai, but there were some in English. Some had no lettering on the spine and seemed to contain files.

Near the far door there were chips of plaster that had fallen from the wall. He looked through the window beyond the insect carnage and saw a line of individual houses. Not luxurious but sturdy. Jeeps or pickup trucks parked outside them on a tarmac road. Front garden plants mostly in pots, suggesting the residents didn't expect to stay long, or the owner did not allow landscaping. Wires overhead. A cat sleeping. Bins for garbage.

One more circuit of the room. Leather chair behind the desk with the stuffing coming out. Guest chair opposite. Lamp with a chain pull. No carpet. He knelt at the litter basket beside the desk, infuriated that he couldn't unscrew the balls of paper there. Only one envelope offered a clue. It had been ripped in half but was clearly visible. An address was written on it: *Than Kritsana Mukum, Dusit Insurance Company, Suan Dusit, Ban . . .* There was an error. The Thai word for Bangkok was misspelled, crossed out and scribbled over as if in anger.

There was only one more oddity in the neat office. Siri was on his hands and knees looking under the sofa that was still wrapped in plastic. Beneath it was a hole puncher. It probably had been dropped there and forgotten. He lay on the floor and looked up at the non-moving ceiling fan, and a hand reached out from under the sofa. It stroked his skin before taking hold of his arm.

"Siri," said Madam Daeng, "I think we should get up now."

He awoke like a man who had jogged to Bangkok in his sleep. His joints and muscles ached. His first conscious uttering of the day was a groan. He would happily have rolled over and made another attempt at a peaceful sleep. His night's slumber had begun badly. The almost full moon through the window had been annoyingly hypnotic, and the amulet burned so hot against his chest he'd been forced to take it off and lay it on the floor beside his pillow. Had this led to the breakthrough in the dream audio and the nocturnal trespass?

They sat together at the rattan table, and he told Daeng all about it. They came to the same conclusion. Yes, it must have been the amulet that blocked his communication with the other side. Sure, it kept him alive, but if he really wanted answers to his myriad questions, he had to break his dependence on it from time to time. They just had to be sure they were in an area low on malevolent spirits, and this certainly wasn't the place to be experimenting.

Siri patted Ugly on the head and walked to the pretty temple garden. The Sangharaj was sitting in the lotus position on an enormous slab of slate beside a pond. His robe was off his shoulders and Siri could see the hieroglyphics of war and age and abuse etched across his back. He was probably in his late eighties, but, unlike the pensioners in fat cities, frugality and common sense had kept him fit and clear-headed.

"Hey, Granddad," said Siri.

"Go away. I'm meditating," said the monk.

"No you're not. You're reading a magazine. I wouldn't be surprised if there were a few glamour girls in those pages."

The Sangharaj put down his newspaper. "What would someone my age need a glamour girl for?" he asked.

Siri sat beside him on the black slab and looked out

over a pond of carp, some big enough to feed a family of ten for a week. "I imagine it mounts up," he said. "All those years of abstinence."

"The secret is to abstain from only those supposed pleasures that have been promoted beyond their true value. The advertisers and the pornographers have created needs in us that don't actually exist."

"Including lust?"

"Especially lust. Lust is not a necessary thing."

"I'll inform Madam Daeng of your ruling."

"She's a levelheaded woman, Siri. She knows."

"Even orangutans scream with pleasure when they mate."

"Perhaps they're screaming with joy because they're propagating the species," said the monk.

"I doubt I'd be too exited if I came back as a monkey," said Siri. "Isn't it funny how it works that way? Man has a good chance to come back as man, or, at a pinch, some superior animal species, but you lot make it hard for a turtle to climb the ladder. I mean, what exactly would an orangutan have to do to amass enough credit to come back as a pornographer?"

"I doubt any self-respecting orangutan would consider that to be an incentive."

Siri laughed and threw a pebble in the pond. The fat fish gathered around it.

"Ah, Siri," said the Sangharaj, "I feel you and I will have such fun discussing our relative values. Me explaining the simplicity of religion. You being wrong about everything."

"You've spoiled that confrontation, I'm afraid," said Siri. "Because it would come down to me sticking to my principles and you floating away from yours on a plastic boat."

"Are you a good Communist, Siri?"

"That's a non sequitur to take my mind off your defection."

"It's relevant, trust me. Do you believe everything they tell you? Are you convinced the system works? Are there times when you're embarrassed to represent the doctrine you've dedicated your life to?"

In his mind, Siri knew the answers, of course. He'd been a paid-up member of the Communist Party since Paris, and there were times when it was beautiful, when he and his colleagues were genuinely excited at the potential. They believed all of the unfairness of the world could be fed into the big pork mincer of Communism and come out fine and dandy. And it would fit burger-sized into buns to feed the poor. And everyone would be full and equal. But it didn't happen. And he wasn't about to spill his ideological guts to the Sangharaj on their first date. He threw in his own non sequitur.

"Haven't you ever sinned?" he asked.

"Unless you're seeking a confession, what would your point be in asking that question?"

"If I really need a point, perhaps it's that nothing is pure. That mankind is basically flawed. That we all pretend to believe in something but we realize it isn't exactly right, or even necessary. Everything's a compromise. There are blemishes and stains, but we ignore them because we desperately want to experience that trust. It's natural. Faith should be at the top of Maslow's hierarchy of needs. We're so desperate for it we gladly allow ourselves to be short-changed just so we can believe in something."

The two men watched the carp roll over each other.

"And love?" asked the Sangharaj.

"The ultimate compromise," said Siri. "It's so important to have a partner that we cut and shape our tastes and likes and dislikes and go to great lengths to tolerate differences. We do this so we have someone beside us. In this insane quest for institutional faith we need a sidekick: somebody to give us a daily burst of faith at the grassroots level. A little shot of home belief. In that way when our religions and our politics and our doctrines disappoint us it isn't so important because we have love. My planet is parched and crumbling, but my bedroom is in full bloom."

"That's the part I was waiting for," came a voice from behind them.

They turned around to see Madam Daeng leaning against a flowering plumeria. The blossoms formed a halo. The monk smiled.

"If only I'd had you two as neighbors in Luang Prabang," he said, "I might have survived. But all I had was sycophants to the right of me and agnostic cadres to the left. Nobody with me in the middle."

"We could have had cocktail parties," said Daeng. She joined them at the pond, keeping a respectful distance from the monk. Her stomach rumbled loudly as she watched the delicious fish, reminding her she hadn't eaten. But Siri appeared not to share her hunger.

"Suppose you tell us about your friend, the abbot," he said.

"You really came all this way to help him?" asked Daeng.

The monk studied the bushy tail of a passing cloud. "I came to offer support," he said. "I'm not sure how much help I can be. We're Lao, and we have no legal right to interfere here. But the abbot is in a terrible fix. It all started in the Western New Year period. There was a murder in this village. Abbot Rayron told me about it on his last visit to Luang Prabang. An ascetic monk had been staying here at the temple. You'll learn today just how . . . different this village is. It attracts a number of tourists and researchers and thrill seekers. The visitor was collecting information to better understand religions and had asked to stay for a week. Abbot Rayron is generally here alone, so he appreciates company. They found the young man's body on the track. It's a sort of shortcut between the village and the temple, but few people are brave enough to use it. The villagers claim it passes through a part of the forest that is densely populated with ghosts. The monk had been hit on the head with a rock that was found lying nearby.

"The police captain came from Nam Som to investigate. Gumron, he's a career policeman. Very thorough. He asked around the village, took statements. He took the rock away as evidence even though there are no questions you can ask a rock to learn who wielded it."

"Fingerprints," thought Siri to himself. He was a great fan of fingerprinting as a crime-solving method and had used it in the past to prove points. He wondered how advanced a rural Thai police officer might be in forensic skills.

"There was no conclusion," said the Sangharaj. "The traveling monk had been here for too short a time to have antagonized anyone. He had nothing to steal and was, according to the abbot, a thoroughly likeable fellow. There were no witnesses, no suspects and the case was suspended."

Ugly staggered across the lawn, looked unenthusiastically at the fish, and crashed sideways into the long grass beside the pond.

"And the second murder?" Daeng asked.

"Exactly a month later," said the monk. "I suppose it couldn't be described as a murder as the victim was already deceased. There's a tradition in the village that dates back to before the temple was built. This compound is comparatively new, you see? It was built in the sixties. Before its arrival the dead would be laid out in a gazebo behind the headman's house. It was a convenient place from which to carry the body to the pyre. The deceased was a young man who'd died mysteriously in his sleep. It happens a lot here in the northeast. They say it was the work of an evil witch who makes love to sleeping men, but I heard he'd been drinking some locally produced hooch of questionable quality. Anyway, the family came in the morning to take the body to the pyre only to find him on the platform with a ceremonial knife buried in his heart."

"What type of knife?" asked Siri.

"I believe it was a prop once used for exorcisms."

"And where might that have come from?"

The monk smiled. "You'll see," he said.

"So two criminal acts a month apart but no evidence they were connected," said Daeng.

"No. But on this occasion there was a witness. A young girl had been doing her ablutions late at night behind her hut. Through the gaps in the bamboo shower room she saw a monk."

"But it would have been dark," said Siri.

"Full moon," said the Sangharaj. "Just as the murder of the traveling monk had been on the night of the full moon a month earlier."

"Not the most sensible night to be doing evil deeds," said Daeng. "No cover of darkness."

"The same police captain came," said the old monk, "Gumron. He asked around again, but this time he wasn't satisfied with the answers. He interviewed Abbot Rayron and asked him why he was in the village late at night. The abbot said that he wasn't. As the abbot was the only monk known to be in the vicinity at the time, either he or the girl was lying. The inquiry again ground to a halt for lack of evidence, but the seeds of suspicion had been sown."

"And the third murder was also on a full moon?" said Daeng.

"A month ago," said the Sangharaj. "The village elders had been playing cards and drinking and getting raucous as they do. Most rowdy of them all was Loong Gan, age ninety-seven, oldest man in the village, illegitimate children in the hundreds. Abbot Rayron had cornered him earlier in the day and told him it wasn't too late to change his ways. Of course it was, but it's a standard pep talk to steer him from the hells. We're obliged to run it by those of little hope. They'd had one of their customary slagging matches, and Rayron had perhaps uttered one or two small insults that he hadn't learned from the temple.

"The next day they found Loong Gan facedown in a paddy, strangled with his own loincloth and slashed to pieces. And here everything comes together. Not one but three witnesses saw drunken Loong Gan being helped back to his hut on the arm of Abbot Rayron. And in front of the police captain one shy boy stepped up to admit that on the night of the death of the wandering monk, the first murder, he'd seen two monks, one following the other in the direction of the temple path. So it was all cut and dried. The captain arrested Abbot Rayron and took him to the police station in Nam Som. There is no tradition here of allowing a suspect one phone call. A local man would rely on his family to prove him innocent as nobody can afford a lawyer. But the abbot was familiar with the head of the police, who allowed him to make a call to a number in Nong Khai to explain his plight. The jungle telegraph carried that message all the way to me in Luang Prabang."

"Why isn't he still in jail?" asked Siri.

"Because, for as long as it lasts, I'm the Supreme Patriarch of Laos, and the police lieutenant is a very religious man. I vouched for the abbot, and he is here under my house arrest, at least until the judge gets here."

"Judges do house calls?" said Daeng.

"Not exactly," said the Sangharaj. "It's complicated. They aren't exactly judges, more like traveling public prosecutors with the right to make judgments on certain issues."

"Like Judge Bao Gong," said Siri who was a huge fan of the stories of the Chinese street judge. "He travels the land dispensing wisdom and justice in even measures. A pleasantly mannered man who can hang you."

"I don't think they can carry out the executions themselves," said the Sangharaj. "But they can refer you to courts in the cities where the prosecutor's assessment of a case is invariably not questioned. So I don't think I'm understating their power."

"So how long do we have to sort this all out?" asked Daeng.

"Prosecutor Suthon will be hearing the abbot's case tomorrow afternoon. They have a sort of courtroom in Nam Som."

"That's not much time, is it?" said Siri. "As I see it, there are two possibilities. The first is that he did it, which makes him a nutcase who deserves whatever the Thai justice system doles out to him. The second is that he's being framed. It really isn't that hard to shave your head and get ahold of saffron robes. They give them away at temple fetes. At night, even under a full moon, all you ever notice are the body shape, the shiny head and the robes. So the method's simple enough. All we need then is motive. Do you suppose there might be anyone in the village with a grudge against the abbot? Anyone who might see the temple as a threat to traditional beliefs? Any possible conflicts of faith?"

The Sangharaj turned to Siri, and another laugh rose from his gut. It was an infectious bronchial chortle, the type you'd expect from quarry workers or smokers who drank too much. He probably hadn't found a lot to laugh about of late, so Siri didn't begrudge him. But they had no idea what he was laughing about. It took some minutes for the rapture to die down.

"I think it's time you visit Sawan Village," said the Sangharaj.

For the first time since his rescue, Ugly the dog wasn't at Siri's heel when he set off along the shortcut trail to the village. The dog sat and stubbornly refused to take another step. So unexpected was it that Siri didn't even notice his absence until they were halfway along the track. He whistled. The dog didn't come.

"Weird," Daeng told the monk. "That dog goes everywhere with the doctor. If he wasn't afraid of being inside buildings I'm sure he would sleep with us."

"It won't be the last weirdness you see today," said the Sangharaj.

"I have to warn you we're rather hard to shock," said Siri.

He had no doubt there was heavy supernatural activity all around them. He could see the spirit shadows in the forest. They looked up nervously like deer when he passed. They were merely ghosts with no ill intentions, but his talisman told him of a deeper presence, one that couldn't be seen. The stone had ceased to be a chunk of rock and had taken on animate qualities. It squeezed his chest like a hand. It squirmed like a warm rattlesnake beneath his shirt. It was alive.

"Why was the temple built so far outside the village?" Daeng asked.

"Neutral ground," said Siri. "It was the only plot left unoccupied."

"By whom?" Daeng asked.

"The bad ghosts. The *phibob.*"

"I see," she said. "So we're heading off into another Siri moment. Marvelous."

Before she was reunited with Siri a few years earlier, Daeng had paid homage to her ancestors and shown respect to the spirits of the land. She'd had no personal dealings with any of them, but it was what her parents and grandparents had done. Just as a Muslim child has no doubt there is Allah, so little Daeng never questioned there were spirits. It hadn't been necessary to touch or be touched by them. But then came Siri with his entourage. Whether it was magic or hypnosis, it mattered not. She had a tail, and the tail had rid her of a debilitating infliction. Her husband saw ghosts. It was merely a confirmation that millions of spirit worshippers in the world were as sane as anyone else.

The trail opened onto the type of village they'd seen thousands of times in their travels. Bamboo and wood houses on stilts with grass roofs, large concrete water pots, pigs, antique-looking farm implements, dirt, fenced-in vegetables, neat gardens and a well-kept village center with a court for rattan ball. Daeng saw nothing immediately threatening about the place, but she turned to Siri, and his face was as white as coconut meat.

"Siri, are you all right?" she asked.

"I feel like an outlaw who's just ridden into town and seen his face on a hundred wanted posters," he told her.

She had no idea what he meant.

Sawan's headman was standing by the rattan ball net with a toothless smile. He was about fifty, muscular and had a face abused, perhaps, in Muay Thai tournaments. Time had healed over the beatings like an ancient ruin covered in moss.

"Welcome," he said, putting his hands together in a *nop* the Thais called a *wai*. Siri and Daeng responded in kind. The Sangharaj did not respond because, well, he was supreme. Daeng wondered how the headman had known to expect them.

"I'm Tham," said the headman.

"This is my wife, Daeng," said Siri. "And I am . . ."

"You are Yeh Ming," said Tham. "Of course. We've been expecting you."

It happened often. Yeh Ming was the name of Siri's resident shaman who had hopped from body to body for a thousand years. Siri had told few living beings about his possession, yet he often ran into those who felt the presence of the old Hmong before they saw the doctor. The Sangharaj raised what used to be eyebrows and smiled in admiration.

"He's mistaken me for someone else," said Siri.

"I don't think so," said the monk.

"Let me show you our dear Sawan," said Tham like a proud parent introducing a new baby.

It was only when they came close to the houses that they could see just how bizarre the village was. Every hut was adorned with some kind of supernatural paraphernalia. But there was no cultural uniformity. It was as if each resident had decided which spirit to worship and which to be afraid of. It was like an open-air museum of paranormal paranoia. There were Hmong gates and bridges for the lost souls to find their ways home, and glass ornaments and mirrors to ward off unwanted spirits. There were smelly portals of dried garlic and gardens of straw or taro root dolls like regiments of tiny terracotta warriors. There were white cotton strings looping down beside the entryways and stuffed animals with looks of horror on their faces. Some huts displayed old coconuts made up to look like shrunken heads, and even though they were five hundred kilometers from the sea there were garlands of seashells strung out on posts.

And, in front of every hut there was a hand-painted board with a menu of services and their costs:

FINDING LOST OBJECTS/PEOPLE—30 baht
FAMILY SÉANCE—50 baht
CURSES AND GOOD WISHES—20 baht

Villagers sat on rocking chairs or on their front steps waving at the visitors, announcing their skills and calling out special offers. Siri couldn't believe his eyes. This was a tourist town: the Disneyland of animism. But it wasn't a scam. He could feel the power. He was certain country folk would travel here to solve their problems. Yet he remembered how the taxi driver had been afraid to bring them. Only the desperate would come. There was something sad about the services they offered. It was as if the true potential of the village was being constrained. Something was holding these folk back.

All around, he could see or sense the limbo people. They leaned against trees, sat on the branches, sunbathed on the grass waiting for assistance that never came. And permeating all of this was a dark fog, a stratum of malevolence where the *phibob* lurked. He could feel their anticipation, the excitement of some impending disaster. He knew his arrival had created a murmur that would change everything in Sawan.

The Sangharaj called a halt to the tour. "Tham," he said, "I believe you have morning tea arranged for your guests."

"Indeed I do," said Tham.

Tea was in the gazebo where, normally, the bodies were laid out before the pyre. As it was impossible for everyone in the village to meet Yeh Ming, they whittled the reception down to nine. They lined up like actors being introduced to royalty. Tham introduced them by specialty followed by name. Tham himself was the senior exorcist, quick to point out that he was retired.

The diviner, Song, was a tall woman with teary eyes and hair streaked white like Frankenstein's bride. The intermediary, Cham, had a shaved head and was fey bordering on effeminate. His superior, a full-fledged medium, was Tian. She was an older woman not unlike Daeng in appearance, with the same unruly mop of short white hair and a wicked smile. Then there were the shaman brothers, Phi and Lek, who were responsible for making bargains with the spirits. They were both missing their left legs, although Tham didn't bother to explain why. The village priestess was Thewa, who had probably been cherubic in her youth but now looked like a potato. The herbalist, Ya, was perhaps the youngest of the group and resembled one of the handsome stars of a Thai television drama. This left only the fortune-teller, Doo. He was stocky and unpleasant both in looks and in nature. His hair was in clumps as if he'd cut it with blunt scissors, and he had a goiter the size of a ripe papaya on his neck. He refused to join the queue to shake the visitors' hands and grumbled continuously under his breath.

Siri and Daeng would have no problem remembering them, as they were named in Thai language after their roles and most of them looked the part. They were dressed in their respective costumes and were a colorful bunch. Tea was served along with a tasteless doughy cake that had no purpose other than to soak up the tea. All but Doo clamored around Siri with the adoration usually reserved for rock stars. The Sangharaj and Daeng were largely ignored.

"I have to begin by asking how you all came to be in this village," said Siri. "I can tell from your ethnicity and accents that you've traveled from far and wide. Why did you settle here?"

He'd planned to avoid mentioning the claustrophobic presence of the *phibob*, but in company such as this, where everyone communicated on non-verbal levels, it was a foolish plan.

"The thing we have in common," said Priestess Thewa, "is that we were all banished from our own villages."

"Because we were possessed by *phibob*," said Intermediary Cham.

"All of you?" said Siri, dumbfounded.

"The first two generations," said Headman Tham. "They haven't got to our grandchildren yet."

"And never will," grumbled Doo.

"We were like lepers," said Medium Tian. "It didn't even have to be proven. You know what it's like in the countryside, Yeh Ming. There's a suspicion that turns into a rumor that overnight becomes a fact."

"Then you weren't all possessed?" said Siri.

"Not completely," said Shaman Phi.

"Perhaps a little," said Shaman Lek. "From time to time. We were all in the spirit trade, you see? There were a lot of currents and waves passing through us. It's likely we'd pick up a *phibob* or two."

"But it's more like the flu than cancer," said Headman Tham. "You get over it."

"Some get it like cancer," grumbled Doo.

Siri had learned his lessons in *phibob*ery very quickly. They were not the spirits of the deceased. Neither were they, strictly speaking, the spirits of the forest. They were the ghosts that existed as a result of the destruction of nature. In a previous incarnation they may have been placid tree-dwellers. Then, one day, their home was gone, their roots lost. And they began to wander aimlessly and became more and more volatile. And as more forests were destroyed, so the *phibob* joined forces and became powerful. They did their evil by possessing a living being like a hand inside a sock puppet. The demoniacs rarely knew they were possessed unless they had their own channel to the spirit world.

Madam Daeng had never attended a meeting such as

this, and she was quite plainly thrilled by the ridiculous-
ness of it all. She smiled at the Sangharaj, who replied with
a slight tilt of his brow. She noticed how Medium Tian, the
oldest woman in the group, would strain her neck from
time to time to get a better look at Daeng's backside. The
woman would give her a knowing smile before returning her attention to the meeting. The thought that her
tail might be visible to this crowd made Daeng feel oddly
self-conscious.

"Look, let's get to the point," said Doo.

"And what might the point be?" asked Priestess Thewa.

"The point," said Doo, "is not to discuss our origins.
These outsiders are here because one of theirs is about to
be executed for murder."

"Oh, do shut up," said Diviner Song.

Doo ignored her. "They're here to find a scapegoat," he
said. "His high and mightiness there thinks we're expend-
able because we're clay doll worshippers. He thinks he can
dangle one of our names in front of the judge, and they'll
do a deal. Free the monk; shoot the village idiot."

"Then that would have to be you," said Headman Tham.

"Why else would they be here lording over us?" asked
Doo. "Looking down at us like all those fancy abbots in
Bangkok."

"Sorry," said Headman Tham to the Sangharaj. "He can
see the future, so I suppose he doesn't have much to be
positive about."

"But he does have a point," said Shaman Lek. "Given
the Sangha's views on the occult, how can the Sangharaj
be here with an open mind?"

"We really don't want to insult our guests," said Headman Tham.

"No, actually I don't mind at all," said the Sangharaj. "I'd like a chance to clear my name."

"It's not nec—"

"Really," said the Sangharaj. "I wonder if our learned fortune-teller realizes that there are as many members of the Thai Sangha Council who condemn our Lao version of Buddhism as those who make fun of your pagan rituals."

"I'm no pagan," said Doo.

"Nor am I," said the monk. "Animism had existed for centuries in my country long before Buddhism arrived. We are a fragmented nation of hundreds of different ethnic groups, each with its own beliefs. All of them were convinced of the existence of a spirit or a soul. Buddhism in other places denied the existence of a self—said that a soul is the source of suffering—but we didn't want to alienate those tribes, did we now? Didn't want to steamroll through centuries of culture. So we conceded that there is such a thing as a soul. That immediately pitted us against the mainstream. There were other contentious differences. Gods, for example. Our deities reside in their own heaven, whereas world Buddhism emphasizes impermanence. There was no room for compromise. We had defied our own order. So you see, in the Sangha's eyes I'm no less a heathen than you."

That was the moment when Siri and Daeng became aware that the Sangharaj had no intention of defecting to Bangkok.

"In conclusion," said the monk, "I am here because my friend is in trouble. I like and trust the abbot, so I have traveled far to be here in order to help prove him innocent. Does anybody here honestly believe a dedicated man such as Abbot Rayron would suddenly go rogue for no reason?"

This sparked a general discussion on both the good works of the abbot and a good-natured free-for-all examining the facts and putting forward new theories. There was nothing insightful nor particularly brilliant about the comments. Siri was always surprised by the day-to-day simplicity of the men and women who, with the right stimulus, tackled demons and rode on the back of stallions to the otherworld. But this was not a philosophical gathering. It was a collection of facts. They agreed that the girl who claimed to have seen a monk at night had no reason to lie. In fact, her future depended on her honesty. Her ambition was to join an order. In Thailand, a woman wishing to become a nun was like a man dreaming of becoming a street sweeper. There was nothing in the way of respect or financial gain to be had by joining a nunnery. Buddhism was an unashamedly misogynistic religion. Women were told that to become enlightened they would first have to be reborn a man. But she didn't seem to care. As lying was sinful she admitted that although she had seen a monk walk away from the village, she could not be certain it was Abbot Rayron.

The boy who had seen two monks walk to the shortcut on the night of the first murder was also unlikely to have lied. It was the abbot himself who had persuaded him to step forward with his eyewitness account. The lad studied at the temple and was one of the abbot's brightest. The village was too far from the nearest government school, so the children in Sawan studied in the temple. All the abbot's students adored him. The parents were pleased he didn't proselytize but instead encouraged the children to form their own view of the world by listening to all sides of a debate, religion included.

"So the abbot incriminated himself," said Daeng. "That hardly sounds like the action of a guilty man."

"Murderers can be devious," said Doo.

"Oh, shut up," said almost everyone.

"But that brings us to the night when your eldest villager was killed," said Siri.

"Nobody mourned that man," said Diviner Song.

"Evil piece of shit," said Shaman Phi.

"That doesn't excuse drowning him in his own paddy and gutting him," said Headman Tham.

"Who was he drinking with?" Siri asked.

Headman Tham, the shaman brothers and Doo put up their hands.

"I liked him," said Doo.

"It's a small village," said Shaman Lek. "If you like a drink you either indulge at home alone and get nagged at by the wife, or you come here to the gazebo."

"This is your pub?" said Daeng.

"We have a communal still out back," said Headman Tham, glancing at the Sangharaj hoping for forgiveness and not receiving it.

"So Loong Gan staggered out of here the way we came in," said Siri. He stood and went to the entrance, retrieving his sandals on the way out. The others followed.

"He went that way," said Shaman Phi, pointing across the clearing beyond the rattan ball court. "We all followed him out."

"And where was he when the monk came to help him?"

"Just at the tree line."

"Even with a full moon it's quite a distance to make a clear identification," said Siri. "And I assume you were all drunk."

Daeng stood scratching her head. "Was it closing time?" she asked.

"What?" said the headman.

"You all left at the same time," she said. "Did they close the bar?"

They laughed.

"It's not the type of bar that closes," said the headman. "You come and you go as you please."

"Then why did you all leave together?" she asked.

They all looked at each other but nobody had an answer. Then, one of the shamans said, "The whistle."

"That's right," said Doo. "There was a whistle. I'd completely forgotten about that."

"What whistle?" asked Siri.

"It was like a police whistle," said the headman. "Loong Gan left and we heard this whistle, and the first thing we thought was that he'd been arrested. Now, thinking back, that doesn't make any sense because who's going to arrest him late at night for being drunk in his own village? And we have no local policeman. But, well, we were all in our cups. So we ran out."

"And that's when you saw him meet the monk?" said Siri.

"That's right."

"Interesting."

Before he retired for the night, Siri decided now was a good time to have a chat with the quiet abbot. He found him in the prayer hall reading by candlelight.

"Are you busy?" Siri asked, sitting opposite the monk without waiting for an invitation.

The abbot put down his book and removed his glasses. "Please," he said.

"Did you kill those people?" Siri asked.

"That's your first question?" said the abbot.

"Always good to get that one out of the way first," said Siri.

The abbot took some time to reply. "What do you think?" he asked.

Siri smiled. "Well, son, that really was the wrong answer. I hope for your sake the judge doesn't ask you that question. I don't know you. I don't know anything about you. So if you ask me what I think, looking at the evidence, I'd say you're as guilty as sin."

He looked around to give the abbot time to rethink his answer. They were sitting cross-legged in the prayer hall. The Buddha image looked down on them, jolly in its new coat of yellow paint. The wall murals depicted scenes of what Civilai called the Indian music hall version of Buddha's life: flying through the air and bursting into flames, taking on Angulimāla, the killer of thousands, walking through mountains.

"Then, no," said the abbot at last.

"Well, somebody's trying really hard to make us believe you did," said Siri. "So if you can think of anyone who might want you put away for life, now's the time to remember."

The long gaps between question and answer were vexing. Siri drummed his fingers on his knees.

"I'm a Buddhist monk in an animist village," said the abbot. "I have a big fine palace to live in because the Buddhist Council has a budget for buildings and ornaments. It's possible the spirit worshippers in the village resent this opulence because in their eyes I'm just another shaman. Brother Ya mixes potions that make a man irresistible to women. Sister Song selects a spot to dig a well. Abbot Rayron performs at funerals. I could branch out. There are monks who bless airplanes and provide lottery numbers and tell fortunes. But I do not. I don't step on anyone's toes. I adhere to my scriptures. I teach. I lead by example. I try to steer the villagers in the direction of better decisions on health and personal relationships and management of resources. But I don't preach. It's not our way. I tell stories. I hope to inspire. But I've never had a heated debate on the benefits of my religion. If you ask me if I'm respected here, I'd say I hope so. If I'm liked? I hope so. If I've angered a man enough to wish me dead? That, I hope not."

Siri shifted his numb buttocks and stretched his spine. One gentle crack echoed through the hall. He stared at the abbot. He was what Madam Daeng referred to as "eventually handsome": a face you don't immediately consider to be good-looking but which grows on you. He was about forty with a body that left no evidence of the sugars and alcohol and starches and fats and tobacco the twentieth century inflicted upon the weak.

"Then what about your personal life?" Siri asked.

"I'm a monk. I don't have a personal life."

"But you did. Before the monkhood."

"Oh, such a distant life. How is that likely to help us, Doctor?"

"In your defense? Probably not at all. But in understanding you there's gold to be panned in a man's origins."

"Then I think your pan might be empty. I was abandoned at the temple when I was eight."

"Really?" said Siri. "Me too. See? Our first scoop, and we come up with empathy. Eight must have been the fashionable age to dump young boys."

"But you broke away, Doctor. I remained with the Buddha because he was the only father I knew. I'd been raised by a woman I loved and who apparently loved me. And then suddenly she wasn't in my life. People I didn't know took over her duties. Then one day a man came to the house. He looked Chinese, but he spoke Thai. He was well dressed. He put me in the backseat of his car. There was a small paper bag beside me that contained my clothes. I'd never been in a car. It was like flying in a magic device. And he dropped me at the temple, told me to be good for my mother's sake, mussed my hair and flew off. Thanks to the mode of my arrival I was instantly popular with the novices."

"Do you know where the temple was?"

"Of course. It was my home as a child. Wat Po in Udon Thani."

"And did you ever return there later in life to ask about the man with the car?"

The abbot contemplated his fists for a long time. "Not until it was too late. The monks I served as a novice were all dead, and there was no record of deliveries. Today people drop off dogs at the temples when they can no longer cope with them or are too poor to feed them. Back then the same applied to male children. I was an unwanted stray, but I found acceptance and peace."

"Until now."

"This is my destiny."

"Oh, don't give me that karma rot."

But this was to be the night when destiny demonstrated her power. It was beneath the light of a single moon that three unrelated women lost their lives: one on the outskirts of Vientiane, one in Pak Xan and one in a village of sleeping shamans. It was midnight and Madam Daeng was woken by the word *"merde"* repeated several times. She opened her eyes to see her husband hurriedly putting on his trousers by the light of the full moon. As she was not unused to emergencies in their relationship, she immediately stood and began to throw on her clothes as well.

"Where are we going?" she asked.

"To the village," he said.

"What's wrong?"

"My brain. I can't believe how stupid I am."

"Anytime you need reminding, feel free to ask."

They were already on their way out of the door with their bags over their shoulders.

"Five years, Daeng," he said. "Five years I was at that temple. They told us those damned stories over and over again until they were big chunks of unwanted gunk lodged in our memories. The Buddha stories. The son of a king decides to renounce his wealth and head off into the world leaving footprints and body parts from Nepal to China."

Daeng's flashlight worked that night although the full moon was bright enough to see the eyelashes on a mosquito. They were out of the temple compound gate and on the haunted path. Again, Ugly balked at the start of the track. The couple ran at a sort of geriatric road-walk pace ignoring the howls and groans coming from the jungle on either side. Siri's lungs weren't what they used to be, and Daeng had only recently reclaimed her leg muscles.

"I wish I'd brought the Triumph," he said.

"And what was it the Buddha did that was so important we need to risk heart attacks?" wheezed Daeng.

"The four . . . things."

"What four things?"

"The things the Buddha saw that made him realize the world wasn't all frangipani leis and champagne cocktails. He climbed over the palace wall and went into town to see what his parents had been shielding him from. And that's when he saw them."

"What? Who?"

"An ascetic, a corpse, an old man . . ."

They were too late for the sick woman. She'd been given some sort of fast-acting poison. When they arrived at her hut, her lips and the inside of her nose had already turned greyish white, and there was some bubbling around her mouth. Siri had seen her earlier in the day when he'd offered to take a look at the village sick. He'd found the elderly folk to be in remarkably good shape. The old woman was the only serious case that the herbs of young brother Ya had been unable to help, and Siri had treated her for hepatitis. The Buddha had seen a sick man on his fact-finding mission, but as there were none available, in this case, a sick woman would have to suffice.

Following Siri's alert, the villagers headed off with their weapons to find the murderer. Some voiced their opinions that they'd find the culprit back at the temple where he'd come from. An old witch suffering from insomnia had been rocking on a chair on her porch when the monk walked past in the direction of the dead woman's house. She had no doubt whatsoever in her mind that the monk was Abbot Rayron.

◎ ◎ ◎

Humnoy, the man who currently ran the Lao national police force, was neither a policeman nor a military man. Nor was he an academic versed in the laws of the country because they were yet to be written. Nor was he a bookkeeper of any standing. His qualifications for the role could be summed up in the phrase, "He's a good Party member and the brother-in-law of somebody important."

The lack of abilities in no way prevented him from doing his job. The buck had to stop somewhere, and he was the perfect man to stop it. He made endless arbitrary decisions based, apparently, upon how to upset the fewest of his superiors. His favorite words were *bo dai,* which naturally meant "no."

"Bo dai," he said having listened intently to the inspector's request. It was no less than Phosy expected. But Phosy was no two-left-footer when it came to circle-dancing with administrators.

"Yes, that was my first reaction too," he said. "Why rile the military? Who really cares that their soldiers kidnapped an innocent civilian on the street in front of witnesses? He probably deserved it. Why, the two young soldiers are probably downstairs right now putting in an official complaint about whatever it was he'd done. Because we all know this is not a country run by a military junta, but a democratic republic with a fully functioning police force charged with the responsibility of keeping the peace."

"I'm not—"

"In fact that's what I reminded Corporal Suwit on Friday."

"Who?"

"Corporal Suwit at the Armed Forces Ministry. Oh, sorry. I assumed you two were acquainted. He knows everything there is to know about you down to your shoe size."

"What in blazes does this Suwit have to do with me?"

"He's the head of the military—national police liaison department. You do know that exists, right?"

"There is no such thing."

Phosy had gambled on his boss having no more knowledge of the department than Phosy himself before he stumbled across it.

"With all due respect, sir, I was sitting in that office just a few days ago. Suwit seemed to have a lot of information about me and my cases. He had a file on my department as thick as a temple lintel."

"But that's . . . that's atrocious."

"Couldn't agree more, sir. Especially given some of his comments about . . . No, doesn't matter."

"Phosy!"

"No, really. I shouldn't say."

"I order you to tell me."

"There was nothing direct. Just comments about . . . about your suitability for this position. What they called 'a poor track record.'"

"Bastards."

"I know, sir. I told him I didn't want to hear any more."

"How dare the army keep files on us?"

"How dare they, indeed?"

The director was a broad man, brawny, easily angered. His cheeks reddened to signal he'd passed his limit, but commendably he didn't raise his voice. He placed his big hands flat on the desk and practiced his breathing. Phosy sat patiently. Finally, the director nodded.

"These witnesses," he said.

"Yes, sir?"

"Would they be prepared to give evidence?"

"I believe so."

"All right. Bring 'em in."

"Are you sure it's—?"

"Just do it."

Phosy stopped outside the director's door. He should have been sitting in that chair. He'd fought and spied bravely for the Pathet Lao during the resistance years. He'd agreed to join the police to convert men of war into peacekeepers. He'd been integral in the writing of most of the temporary regulations they were using as their flimsy legal base. But it seemed that for every competent man or woman there was an incompetent man above. It was the law of trickle-up irresponsibility. And the competent man and woman spent so much time manipulating the incompetent men they had neither the time nor the motivation to do their jobs properly.

Phosy took a police jeep out to the kiosk of the cordial seller. He had a young sergeant by his side. He'd omitted to mention that the innocent civilian was not Lao. And there was, of course, just the one eyewitness, and she had no idea who the kidnappers were. All she had was an instinct, and that wouldn't carry any weight in the court of law—if in fact they had such things. But Phosy had people who owed him favors. He was certain one or two of them could be diverted retrospectively to the scene of the crime. And with backup, who knew what the cordial seller might recall?

She wasn't sitting behind the bottles when they arrived. He drove off the road and down the track that led to her bamboo hut. The pile of empties still dominated the yard. The hut wasn't a complicated structure: A single room on stilts with barely enough space for a pig below. A ladder up to an unfenced balcony.

Phosy stood on the middle step and banged on the banana-leaf door. There was no answer. The balcony was caked in dust from the road, but out of courtesy he kicked off his sandals and climbed up.

"Anybody there?" he called.

No answer. Even before he pushed the flimsy door a familiar smell hit him. He knew what to expect. The room was buzzing with flies. They seemed to congregate mostly around the far side of the room where a window shape was cut out of the panel. There was a dark, dry puddle. There had been a lot of blood, although much of it would have seeped down through the gaps in the bamboo flooring. He sighed and looked through the window. The scenery was beautiful: white terns on the backs of buffalo, lush green paddies, and verdant trees that looked like they could defy the advance of development forever. The only nature that ever disappointed him was of the human variety.

◙ ◙ ◙

It was an odd breakfast. Captain Gumron had been dragged out of his bed at two to investigate yet another murder at Sawan Village. As there was no phone line to Nam Som, Yuth, the headman's slow-witted son, had taken the village motorcycle to alert the police. The captain, having talked to some peculiar Lao coroner and his wife— both apparently in the country illegally—had interviewed the eyewitness to the crime. She was riddled with cataracts in both eyes, but he really had no choice but to re-arrest Abbot Rayron. The sun was up, and he and his constable were tired and in need of a feed. As the alms at Sawan village were legendary, they decided to accept the offer of breakfast before dragging the suspect off to jail. The only other good news was that this was court day. They would have had to come anyway to cart the monk off to hear the judge's decision on the previous month's hearings. So, in a way, they were killing two birds with one stone.

As Abbot Rayron was accused of multiple homicides, the Sangharaj had graciously agreed to take on the abbot's alms that morning. He returned with a feast worthy of a five-star hotel. Abbot Rayron sat a few meters behind the Supreme Patriarch, eating meagerly.

"Well, if you didn't do it, brother," said Captain Gumron, slurping up spoonfuls of delicious rice porridge, "you must have really pissed somebody off. Because it means there's a character out there pretending to be you killing folk and defiling corpses. Anybody hate you that much?"

"Not to my knowledge," said the abbot.

"It might not be personal," said Siri.

The captain had long since tired of the old Lao man's theories. He was on the verge of making this a double arrest.

"What do you mean, Siri?" asked the Sangharaj.

"Well, think about it," said Siri. "An anonymous monk committing crimes that mirror the revelations of the Buddha. This isn't a murderer who hates Abbot Rayron. It's a murderer who hates the religion."

"I'd like to remind you all this is an ongoing investigation," said the captain. "And I am not at liberty to discuss theories or wild accusations."

"Then don't say anything," said Madam Daeng. "Just listen."

The captain laughed. "One more comment like that, young lady, and I'll have you in handcuffs," said the captain.

Siri's haunches rose. The policeman was clearly flirting with his wife. The Thais had no scruples. The doctor had no choice but to lock horns with this rival.

"Whilst doing my rounds of the elderly and infirm of the village," he said, "I noticed how few villagers had hair above their collars. I think it's something the Thai police should have taken into consideration."

"What?" said the captain. "Hair fashion? Isn't that more the role of your morals police up in Laos? Length of hair. Length of hem. We've got better things to do."

"I'm talking, of course, about beginning the search for the man who's impersonating Abbot Rayron. Something you should have been doing months ago."

He stared at the Thai policeman, who was stuffing his face with food meant for the monks. He was in his fifties, and, despite the restrictive qualities of the Thai police uniform, he had a considerable paunch. He walked as if he expected a wild boar to run between his legs. He wasn't at all Madam Daeng's type, yet she fluttered her eyelids every time he looked her way.

"In fact," Siri continued, "if I were a Thai policeman I'd be looking at the elders of the village. One or two of them are losing their hair. I'd be focusing on men over forty."

"Mr. Coroner," said Gumron, using the derogatory term, "ghost doctor," suggesting Siri's role was more a vocation than a profession, "from getting out of bed this morning to my arrival here took thirty minutes. Anyone with a motorcycle or car can come here. Why would I concentrate my efforts on the village when anyone from the town could have done it?"

Siri smiled. "Because," he said, "this is a crime of hate. You have so many more splendid temples around Nam Som with many more monks to abuse. Much more explosive points to be made. But he chooses a small temple in the jungle. No. Whatever inspired these murders has its roots here."

"Of course," said the captain. "A man of science. You'd be delighted if the murderer was a shaman or an exorcist or any one of the weird characters who practice pagan rituals here. You're prejudiced."

Daeng wiped a tissue over her lips, smiled and left the men to their duel. Siri would have loved to race after her, lift her tail and shout, "Is this prejudice?"

He would gladly have disappeared right then and reappeared five minutes later to see the look of amazement on the man's face. But there was something about the captain. His ease around the villagers. His willingness to come to Sawan alone when other townies dared not unless they were in a tour group. Siri understood.

"You're from here," he said.

"What?"

"You're a Sawan lad. A child of the sages. These are your people."

"Grandfather, I think you've done enough amateur detective work, don't you?" He turned away from Siri's satisfied smile and addressed the abbot. "The constable and me came on two motorcycles. Do you want the boy to go back to bring a van, or . . . ?"

"I'm fine on the back of a motorcycle," said the abbot.

"I thought so," said the captain. "I don't suppose you have much in the way of belongings?"

The abbot held up his small saffron shoulder bag.

"When will the judge hear the abbot's case?" asked the Sangharaj.

"Well, sir, it's not exactly something you could set a clock to," said the captain. "We're on what they call the judicial circuit. Prosecutor Suthon is here once a month. When he's in town he gets through as many cases as he can in three days. He got here yesterday. Now, the more serious the case, the higher the priority. He'll be expecting to pass down a verdict on last month's murder. He won't be prepared at all for what happened last night. I'll have to type up the report of my findings here and that takes time. I don't know if he'll want to make a judgment without looking at the new evidence. So I'm guessing he'll not say a lot today."

"The abbot doesn't have the right to have witnesses speak on his behalf?" asked Siri.

"Usually not," said the captain. "All that stuff will be in my report."

"Doesn't that make you the judge?" said Siri.

"I don't write down opinions, Grandfather. I just make a note of what I see and what people tell me."

"That's what most of the newspapers in the world claim to be doing, but you'd be surprised how slanted the finished text turns out."

"Yeah, and you'd really know something about the world's newspapers."

"A bit."

"Nobody's ever questioned my reports," said the policeman. "I spend a lot of time getting them accurate."

His defensiveness was turning to annoyance, his tolerance taut as a piano wire. But still Siri pushed. "And meanwhile the accused rots away in a cell for a month waiting for the next judicial visit," he said.

The Sangharaj cut in like a boxing referee. "I too am concerned with the amount of time the abbot will have to wait before the next hearing."

"That's the system," said the captain. "We have cases ongoing for four or five years. We have witnesses and suspects die of old age before they hear a judgment."

"Isn't there any way to expedite the process?" asked the Sangharaj.

"In this country I'm sure money would speed things up," said Siri in the background.

Gumron ignored him. "Only one that I know," he said.

"And what would that be?" asked the Sangharaj.

"Publicity," said the captain. "If for some reason the press picks up on a story, especially if some celebrity's involved, and the TV people hop on board and the public weighs in on the side of the accused, then you'd be amazed how a case can speed up. Pressure from Bangkok to be seen doing its job. Good exposure overseas. But, then again it could all be over today."

"How so?" said Siri.

"Well, the judge has had time to go over the reports of the first three incidents. After the first two he said there wasn't enough evidence. But since then we had another murder, and now this. He might just recommend the death penalty this very day, and your abbot will be shipped off to Udon."

Siri looked at Abbot Rayron, whose expression hadn't changed since the doctor arrived. There had been no delight, no shock, no horror registered there. The doctor couldn't tell whether it was the look of enlightenment or resignation.

"And this all based on a couple of informal chats with villagers and scribbled notes and circumstantial evidence," said Siri. "No cross-examination. No research. No appeal. And I thought our system at home was barbaric."

The policeman had reached his limit. "Listen, you hick, Commie senior citizen, we do what we can on a low budget. We're swamped out here. It wasn't that long ago that all these cases were settled by village headmen with vested interests. You upset some old idiot today, and you find yourself in his court tomorrow. We've come a long way since then. You get your own house in order before you start throwing rocks at ours."

◙ ◙ ◙

Madam Nong had traveled back to Vientiane with the driver. Civilai was at the council office at exactly opening time. The officials of the district council office arrived between twenty and forty minutes later. Civilai continued to sit on a concrete bench in the garden where brown vines strangled the few surviving flowers and the grass was too high to walk through. Nobody asked him who he was or what he wanted. He noted how Communist bureaucracies constantly shifting cadres had created an impersonal, non-caring system.

He wasn't absolutely sure what he was doing there. Perhaps it was just that there had been nobody to complain to in the village, and the desire to vent one's frustrations could be a powerful thing. But there was something else. He'd felt ill at ease in Ban Toop. It wasn't a normal Lao village. He hoped that the government administrators could explain what was going on there.

At last he walked inside, where a greasy-faced girl was filing. "Where's your director?" he asked.

"Just sit down, Granddad," she said. "We'll get to you."

"I don't want to be got to," he said. "I want to speak to your director."

She sighed as if she'd had her fill of grumpy old people. Then she ignored him. She just carried on with her filing as if he didn't exist. Civilai hated being ignored almost as much as he hated the Chinese. He walked up behind her.

"What's in those files?" he asked.

"Oh, just sit down," she said.

"I wouldn't be surprised if one of your cabinet drawers was labeled something like . . . ooh, I don't know. Politburo? Am I right?"

She disregarded him, but she was clearly feeling uncomfortable. He walked along the bank of cabinets calling out the labels alphabetically until he reached the drawer he'd been looking for. He'd pulled it open and thumbed through the files before she could react. As he expected, the photographs of politburo members who had been retired from both the cabinet and the frames on the wall had been placed in the drawer. There was an expanding number of pictures of those who had passed away. He found the photo of himself just as the girl reached him. She made a lunge for it but his backward step was too quick for her.

"Well, look at this," he said. "I wonder who this vibrant young character is. He was a little thinner back then before the kitchen gods possessed him, but I think he's filled out quite nicely now, don't you?"

She looked at the photo, looked at the man who held it, then looked at the photo again. And her legs seemed to give way beneath her.

8

A Living Skeleton in the Closet

Civilai stood in the office of Comrade Luangrat, director of the local council, having refused water, juice, Coca-Cola, tea, coffee, snacks, cigarettes and "something a little stronger." He refused to sit as he listed the failings of the office. It was then that he added the debacle of his own official visit to the region and the absence of pomp and ceremony. The director was not the dynamic type. He looked like an old cinema usher who'd spent his life in the dark showing people to their seats. Even his embarrassment was subdued.

"We got the notification from Vientiane," he said.

"And threw it in the bin?"

"No, comrade," he said. "Naturally we informed the headman at Ban Toop. He insisted on making the arrangements for your visit himself."

"But it's the responsibility of you and your office to follow up on that. At the very least you should have been there to greet my wife and me. That's protocol."

"I know," said the director, timidly.

"So why weren't you?"

"It's . . . it's a little difficult to explain."

"Good. I have until my heart finally gives out to hear that difficult explanation."

Civilai sat behind the desk. The director was silent for the longest time.

"Well?" barked Civilai.

"The headman at Ban Toop is a very well-respected and powerful man."

"More respected and powerful than your office? More powerful than the administration you represent?"

"At the local level, I suppose one could say yes."

"You're afraid of him."

"Goodness, no. But my role here is to maintain cordial and productive relations with village communities that have been established for generations."

"Did he tell you not to send anyone to meet me?"

"Not in those words."

"Then, give me the words."

"He said they would welcome the esteemed visitor according to the traditions of the village."

Which means not welcoming him at all, thought Civilai, but he said nothing. He'd had enough. It was clear he was talking to the wrong man.

"I need a car," he said.

"We . . ."

"Yes?"

"We only have the one."

"That should be enough."

"There's no driver available."

"I've been driving since 1921. I think I remember how."

"But . . ."

"You really have a 'but' after all this?"

"No."

"I assume you have a fax machine?"

"Yes."

"Then I want you to contact my office in Vientiane. I'll give you the number. Tell them we have a village that could use a little discipline. You can use your own words. Explain to them what's happened and tell them to send out a team immediately. I'll stay until they get here. I'll come by this office tomorrow to collect the reply."

"You won't . . . I mean, this won't endanger my position here, will it?"

"Honestly, Comrade Luangrat," said Civilai, "I'm surprised you *have* a position here. Now, where's my car?"

◙ ◙ ◙

Nurse Dtui and Mr. Geung had been sitting in the reception area of the Ministry of Justice for forty-four minutes. There were only four hours between the lunch and dinner shifts at the noodle restaurant, so time was precious. Manivon, the chief clerk and secretary to Judge Haeng, had apologized every ten of those minutes. Apologizing took up a large chunk of her time most days. Dtui and Manivon had known and liked each other for a long time, so if strings could have been pulled to get Dtui into the judge's office they would have been. But her boss reminded everybody that these were particularly hectic times. The republic was a week away from formalizing diplomatic relations with Bulgaria. The Thai prime minister had visited, which had entailed setting up a number of impromptu meetings. The Soviet Development Commission had been touring the disastrous cooperative farming

projects in the south, and there were moves afoot to recognize a Vietnamese puppet government in Cambodia led
by an ex-officer of the Khmer Rouge.

In fact, Judge Haeng had been involved in none of
these political matters but he used them as an excuse to
hide out in his office with the blinds closed. Whenever
Manivon knocked on his door he would jump out of his
skin. He flinched at any loud sound and had stopped eating. Rumors were circulating in the ministry that he'd
become an opium addict.

Dtui tapped Mr. Geung on the knee. "Let's go," she said.

"Go wh-where?" asked Geung.

"To disturb a rude judge," she told him.

"Poor judge," he said but followed her along the open
corridor. If anyone had cause to hate the little judge—and
many did—Mr. Geung should have been at the front of the
queue. Haeng had gone to great pains to remove Geung
from his position of morgue assistant at Mahosot Hospital. He'd called him a freak, said there was no budget to
employ morons. Yet even though he understood all of
these terms, honest, sweet Mr. Geung hadn't been able to
find hatred in his heart.

They arrived at the unmarked door and Dtui knocked
lightly before barging inside. She was just in time to see
the judge drop to the floor behind his desk.

"Ha, ha. I spy you," said Geung.

"Judge Haeng," said Dtui, "it's me, Nurse Dtui."

"What do you want?" he asked.

She got on her knees. "Why are you under the desk?"
she asked.

"Paper clip," he said. "Dropped one."

"Can I help you?" she asked.

"No." He banged his head on the underside of the desk when he tried to return to his chair. When he was finally seated he noticed Geung standing in the doorway.

"What's that doing here?" he asked.

"He's with me," said Dtui.

"I can see that," said the judge, slowly regaining his composure.

To Dtui, Haeng looked like a roll of moldy flannel.

"Are you all right?" she asked.

He was twiddling a pencil between his fingers to disguise his trembles.

"What gives you the right to inquire about my mind?" he asked.

"Err, I wasn't," she said. "I was asking after your health."

"Then don't," he said. "I'm perfectly well. Now, I don't believe you have an appointment." He looked menacingly at Geung, who waved his fingers in reply.

"In a way we do," said Dtui. "The doctor thinks he can help you with your little ghost problem. So he sent us."

"Siri?" said the judge. "Where the hell is he? I've been sending messages for two days."

"The doctor and Madam Daeng had to go . . . away on business."

"Damn. And what do you suppose a chubby girl can do for somebody like me?"

Dtui took one last gulp of her pride. She had promised Siri, after all. She remembered one of her mother's sayings. *When you're removing a splinter from a bear's paw, expect a few scratches.* Judge Haeng was a hard man to help.

"Look," she said. "Everything Dr. Siri knows about you—medically, politically, mentally and morally—I know about you too. The doctor and I have no secrets. So don't play the

tough judge with me. I don't have to be here. I have noodles
to boil and nurses to teach and a daughter to play with."

"Me too," said Geung with a grin.

"And, in fact, I'd be happier digging up beets in the
communal garden than helping you. So either show a little
humility, or we're leaving and you can spend the rest of
your life haunted by a dwarf." She headed for the door.

"No, wait," he called.

Before heading to Comrade Koomki's apartment, they
stopped off at the market for some supplies the doctor had
recommended. At first they couldn't get Haeng to walk
through the communal front doorway of the old colonial
house.

"Tell me why we're here," he said.

"We're following up on a Dr. Siri hypothesis," Dtui told
him. "Do you have the keys?"

She knew he did because she could hear them rattling
in his shaky hand. She took them from him, walked along
the corridor to Koomki's room and opened the door. The
apartment smelled of excrement but not death. Dtui considered that a good sign.

"We might be in time," she said.

"What for?" shouted the judge.

"To prevent a loss of life."

"Whose?" asked the judge, slowly edging along the dark
corridor toward the room.

"Let's see."

Dtui went immediately to the wardrobe and unlocked it.
The stench from inside was horrendous. She put her hand
over her mouth and nose and looked inside. The contents appeared to have been attacked by a madman with

a machete. Clothes were ripped to shreds, the wooden shelves where split and scratched, and there were blood-stains around the lock. She took down a metal coat hanger and used it to poke around in the debris. It was on the bottom shelf beneath the folds of a nylon bedcover that she found it, as good as dead. Its claws were caked in dried blood from its attempts to escape. Some teeth were broken. Hair was shedding in clumps and it was as skinny as a lattice of toothpicks. But it was alive.

"Not dead yet!" shouted Dtui.

Haeng came tentatively into the room. "What is it?" he asked.

"A cat," said Dtui.

"A what?"

"Koomki kept a cat," said Dtui. "When you came to inspect the apartment, you locked her in the wardrobe."

He looked over her shoulder. "Are we too late?" he asked.

"Might be."

Mr. Geung gently lifted the body. She weighed no more than a lightbulb.

"But that was a month ago," said the judge. "This is impossible."

"You'd think so," said Dtui. "Defies all logic. But here it is."

She opened the bags they'd brought from the market and unwound the rubber band that fastened a plastic pouch of coconut water. Mr. Geung dipped his finger in the liquid and rubbed it over the cat's lips. There was no reaction. He tried again.

"Coconut water," she said. "Lot of nutrients and easy to digest. In a pinch it can be used in place of a saline drip.

I'd sooner she took it by mouth though if she's got the strength."

"But how?" said the judge. "How did Siri know it was in there?"

"Intelligent guess," she said. "Instinct. A whisper from the beyond. Who knows? But the doctor figured even a man like Koomki needed company, and cats don't really care about body odor or bad personalities as long as you feed them. Siri put two and two together. Saucer and towel on the floor, animal comics, the sound of crying. And he decided Comrade Koomki wasn't as tough as he pretended to be. He loved his cat and he couldn't move on as long as it was suffering."

"And that's why he's . . . he's . . ."

"Haunting you? Probably. We'll know for sure if we can't bring this little fellow back from the edge."

"Little girl," said Geung.

"I imagine if you killed his cat Comrade Koomki would dedicate the rest of his afterlife to making you miserable."

Geung put the cat on the table and tried again with drips of coconut water. Judge Haeng stood over her like a grieving parent.

"Will she . . . ?" asked the judge.

"She can't find her swallowing instinct," said Dtui. "Let's give her a hose job."

Dtui bit a corner off the plastic bag and squirted the juice into the cat's mouth through the hole. Most of it ended up on the table but some found its way down the throat and made her cough.

"I reckon that got through, don't you?" said Dtui.

A little tongue appeared between the cat's lips and licked at her wet whiskers.

"There you go," said Geung.

He left the cat with Dtui and went to take a look in the wardrobe.

"In-in-instant noodle packets," he said thumbing through the contents of the shelves, "leather boots chewed down to-to-to the soles. Shreds of p-p-paper."

He knelt down to look on the bottom of the cupboard and let out a victorious cheer.

"Here we, here we are," he said.

He pulled out a twenty-five liter water bottle that lay on its side. It was made of heavy duty plastic. The top was screwed on tightly and still had the water distributor's tape stretched over it.

"It must have been a frustrating obstacle for a cat dying of thirst," said Dtui. "But it's not full, so she got in there somehow. See anything, pal?"

"Here on the side," said Mr. Geung. "She scratched her w-w-w-way in."

"And wore her claws down to the stubs," said Dtui holding up one front paw.

The cat was lapping weakly at the puddle of coconut water in Dtui's palm, still with no strength to stand. Her eyes were closed, and her body shuddered from time to time.

"Lucky she wasn't a dog," said Dtui. "Cats originated in warmer climates. They don't drink as much as dogs. Just as well. It isn't exactly flowing out of the bottle, is it?"

"Only one drip so far," said Geung.

"Right," said Dtui. "One drip every ten minutes. She'd have to be one patient cat."

"She's a survi-vi-vivor," said Geung.

"She sure is," said Dtui. "I think we should take her home and fatten her up."

"No," said the judge.

"No, what?" said Dtui, about to get on her high horse.

"I mean, I'll take her."

"That's all right," said Dtui. "It'll be a burden for you. We can—"

"Seriously," said Haeng. "Give her to me. I'm responsible for what's happened to her."

"If you insist. But there are any of a hundred reasons why she might not make it through the night."

"I know."

And so, Dtui handed over the cat to a person she'd never imagined to have any compassion for man or beast.

◙ ◙ ◙

Civilai found himself at the wheel of a Renault that could easily have been the one he first drove back in 1921. Admittedly, some parts were held together with tape, but she was much tougher than she looked. She bounced along over rocks and ruts as if she were designed for such a terrain. There wasn't much to see on the forty-minute journey. The rice farmers had deserted the fields sooner than join cooperatives, so the paddies sat crusty and dry in the midday sun. In the far distance a storm was gathering as if Mother Nature had made a mistake with the sky design and tried to scribble it out. The only other vehicle he saw was a homemade tractor powered by a two-stroke diesel engine carrying twenty or so workers in straw hats. Civilai waved and smiled, but they all looked at him sourly.

Nor were there smiles upon his return to Ban Toop. He cruised slowly down the dusty main street with an elbow on the window ledge. He called out "Hey, you" to one child he saw there, but the boy looked away, pretending not to have heard. Despite the car's lack of speed, a suicidal chicken threw itself under the front wheel of the Renault. There was an almighty scream before the bird expired. In a normal world this would have resulted in the chicken's owner rushing from her house to claim compensation for the dead bird. But in Ban Toop, nobody reacted. Not a face peeked from a doorway.

"What if I strip off and do a jig on the roof?" Civilai shouted. "Would that get your attention?"

He continued to drive at the pace of a government committee meeting. He passed the old colonial building and once again noted its abnormal state of conservation. He parked in front of the headman's house. From recent experience he wasn't expecting the man to be home, and he wasn't disappointed. Even the wife was absent. But there was suddenly a flurry of activity. He went to the side of the house in time to see a lanky youth run out the back door and across the field. It was the fastest he'd seen anyone move in the village. Then, as he was walking back to the car he caught sight of a pedestrian. A crooked old lady with a gnarly staff was edging her way along the far side of the road. He calculated she'd reach the other end of the street sometime in the next millennium, which made her something of a captive audience.

"Any idea where the headman is?" he shouted.

She ignored him. Goodness knows how Civilai loved to be ignored. He decided there and then that he'd wrestle her to the ground sooner than have her take no notice. But all it took was for him to cross the road and stand in front of her.

"Get out of my way, baldy," she said.

"Oh, good," said Civilai. "You can see me."

"'Course I can. I'm not blind."

"Deaf, perhaps?"

"What?"

"I asked you if you knew where the headman was."

She was in a quandary. She wanted to keep going but her way was blocked, and it would take several minutes to go around the annoying man.

"Move!" she said.

"Not until you tell me where the headman is," he said.

"I don't know."

"I don't believe you."

Her face was parched and grooved like a terraced rice field left fallow for a hundred years. Little beads peered out from between the furrows.

"Let us be," she said. "We've found some kind of peace at last. Don't stir it all up again."

She shuffled a foot forward, and Civilai stepped out of her way. He didn't know what she meant, but he felt an overwhelming despair in her. He didn't want to add to her suffering, whatever it was.

He drove to the only other place he knew in Ban Toop, but the Tasitu mechanic's yard was also deserted. The scattered debris looked even more ancient. There was no jolly topless mechanic running out to meet the Renault. Civilai parked and walked to the brick building and called out.

"Maitreya, are you there?"

There was no answer, so Civilai walked in to the workshop. It smelled of old grease and flat petrol. Even the smells were odd in this odd village. In a working mechanic's shop the scents were fresh: oil bled from an engine, grease newly slapped on axles. But this shop had only lingering

ghosts of the work once done there. Civilai doubted Maitreya had worked on a car engine since the turnover. So
how did he make a living? How did anyone here make a
living? Before he left Vientiane he'd checked the roster
and found Ban Toop had rejected an offer to join a cooperative, citing a lack of able-bodied workers. That usually
meant the rice farmers were doing very nicely, had access
to the black market and would make a lot more money
by going it alone. But in this area the fields were deserted
and unloved.

Civilai walked to an alcove behind a cloth curtain in the
back of the workshop. The space was barely broad enough
for a workbench with a vice and an acetylene tank with a
blowtorch. And on the bench was the oddest thing he'd
seen in a very long—

"This how you do it in Vientiane?" came a booming
voice from directly behind him.

Civilai's old heart missed a short run of beats. He
looked over his shoulder to see Maitreya with a large rust-
ing wrench in his hand. The old man gathered himself.

"Do what, young fellow?" he asked.

"Walk into people's places without an invite."

"It's just a workshop," said Civilai. "In fact I was hoping
you might have a toilet back here."

The mechanic frowned. "Plenty of trees and bushes outside," he said.

"Ah, young Maitreya," said Civilai pushing past the
younger man and back into the garage where there was
space to avoid a swinging wrench, "my crouching tiger
days are over. If I can't find a French *toilette* with a comfortable seat I'd sooner let it back up for a week. That's what I
fear will be the death of me."

"You thought you'd find a French toilet in a workshop?"

"Why not? Judging from that fine old French villa back in the village, you had foreign influence here in Ban Toop. And the froggies always put in the bathroom before the walls and roof. It's a known fact."

The mechanic smiled and dropped the wrench onto the dirty floor, which surprised Civilai.

"You should be careful," said Maitreya. "I come back to find a strange car in the yard and someone nosing through my things. A man might act rashly, if you know what I mean. One of the boys just told me there was a stranger rooting around."

"I didn't hear you come back," said Civilai.

"Bicycle. Great weapon of war. The Japs used them a lot against the British. Whole units sneaking up on a garrison without a sound. Slit their throats before they knew what had hit 'em."

"I've never heard that."

The two stared at each other for a while.

"Tea?" said the mechanic.

"Thank you."

They sat on old Shell oil drums drinking their tea under a lush American iron filings tree. The fig tree beside it hadn't faired so well. Someone had used it as a notice board. There were hundreds of nails hammered into the trunk. It stood leafless and riddled with disease, its only fruit a truck tire hanging from a rope. The tree's demise probably paralleled that of the mechanic's business.

"I thought I made it clear I wasn't interested in any of this Buddha nonsense," said Maitreya.

"You did," said Civilai.

"Then why didn't you go back with your wife?"

Civilai smiled. "Well, you're right," he said, "you're not the next Buddha. I have no doubt about that. But I have a report to write, and just as we were about to leave something peculiar happened. I'm the type who can't sleep when there's a mystery left unsolved."

"I hope I can help," said Maitreya.

"An old woman came to see us at the guesthouse. She claimed to be your mother."

Maitreya laughed. "Spindly? Hair like an old carpet? Shaking hands?"

"That's her."

The mechanic took an unnecessarily slow draft of tea. "Wan's her name," he said. "They call her the fruit bat. She should have been locked up a long time ago."

"She's not your mother?"

"She's nobody's mother. Mad woman. Did she pull the virgin birth routine on you?"

"She had a note from the hospital."

"And did you notice there wasn't a name on the note? Every time there's a stranger in town she comes up with the same story claiming to have given birth to whoever it is the visitors have come to see. I don't know who wrote the note for her. I know for a fact she can't read or write. She just memorized the words. It's sad, Uncle, but it's hardly a mystery. But if you're into unanswered questions I imagine you're wondering why the village is empty."

"That had crossed my mind."

"Simple. We're preparing for our village festival. Everyone's off in the hills gathering wood and hunting for meat. It's a big deal for us. It was very bad luck that your visit coincided with it. The headman would have liked to meet you."

Maitreya tuned the Renault before he'd let Civilai leave. It was strange that a car mechanic wouldn't recognize the only car within fifty kilometers of the village. But as Civilai drove back to Pak Xan, he put together a long list of bizarre points. Strange it was that the village would be celebrating a festival that wasn't on any calendars. Strange that the town's only guesthouse should claim they'd never seen the fruit-bat woman before. Where else would she stalk strangers? Strange that a villager would call a government official "uncle" rather than "comrade." Strange that a man in an isolated village should know Madam Nong had already left. Strange that a poor village would reject the opportunity to join a rice cooperative. Strange that a mechanic would show such little respect for his tools.

But, as he drove back into a shocking pink sunset, Civilai couldn't make head or tail of the strangest thing of all. On the bench in the alcove behind the workshop was a Buddha image some sixty centimeters tall. But the top of its head was flat. For some reason, somebody had sliced off part of its skull and placed it on the bench beside the Buddha like half an unexploded bomb.

◙ ◙ ◙

Inspector Phosy had made an appointment by telephone, a rare occurrence in the People's Democratic Republic. It was often simpler to turn up at the place, ask whether the person you wish to see is there, announce your arrival and wait. But there was something ceremonial about a meeting at the Armed Forces Ministry. The telephone operator at police headquarters called the telephone operator at the ministry to make an appointment. Twenty minutes later, the telephone operator at the ministry called back and said the appointment was as soon as the inspector could get there.

Upon his arrival Phosy felt a little like royalty. He was met at the gate by a high ranking official and escorted to the police liaison office. The official knocked, opened the door and left. There were three men in the room. Corporal Suwit sat at his desk and two more officers sat on the plastic couch. They were wearing green uniforms that fit, another rare occurrence in Laos.

Phosy toured the room shaking hands, first with the two officers he didn't know. They stood (reluctantly, to Phosy's mind) to return the handshake.

"These are Colonels Viboun and Vinai," said Suwit. "I've asked them to join us because we're all concerned about this misunderstanding. The officers are keen to clear it up as soon as possible."

"Well, a big 'yes' to that," said the policeman. He sat not on the lone wooden chair in the middle of the room but at the end of the couch. Its two occupants had to shuffle along to give him room.

"I can't tell you how many nightmares this case has given me," said Phosy.

"We hope you've made some progress," said the man directly beside him. He spoke without turning his head in the inspector's direction.

"Oh, comrade," said Phosy, "you wouldn't believe how many wrong turns we've made and how much bad luck we're having."

He thought somebody might ask a question, but nobody did.

"Look, I know this will probably turn out to be totally unrelated to you fellows, but I'd really appreciate it if you'd allow me to just get it all off my chest."

"Feel free," said the farthest colonel.

"Well, first," said Phosy, "we discovered that the cyclist who was kidnapped isn't even a Lao citizen. He's Thai."

"How did you learn that?" asked Suwit.

"We found his ID at the guesthouse he'd been staying at," said Phosy. "So naturally, we had to contact the Thais and they insisted on sending some of their people to assist with the inquiry. We told them we're perfectly capable of finding him ourselves. They said there'd be an international incident if we didn't, so we assumed he was connected . . . if you know what I mean. They wouldn't kick up such a dust storm if he was just a tourist. So that raised the profile of the investigation, and, I tell you, that's all I needed because I'm dealing with some nervous witnesses already."

"Witnesses?" said the nearest colonel.

"Right," said Phosy. "Our main witness, the one who saw the actual abduction directly in front of her, she got cold feet because her sister was killed by—we suspect—a jealous boyfriend and she—the witness, that is—she came home to find blood everywhere and her sister buried under a pile of empty bottles. It took us an age to calm the witness down. Am I going too fast for you? No? Good."

He took the opportunity to help himself to one of the unchilled soft drinks on the coffee table in front of him. The couch soldiers were being oddly quiet.

"I hope you found somewhere secure to house the witnesses," said Suwit.

"Not sure I'd call it safe," said Phosy. "And I'm trusting you boys to keep this to yourselves, but we've got the main witness above a friend's noodle shop on Fa Ngum. We doubt the death of her sister is connected to this case but you can never be too sure. Am I right? Of course I am. But if the boyfriend does turn up we'll know he did it because we have his fingerprints from the crime scene."

"His fingerprints?" said the nearest colonel.

"One or two sets still unidentified," said Phosy.

The other colonel laughed. "This isn't some American thriller," said the farthest colonel. "Are you sure you aren't overestimating the capabilities of your department?"

"I know what you mean," said Phosy. "A few months ago I was just as skeptical as you. But this—I don't know what to call him—this forensic-evidence genius shows up, trained overseas, and suddenly we're not only keeping up with our neighboring countries, we're leaping ahead of them. Things we wouldn't have noticed before, like the motorcycle tracks."

"What about them?" asked Suwit.

"We've made a plaster cast of the tracks of the motorcycle that the kidnappers were riding. And now we've got the tire tracks of the man who killed our witness's sister. Of course, they aren't connected, but if they were we'd know it soon enough."

There followed another silence.

"You mentioned witnesses, plural," said the nearest colonel.

"Yes, it's astounding how many people have nothing better to do than sit and observe," said the policeman. "I personally think we're being too generous to the elderly. They should be put to work on the drains or digging ditches. But that's just me. Once we had a witness who could describe the kidnappers it wasn't so hard to work backward along the route they'd taken. We found people who'd seen the cyclist and others who remembered him being tailed slowly by two young military types on a motorcycle."

"That's speculation," said the farthest colonel.

"You're quite right," Phosy agreed. "But we should know exactly what they look like soon enough. The Thais came up with a police portrait artist and the witnesses are really excited about the results. But listen to me. Here I am going on and on and not giving anyone else a chance to speak. I really do apologize for taking up your valuable time. I know you have a country to protect. I just wanted to keep you informed. Keep that old Armed Forces–National Police Force channel open. I'm so excited about the potential of us all working together in the future. Thank you."

He stood and had completed another round of handshakes before anyone realized the meeting was closed. He went to the door, opened it and stopped in the doorway.

"Really, thank you," he said. "I'll see myself out."

He sighed heavily on his way down the echoing staircase. Of course it was all fiction. Lies. His only witness was dead. There were no plaster casts or fingerprints or sketch artists. The police department didn't even have enough whistles to go around. Two muggings over the course of a week would have been considered a crime spree. The slick police force he'd described to the soldiers was one he'd learned about from the stories of Dr. Siri. They had no forensics department. His only reason for exaggerating the progress on Noo's kidnapping case was to poke a very short stick into a very scary hornet's nest. Now all he could do was stand back and see if they'd bite.

But first he had to return to headquarters and arrange protection for his wife. Nurse Dtui looked passably like the dead cordial seller. If the killer thought he'd murdered the wrong woman, there was a chance he'd try again. And Phosy had set up his wife, even given them a location. If the military was connected to this whole affair as he believed, there'd be a visit to Madam Daeng's noodle shop soon enough.

As he rode his lilac Vespa along Lan Xang Avenue, he reconsidered his actions. What was he doing? Could he be more irresponsible? What if the assassins shot first and asked questions after? And for what? For one man's life. For a man he hardly knew. After so many years of bloodshed, who really cared whether one trouble-making Thai monk vanished from the face of the earth? Or a cordial seller? Or his own wife and child? And that, of course, was the key. The victims could have been Dtui or Mali. The re-educators had pummeled it into him back in the seminars. In this new system even the poorest, most feeble rice farmer would have the same rights as the greatest general. That's what they'd said. That was the myth of socialism. It wasn't the army he was up against; it was the sagging ideology. It was the duty of the community to protect its weakest members. He never thought he'd hear himself say it but, damn, it was the principle of the thing. Dtui was a fighter. She'd take it well. That's why he'd chosen her as a wife.

◙ ◙ ◙

Before returning the Renault to its owner, Civilai filled the tank at one hard-to-find rusty pump and asked for directions to the high school. When he arrived he was too late for classes, but he hoped there might still be staff around. The school looked new and dilapidated at the same time. Unlike the French colonists, who weren't huge on wasting education on the locals, the Americans veritably vomited schools all over the place. Their policy was to use local tradesmen and materials wherever possible, which explained why the buildings had already started to fall down.

As it turned out, there were a number of teachers engaged in after-school activities: the band, the vegetable allotments, after-hours political classes for the remedial and, although the light was fading fast, a football match was in progress. The two teams playing shirts against skins were just about to start the second half. Despite all his years of rhetoric in favor of women's rights, he found himself surprised and disoriented to see that the referee was a young woman.

"Good game?" Civilai asked her.

"A bit one-sided," she told him.

"Are you a teacher here?" he asked.

"Yes, comrade."

"I'm looking for someone who might have been teaching in Pak Xan back in the old regime."

"Then you're looking for Teacher Grit," she said.

Teacher Grit taught math and had been doing so, he said, since before the birth of Pythagoras. For all its lines and wrinkles his was a face anyone would want to nuzzle. He'd been at the school since it was built by the Americans, whom he remembered fondly. He dropped one or two English words into his reminiscences. In fact, they'd leveled his family compound in order to build the school and had relocated his family to a sturdy but cultureless home just opposite.

"We teach upon the hallowed ground of my ancestors," said Grit. "I wouldn't be surprised if we were sitting here above the potted ashes of my great-grandmother. They didn't mark graves back then."

"You'd remember the French then," said Civilai.

"*Bien sûr,*" said Grit. "Those bastards wouldn't let me go to school. They reminded my mother I was Lao and the French and Vietnamese were the elite classes. We were laborers."

"Then how did you become a teacher?" asked Civilai.

"We crossed the river. My mother convinced the administrators over there we were Thai so my three siblings and I all studied in Beun Kan. I went on to the teachers college in Chiang Mai. Came back here and labored for the bastard French until the Americans turned up. Damned fine colonists, the Americans."

"What do you remember about the French administration here?"

"Bastards."

"Apart from that."

"Pig ignorant. Arrogant."

"I'm thinking specifically about the owner of a colonial home out in Ban Toop," said Civilai.

"Ah, yes. Now you're talking about the most arrogant and ignorant of them all, Administrateur Marche. He was based here for almost ten years."

"And what was his connection to Ban Toop?"

"He *was* Ban Toop. He established the village. Nobody

knew why he chose the place. Not beautiful at all. He had a fine house here in Pak Xan. He was like an emperor here. He was in charge of everything. When I returned from Thailand everyone was afraid of him. I offered to teach at the temple, and he laughed in my face and put me in a quarry."

"Who built his house at Ban Toop?"

"He had a team of Vietnamese builders there for three months. When it was finished they returned to Vietnam and Marche had a fine house in the middle of nowhere. Really, there was nothing there. We assumed he wanted a country home like they do in Europe. Somewhere to escape. He'd drive out there on weekends with his assorted concubine whores."

"What did he do there?"

"Heaven knows. He was a very secretive man. And there was something . . . dark about him. There were many rumors, but rumors are our national pastime."

"Do you remember any of them?"

"There was talk of children disappearing. Never children from the town. Always the daughters of travelers."

"You think he had something to do with that?"

"Who can say? When you dislike someone enough you will the gossip to be true. But I do know for certain he was removed from his post very suddenly by the French Protectorate. One day he was gone, and there were parties in the streets. But by then a small community had grown around his house in Ban Toop. It continued to grow even after he left."

"And what do you know about the place now?"

"You know? I'm not really the person to ask. I haven't been there for ages."

"You're probably more trustworthy than anyone I'm likely to meet in an official capacity."

The old teacher got to his feet and started to wipe the equations from the blackboard with a damp rag. "There are those who say Ban Toop is a law unto itself," said Grit. "The local government cadres are afraid of the place. But in a way I can see why. After decades of minimal help from Vientiane, a community learns to fend for itself to survive. It builds walls. The next leader comes along and tells them, 'We're in charge now. You have to do what we say.' But who knows who'll be running the country next year, or next month even? So the local communities put on their armor."

"You're not shy about being an anarchist, are you?"

"When I came back from Thailand I was hotheaded and angry," said Grit. "But I soon learned to keep my mind open and my mouth shut. Then you get to an age where your mind's shut, and you can't stop your mouth from running off. But by then everybody's stopped listening."

"You're not wrong there, comrade. Do you know the headman at Ban Toop?"

"I've met him. He seems harmless enough. Why are you interested?"

"Just curiosity really. I went there on an official visit and he was too busy cockfighting to see me."

"Yes, I've heard he's not that sociable when it comes to Party activities."

"It sounds like exactly the type of place for the government to be running back-to-back political seminars. Somebody needs to teach the Ban Toop leaders a lesson in good manners."

Civilai stood and shook the old teacher's hand warmly. "One last matter," he said. "Would there be some type of local repository of documents dating from the French administration days?"

"There would if your crowd hadn't marched into town and burned everything."

"I was afraid you'd say that."

"But . . ."

"Yes?"

"If you promise not to set fire to it, there's a . . . I wouldn't call it a repository exactly, more like a suitcase."

"A suitcase?"

"Two, if I remember right. I assume the last administrator had planned to take them with him when he left, but there wasn't enough room in the getaway car. They're in a cupboard in Sirimongkol Temple."

"Do you suppose they'd let me take a look at them?"

"I doubt anyone would care one way or another."

Civilai dropped off the Renault at the district council buildings, expecting the place to be deserted, but one lamp still burned inside. He went to the door to find the same greasy-faced clerk engaged in the endless pursuit of solving the world's filing problems.

"Comrade," she said, startled.

"Don't you have a husband to go home to?" he asked.

She smiled for the first time. Her teeth were all over the place. "Last-minute duty," she said.

"Do you know whether Vientiane got back to me about my fax?"

"Fax? Nothing as far as I know."

"Who operates the fax machine?"

"Me, usually. But I'm sure Comrade Luangrat took care of it personally if it was important," she said.

"Look," Civilai put on his charm voice. "I can see you're really busy, but I don't suppose you could dig out a photograph of all the regional headmen by any chance?"

"A photograph?"

"Yes, you know. Headman seminar, workshop, pep talk. They always take pictures at the end of those things. Give out certificates."

"Probably," she said and walked directly to the correct cabinet. Filing was her life. "Here, October last year. Cooperative Farm Training Programme for Village Leaders."

Civilai riffled through the photographs. A hundred men in three rows in front of the council office. None of them was smiling.

"Which one's Comrade Noulak, the headman at Ban Toop?" he asked.

"Oh, he wasn't here," she said.

"Why not?"

"He had a cold, or malaria. I can't remember which."

"Then, his deputy?"

"He wasn't here either."

"Must have been an epidemic. Lucky the whole village wasn't wiped out completely."

She looked blank.

"Any other meetings?" he asked.

She produced graduation photos for the July Workshop on Water Management and Sewage, and the February seminar on Fruit for a Healthy Future. Again, she was unable to pick out the headman.

"He isn't so enthusiastic about meetings," she said.

"I'm astounded he's still the headman," said Civilai. "He has no choice but to attend."

They looked at five more photographs of serious men at local government events, but the clerk was unable to point to anyone from Ban Toop.

"I'm beginning to believe he doesn't exist," said Civilai.

"Oh, he does," said the clerk. "I've met him. He's a very polite man. Perhaps . . ."

"Perhaps what?"

"They aren't official photographs so they're filed under 'unofficial photographs,' but I remember he was in town for the rocket festival last year."

"The rocket festival that was banned?"

"Yes, that's the one. Our official photographer wasn't around but one of the Soviet experts from the road survey project had a camera. He made copies and sent them to us. Here they are."

She pulled out a paper pouch with the name of the pharmacy that had developed them written on the front. It was in Thai. Only five months on, and the photos were already starting to fade.

"I'm sure he's in here somewhere," said the clerk, thumbing through the pictures.

Civilai was fatigued from the long day and the even longer life. Each evening reminded him he was no longer forty.

"Look, never mind," he said. "I'll probably never get to meet him anyway."

"No, I'm sure . . . Yes, here he is."

She handed Civilai the photograph. It depicted a typical Lao party scene. A lot of drunken men. Some equally drunken wives. In the background the words PAK XAN WELCOMES OUR SOVIET BROTHERS had been cut out of polystyrene and glued onto the wall. And standing beside a ridiculously large black music speaker with a glass in his hand was the elusive headman of Ban Toop. The shot was a little fuzzy, and Civilai couldn't tell whether the man was drunk or had merely blinked when the flash went off. He was wearing a traditional collarless Lao shirt that flattered his stomach, but there was no doubt in Civilai's mind: Comrade Noulak, the headman of Ban Toop, and Maitreya, the imminent reincarnation of the Buddha, were one and the same person.

9

The Case of the File in the Case

Everything looked normal. But when you're expecting trouble, when you have that voice in your gut that says, "Something's coming," even the smallest of abnormalities have to be checked out. They'd all seen the motorcycle earlier that evening. The rider stopped opposite Daeng's noodle restaurant and had pretended to be looking out over the river. He was about thirty, fit, and he wore a baseball cap, but you could tell his hair was cropped close to his scalp.

As arranged, Mr. Geung had carried a bucket of slops across the empty road to dump on the riverbank. They'd told him to act as if he had mental problems. He'd been practicing all afternoon. Crazy Rajhid was perched unseen in the tree overhead for backup.

"Hey, retard," said the man.

"Y-y-y-yes, comrade?" said Geung.

"That woman," said the man, nodding in Dtui's direction. She was wiping the tables. "How long's she worked here?"

"No noh, noh, noh, noh . . ."

"Oh shit."

"Noh, noh, not long," said Geung.

"What does that mean," said the man. "A month? A week? A day?"

"Yes," said Geung.

"Which?"

"I'm no, I'm no, I'm not very good with numbers."

"Was she here last week?"

"Ta, ta, ta"—he could tell the stutter annoyed the man intensely—"ta, ta . . ."

"I'm not here all week, you moron."

"Ta, ta, ta two or three days. Whaaaa why you asking?"

"I like the look of her," he said. "Think I'll ask her out." The man smiled. His teeth were neat and white as a row of coconut chunks.

"She, she, she, sheeee's sad," said Geung. "Her sister die-die-di—"

The man revved the engine on his bike and kicked down the stand.

"Don't worry, retard," he said. "I'll make her happy. She sleeping here?"

"Yes, comrade."

Geung was left in a cloud of exhaust.

Agent Geung had been able to recite the conversation verbatim, which is why they were expecting a late night return from the motorcycle rider and his cohorts. Upon his arrival at police headquarters after the ministry bluff it had occurred to Phosy that he had no legitimate reason to request a squad of men to protect his wife. So he'd been left with his old friend and colleague,

Sergeant Sihot, who was rarely busy in the evening, and Tumsin the butcher, who was so backed up on favors for the detective he'd need another lifetime to repay him. At the end of the evening noodle shift they'd sat around the restaurant with warm tea and Chinese donuts and weighed the odds.

"Hand grenade," said Sergeant Sihot.

"That's how I'd do it if I wanted to teach the restaurant owner a lesson," said Phosy. "But this is an assassination. I'd need to confirm my target had been taken out. A hand grenade's too random."

"Then they'll shoot me," said Dtui, surprisingly cheerful.

"Possible," said Phosy. "But they know I'm on the case, and I probably have backup."

"That's me," said Tumsin the butcher.

"They wouldn't want to risk a shootout or a fistfight," Phosy continued. "I guess a sniper on the riverbank or in a boat might work, but he'd be sitting there all night hoping Dtui walks past a window."

"And the military couldn't hit a buffalo from two meters," said Sergeant Sihot.

"Things have changed since you were in the army," Phosy told him. "They have time to train them now."

"Let's face it," said Dtui. "The motorcycle rider asked if I'm sleeping here. They'll go the ninja route. Wait till everyone's asleep, tippy-toe over the rooftops, drop down through an open window and garrote me before I have a chance to let out a scream."

"That's the way I'd do it," said Phosy.

"See why I married him?" said Dtui. "We have so much in common."

Mr. Geung turned to his fiancée, Tukta.

"I wo-won't let anyone garrote you, darling," he said, and they kissed. Everyone turned away.

With Sergeant Sihot on point on the riverbank and Rajhid still clinging to the upper branches of his tree, the front of the restaurant was taken care of. Mr. Geung with Tukta on pillion rode the restaurant bicycle in the direction of Siri's house just in case they were being watched. At the Lane Xang Hotel they dismounted and crept back through the shadows to take up their positions. The others pulled down the metal shutters, and turned out the lights. With butcher Tumsin on a stool in the small backyard clutching his favorite cleaver, Phosy and Dtui went upstairs confident that every eventuality was covered. Their inquisitive daughter was absent, and they weren't expecting to be slaughtered in their beds until after midnight, so for half an hour they took advantage of the comfortable mattress and the abundance of adrenalin before retiring to their respective rooms.

The motorcycle ninja was not spotted when he returned to the restaurant at 2 A.M. because he had hopped over the small wall into the backyard and not disturbed the sleeping butcher. The upstairs window shutters were open. His equipment was simple enough: a rope with a football sock tied to one end. Inside the sock was a metal *petong* ball. He aimed for a point between the shutters and tossed the rope. The ball arced and looped over the left shutter, pulling the rope back into the hands of the waiting ninja. And there it hung. He pulled on the ends to test the hinges then hoisted himself up with the agility of a gibbon.

It could not have been simpler. He perched on the window ledge looking down at the fat girl. She was alone. It was a dark, cloudy night, but she was burning a scented candle beside her sleeping mat. The flame flickered. She wore a figure-hugging nylon nightdress. Her hair fanned out across the pillow. He liked them big. It was almost a shame he had to kill her. But he'd screwed up once. He couldn't get it wrong again. His bare feet made no sound on the parquet floor. The blade was in a holster at his belt. It was a ballet he'd choreographed. Two steps forward, slash, two steps back to avoid the blood. He took the first step, except . . .

Some dark angular shape appeared in the window frame through which he'd just climbed. He turned his head and saw some half-naked Indian sitting on the ledge. And the naked half was not the top. Then, in an instant, someone was on him from the other side. One strong hand grabbed the wrist that held the blade in an unbreakable grip. The sleeping woman had been neither asleep nor a woman. The wig remained fanned out on the pillow bereft of a head. Crazy Rajhid leapt from the sill and positioned himself so he could kick the motorcycle ninja in the groin. No martial art on the planet can counter that. Then another man came, then a woman, and the ninja was pinned to the parquet tiles like a moth in a museum display cabinet.

"Bugger it," he said.

◙   ◙   ◙

An unused foreign language could fade as rapidly as the flowers in a wreath. For fifteen years in Paris, French had come more naturally to him than Lao. Now here was Civilai in a dusty temple office with stacks of mildewed papers on the table in front of him. Every one of the reports he read was a challenge to his eyesight and to his memory. Sirimongkol Temple was more functional than decorative. Its large events hall had become a community center with Vietnamese language classes, bomb disposal workshops and lessons in beekeeping. Hives were spaced out across a yard that was once gay with festivals. But early that morning when Civilai had arrived the only movement was from a flock of chickens being shooed out of the prayer hall.

There was just the one monk in residence, a feeble-minded young man more used to following orders than making decisions. He'd remembered the two old French suitcases and had led Civilai to a tall wooden cupboard where they'd remained untouched for decades. He hadn't asked Civilai his name or what his business was. He didn't tell the visitor to be careful with the old documents. He just laughed a little when Civilai said "thank you."

One suitcase contained paper spaghetti and droppings. There were several entrances and exits in the vinyl that were the shape of mouse holes in cartoons, which gave Civilai cause to chuckle. The contents had served the temple rats better than they would him. The other suitcase had proven too much of a challenge for the rodents. It was also almost beyond Civilai. He'd spent about half an hour with his penknife attempting to free the spring locks from their rusty shrouds. He'd feared the documents would be unreadable. When the lid finally lifted the stink of mold on the leather case overpowered him. But the lettering was so clear on most of the papers they might have been typed a week earlier.

From the dates Teacher Grit had provided, Civilai narrowed down the search to the period around 1942. He worked his way down the stack, wondering whether he might succumb to lung infection before he found what he was looking for. It had been a fruitless search so far. In fact the only personal communication he'd found referring to Administrateur Marche was a formal letter from Paris telling him the Vichy would honor its agreement to ship the administrator's luggage to France at the end of his truncated tenure. The phrase that Civilai found interesting in the letter was, ". . . despite the unfortunate circumstances." It went on to give details on how to itemize personal belongings but did not elaborate on what the unfortunate circumstances might be.

It was not until Civilai started to sift through the personal correspondence of Administrateur Lebouef, Marche's successor, that a plot began to unfurl. Shortly after he took over, Lebouef had been asked to host a Monsieur Gallas, a junior detective from the French Sûreté Nationale. He had been appointed to conduct inquiries into the activities of Administrateur Marche during his stay in Laos. Evidently, somebody of importance had curtailed Marche's contract and ordered an investigation. There were no copies of Monsieur Gallas's reports, but Administrateur Lebouef had included the original mission statement with his letter to the protectorate.

It appeared that Marche had been less than candid about his background when applying for a post in French Indochina, and the Paris police had been less than conscientious in their examination of the man's past. If they had been more thorough they would have found the records of his involvement in two court cases dealing with the disappearance of teenage girls. In both cases, the prosecution had failed to make a strong enough argument against

Marche, who was subsequently acquitted. Thus, Marche had had no legal obligation to disclose the arrests. The mission statement went on to say:

Our office became involved in this affair following M. Marche's written application for acquiescence to take up a government post in Paris upon his return. It is the guiding principle of the Vichy administration to thoroughly scrutinize applicants for official positions. Whilst examining the administrator's affairs prior to his appointment in Indochina we uncovered the court dealings and a number of other complaints which had, for some reason, not been investigated. There were also several grievances from French and Vietnamese citizens reported during his tenure in Pak Xan. We came upon one complaint, for example, from a French accountant, M. Charles Delon, who was employed by the Vichy throughout the region during that time. He claimed that Administrateur Marche had been integral in the procurement of teenage girls in Laos. The accountant had been made aware of this matter by his clerical assistant, a French citizen of Vietnamese origin, who was the mother of one of the girls concerned.

As the procurement of teenage girls was not a rare occurrence in Laos and the arrangement was usually deemed to be consensual, the matter was not further pursued at the time. It was only when viewed in relation to the earlier cases that we began to see a pattern. Our department commenced an investigation into the actions of M. Marche with more vigor, and it was then that we uncovered suspicion of crimes far more nefarious than mere kidnapping. This is the rationale behind Marche's

recall to France and Inspector Gallas's journey to Indo-
china and specifically to Pak Xan. It is hoped he will be
able to gather sufficient data to support our suspicions
and build a strong legal case against Marche. We appre-
ciate your cooperation in this matter.
     Yours sincerely,
     Police Commissioner Alain Boyer

"Crimes far more nefarious than mere kidnapping,"
said Civilai aloud. "Damn, if that doesn't leave a reader on
the edge of his seat."

He huffed and coughed his way through another half
hour of administrative dross but found neither a word of
the progress of Inspector Gallas nor reports on a trial nor
further mention of the Vietnamese clerk's missing daughter. But Civilai persevered because, as Siri often said, "A
story without an ending is like a tin of corned beef without
a can opener."

The sun had reached its highest point by the time Civilai found another mention of the case. It was in a copy
of a monthly report from Administrateur Lebouef to his
desk officer in Paris. It was the seventeenth of forty-two
asterisked items on issues pending. It was a short but tart
reference—one that made the hairs stand up on Civilai's
arms.

Six months on and still no news of the whereabouts of
Inspector Gallas.

Civilai walked back to his guesthouse with no great
urgency. He found it hard to walk fast and be brilliant at
the same time. And this matter needed all the brilliance he

could muster. He hoped the team he'd requested would be there soon. There was something eerie, threatening even, about the whole situation. Having some ministry people beside him would buoy his confidence. Initially his inquiries about the old colonial building had been unrelated to the reception he hadn't been given. It was just idle interest. But he'd been uncomfortable about the place since they'd first parked in front of it. Innocuous but imposing at the same time, it stood out like an Arc de Triomphe in the desert. There was no logical link between a reluctant would-be Buddha and a French child abuser more than thirty years earlier, but Civilai was certain a connection existed.

At the guesthouse a sweaty man in a dark grey shirt rose from the only chair in the reception area and nodded curtly. His haircut made him look like he'd run his head through the blades of a combine harvester.

"Civilai Songsawat?" he said.

"Yes."

"I'm Sergeant Savath of the Pak Xan police force."

"You're a policeman?" said Civilai, looking him up and down.

"Yes," he said.

"You're wearing rubber flip-flops."

"They're comfortable."

Until Civilai's visit to Pak Xan, anarchy had been just a theoretical concept. Perhaps he'd been sheltered as a high-ranking official because he'd never actually felt it. But this area was crawling with a tangible sense of disrespect. Pak Xan anarchy exposed itself through its bad attitude.

"Do you have official police business with me?" Civilai snapped.

"Yes."

"Then go home and come back appropriately dressed."

He tried to push past the solid man to get to the stair-case, but the policeman grabbed his arm. Civilai pulled away and was about to play his "Do you know who I am?" card when the policeman beat him to the payoff.

"Early this morning a woman's body was found in the reeds a few meters from where you and your wife were get-ting drunk on Sunday night."

Civilai took a step back, and the policeman released his grip.

"She'd been dead about forty-eight hours," Savath con-tinued. "She'd been beaten so bad we couldn't recognize her at first. When we found out who she was we learned something interesting. The evening she died, guess who the last person she was seen speaking to was?"

◙ ◙ ◙

Siri's experience with real judges was limited. In fact the only arbitrators he'd ever appeared in front of were either military officers appointed to settle disputes or Haeng, who everyone agreed was a poor excuse for a judge. Siri's idea of what a judge should look like had been fashioned from early Hollywood, where the man in the chair was always balding and had white muttonchops and wise, saggy eyes.

So when Suthon, the traveling public prosecutor of Udon Thani entered the temporary courtroom Siri looked behind him for the real judge. Nobody else came. In Siri's eyes, the prosecutor was a boy. He was pale with no chin and had an ill-fitting piggy nose. He didn't even have a robe and instead wore a white shirt with a tie and black trousers like a college student. Siri's first instinct was to shout out, "How old are you exactly?" But to Madam Daeng's relief he kept his mouth shut.

They'd arrived three hours earlier in the back of the Sawan truck that was only ever used on special occasions. The Sangharaj had climbed aboard the truck's flatbed without complaints. He'd pulled his robe over his head to protect himself from the sun and hummed some non-ecclesiastical tunes all the way to Nam Som.

Siri had stared at him and imagined himself as a supreme patriarch. He was certain he wouldn't be at all humble. He'd ride around the country on his Triumph in his American sunglasses rooting out sinners. He'd have *S.P.* stamped in gold lettering on the back of his leather jacket. Perhaps that was why nobody had asked him to be the supreme patriarch.

The young judge was going through cases at a cracking pace. Siri noticed he dispensed wisdom only when he thought the accused might appreciate and understand it. Otherwise he'd hand out punishments with no embellishments. He knew the law and the penalty for breaking it. He spoke well and not over the heads of the uneducated. Despite the fact that the man, perhaps in his forties but clean shaven, was far too young for his position, Siri found himself admiring him.

Some of the accused entered the room in leg shackles led by uniformed police officers. When they'd heard the verdict they'd be escorted either back to the cells or into the arms of freedom. In most cases the only words they spoke were, "I do," when the administrator asked whether they understood the judgment. There was no schedule posted, and the only list of cases to be dealt with was the one on the table in front of the judge. So it was a pleasant surprise when he looked up and said, "I see Abbot Rayron is in the room and unchained."

Captain Gumron had been sitting at the rear of the courtroom writing reports. He hurried to the front and *wai*'d the judge. To Siri's further surprise, the judge *wai*'d him back.

"The abbot has been under the supervision of the Sangharaj of Laos," said the captain.

"And that's gone well, has it?" asked the judge.

"Quite well, sir. That is . . . until this morning."

"Don't tell me there was another incident," said the judge.

"Murder. The report should be on your desk, sir," said the captain.

"Witnesses?"

"One."

"Reliability?"

"Blind as an earthworm, sir."

The young judge looked at the abbot. "It seems like I have a new accusation against you every time I come here," he said. "What are we going to do with you?"

It was undoubtedly a rhetorical question, but Siri felt an uncontrollable urge to answer it.

"Release him," said the doctor.

Daeng pinched his arm.

"What was that?" said the judge. "Somebody have something to say?"

"It was me," said Siri.

Daeng sighed loudly.

"And you are . . . ?" said the judge.

"Sir, he's just . . ." began the captain, but the judge waved him off.

"Just an old student of the process of law," said Siri.

The judge smiled. "Your name, sir?"

"Dr. Siri Paiboun."

"And what is your assessment of this case, old student?" asked the judge.

Siri stood. "That the evidence is scant and largely circumstantial, the witnesses are unreliable and above all there is no motive."

Siri saw what he hoped was a smile of admiration on the young judge's face.

"I can tell from your accent that you hail from a country that currently has no laws," said the judge.

"Which is why I admire a legal system that has such clearly defined parameters," said Siri.

"Good response, old fellow," said the judge. "I don't often find men in my courtroom who can put together such long, grammatically correct sentences. Perhaps someday we can sit down over a beer and discuss the relative values of law versus lawlessness. But in the meantime I think I'll have to run with the premise that if enough circumstantial evidence falls repeatedly on the same suspect we cross the line of coincidence and enter the realm of probability."

"But you haven't even read the latest report," said Siri.

"Indeed I haven't, comrade counsel for the defense," said the judge, still with a pleasant smile on his face. "But it seems whenever I fail to put the abbot in a cell somebody else ends up dead. And being a coincidence doesn't make them any less dead. So, Abbot Rayron, I am ordering your detention here in a lockup at the Nam Som police station until we can transfer you to Udon Thani provincial court to face the charge of three counts of premeditated murder."

"But that's not—" began Siri.

"Quiet," said Captain Gumron.

Ugly began to kick up a fuss in front of the courtroom.

"I take it that's your dog outside?" said the judge. "I believe I saw you arrive together."

"I apologize," said Siri. "He's not that fond of police."

"Apology accepted and understood," said the judge, still smiling. "Now if you'd perhaps allow me a few minutes to take back control of my court, I was planning to mention that there's a month before that initial hearing in Udon. I'm sure if someone contributed a little brilliant detective work to the case before then and came up with a new suspect, we could also apologize to the abbot and pursue proceedings against a more likely murderer."

Interestingly, he looked not at the police captain during this speech, but at the abbot's entourage, specifically Siri.

"Your Honor," said Abbot Rayron.

It was the first time the monk had spoken, so everyone was surprised to hear his voice.

"Yes?" said the judge.

"I also apologize," said the abbot.

"For what?" asked the judge.

"For forcing you to make such a difficult choice."

Everyone looked on in amazement. The abbot had apologized to the judge for the inconvenience he'd caused. Even the unflappable judge was stunned. He stared at the monk mystified for a few seconds before waving him away.

Very few suspects sent to Udon had returned to tell the

tale. The provincial justice department frowned upon paying for two-way tickets, so only non-returnable certainties made it to the central courthouse. Yet the judge had given them hope. A uniformed officer *wai*'d the abbot before handcuffing himself to him. He nodded when the lock was secure and led the monk outside. Siri and the team followed with their heads bowed. By the time they reached the door, the next case was already being heard. For once, Siri and Daeng could think of nothing to say. They followed the Sangharaj out through the double doors into the glare of a late afternoon filled with shouts.

"How many have you killed, Abbot?"

"Are there other bodies we don't know about?"

"Is this the temple's way of clearing out the shamans?"

The abbot, chained to his grinning guard, was surrounded by reporters. There were the whirrs of cameras and the orders to "Look this way, Abbot."

They pushed rudely against him. One prodded a cassette recorder into his face. He had no chance to respond between the questions. The police guard enjoyed the attention and had no intention of hurrying the abbot to the cell. It wasn't until Siri, Daeng and Yuth, the headman's son, forced their way into the crowd and hustled both abbot and guard out of the forecourt that the madness abated. Most of the reporters were local, but there were one or two from Bangkok.

Someone had blabbed.

10

The Devil You Don't Know

Phosy had been sitting for an hour on an uncomfortable wooden bench one floor below his superior's office. With every minute he waited, his overactive policeman's instinct nipped at his nerves. He shuffled through the possible courses of action. Sergeant Sihot had said immediately after the ninja's capture that they should rope and gag the guy and throw him in the Mekhong. Show the enemy what they were up against. Half the detectives at headquarters would, at the very least, have beaten a confession out of the man. There on the itchy seat in the cold light of day neither of those scenarios seemed so bad. Even when the cocky ninja had stared Phosy in the face and mocked him, the detective had kept his hands to himself.

"You know it doesn't matter, don't you?" was what he'd said.

"What doesn't?" Phosy asked.

"Whatever you do to me, whatever information you extract from me by, whatever means—it's not going to make any difference."

"Beating you up would make a difference," Phosy had said, although he wasn't the type to hit a man in ropes.

"Only to you, Cop. Not to your case."

"Oh, I don't know. Tomorrow I file criminal charges against you. Then we see who attempts to bail you out. Then we'll know who your boss is at the armed forces ministry. And he'll find out that the police force has come a long way since the old regime."

"You have no idea, do you?"

"Tell me what I don't have any idea about."

"No idea who we are," said the man. "No idea how deep you are in something you should have kept out of. No idea how small and pathetic you are. How unimportant."

"Oh, kid," said Phosy, "when will you learn? There's no 'we.' You're a hired thug and not a very good one at that. Even if you're on a salary you're still a hired ruffian. You just do what your boss tells you. People like you are never let into the inner circle. You're a soldier ant, pal, and you just got squashed tonight."

"You should have let me kill her."

"What?"

"A killing would have given you something to charge me with. But what have you got? Breaking and entering? A petty thief. They won't even bother to charge me. I'll be out of there before lunch. Really, Constable. You should have let me slice open that ugly fat bitch."

Phosy reached in his shoulder bag.

"Bang," said the ninja.

But Phosy produced a Brownie Instamatic camera. The police department had three of them.

"Souvenir?"

"Kind of. I want to take a picture of you before you have your accident."

One of the few benefits of being a policeman in the People's Democratic Republic was that nobody cared about brutality in police custody. So that morning he'd merely had to tell the desk sergeant his prisoner got those two black eyes by dancing with a tall Ukrainian woman with a reinforced brassiere. The sergeant almost fell off his chair laughing. But now on that hard wooden bench with his instincts twitching, Phosy was starting to believe he should have fed his ninja to the giant catfish.

Most of the government buildings had open-air corridors, so Phosy heard the voice from the floor above clearly enough.

"Phosy? You down there?"

"Yes."

"Come up."

It was the Lao version of the intercom.

The supervisor was leaning against the wall in front of his office smoking a Marlboro.

"Smoke?" he said.

"No, thanks," said Phosy when he arrived. "You have something to tell me?"

The supervisor puffed on his cigarette. Four years on and they were still finding stashes of them. It was as if the royalists had planted them before they fled the city to wipe out the enemy one lung at a time.

"*Bo dai,*" said the supervisor.

"*Bo dai,* what?" as if he didn't know.

"You have to drop your investigation."

"I thought it was *our* investigation."

"It's not going anywhere. It's time to stop."

"We have a military hit man downstairs and seven witnesses prepared to state—"

"He's out," said the supervisor.

Phosy accepted one of the cigarettes. He didn't smoke, but he wanted to crush something in his fist.

"Had visitors, did you?" he asked.

"Phosy, don't—"

"You know we could save a lot of money on rent by moving into the armed forces ministry. They even have a lady who delivers tea and biscuits right to your office."

"Phosy!"

"Of course we'd be answerable to the general, but that's not much different than . . ."

"Phosy. It's not them."

"Not who?"

"The army didn't do it."

"Rubbish."

"It's true. They weren't responsible for the kidnapping. You were wrong."

◙ ◙ ◙

From the roof of his guesthouse Civilai could see Thailand. The Thais had long-distance telephones and faxes and even courier services where you'd give a man a letter and he'd speed off on his motorcycle and hand it over in person. So close—just across the river—but so far. In Pak Xan, the public phone at the post office wasn't active. A line was down somewhere. The postal worker even had the nerve to say, "But we do have a fax machine."

Two buses passed through town every day on their way to Vientiane. Civilai had entrusted notes to the drivers of both and handed over generous tips for the trouble of delivering the messages to the ministry. The odds of that working were as narrow as Laos winning a medal in the next Olympics. Like so many times before, he was being held prisoner by his country's non-communication system.

He went to the council office to see whether they'd had any luck with their own phone. But the greasy clerk was nowhere to be found, the director was off "in the field," and the telephone had a padlock that prevented unauthorized users from dialing. The second-in-command assured Civilai they'd bring him a message whenever they had a response from Vientiane. The only response Civilai wanted was a pickup truck with half a dozen embassy officials on board. The director had taken the Renault, so the assistant suggested in a most condescending fashion that the old man take advantage of this quiet period and relax. If he was lonely the man said he knew of a pretty young lady who was a most competent masseuse. This suggestion was punctuated with a wink.

Civilai had reluctantly agreed to stop at the police station to pay a courtesy call on the rude flip-flopped police officer. He was eating sweet suet balls at his desk and didn't offer one to his visitor.

"How did you know the dead woman?" he asked, dribbling sauce down his chin.

"I assume you have a remarkable memory," said Civilai, helping himself to a seat.

"Why?"

"Because you're beginning an interview without a pad or a pen. Unless you're planning to bite my replies into your suet balls in Morse code I'm assuming you'll be memorizing everything," said Civilai.

That entire speech was apparently meaningless to the policeman. "I asked you a question," he said.

Civilai sighed. "My wife and I encountered her on Sunday evening for the first time," he said. "We'd never seen her before."

"But she knew you," said the policeman.

"Knew of us, more like. She knew we'd been to Ban Toop."

At this point, one of the five framed black-and-white photos of senior Party members that lined the wall behind him came unscrewed. To prevent warping, very common of wooden frames in the tropics, a second screw anchored the frame at the bottom. This screw held, so the president now hung upside down and out of alignment. To his credit, the policeman barely reacted to this decoration malfunction and continued his interview. Civilai, on the other hand, found the sight of this upside-down ex-royal, now with a single eyebrow above his nose, rather hilarious. His replies to the policeman's questions were seasoned liberally with giggles. This riled the policeman, who took it as a personal insult. From that moment on any pretense at détente was canceled.

But all at once the dangling photograph took on entirely different characteristics in Civilai's mind. The fall from alignment was symbolic rather than accidental. And as he went through the motion of replying to the policeman's questions he rummaged through the clutter of his memory in search of a story. Scary tales around a campfire as a teenager. Gossip and rumors that had become folklore. He searched desperately for a connection.

"Are you listening to me?" said the policeman.

"No, not really," said Civilai. "Look, I need a library."

"You what? Do you want me to arrest you?"

"Do you want me to take your job from you?"

"What?"

"Take a look at me. Don't you know who I am?"

Nobody outside Vientiane and very few in it took any notice of who was on what board or which committee. Just a lot of old fogies in jackets and ties.

"I . . ."

"You'd better remember because in an hour my team will be here from Vientiane and right now, your position is hanging by a thread. Write down the name Civilai Songsawat, Lao Politburo. Oh, wait. You don't have a pen, do you? Then memorize it. And when you've done that and you've considered how much trouble you're in you can tell me where I can find some books in this town."

Of course there was no library. Even the national *bibliothèque* on Sethathirat looked more like a poorly stocked bookshop. The country had few tomes in its own language beyond the palm leaf manuscripts lying unread in the temples. But, like Siri, Civilai had hope that not all the French or English books had been destroyed. That besides Siri's ill-fated goldmine of classic French literature there might be other caches of gems hidden away until a day when the country regained its common sense. Naturally, the policeman knew of none. Nobody would confess to owning contraband literature. But there was one likely source.

Civilai was back in Teacher Grit's classroom. The children were huddled around mathematical puzzles and barely noticed the stranger's arrival.

"Ah, brother," said Grit, shaking Civilai's hand warmly. "How was your visit to the temple?"

"Frustrating," said Civilai. "Your local rats enjoy a good French report."

"I'm sorry," said Grit, "but you haven't given up?"

"I need an encyclopedia."

"And a submarine and a Rembrandt?"

"Is it that difficult? The lady football referee said you were the fountain of all knowledge."

"I disappoint often."

"Come on. You were angry about the cadres burning books here. Somebody like you would have found a way to hide a small stash. I'm not going to report you. I just want to look something up."

The old teacher puffed up his cheeks. "English or Thai?" he asked.

"No French?"

"Sorry."

"I'm not sure the Thais will have what I want, and my English is pretty horrible."

"Give me twenty minutes till the break, and I'll help."

The eleventh edition of the Encyclopedia Britannica was published in 1911, and it looked its age. Whilst its spies waged war against the Communists, American educators and volunteers stocked its school libraries in Laos mainly with secondhand books. A lot of the material was overt pro-paganda: abridged readers on great Americans and the like. Many of the schools destroyed their stock in '75, not know-ing how the Pathet Lao would react if they found them. Others, like Teacher Grit, hid them and returned them to the school when the coast was clear.

"Bit dusty," said Grit, "but all here, thirty-five volumes.

We boarded off the alcove during the early paranoid years but as you can see there's a little flap that worked its way loose and this paraffin lamp always seems to be alight during school hours. It's a sort of secret cave. The children love it. So, brother, what are we looking up?"

"Missa Niger," said Civilai, "although I doubt you'll find that. These are just words I vaguely remember from my youth. Perhaps you could try, La Messe Noire. The black . . ."

"Black mass," said Grit, in English. He was already thumbing through the battered B volume. He didn't seem at all fazed by the choice of topic. Civilai assumed he couldn't have known what it meant. He wasn't that sure himself. It was just an expression that had returned to him from stories he'd heard as a boy. From a picture he'd once seen in a book in his high school library of cloaked figures and a crucifix hanging upside down on the wall. He'd been thinking about the Buddha images in the mechanic's yard. Their defilement had been deliberately sacrilegious.

Grit found the entry, moved the lamp closer so he could make out the small lettering and translated as he read.

Black Mass: a blasphemous and obscene burlesque of the traditional Latin Mass performed by satanic cults. It is a ritual characterized by the inversion of the true Mass as celebrated by the Roman Catholic Church. Charges of satanism and celebration of the blasphemous black mass have been made against persons accused of heresy and witchcraft since early Christian times. It is invariably linked to a belief in a pagan deity.

The rite commonly incorporates other elements of satanic magic such as philters *or* abortifacients.

(These last two Grit was unable to translate.) *The naked back of a woman often serves as an altar and a consecrated but defiled host such as altar bread is generally used to intensify the mockery. Allegations have been made that the mass extended to perverse sexual rituals, and the sacrifice of children. The mass may include inverting, spitting and stepping on the cross, stabbing the host and other obscenities.*

Once he'd finished, Teacher Grit looked up at Civilai, whose face was etched with questions.

"Helpful?" he asked.

◙ ◙ ◙

"But to whose advantage would it be to get the press involved?" asked Daeng.

She was shouting above the growl of the Toyota engine. Headman Tham's son, Yuth, drove the village truck, but everyone had chosen to sit in the back to vent their frustrations.

"The policeman," shouted Siri.

"Now, how did I know you were going to pick him?" said Daeng.

"He gave it away," said Siri. "All his talk about the influence of the media on a case. He's exactly the type who'd want to get his face in the newspapers to advance his career. He'd be the local cop who caught the shaman village serial killer."

"Then why announce to us what effect alerting the press would have?"

"He's not very bright."

Daeng smiled and kissed his cheek. He was a little self-conscious in front of the headman and the Sangharaj.

"I love it when you're jealous of other men," said Daeng. "I'm . . ."

"Could we perhaps get back to the subject?" said the Sangharaj. "We have an innocent man in prison awaiting a tainted trial. He now has the press and half the country against him. And with the sudden interest of the media, we have less time to collect evidence in his favor. My guess is that the real killer was the one to involve the press."

"Someone in the village might have told the newspapers," said Headman Tham.

"Why?" asked Daeng.

"Most of our income is from tourists," he said. "Most of what we do is, you know, simple stuff. Guests don't come with very serious problems, so we can't charge too much. They buy souvenirs and take pictures and have a traditional Sawan lunch and some rice whisky and they're gone. If Sawan got on the news we'd be set. We'd have a bit of a surge, like they say. We're due for one."

"But it's not as simple as that, is it?" Siri shouted.

Tham looked at him and at the Sangharaj, and he smiled and shook his head. "No, Yeh Ming," he said. "It's not. It's not that simple at all. We've got a balance there in the village. It's all we can do to keep this or that pot from boiling over. We've all come there with our own demons. We're none of us perfect."

"What's he talking about?" asked Daeng.

"They're afraid," said Siri. "They have to avoid all the serious stuff: the exorcisms, the spirit séances. They can't control them anymore."

"I haven't put on my red hood for two years," said

Tham. "You know, Yeh Ming? I never know what I'm going to meet down there on the journey to the otherworld. Never know what I might accidently drag back with me. Or worse, never know whether they'll get me before I can make it back. I'm scared of them. We all are."

"Who?" asked the Sangharaj.

"The *phibob*," said Tham. "We were all thrown out of our villages because of them. All found our way here to Sawan because of them. We knew we had *phibob* in us, but we didn't really know what that meant. They're all around us, waiting for us to let them out of the cage."

"You do know that together you have the psychic power to discover exactly who it was that killed your people," said Siri.

"We dare not," said the headman.

"So you're prepared to let Abbot Rayron be executed because you're afraid of ghosts?" said Daeng.

Headman Tham looked at Siri pleadingly. "You know them, Yeh Ming," he said. "You know what they can do."

"Yes, I know them," said Siri. "But I've beaten them before. I'm not afraid. Do you think your elders would stand together if I coordinated it all? Would they trust Yeh Ming not to let loose a plague of evil spirits?"

The headman gave it some thought. "If it was Yeh Ming," he said, "I think I could convince them."

Yuth dropped Daeng, Siri and the Sangharaj at the temple and Headman Tham went off into the village to win over a ragged band of scared elders. Siri had picked up a crate of beer in Nam Som: Singha. It was a third the price of the version on sale in Vientiane. He wished he had Civilai there beside him to chug the beer and formulate theories and solve mysteries. Because he had stupidly given himself a problem bigger than the afterlife. Siri, a veritable novice in the world of spirits, had promised a career shaman he could keep down a *phibob* rebellion. That he could stop them from dragging every man, woman and child in the village into the cauldron of insanity. Possess them to death. Yet he hadn't the first idea how. Yeh Ming could tell him. Yeh Ming, the thousand-year-old immortal enemy of the *phibob*. He'd wrestled with them all his life and centuries into his afterlife. And he was there renting a small corner of Dr. Siri like some feeble retiree saying nothing at all.

Siri put the beer in its wooden crate into the carp pond. The water maintained a pleasant coolness during the day and chilled at night. He set out three triangular cushions on the slab of slate with a view of the sky and heaven and all that. The moon was pudgy but no longer full. Siri opened a beer with his teeth and took a long and blissful first draft. Ugly came to lie at his feet.

"Yeh Ming, mind if I join you?" said the Sangharaj.

Siri turned. "In a beer?" He smiled.

"In a meaningful dialogue."

"Then you're lucky you caught me before the sixth or seventh bottle."

The monk sat on his allotted cushion. "You can feel it here, can't you?" he said. "The tension."

"Yes," said Siri. "You?"

"Not of the dark spirits. But of the deceased. I just feel their presence. I imagine you see them. Does it become overwhelming?"

"Here or in Vientiane, no. They're more like decorations. Like statues that breathe and shuffle around. They're just souls waiting to move along. Nothing threatening. It was in Cambodia that I was overwhelmed. It was like a plague of desperate butterflies hitting your windshield. There was no time to be compassionate. You just turned on the wipers and drove through. I had no idea how to cope."

"Hence the alcohol?"

"No. I drink so I'll always have something to blame my stupidity on."

The Sangharaj tried his best not to laugh but failed. "Where's Madam Daeng this evening?" he asked.

"I imagine she saw us talking and went back to the room."

"Why?"

"She knows we have things to discuss."

"She'll be thirsty."

"She took a couple of bottles."

The moon slipped out of its cloud and bathed their faces.

"What went wrong?" Siri asked.

"In Laos?"

"Sangharajs don't run away unless there's no hope. When did it go belly up?"

The old monk shook his head and rearranged his robes as if he were about to deliver a sermon.

"Where does anything go wrong?" he said. "On paper everything seems logical and sensible and right. But you put it in the hands of the illogical and nonsensical and wrong people, and its flaws are revealed."

"Are you talking about socialism?" Siri asked.

"I'm talking about any delicate flower you leave in the hands of a gorilla. We were worried at first when we heard the Communists were getting support from Vietnam and

China. We were the opium of the people in their eyes. They killed and incarcerated thousands of monks in the Soviet Union. We were expecting a purge.

"Then these Pathet Lao cadres arrived in our villages, and they told us how, in their view, Buddhism wasn't so far from socialism. The Lord Buddha worked with and for the people. They had us believe he was the original Marxist. And we respected them. They weren't the plump government officials who stopped by once in a while to tell us there was no funding available for temples. The same corrupt beasts who were pigging their way through five hundred million dollars of US funding a year.

"Those young socialist people lived frugally like us. They were country boys and girls. They knew how the population had suffered from the years of civil war. They knew that villages paid tax to the government but saw nothing in return. We were undergoing the indignities the Lord Buddha had challenged two thousand years earlier. We admired the young soldiers who traveled by night and sat in the temples with our novices and patiently explained with charts and statistics how Laos had more than enough natural resources for every man, woman and child to live comfortably. And they recruited us. Our young monks would travel from temple to temple giving the same optimistic talks. And our new best friends the Pathet Lao assured us that as soon as they assumed power they would take up the Buddhist portfolio and improve the lot of the Sangha.

"And briefly, thanks to some diplomatic jiggery pokery in Europe, a coalition government was set up there that included the Pathet Lao. And true to their word, they took up religious affairs that nobody else wanted. Immediately, they issued orders that the temples were to multiply their efforts to spread the word of Communism in the country-side. It was perfect, you see? In a country with no modern communications system, they had a long-established net-work at their disposal. In more developed countries an invading force might take over the radio stations. In Laos they had us, and now they weren't passing on directions as our friends. They were dictating as our superiors."

Siri went down to the pond for two fresh beers. The monk's monologue had rendered Ugly comatose. Siri opened one of the beers with his teeth and handed it to his wife, who had arrived silently and was sitting away from the men on a raft of sweet-smelling grass. He winked at her and returned to the monk.

"The coalition soon broke down," said the old man, "and the Pathet Lao lost its seats, but the bush temple network was at full strength. Just as kings and warlords throughout history pumped vast wealth into the temples to unite and pacify the peasants, so the PL was using us to do exactly the same thing but without the vast wealth. In 1975, with not a little help from Hanoi, the Pathet Lao took over the country. The Chinese and Soviets were over the moon. The Americans had failed to prop up that most important Indochinese domino. And just as the Americans in defeat had abandoned their Hmong allies, so the Pathet Lao in victory forgot its pledges to us. They were reminded by their socialist relatives overseas that religion was 'the sigh of the oppressed people.'

"I suppose they could have destroyed our temples as the Siamese and the Ho bandits had done. They could have lined up the monks and beheaded us as the Khmer Rouge was so fond of doing. But I suppose some Laoness still had a pulse in them, and they merely let us starve. Neglect can be a far more effective form of abuse."

"So why did you wait this long?" Siri asked.

"Patience, friend Siri, is a very Buddhist trait. It sometimes stretches over centuries as we wait for our enemy to be reborn a quail. I hoped things would improve."

"But . . . ?"

"But then in January this year the new Ministry of Tourism announced that Buddhism would be their focus for 1980. The temples would be the bait to attract tourist dollars. They said they were disappointed at how little the monkhood was doing to help promote our wonderful country. We received a memo telling us to stop being lazy and clean up our act. Last straw. Here I am."

"And how was our friend Noo recruited to aid in your escape?"

"He had a Thai identity card and contacts on this side. He knew what we were going through. We respected him for the articles he wrote."

"Articles?"

"Oh, yes. He produced a large body of work describing our abuse. His pieces were published in a number of international journals and magazines. He didn't tell you?"

"He didn't tell us a lot," said Daeng, who had been quiet for long enough.

"That's why I was surprised to find Dr. Siri, deep in his cups, as Noo's replacement," said the monk. "Do we know what happened to him?"

"I have a policeman friend who's looking into his disappearance," said Siri. "He still doesn't know that you were Noo's top-secret assignment. I think it would really help if he had that knowledge."

"I'll get on to it in the morning," said the Sangharaj.

And that was the end of seriousness for the evening but not the end of mystery. Siri was never at his most comfortable sleeping in temples. He was always conscious of his own atheism and suspected the walls and ceilings resented the disbeliever. So he woke often. It was during one of these sleepless moments that he witnessed something odd from his window. He saw the Sangharaj on his hands and knees digging in the garden by moonlight. He dug a hole as deep as his arm's length and put something into it. He hurriedly filled the hole with earth and left. Siri shook his head and smiled to himself.

◙ ◙ ◙

"If it wasn't the military, who the hell could it be?" asked Nurse Dtui.

She and Phosy sat with Mr. Geung and Tukta at the end of the evening shift.

"Of course it's the military," said Phosy. "Of course the commissioner's going to say it isn't. They would have come and made threats and put pressure on him. What else could he say?"

"But the nin-ninja said we got it wrong, too," said Geung.

Tukta nodded. She rarely spoke in public, but Geung led everyone to believe he couldn't shut her up when they were alone. He said that some of his most insightful observations had originated from her.

"He wanted to put me off the trail," said Phosy.

"You said he was a-a-a thug," said Geung.

"He's right," said Dtui. "A thug isn't going to start

thinking about providing misinformation. He'd gloat over the fact you got it wrong."

"Which brings me back to the same question," said Phosy. "Who else could it be? I know it's not the police, and we've counted out immigration. That only leaves us with the girl scouts."

Both Geung and Tukta thought that was hilarious.

"Didn't your boss give you any clues?" asked Dtui.

"Nothing," said Phosy. "In fact he's closed the case. I don't have any resources to follow up. He told me to back off. I don't have any allies."

"You have them," said Tukta.

They all stared at her in surprise.

"Who?" said Mr. Geung.

"The army," said Tukta.

◎ ◎ ◎

Civilai's last stop on his fact-finding mission was back at the temple. He'd studied Buddhism the way a naughty schoolboy might study physics and chemistry, picking up the basics without knowing how the elements joined together to make an atomic bomb. He'd forgotten most of it. What he needed was a primer, but the only monk he knew in Pak Xan was of limited capacity. Still, it was worth a try.

He found the monk sweeping leaves from the prayer hall with a long straw broom. The monk laughed when he saw Civilai approach and sit on the top step in the shade of the overhanging roof.

"All alone?" said Civilai.

"I have the nagas and the *garuda* and the bees," said the

monk. He was a soft fifty with leaky eyes and asymmetrical bald patches in his short hair.

"Not much of a conversation to be had there," said Civilai.

"Better than some people," said the monk, "and good enough for me."

"Then, would you be kind enough to postpone your conversation with the bees and answer an old man one or two questions?"

The monk laughed. "I don't know much," he said.

"But you know about the Buddha?"

"Oh, yes. That I do know."

"Much?"

"Everything."

It was quite a boast, so Civilai put him to the test. He patted the step beside him, and the monk came to join him. He still held on to his broom.

"They tried to raise me a Catholic," said Civilai.

"That's a nice religion," said the monk. "Lots of singing."

"It has its good points. But very clearly it has a devil. You know what a devil is?"

"Of course," said the monk.

"Now when they taught me Buddhism nobody mentioned a devil," said Civilai. "There were hells, lots of them, but none of them had a scary old creature with horns. So am I right in saying there is no devil in Buddhism?"

"No."

"No there isn't?"

"No, you're not right," said the monk. "There's a devil."

"Can you tell me about him?"

"Yes."

Civilai waited. The monk didn't speak until Civilai coughed.

"Now?" said the monk.

"Yes, please."

"Mara," said the monk. "It was Mara who tempted the Lord by offering his three daughters. It is Mara who interrupts our meditation and puts temptation into our minds."

"He sounds more naughty than evil," said Civilai.

"Oh, he is evil, Uncle. It was Mara who caused a shower of rocks to smite the Lord. He holds the wheel of life in his hands. The word Mara means 'death.'"

"I see," said Civilai. "And are you afraid of Mara?"

"No."

"Why not?"

"Because I have a loaded .32 ACP automatic under my bedroll."

The two men laughed. Civilai patted his friend on the back, walked down the steps and crossed the dirt yard. He stopped and looked up at the lush, flowering fig tree that stood guard at the temple entrance. All of the ridiculous parts had come together to make a ridiculous whole in his mind.

Civilai returned to the steps and said to the monk, "There's one favor I'd like to ask."

1 1

Dr. Siri's First Official Public Disappearance

Phosy picked out his name from the guard's list of welcome guests, marched across the parade ground and
entered the Ministry of the Armed Forces. Corporal Suwit
sat at his desk staring at the door as if he'd been expecting
someone to enter. But there was surprise in his voice.

"Inspector Phosy?"

Phosy had spent much of his time in this office bluffing
and, yes, lying blatantly. So he saw no point in changing a
winning formula.

"Your man paid us a visit last night," he said.

"I beg your pardon?"

"You may recall that I provided you and your colonel
friends with some information—false, as it turns out—that
the witness to the kidnapping of the Thai citizen was alive
and staying at a noodle shop on Fa Ngum."

Phosy again ignored the guest chair and sat on the sofa.
Corporal Suwit seemed to be looking around his office for
some assistance.

"That information was erroneous for a number of reasons, in particular that the witness had indeed been killed

already. But the interesting thing is that you and your two superiors were the only people I passed on the location to. And who should turn up there but a soldier, highly trained in the arts of suburban subterfuge. He found his way into the building through a rear window and attempted to kill my wife with a twenty-centimeter blade. The latter, I'm sure you know, is standard military issue for discreet missions."

"I think I should go and fetch the colonels," said Suwit. He got to his feet but Phosy continued.

"Even though the soldier displayed much skill in the martial arts as taught to our elite troops by the Russians, he was overpowered and arrested. During interrogation he confessed he was a decorated soldier but refused to give us the name of his unit or his commanding officer. He was taken to police headquarters, charged and put in a holding cell. In under two hours he was released by the order of my boss, who wasn't at liberty to disclose who'd put the screws on him to sign the release."

Suwit seemed exhausted just listening.

"I really need to bring in . . ." began the corporal.

"Here's where we stand," said Phosy. "I have written a report outlining all the details of the case. The Thai ambassador is currently in his office awaiting its delivery. The Thai high command is on alert and waiting to hear from the ambassador."

"I don't . . ."

"But, here's my dilemma," said Phosy. He left the sofa, dragged the wooden chair to the desk and sat astride it. "I don't believe the military is responsible," he said.

"What?"

"It's true, everything points to you fellows: the leaked information, the identity of the witness, the description of the kidnappers and the admission of the assassin that he had a military background. Oh, and here's his photograph, by the way."

Phosy produced a copy of the photo he'd taken the night of the attack and laid it on the table in front of Suwit.

"And I'm sure that's the way the Thais will see it," Phosy continued. "But I have my doubts."

"You do?" said the corporal.

"Yes. I'm an old soldier, you see. Of course you know that from my file. Twenty years fighting for the revolution. Five years undercover. I've given much of my life to the defense of our great nation. I'm one of you at heart, and I don't want to send my report."

"Then don't."

"The ambassador's waiting for it."

Suwit returned to his desk and sat heavily. He was no longer a cartoon.

"I'll see what I can do," he said.

"About what?"

"Since you first arrived here we've been conducting discreet investigations of our own. We are keen to dispel rumors that we may have been involved in this matter."

"Meaning you have information as to who's responsible?"

"It's possible."

"If I don't hand over the report to the Thais they'll assume we're pulling the old Lao cover-up. Their prime minister's a military man. We promised there'd be openness in inter-military dealings."

"And there will be," said the corporal. "Give us twenty-four hours."

Phosy couldn't wipe the smile from his face as he rode

the lilac Vespa through the barrier in front of the ministry. Tukta had been right. He did have allies. In fact the army was off investigating on his behalf. All he had to do was sit with his feet on his desk and wait for the results.

Perhaps he should have been giving more thought to his riding because from out of nowhere a monk stepped in front of him. The Vespa was not a Harley, and it had never actually built up enough speed to kill a man. But it could give a monk a hefty thump and bounce him a couple of times on the road. Phosy stopped and looked down at the dusty man.

"You all right?" he asked.

As monks were already a rarely sighted species on the roads of Vientiane, Phosy didn't like to be responsible for further decimating their numbers.

"I'm fine," said the monk. He was ugly, but Phosy doubted the collision had much to do with that. He had the features of a horse, which were handsome on a horse but somewhat grotesque on a man. Phosy helped him to his feet.

"I have a message for you," said the monk. "From Dr. Siri."

◎   ◎   ◎

It was probably Dr. Siri's first official public disappearance. Until that moment he'd vanished mostly in his bed, which often went unnoticed by his sleeping wife. Then there were dematerializations from the bathroom or those that occurred when he was alone. But on this day Siri was not only present at the meeting of elders but was chairing it.

They'd had a lively hour of good-natured arguments,

jokes, scary stories and tea. Madam Daeng had been aware from the first sip that the cup contained something other than tea leaves. It was spicy and gingery, but it had a certain tang that gave them all a pleasant buzz. Perhaps that was why the meeting had gone so well and achieved so little. By 10 A.M., nobody had agreed to go back into what Headman Tham described as "the cesspit of no return." All of those present had experienced possession by the *phibob* and had felt the increase in the spirits' power from mischievous to downright nasty. The *phibob* had committed acts of spite and cruelty, and there were unexplained incidents that had lead to death.

On three occasions Siri without his talisman had been a target of the malevolent ones and had lived to tell the tale. Yet despite his assurances that the situation wasn't nearly as bad as it seemed, he had been unable to sway the group. So, either as a result of desperation or of the tea, Siri vanished. Everyone had been looking at Priestess Thewa at the time, so she was the only eye-witness to the disappearance. But when her eyebrows rose almost to the wooden rafters, everyone followed her gaze and saw the empty space that used to be the doctor.

"He's gone!" she shouted.

Daeng looked up from her notebook and smiled. "He does that," she said, and returned to her shorthand.

"Fine," said Intermediary Cham. "Damned fine."

Nobody in the room considered for a second that the doctor might have merely slipped out for a minute to use the toilet. They were professionals. They knew where he'd gone.

Siri was between the adjoining doors in the dark. He wished he hadn't come up with the hotel door analogy when he'd first explained the feeling to Daeng. Now it seemed he was doomed to be a casualty of his own imagination. He felt for door handles. There was one behind him, but he didn't feel like returning to the meeting. He had no good argument, and even if they agreed to delve back into the world of the extreme supernatural he had no way to guarantee their safety. So perhaps the connecting door could help.

He stood there, patiently at first, checking the forward door for a handle, calling out, "Anyone there?" and clenching and unclenching his fists. As time there didn't seem to matter, he wasn't sure whether he'd waited long enough or been too impatient. But he was bored, so he reached behind him and opened the door to where he'd come from. He heard rain dabbing onto a tin roof, which became the sound of hands clapping, and he was back in the meeting receiving a standing ovation for his trick. Even Daeng was on her feet laughing and wagging her tail. Another breakthrough.

"Remarkable," said Medium Tian.

"Yeh Ming, my hero," said Diviner Song.

Siri waved down the applause, not because he was modest but because he'd done nothing but stand between two doors for . . .

"How long was I gone?" he asked Daeng.

"About thirty seconds," she told him.

"Tell us of your journey," said Headman Tham. "Where did you go?"

"What did you learn?" said Shaman Lek.

They sat like first graders at story time anticipating Siri's tale.

"I didn't . . ." he began, but then he understood. He'd

disappeared for a reason. This was an opportunity. So he told them of flying through space to a place where the earth was cracked. He jumped into one of the fissures and landed in water, but he didn't drown because he'd taken swimming lessons at the Lane Xang Hotel pool. He floated for six days and six nights until he . . . Well, it didn't matter because it was all bull. But they ate it up, even the part where he took on a dozen armed *phibob* and crushed them to talcum powder. Before their demise the spirits had told Yeh Ming his magic was much more powerful than theirs. And when the story ended and everyone sighed with exhaustion, they all agreed there would be a grand séance in the village to cast out the *phibob*.

"You made it all up, didn't you?" said Daeng as they walked back along the haunted shortcut.

"Yes," said Siri, who never lied to his wife.

Siri thought about the mess he was in as they walked. The spirits behind the bushes were whistling pop tunes.

"Kurosawa," he said at last.

"Sounds Japanese," she said.

"Correct. Director. Made a movie called *Seven Samurai*. It's about a group of warriors in a village that's about to be overwhelmed by the army of an evil warlord. The warriors harness the skills of the villagers and train them to defend themselves."

"And you're the head warrior?"

"Metaphorically. We just gave the villagers enough confidence to believe they can overcome the *phibob*. It's faith in the most powerful of forces: belief in themselves."

At the end of the trail Ugly was there waiting for them,

his tail stub waving like a windshield wiper. They gave him some love.

"So what happened?" asked Daeng.

"In the movie?"

"Yes."

"Oh, I can't remember."

"Siri?"

"The village was almost totally destroyed, and the head warrior met a horrible death."

◙ ◙ ◙

Civilai sat on his bed and wondered about the girl who might keep him company. Not how she looked or what skills she'd have but whether she'd saved up enough to buy a motorcycle. He needed one. He'd had plenty of time to think as he waited for the arrival of his team from the ministry. He'd thought about potential allies there in Pak Xan and decided there were none. He'd considered jumping on the next bus to Vientiane and regrouping. He'd considered walking or riding a bicycle the thirty kilometers to Ban Toop. He'd considered hiring a local to ferry him across the river where the odds of successful communication were exponentially greater. In Laos, officials vanished when they went to the countryside. They invariably reached their destination, performed their tasks and had no problems. But their co-workers would not know for sure until they returned.

And, honestly, what was there to tell? He had no evidence to support his theory. There were no facts. Even if he returned to Vientiane he'd be unable to convince anyone there was evil afoot in the provinces. He took out his notebook for the fiftieth time and looked at the notes he'd written there.

1. *FRENCH ADMINISTRATOR MARCHE ACCUSED OF PROCURING TEENAGERS. SUSPECTED OF NEFARIOUS ACTS.*
2. *TAKES JOB IN INDOCHINA. BUILDS HOUSE IN COUNTRYSIDE/POWER.*
3. *LOSES JOB SUDDENLY AND IS INVESTIGATED.*
4. *FRENCH POLICEMAN DISAPPEARS.*

He then made a list of the elements of the black mass and connections to Ban Toop:

1. *INVERTED CROSS/SAWN-THROUGH BUDDHA IMAGE*
2. *REVERSING TEXTS/BAN TOOP POSSIBLE REVERSAL OF THE WORD POOT—BUDDHISM; TASITU REVERSAL OF TUSITA*
3. *WORSHIPPING DEVIL/MARA*
4. *SACRIFICES/MISSING TEENS*

He wondered if he was being ridiculous, trying too hard to match unrelated points. But when he saw the healthy fig, the Buddha tree in the temple, it reminded him of the dying fig tree at the mechanic's yard with hundreds of rusty nails hammered into its trunk. And as unlikely as it sounded, he was convinced someone in Ban Toop was involved in the dark arts.

He went to the window and stared at the treetops where the birds twittered and tweeted in their social network. Somebody had put in a claim that Noulak, aka Maitreya, the headman, the mechanic, the liar, was the next Buddha. But he'd done all he could to refute the claim. Nobody in the village was interested. So what if the claimant was a concerned citizen who knew what was going on in Ban Toop? What if he invented the assertion just to draw attention to the village? To get someone in a position of authority to visit and see for himself? What if the purpose for Civilai's mission was not to investigate the claim, but to uncover a much darker secret?

The only thing to connect Marche forty years hence to Ban Toop in 1979 was the house. If there were any evidence of illegal activity, that's where it would be found. He needed to go there to take a look inside. And if any further incentive were needed, it came with a knock on the door.

"Comrade Civilai," came a voice, "we've found you a motorcycle."

◙ ◙ ◙

Phosy and Nurse Dtui sat beside the hammock playing with Malee. She was a ticklish child, and her tinkly laughter never failed to fill her parents with joy.

"Will you tell them?" asked Dtui.

"The military?" said Phosy.

"Yes."

"You know, I'm not sure anyone knows the Sangharaj has gone. I've not seen any memos. There's been no gossip at the market. I don't think I want to be the one to break the news. And I'm not sure knowing would help at all in the search for Noo. And if Siri and Daeng are still with the Sangharaj, I don't want to put them in any danger."

Dtui stroked her daughter's hair. "Do you think we'll still be having life-threatening adventures when we're their age?" she asked.

"I hope not. I'd be happy to spend my old age drinking whisky and fishing."

"You hate fishing."

"It's a taste you acquire when you're old."

They were interrupted by a shout from the entrance of the police dormitory.

"Phosy, you there?"

"Don't answer," said Phosy.

"He's here," said Dtui.

"You've got a parcel," said the voice.

The parcel was just a large manila envelope. It was sealed with thick tape, and it took Dtui's old scalpel to get through it. Inside was a second photograph clipped to the picture of the ninja Phosy had left with Corporal Suwit. The new photo was clearly of the same person, but it placed him in army fatigues and made him four years younger. His hair was longer. Phosy flipped it over and read the handwritten note:

> NAME: MAJOR AGOON PREVIOUSLY STATIONED HOUAPHAN PROVINCE.
> CURRENT POSITION, PRESIDENTIAL SECURITY DETAIL.

◙ ◙ ◙

As Yeh Ming, Siri made the executive decision to call on the spirit of Loong Gan, the last victim of the murderer at Sawan. This was not, of course, as easy as it sounded because in spite of an abundance of spirit doctors in the village, few of them had even fleeting experience of making contact with humans. Most of their work had been spent placating the natural spirits of the earth. Those who claimed to talk to human phantoms had invariably been chosen by the spirit rather than the other way around.

In Vietnam, the mediums had established a thriving trade by talking to the spirits of dead soldiers. But of the group assembled in Sawan that afternoon, the only experienced ghost communicator who settled matters with ancestors was Intermediary Cham. But even he avoided conducting séances. The medium would ask her assistant spirit guide to run off and discover what the ancestor was so het up about. The ancestor would ask for a little more attention at the altar or for the sacrifice of a chicken, and the matter would be settled.

Siri had not been able to convince the Sangharaj to help out at the rehearsal. The doctor was sure the old boy would have enjoyed himself, so it was a shame. There was a carnival atmosphere in Sawan that afternoon. They'd decided from the signs that the weather would be kind to them in the evening, so they'd perform the ceremony under the stars. They took down the rattan ball net, and the skilled men of the village were assembling some kind of wooden structure. Paper lanterns were hung all around and colored strings with ghost money dangled from the trees.

Siri and Daeng had arranged the junior practitioners into teams with an elder in charge. Siri would pull a group to one side and go over their lines. They talked about escape plans, what to do if they lost control of their respective contributions to the grand séance. What to do if there was a fear the *phibob* might take over. Everyone had home-made remedies to counter the effects of malevolent spirits: powders and fire water in plastic spray bottles and holy water in buckets for a good dousing. Headman Tham practiced his old *pali* chants and Fortune-teller Doo overcooked a chicken until its bones were soft and pliable. Rather than promoting one method over another, they agreed to try everything. It couldn't hurt. The overwhelming sense on the day of the rehearsal was of invincibility. They'd overcome individual *phibob* in the past, and as a team, a powerful force of spirit doctors with Yeh Ming leading the charge, they would be able to overpower an army.

The wooden structure turned out to be bleachers, not big enough for everyone in the village to sit but perfect for honored guests, senior citizens, the pregnant and the frail. Everyone else would sit back behind a white-painted boundary rope. As the candle lanterns would offer only an atmospheric glow several wooden pyres were constructed around the perimeter like Neolithic floodlights.

Of course Siri couldn't handle a war by himself. But he knew Yeh Ming must have been observing that afternoon. He knew once the almighty battle began, Yeh Ming the thousand-year-old shaman would be there in his battle dress fighting side by side with his great, great—however many greats—grandson, fighting to the death.

"Ah," said Siri to his wife, "if only we had a film camera. Can you imagine how glorious this would look on the big screen?"

Madam Daeng had more faith in Siri as a surgeon, a coroner, a soldier and a thinker than in any man she'd ever met. He was the only man she'd ever truly loved. But she had to admit, as a shaman he was somewhat out of his depth.

"Siri," she said, "can I say something?"

"I'm disappointed you'd need to ask," he said.

"In my humble opinion," she said, "you have only progressed from not knowing what you're doing to not knowing what you're doing spectacularly. You've motivated an entire village to throw itself over a cliff."

He looked hurt. "I think you're underestimating my potential."

"You've made one shamanic trip to the otherworld quite by accident," said Daeng. "You've only recently learned how to communicate with spirits . . . or, should I say, one spirit? You host a shaman you never hear from, and you have a grand total of one party trick."

"It's hardly a trick, my love. I disappear."

"And only when you're alone or in the company of people who will you to disappear."

"What are you saying?"

"I'm saying that if your one skill is your only weapon for tonight's show then I'm just as qualified as you."

"Oh, be my guest. Feel free to stand up in front of a village of shamans and wag your tail."

"Apart from cooling them down a little I don't think that would help. Siri, the point is neither of us is qualified."

"Daeng, it doesn't matter what we can or can't do. Nobody in this village is able to function due to the fact they've been traumatized by the *phibob*. This is a show of strength. A chance for us to regain control."

"Oh."

"What?"

"I thought the whole purpose of this was to prove Abbot Rayron's innocence."

"Well, yes. Of course it is. That too."

"You know I'd be very disappointed if I thought this was just Dr. Siri plotting revenge on ghosts."

"Don't be silly."

He was sorry the words hadn't left his mouth with more conviction. He'd motivated all but one person. He watched his wife walk away. He loved how her new legs gave her the gait of a middle-aged woman, that little swing as she got the rhythm of the tail going. Of course he'd loved her just as much tailless and arthritic, but this was a gift from heaven.

◙ ◙ ◙

It wasn't so much a motorcycle, more a vacuum cleaner with uneven wheels. The Indian Motorcycle Chief went out of production in 1953, so to keep the creature alive after all those years, some loving owner had grafted on parts of everything from military jeeps to discarded lawn mowers. It looked abstract, but it was mobile. It chugged along at twenty kilometers an hour and sounded in remarkably fine health. Civilai knew it would be useless in the event of a hasty retreat, but he hoped that wouldn't be necessary.

He'd left notes at the guesthouse, the school and the temple. They were "Should anyone read this after my unexplained disappearance . . ." notes. They contained copies of his theories and his research and the reason, beyond all reason, why he'd decided to head off into the valley of death alone. He was no Bruce Lee, no James Bond, no Siri Paiboun. He was a weak old man with a paunch and hardly enough strength to unscrew the lid from a jar of pickles. But he had a brain, and if that failed, he was seventy-five, and that was a damned fine innings in a place like Laos. Better to go in a fistfight than an oxygen tent.

The sound of the old Chief would have been heard a few kilometers away if there'd been anyone to hear it. Civilai rode proudly into town like Gary Cooper. He saw nobody. He parked by the low wall of the colonial building, switched off the engine and sat there thinking, *It's mighty quiet.* The motorcycle ironed out its nuts and bolts a while, but there were no other sounds. No dogs barking. No birdsong. No breeze rustling the trees. Nothing.

He climbed down from the saddle and rearranged the discreet package he wore beneath his underpants. After thirty kilometers on a vacuum cleaner it took a few minutes to rise to his full height. But, by the time he was halfway along the garden path he was striding confidently. Before him was a large solid single-story building with enough space for nineteen families. There had been a propaganda campaign following the revolution to house poor families in the opulent homes of the usurpers. But there were no bare-bottomed toddlers running around, no lines of washing or rows of cabbages in the yard.

He stopped at a splendid blue door with opaque stained glass panels. After so many years he would have expected the glass to be cracked, the paint to be chipped and sunburned. But it looked as proud as the day it was first hung. And the door was ajar.

"Anyone home?" he shouted.

The building was as silent as a tomb.

He was half tempted to kick off his shoes before walking inside. Beyond the door was a typical front room: a large space with doors leading off it. There was no furniture, no tapestries or pictures on the whitewashed walls. And it was spotless. It was as if the area had been primed for a surgical operation. He didn't see so much as a ceiling lizard.

He walked to each door, knocked and stepped inside. But the rooms were just as empty and spick and span. The bathroom, the large kitchen and the maid's quarters were pristine and deserted. He walked to the back porch, which was surrounded by French windows. There was no table, but he could imagine the administrator dining there with his guests looking out over the lush garden. It would have been pretty in its day. There were small but cared-for non-native trees of both fruit and blossom. There were the outlines of flowerbeds and borders, and, although local weeds had grown through it, somebody had taken the trouble to keep the lawn even. It was a well-kept garden by Lao standards, but it had lost its class.

One of the many questions Civilai asked himself as he sat there on the garden steps was why anyone would care for a garden of an empty house.

He was so used to being alone in Ban Toop that when the figure emerged from the bushes to his right, he assumed it was one of Siri's ghosts. But it soon became clear that this was a young girl in her teens. She wore a colorful *phasin* skirt and a white blouse, and she had long, thick ebony hair. To complete the picture of the classic Lao beauty she should have been smiling, but she had a look of disappointment on her powdered face.

"I don't suppose I could order a glass of lemon juice?" said Civilai when she was close enough to hear. "I'm parched."

He noticed she was holding some sheets of paper in her pretty hand. He recognized the handwriting. There was no way of knowing how his farewell letters could have made their way to Ban Toop almost as fast as himself, or whether the collection was complete, but there was something final about the ache that squeezed his chest like a heavy concertina. It was as if the escape tunnel had caved in behind him.

He smiled at the girl. She looked at the ground in front of him.

"You have two choices," she said, her voice thick with rancor. "They both involve you dying. You can get on your bike and start riding back to Pak Xan. On the way you'll be killed in a tragic accident. They'll send your body back to Vientiane."

Civilai lowered himself down the steps, so she'd have no choice but to look at him.

"If you don't," she said, "you'll die here and your wife will never know what happened to you."

He was shocked that such a dark message could come from the lips of one so young and lovely.

"Not particularly good options," he said, "but I'll go for scenario B, the mysterious disappearance. At least then I might get a few answers."

She glared at him for longer than a Lao girl should stare at an elderly male.

"Go," she said.

"So you won't have to clean up the blood?" said Civilai.

"No . . . I . . ."

"Darling," said Civilai, "I understand you're just a messenger, albeit a rather scary one, but if I'm to be killed either way I prefer to die in front of you, so the image will stay with you all through your life."

She spat on the ground and continued to glare like a feral cat, but he noticed a tear in her eye. It was fleeting and was swatted away in a second, but it was there. She turned and walked across the freshly cut grass and disappeared behind her bush.

Civilai shuddered and looked around. "Cue the dark assassin," he called out. But nothing happened. And that lull was far more unnerving than any murderous intent. He walked back through the clean house along the garden path to the road, and he looked left and right. He strained his ears for human noise. He imagined this was what deafness must be like: the knowledge that there must be sound, but it couldn't be heard. All he had in his head was the imagined thump, thump of his heart.

He walked to the center of the road where he stood and shouted, "I am Civilai. I am seventy-five years old. I know what's happening here. I am not afraid."

Those last two points were not necessarily true, but he wondered even at this late hour whether he might elicit some sympathy from the villagers. He wondered if the over-seventies might rush out into the street and say, "We're with you, Civilai." As it was he felt silly standing there alone. The whole scenario was so ridiculous he laughed. It was true. He no longer felt afraid. He realized that you can only fear death if you lust for more life, and he didn't.

So when the old Renault appeared at the end of the road and figures in black hoods with slits for eyeholes emerged from the houses, it all struck him as rather amusing. While he still had the stage in this silent theatre he shouted his last thoughts.

"This is not . . ." he began.

One of the black hoods thumped him in the back of the knees with a tree branch. It hurt. He dropped onto his shins.

"... not the Lao way," he called out. "We are a peaceful people."

A second branch slammed into his upper arm, and the old bone snapped. A slither of nausea ran through him. He barely had the strength to finish.

"The Buddha taught us to love, not to—"

The last branch shut him up. It bounced off the side of his head, and he dropped flat on the roadway.

12

I Shot the Buddha

"So here's the bottom line. I've organized this . . . event. It's in a village so riddled with evil spirits you could poke a stick in the ground, and they'd spurt out. Daeng thinks I arranged it because I've lived in fear of the *phibob* long enough, that I want to show them who's boss. And, to be perfectly honest, she's right. She's usually right. She also thinks I don't have the wherewithal to pull it off. She's right on the button with that too. So I was wondering if you're not busy whether I might, you know, evoke you."

Dr. Siri sat there on the little stool and waited for a response. Surely they knew what was going on: the guardian spirits, his dead mother, Auntie Bpoo, Yeh Ming. Surely someone was tuned in to the Siri channel. He wasn't even in the space between the two doors. He was in the bathroom with a loofah in one hand and a cake of soap in the other. He decided at the very least he'd go to the grand séance clean. His inadequacies were another matter. He couldn't even will himself to disappear again. He'd never felt so naked.

He splashed himself with cold water from the tank,

dried himself with one of his two loincloths and wrapped the other around his waist. He walked to the door of the bathhouse and stepped outside. He thought his sandals were gone, but he'd left through a different door. He tried to go back, but the door didn't have a handle and had locked itself. Ahead, along a neat stepping stone path, was another door. It looked remarkably like the door he'd taken to get into the bathhouse in the first place.

"What is it with the doors?" he asked, looking up at the rapidly darkening sky.

He went through the other door, but it opened into a waiting room. There were chairs lining the walls and a bamboo table in the center with magazines. There were posters of cartoon dogs with worms eating their hearts, cats with cartoon lice laying eggs under their skin. There was a calendar of livestock sponsored by an artificial insemination clinic.

Siri tried to take one of the magazines, but it was stuck to the table, so he sat on a chair and waited. There were no doors now, not even the one he'd come through, so he couldn't go anywhere. And he couldn't speak or shout or sing because his mouth was sealed like a wound that had healed over. A man leading a monitor lizard on a rope entered through the far wall. Siri was so distracted by the lizard he didn't notice the man at first. It was Civilai, and he was bruised and covered with blood. Siri called out, but of course there was no sound. Civilai seemed not to notice Siri. He sat on one of the chairs, and the lizard curled up under the seat.

The wall to the right opened a crack and in walked Phosy. He too was walking a monitor lizard on a rope. He sat beside Civilai without acknowledging him. His lizard also curled up beneath the chair and went to sleep. Phosy perused the posters around the room. He was apparently unfazed by the twenty-centimeter blade sticking out from his stomach. Both men looked at their left wrists from time to time even though they were not wearing watches.

A nurse in a glossy white uniform entered through the wall immediately beside Siri.

"You," she said, slapping Siri across the back of the head. "You nex."

She had the type of Chinese accent Thai comedians adopted to make fun of the Chinese. Siri stood and wondered where he was supposed to go.

"Don't forgeh you dog," said the nurse.

Siri was holding a rope at the end of which was Saloop, his old dead mongrel. His tail was wagging and a broad, toothless grin filled his face. Siri smiled back.

"Folla me," said the nurse. She turned to Civilai and Phosy. "You two gotta wait," she said. "You both pendin."

Siri followed her through the wall. The vet was delivering a piglet. The mother pig lay on her back with her legs akimbo. The nurse told her to push as hard as she could.

"Might hurt," she said, "but it worth it."

Siri focused on the vet. He was older than the black stupa and wore monk's robes with an apron to keep off the blood. He was holding a bottle of whisky from which he took the occasional belt and encouraged the nurse to drink with him, swig for swig.

The pig produced a piglet that smelled of a hot cooked breakfast. The nurse took it and, unseen by the mother, dropped it down the garbage chute. Saloop the dog dived in after it. The nurse went to a small cupboard and took out a rubber duck. She carried it to the mother pig and held it up.

"I sorry," she said. "Baby no make it."

The pig, evidently not very smart, walked out in tears holding the rubber duck.

The vet shrugged, took a long draft of his whisky, handed the bottle to Siri and fell dead on the floor. Siri finished the bottle and fell beside him.

"Is there anything you'd care to tell me now that you're dead?" Siri asked the vet, but the question came out in a stream of bubbles from his ears.

"People believe anything," said the vet.

"I see that," said Siri.

The vet shriveled up, and his remains were blown away by the ceiling fan. Siri stood and walked back through the waiting room where there were now only the two monitor lizards sitting on chairs reading newspapers. They ignored Siri, who continued through a new door that had appeared leading back to the bathroom. There, sitting on a small plastic stool, he saw a naked Dr. Siri splashing himself with water. He didn't consider stopping for a chat. He turned around three times and went through the same door he'd just used, but this time his sandals were outside on the step. He walked through the dark temple grounds bathed in the floral scents of evening and paused to note how beautiful life was.

He returned to his room where Madam Daeng was sleeping on the floor mat. He lay beside her.

"Daeng," he said.

She was hard to rouse.

"Daeng?"

"Yes, my husband?"

"I've just had a surreal moment in the bathroom," he said. "In fact there might be another one of me arriving here sometime soon."

"Hmm, that would be kinky," she purred.

"What? Oh. Well, the point is, I feel a little drained. I'm probably going to need a quick nap before we head off for the séance."

She heaved herself up on one shoulder. Sleep was caked around her eyes. The room was already in darkness save for an arc of moonlight through the window.

"You don't remember?" she asked.

"Remember what?"

"It's all over, Siri."

"It is?"

"Yes. I was worried. I didn't think you'd ever come down."

"Down from what?"

"From your trance. What's the last thing you remember?"

"I don't . . . I went to take a bath."

"Yes, after lunch. And you came back from the bathroom pumped up like a tractor tire. You were magnificent."

"I was?"

"Oh, yes, Siri. We had the séance. You ran it like a circus master. The mediums mediated and the exorcists exorcised and the crowd yelled. And this shaman was possessed and that shaman was possessed. And there was a display of fireworks and a couple of bamboo rockets, and everyone agreed it was the most fun they'd had in years. Even the Sangharaj was impressed."

"He was there?"

"He was beside you all evening. You held his hand. Even when you were in your trance you didn't let him go."

"I was unconscious?"

"In a sitting position on the bleachers. We assumed you were drunk from the rice whisky or high from the opium. You went through a lot. But your eyes were wide open, and you smiled the entire time."

"I remember nothing," said Siri, shaking his head. "But it doesn't seem right to me. What about the *phibob*?"

"No show. The elders put it down to their own superior mental power. You were right. You gave the villagers their confidence back. Mediums reunited with their spirit guides. The shamans reopened pathways to the otherworld. It was as if everyone suddenly believed again. You gave them faith. They're back in control." She took his hand. "Siri, you're shaking."

"They're not," he said.

"Not what?"

"In control. They're not in control. All it means is that the séance wasn't important enough for the evil spirits to make an appearance. There's something bigger afoot. Something vast."

"Siri, aren't you being a little melodramatic?"

He touched the talisman around his neck. It was as cold as Antarctica. "They're not even interested in me tonight," he said. "They've found someone else to haunt. Someone powerful. Someone without defenses. Who . . . ?"

"You're making me feel a bit uncomfortable."

"What would an evil spirit value?" Siri asked. "What would they envy?"

"What?"

"Purity, Daeng. They'd be all over purity like ants on a dying caterpillar. Him! I held his hand. I wasn't being friendly to the patriarch, the *phibob* were using me to channel."

Daeng was already on her feet and fishing the repaired flashlight from her bag. Siri was at the entrance and moving fast. The Sangharaj's quarters had no door. Siri froze in the doorway, and Daeng arrived in time to shine the lamp over his shoulder.

"We're too late," said Siri.

The pages from the Sangharaj's canon were torn and scattered around the room. The monk possessed two robes. Both were folded neatly at the end of his sleeping mat. Wherever the monk had gone, either he was not dressed as a monk or he was not dressed at all.

◙ ◙ ◙

"He must be back by now. He's a field surgeon with battle-front experience. We should find him."

"Dtui, we have qualified surgeons. They were all in the military."

"But I want him. I want Siri. He'll know. He'll know what to do." She was irrational now, her voice loud and shrill. Her hands shaking.

"We all know what to do," said the hospital director. "But this isn't just about skill. The blade went in through his stomach. We can't just pull it out. We might cause more damage. We have to be careful, look at the x-rays, consider the options."

Dtui had worked at Mahosot Hospital for nine years both as a nurse and as a morgue assistant to Dr. Siri. She often heard the words "options," "careful," and "we know what to do." All those options lacked equipment, cleanliness, experience and accountability. If you lost a patient it was an unfortunate but unavoidable statistic. She'd arrived at the conclusion that you stood a better chance of survival in the morgue than on the ward.

The evening had begun in an innocent enough way. Dtui and Phosy had been walking along the riverside after her evening at the restaurant. He'd been discussing the connection with the presidential security division and the fact that someone at the armed forces ministry had leaked news of his visit with them. It didn't matter who it was. He'd come to believe there was nowhere to go, that he might as well be investigating the whereabouts of the Lord Buddha. People were disappearing, and he didn't want to be a part of such a system.

They'd been discussing other lives in other places. They wondered what type of life Malee might have in a Thai refugee camp. How many years they'd have to save before they could afford to open a little cake shop in Milwaukee. Everyone needed cake to take their minds off their humdrum lives.

And he'd walked toward them boldly, the ninja. In the shadows, the bruises around his eyes made it look as if he was wearing dark glasses. He smiled as if he knew something Phosy didn't and held up his hands to show he wasn't armed. Phosy stepped in front of Dtui. He had no weapon, but he'd have his wits about him in a street fight. He knew that the dynamics changed when forced to defend a loved one.

"Well, look at that," the man had said, "the fat girl and the bodyguard. Beautiful."

"You've got one chance to turn around and walk away," said Phosy.

"Or what?" said the man. "You'll throw her at me?"

Phosy wasn't easily riled. He was an expert at taking in

his surroundings and assessing his chances. Although the policeman couldn't yet see it, he knew the man would have a blade at his belt. The moon was behind them, so the ninja wouldn't be able to tell whether Phosy had anything in his hand. The man was approaching fast, which meant he'd be slightly off balance. All things being even Phosy would step forward, feint left and have the younger man in an armlock.

But all things were not even. Out of the corner of his eye he caught sight of the other man approaching Dtui from behind. Phosy dropped and kicked his wife's feet from under her. She landed with a thud on the packed earth of the street, but it made her a harder target. The second man stopped and looked on in surprise, but when Phosy looked back the ninja was already on him.

"Nobody hits me and gets away with it," he said.

They were interrupted by shouts from along the riverbank, shadows running toward them. But by then the blade was already in Phosy's gut. The assassin's work was done. When Geung, Tukta and Crazy Rajhid arrived, the inspector was on his side on the ground in a pool of blood.

Now Phosy lay on a gurney in an open-air corridor at Mahosot waiting for an x-ray, waiting for the arrival of a surgeon, waiting for death to take him somewhere more organized. Dtui continued to press the bunched-up sheet against his stomach to stem the blood. She'd disinfected the wound as best she could, but her dilemma was the blade. Was the director right? Would its removal cause more damage? She didn't know. But it was as if Mr. Geung read her mind.

"Better chance in the m-m-morgue," he said.

◙ ◙ ◙

Civilai took some time to open his puffy bruised eyes wide enough to see where he was. He felt like he'd been hit by a buffalo. The pain punched at him from the inside. He couldn't lift his left arm. It was obvious they'd continued to beat him even after he was unconscious. There were voices.

"Wait," said one. "He's alive."

"Don't talk shit," said another. "He's got no pulse."

"Then come here and tell me his eyes aren't moving," said the first.

Three figures in black cloaks without hoods gathered around him. Civilai clenched his fist but had no strength to throw a punch.

"Shit, he is," said the second man.

They ran out of view then returned a few seconds later wearing their hoods. If his face hadn't hurt so much Civilai would have laughed at that. He had no doubt at all he'd been dead for a few seconds, but there had been no distant light, no limbo, no out-of-body experiences. It had been a good atheist's death. He didn't know why his body had rebooted. He wasn't in the best of shape to take advantage of his second chance, but he was aware he had one last shot.

One of the hooded men grabbed him by the foot and dragged him across the floor. It gave the old politburo man a chance to look around. He was back in the house, the large room. It was nighttime, and the place was gloomy, lit only by thick black wax candles. There was an altar, the type you'd expect to find at the front of a church with a white lace tablecloth. It held expensive-looking silver

items: decanters, snuff boxes, a candelabra. But on an
upper tier were three Buddha images like the one he'd
seen in the mechanic's yard but much larger. They too
had experienced lobotomies and were standing on their
heads. The meaning was clear. In his research, Civilai
had been reminded that, in the Catholic version of the
black mass, the crucifix was inverted to indicate the
absence of respect. This was a cult conceived by a per-
verted Frenchman forty years earlier to test the bonds
of Buddhism. There were sweet joss sticks burning on
either side. From their scent, Civilai suspected they'd
been fashioned from marijuana. The altar candles were
phallic. To one side there was an opulent throne.

He lay there in the center of the room for some time
before the performers arrived. He and Siri had seen Boris
Karloff in *The Black Cat*, so he knew what to expect: satanic
cult, scary leader, horrible death. But it was one thing to
watch it on film and something else entirely to be in the
middle of it. The black-hooded actors formed a circle
around him. In all he counted eighteen. His sight was
returning. His arm throbbed.

One of the hooded eighteen spoke. "Brothers of the
Sacrilegious Order of the Almighty and Most Powerful
Mara," he said.

Civilai recognized the voice.

"We are gathered here this night to purge Nirxana
of one of its most odious enemies. We call on the spirit of
Marche to guide our hands today and to give our great
leader Mara the wisdom of the ancestors to make a
judgment."

The speaker was Comrade Luangrat, the director of
the regional council office, which went a long way in

explaining why Civilai had received no backup from the ministry. The speech Luangrat gave was grammatically incorrect, as if it had been written by a non-native speaker. It had probably been passed down from the pen of Marche himself. Civilai tuned out and thought back to those early days. An educated but flawed man with a hatred of organized religion had established a dark cult amid ignorant country people. Of course they had been too afraid of the great white master to argue with him. A secret organization with magic imported from the great capitals of Europe. A charismatic but feared anti-Buddha. A society that still embraced animist beliefs. And that cult held on through the wars and the peace and the takeover in a village that lived apart from the rest of the country—from the rest of humanity. Funded perhaps by cultists in the West. New leaders had emerged, and generation after generation had prolonged the dread. The membership and influence spread its tendrils through the province. A belief system based on something quite absurd had taken over to control the lives of citizens desperate for something to depend upon.

The councilman was still spouting, but now the circle of idiots had begun to chant in the background. It made no more sense than anything else in that place because the chant had been memorized backward. Civilai was about to conclude that Boris Karloff had done it all so much better when a door opened on the far side and two naked girls appeared. One of them was the teenager who had threatened Civilai that afternoon. They plodded across the room with no elegance or élan to the closed double doors. They stood one at each handle and pulled the doors open.

The circle chanters dropped to their knees and

performed a reverse *nop* where the backs of the hands were together. It looked uncomfortable. And, to the accompaniment of an unseen gong, Mara, the devil incarnate, entered the room. He looked serene, even in his dark glasses and his pool-table-green monk robes. The two naked girls fell in behind him and followed him to the throne. But even that small performance lacked class. Before taking his seat, the devil motorcycle mechanic looked up to the nine-tiered umbrellas suspended from a hook on the ceiling and clenched his fists and intoned some quiet words in their direction. When he finally sat, the two naked girls knelt on either side of him.

Civilai sighed. Satanism, animism, the world's religions, they only worked if you were afraid of them. And if you weren't in awe you'd see through it all. He recalled the story of the Mexican child who ate the taco with the Virgin Mary's face on it—a taco that attracted hundreds of devotees—because he was hungry. Civilai was not afraid of the power, just of the fools who wielded it. But hopeless as it seemed, he had one gambit. The only way to pull it off however was to overcome his own sarcastic nature. This, possibly his final performance, called for the surrender of his ego. He had to prostrate himself before a mechanic and resist the temptation to make smartarse comments. The odds were against him.

The chanting stopped. Those in the circle changed to a sitting position with their feet pointing directly toward Mara. One of the naked girls handed him a cheap palm leaf temple fan. He produced a Zippo lighter from somewhere deep in his robes and set light to it. It burned rapidly and flew off as ash. Civilai wasn't overwhelmed by all the symbolism. He could feel the big scene coming.

Mara stepped down from his throne and paced around the circle. With the sunglasses on it must have been difficult not to step on a disciple. Each hooded man nodded respectfully as he passed behind. When Mara stepped inside the circle, he was directly in front of Civilai. The old man cringed as if the power emanating from the part-time Satan was too much to bear. Mara looked at him but addressed the circle.

"He dared to come here," he said, "this lover of the Buddha . . ."

The audience hissed.

". . . to question our faith," he continued. "He accused us of being a descendant of his God."

Hiss.

"He said the senate of morons in Bangkok had sent him. But that was a lie. He is a spy."

Groan. Hiss.

"He investigated our heritage. He cast aspersions on our great founder, Marche, the first and most great Mara."

"Mara the first. Mara the first," they chanted.

"He called for his gang of Satan haters to come here to destroy us. But we thwarted his attack."

A cheer from the circle.

"But his arrogance knows no bounds. He dared to come to us alone. To challenge us. A decrepit old man with no control over his bladder."

Gales of laughter from the hooded men.

Civilai looked up. "How could you know that?" he asked.

"You were searched, you idiot," said Mara. "Do you know how insulting it is to be invaded by an opponent whose only weapon is a colostomy bag?"

Raucous laughter. Some rude comments.

Civilai reached for his bag. Technically it was a urostomy bag, but he wouldn't haggle.

"Don't worry, Great-grandfather," said Mara. "It's still there. We didn't want you to have an accident on our nice clean floor. We pride ourselves on our hygiene. It's full, by the way."

The men in the circle had never heard anything so hilarious.

"Please have mercy," said Civilai. "I'm just a weak old man following orders from Vientiane. I didn't realize what harm I was causing here. I can see it now. I admire what you've achieved so much. I have no resp—"

Mara kicked him in the side of the head.

"Shut up, old Father Time," he said. "How stupid do you think I am? A man will say anything at his execution."

"Exec . . . ?"

"Oh, dear. We didn't tell you? Our sacrifices are usually a lot fresher, but there will be some value in your death. The letting of your blood should appease some of the lesser devils in heaven. In fact they were disappointed when we thought you were already dead."

The circle had started a wordless, monotone dirge. Mara snapped his fingers, and one of the naked girls, shivering either from the cold or the embarrassment, walked to the edge of the circle with a long flat box in her hands. It was beautifully embossed. She held it out for Mara, but her eyes were on Civilai. He wondered if she was thinking about his words from that evening or if all personal opinions had been deleted from her head.

Mara opened the box and took out a ceremonial dagger that glinted in the candlelight. He held it with great reverence in his palms and walked slowly counterclockwise around the circle. The dirge increased in volume and intensity until the room had filled with an audible menace. Civilai had to admit the situation was getting rather disturbing, eerie, even. Every head followed the dagger, the instrument of generations of misguided executioners. Nutcases who had been brainwashed into believing that violence was the route to heaven. Mara offered up the dagger to the three lobotomized Buddhas.

"Oh, great Marche," he shouted, his weak voice barely audible above the chanting. "We offer you this unbeliever, this naysayer. And with his blood may you feast this night and—"

The shot was so loud the men in the circle covered their ears before dropping to the ground. Most were disoriented, but there must have been one or two who saw what happened. Some witnessed it in reverse.

One man in the circle had clearly been shot because he shouted, "I've been shot," and clutched his chest.

The bullet that hit him had passed through the shin of the all-powerful Mara and shattered it. And at the source of the shot sat Civilai in a pool of cold orange juice. The gun in his hand shook a little. When the blast faded from their eardrums all anyone could hear was the whimpering of a wounded motorcycle mechanic and the unenthusiastic screams of the naked girls. Mara managed to say, "Get him," before the sight of his own blood caused him to faint. The men in the circle reacted slowly. One, to Civilai's right, got into a crouch, but Civilai didn't train his weapon on the would-be attacker. It remained aimed solidly at Mara's head.

"If anyone comes near me I'll shoot him again," he said.

There followed a particularly subdued pandemonium

caused in part by the lack of peripheral vision through the eyeholes.

"What's happening?" someone asked.

"He shot the grand priest," said someone else.

"Who did?"

One man directly behind Civilai ripped off his mask and made a play for the sacrificial politburo man. The gun fired again, this time passing through Mara's foot and finishing off the poor fellow who'd caught the first ricochet.

"He's killed Mon," someone shouted.

The naked girls' screams had become more like the bleating of hungry goats.

"This is what's known as a standoff," said Civilai. "My guess is that one more bullet will see off your high priest. As things stand, no matter how fast we drive it's still touch and go whether we can get him to a hospital before he bleeds to death. So you, Comrade Luangrat of the council office, I want you to bring your car right up to the front gate. Two of your accomplices will then carry your unconscious leader and put him on the backseat. This group will be followed by me with my four remaining bullets propped up on either side by our young lady friends there. One false move and this particular incarnation of the devil will be terminated. I'm a very good shot."

◙ ◙ ◙

The Mahosot morgue wasn't what you might call sanitary. But then again neither were the operating theaters. Nurse Dtui, scrubbed up and masked, looked down at the blade sticking out of her husband's gut. The blood was oozing now rather than gushing, but Phosy had lost a lot of it.

"I can't do this," she said.

"You or nobody," said Mr. Geung.

The last straw had been drawn when the wife of the surgeon on call told the Mahosot telephonist her husband was at a wedding party and wouldn't be back till midnight. So the x-rays wouldn't have been much help anyway. By that time Phosy would have been dead.

Dtui was a fine pathologist. Over the last year of their tenure in the morgue Siri had invariably handed over the autopsies to his bright nurse. Had it not been for one of those surprise pregnancies that sneak up on a woman she would now be in her second year in the soviet bloc, set to return as Siri's replacement. She was nimble-fingered and observant, and she would often spot tiny clues the doctor hadn't yet seen. But if she made a mistake, her clients wouldn't be any more dead. She'd never practiced surgery on a live body.

"He's going to die," said Tukta from her seat way at the back. She had no tolerance for the sight of blood. "If you don't do it, you don't love him."

It was a horribly cruel thing to say. Dtui glared at her angrily, had an urge to slap the girl's face. But Tukta raised her eyebrows as if to say, "Tell me I'm wrong." And, of course, she wasn't.

◙   ◙   ◙

At one point, Civilai was forced to pull off the road to throw up, and collapsed across the seat. When he came to, the Mara was still unconscious on the backseat. They were only ten minutes out of Ban Toop. Civilai wrapped the man's wounds tightly with some old rags he found in the boot. It would be useful to keep him alive, but Civilai wouldn't lose any sleep if he didn't make it.

Everything in his escape had depended on timing and bluff. The automatic he'd borrowed from the monk had only ever contained two bullets. And Civilai was only a few minutes away from succumbing to his own injuries. He could already see the black moths of the unconscious flapping around his eyes. But the followers' respect for their leader and fear for his life had expedited the move to the car. Some of the men had insisted they travel with the high priest, but they stood down when the gun was raised to their faces.

And now the car sat beside a silent road. No fear of being followed, as beside the painfully slow motorcycle, there were no other vehicles in the village. He knew he had to drive the hundred kilometers to Vientiane because he could not trust any local officials in Pak Xan. He knew he was unlikely to make it. But he smiled at his coup. Nobody ever looked that closely at a urostomy bag. He'd taken the largest one they had at the pharmacy, slit open the top, put the gun inside and filled it with watered-down orange juice. He re-fastened the bag and taped it to his stomach. If only he'd had a video camera. What a hit that would have been.

Satan groaned in the rear seat and opened his eyes.

"Good morning," said Civilai. "Ready for some grape-fruit and warm toast?"

"What . . . happened to me?" he asked.

"I shot you," said Civilai. "No offense."

"It hurts."

"I know. Bullets do that. Just in case you don't make it, I was wondering whether you might answer a few questions that have been annoying me."

"I'm not saying anything, you bastard. You're a dead man. You wait and see."

"No, you haven't quite grasped the situation. We're just outside Vientiane. You're out of your comfort zone. Nobody's afraid of you down here. You're going to prison, and if you don't cooperate you'll be put in front of a firing squad. So would you mind terribly if I asked you one or two questions?"

"It hurts."

"I know. Look. How about this? You answer my question and I'll give you a shot of this morphine."

Civilai held up a paper bag. The man was too weak to argue.

"Ask," he said.

"There's a good Satan. Now, first the virgin mother. She really was your mother, right?"

"Yeah."

"And she hated your father so much she pruned him out of the family tree. Went around telling everyone you were an immaculate birth."

Mara nodded.

"But what was it about your dad that she hated so much?"

"He was . . . he was the Mara before me. Thirty years. As many wives. Twice as many mistresses."

"So she felt neglected."

"She turned to drink. He kicked her out. He could have any woman he wanted. Had power over every man in the district. He had command over life and death. Anyone came to pry, and he'd arrange for their disappearance, Lao and foreign alike. He was afraid of nobody. I inherited his greatness. He started as a common mechanic like

me. But that's the secret. Greatness comes from humble
origins. He was a great leader, but the minor devils got into
his head. It happens. The Buddha has an army of demons
that screw with people's minds. When he got older he got
confused. Got it into his mind he wasn't Mara at all, that
he was Maitreya. Started telling everyone Buddha was the
real savior, and when he was reincarnated he'd bring all
his lost souls back together."

"So it was your father who put in the claim."

"He wrote to the Sangharaj. Told him he used to be the
devil, but he'd been reborn as the Buddha."

"And he described in detail what was going on in Ban
Toop," said Civilai. Not a question.

He could see the moths again. Knew he was on his way
out. But he had to put the last link together.

"And the first thing you knew about this was the
communiqué from Vientiane telling you a representative—i.e. me—would come here to assess the situation,"
he said.

"Morphine," said the Mara.

"Nearly time," said Civilai. "Finish the story."

"My father had been ousted by then," said Mara. "I'd
been the headman for a year in his stead, and the assem-
bly elected me unanimously to be high priest. We were
Marche's bloodline. Then we got the letter. And we
couldn't let you meet my father. Not the way he was."

"The Buddha I was sent to meet wasn't you. It was your
father."

"He would have told you everything."

"You killed him."

Mara shrugged.

"You killed him and you killed your mother because

either of them would have blown your silly operation here."

"It was for the greater good."

"It was for the greater evil."

"Morphine."

"You mean this?" He held up the bag. "Sorry, found it in the glove box. I think it contains lemon drops. Really old ones."

"We had an agreement."

"I don't do deals with the devil."

13

The Leap of Faith

Compared to the Eiffel Tower, the water tower in Sawan should have hardly rated as a tower at all. It was thirty meters high and was basically a zinc box resting on a precarious bamboo platform. Two bamboo ladders, one atop the other, were attached to the wooden tower with rope. It had been built five years earlier by two keen but inexpert members of the American Peace Corps, and the villagers were frankly amazed it was still standing. Although the odds of dying as a result of a leap from the Eiffel Tower were greater, the base of the Sawan tower and its vicinity was solid concrete. A jumper might survive, but it would be awfully messy.

The Sangharaj, naked as the day he was born, was pacing the top of the tank. He had his hands behind his back and, to Siri, looked like a submarine commander in a low-budget film. They'd found him not from reports of a naked man running through the village but from the din. Walking on a half-empty zinc water tank makes a lot of noise at one in the morning. He was illuminated in the beam of Daeng's flashlight. It was cloudy, and the night was as dark as pitch, so it was a wonder the old monk had found the tower at all. But Siri knew from experience that every move the man made was not of his own volition. Everything that passed through his mind was manipulated. Everything he believed he saw or heard was a lie. There was no tangible difference between reality and the world the *phibob* created in a man's head.

"Do you think he'll jump?" asked Daeng.

"He won't need to," said Siri. "They'll convince him there's a bridge to the next tower or a helicopter waiting to take him for a ride. They have a hell of an imagination."

Siri's amulet had been so hot when they set out that he had Daeng wrap it in her shawl and tie it with string so his skin wouldn't sizzle. Yet her fingers could feel nothing but a cool chunk of stone. Siri knew the ultimate showdown was on its way.

"What should we do?" asked Daeng.

The entire village had left their houses to witness this peculiarity. This was the ambush the *phibob* had planned. Already some of the children had begun to growl and salivate, a sure sign the malevolent spirits were recruiting in numbers. Soon they would have control of everyone. In the village, if a person was inhabited by demons, and the spirit doctors were unable to exorcise those evil spirits the victim would, of course, become insane. But the mad person would be allowed to remain in the village to remind the elders of their failure. They were obliged by the rules of exorcism to provide care. In Sawan, possession was nine-tenths of the law.

But what would happen if nobody was spared? What if the spirits spread like a plague through the region and took over? How far could their influence reach? These were the fears that ran through Siri's mind. Although Daeng could feel none of this, Siri insisted she hold his hand. He called for all the villagers wearing amulets to step forward.

"We have to act fast to avert a disaster," he said. "Anyone here not wearing an amulet should return to their huts immediately. You may have to escort them, even drag them if necessary. Get them blessed and under the protection of the house spirits. The families are going to need a lot of support tonight."

One of the young men who'd left his hut without protection had already been taken. He stood beneath the water tower snarling and brandishing an imaginary sword. In the crowd a woman began screeching like a monkey, bouncing up and down. The elders, each of whom wore a lei of amulets day and night, hurried everyone back to the village. Parents held their children close, whispering healing chants into their ears. Two other males had broken away from their loved ones and joined the crazed swordsman at the tower ladder. They shouted obscenities, although the voices were clearly not their own. And all the while the naked monk strutted and stared downward at the escalating chaos. He edged ever closer to the sheer drop.

It was like two armies gathering for battle. As the possessions took hold, more and more swordsmen and monkeys joined the expanding *phibob* army around the tower. At the same time, the returning elders and newly arrived shaman warriors gathered around Siri with their talismans strung around their necks.

"What do we do, Yeh Ming?" asked Headman Tham.

Siri had no idea, but he was obviously the general, so he figured things out logically one step at a time.

"We need a parachute," he said.

"A parachute, like a metaphysical symbol of safety?" asked Priestess Thewa.

"Like a big nylon sheet that drops out of airplanes," said Siri.

They looked at him blankly.

"Come on," he said. "This is Udon. You had more American planes landing and taking off here during the secret war than dogs have fleas. Someone must have one."

"I do," said Shaman Lek. "We use it for—"

"Doesn't matter. Go and get it," said Siri. "Fast as you can."

"That's it?" said Headman Tham.

"For now," said Siri.

Villagers whose evil-spirit home security systems were apparently bogus or not up to the task came running back to the clearing and joined their evil colleagues at the tower.

"We have to engage them," said Fortune-teller Doo.

"Patience," said Siri.

"We need an all-out exorcism," said Intermediary Cham.

"Difficult," said Siri, "given that the chief host is thirty meters above the ground. But we could use a distraction. If we set up a little séance right here, how many of you think you'd be able to get in the mood to call on your spirit guides?"

"I don't have my equipment with me," said Medium Tian.

"Me neither," said Shaman Phi. "I can't just turn it on like a water tap."

"I understand," said Siri.

"I'm feeling a bit odd," Daeng whispered in his ear. Her hand had briefly slipped from his grasp in the confusion.

He took hold of it again, but she was already starting to bounce. Siri was concerned, but there were priorities. He addressed the shamans.

"Individually," he said, "you will never be prepared or well-enough equipped for a battle of this magnitude. But consider the know-how you have as shamans. Think of all the contacts you've made on the other side. As a team you are frightening. Even Yeh Ming trembles in the presence of such power."

"Siri, I . . ." said Daeng.

Daeng dropped the flashlight and ran off. Siri had no choice but to let her go. She made a good monkey. She already had the tail for it. Siri formed the elders into a simple circle, holding hands, cross-legged on the ground, no props, no costumes, no show. Just seven hundred combined years of experience.

"Just think of the power you hold in those hands," he said.

He knew that since they'd come from their own villages to live in Sawan they'd practiced as individuals. There was no common ground. Most of them had little idea what was happening in the next hut. His instinct told him they needed some simple unifier to bring them together.

"Do you think there's a chant you all know?" he asked.

They offered their favorites, but none were known to all.

"Songs?" asked Siri.

"You mean religious songs?" asked Priestess Thewa.

The number of enraged swordsmen had swollen to fifty. The monkeys, who now included Madam Daeng in their ranks, were starting to advance on the shamans.

"No," said Siri. "Just any song you all know and like."

"I'm very fond of 'The Person Who Rides the Buffalo,'" said Herbalist Ya.

"Yes, by Caravan. I like that," said Diviner Song.

"It's all right," said Fortune-teller Doo. "But I haven't wasted my life memorizing the words to pop songs at my age."

"You don't need the words," Siri told them. "Do you all know the tune?"

They nodded.

"Then that's it," said Siri. "Forget everything that's happening here at the water tower. At the count of three I want you to hum or whistle or 'la la la' the tune of 'The Person Who Rides the Buffalo.' Slow it down a bit. Just focus on the beat and the circle and the camaraderie."

"You have to join us," said Shaman Lek.

"Of course," said Siri. "I'll be with you. Yeh Ming will be with you throughout. First you have to gel."

"But what do we do then?" asked Headman Tham. "When we've gelled?"

"You'll know," Siri told him, and left them to it.

The parachute had arrived, still in its pack. The younger shamans and the assistants were awaiting instructions. They had one eye on the approaching monkeys, who appeared to be collecting rocks. The shamans unpacked the pale-blue chute and stretched it out. Siri spaced the strongest members around its perimeter, and they experimented with gathering the folds so that nothing was touching the ground. To test it, Siri had one of the younger men take a running leap into the canopy. He landed with a thump on the earth.

"Right," said Siri. "Now you'll understand how tightly you'll have to hold it to prevent that man on the tower from ending his life on the concrete."

The young shaman looked surprised.

"You want us to stand over there?" he said.

Siri nodded.

"But . . . they're over there," he said, nodding toward the mad swordsmen.

"'They' are your comrades and your relatives," said Siri. "Do you see swords? No. Why? Because they have none. They believe they can slice off your limbs with their weapons but they cannot. The worst you'll experience is a whoosh of air. They might try to convince you to remove your amulets and join them, but they cannot harm you. And look there at your seniors. They are launching an attack on the right flank. You will slide around to the left with your parachute and take up a position beneath the tower. You won't be able to see what's happening on top of the tower so, you . . ."

He pointed to an enthusiastic girl with a life belt of amulets and posies around her waist. He picked up Daeng's flashlight and handed it to her.

". . . you will be the beacon," he said. "I want you to stand back here with the light trained on the Sangharaj and call to your allies to let them know where he's located and what he's doing. You others will all follow her instructions. Be prepared for sudden movements and the unexpected. Always remember if he falls and you fail to catch him, you will be responsible for the demise of a great and powerful monk."

It wasn't the most positive pre-match team talk, but there was no time for pleasantness. A rock flew a meter past his ear. The monkeys were on the offensive.

"Off you go," he said and they carried their parachute around the left flank. Meanwhile, the strains of "The Person Who Rides the Buffalo" with the odd lyric thrown in were emanating strong and soulful from the elders. They didn't exactly look confident, but the song was more recognizable now. So Siri decided then was as good a time as any for a full-frontal attack. He walked directly toward the tower.

"Where are you going?" shouted the girl with the flashlight.

"Confrontation," he said, and strode manfully forward. He had a theory. This show of force by the *phibob* was to demonstrate their power. How better to do that than to humiliate and destroy a great Buddhist general? The only reason the Sangharaj hadn't stepped off the tower so far was that His Sublimeness, strengthened from a lifetime of purity and devotion, was waging his own battle with the spirits. He was outnumbered, but his will was holding. He needed reinforcements.

Siri wasn't even slightly intimidated by the swordsmen who came at him like wild beasts, drooling and cursing, slashing at him with weapons they didn't have. They were incensed that he could brush past them with such nonchalance. He even dared punch one stocky man on the nose. He yelped like a puppy.

Siri had made one error. He had dismissed the role of the monkey women. They were bold and approached him without fear. It was one slim, attractive monkey who made the first lunge. She came screaming, not for his throat but for his amulet. Siri stepped back and pushed her off. She snarled and prowled away. He cursed himself for his lack of foresight. Of course. All the *phibob* had to do was remove his amulet and his cloak of invulnerability would be stripped from him. Then he'd be bouncing and brandishing with the rest of them.

Siri was completely surrounded by monkey women. If they attacked en masse he'd be lost. He continued to walk forward, but the pack was circling, drawing closer. A second monkey woman lunged. She was in her sixties, but she flew through the air with amazing agility and wrapped her arms and legs around his middle. He didn't have the strength to peel her off. She reached up inside his shirt and yanked on the string that held his talisman. He grabbed her wrist, but she was improbably strong. All he could do was prize her arm away from the package and hold it.

That was when the monkey previously known as Daeng attacked him from the rear. She yanked the cord over his head, snatched the package from his shirt and held it aloft in victory. The other monkey women screeched with delight and danced. Siri was still locked in a simian embrace with the old ape woman. All he could do was watch his monkey wife walk away on her knuckles through the crowd. Almost immediately he felt the crush as the *phibob* moved in on him. It was as if the portcullis was open, and the invaders could enter the castle at their leisure. There were millions of them. Tens of millions. He couldn't see them, but he sensed that there would never be an end to the invaders. Already he was losing his sense of self. He had no willpower. Sights and sounds around him were becoming fainter. But he recognized a voice. It wasn't a human voice. It was the bark and snarl of a dog. It was the familiar sound of Ugly's growl.

Siri opened his eyes in time to see his dog bury his fangs in Madam Daeng's arm. The mongrel was suspended in midair, but shaking and rolling his head until Daeng had no choice but to drop her package. Other monkey women went for it, but Ugly was faster. He snatched it up in his jaws and ran it back to his drowsy master. Siri was disoriented and could not take hold of the talisman, but Ugly held it against the doctor's head and growled when the monkey women came close. Its power was like an injection of cocaine. Siri felt the surge. He fought off the old lady ape and took the amulet package in both hands. The monkey women came at him again. There was a wall of monkeys and swordsmen between him and the ladder. He adopted his rugby stance, amulet cradled in right arm, left arm out in front, palm forward, and he charged them. Ugly was at his side.

He pushed through one then another, but the monkey women were unbreakable. They'd fall to the ground then be on their feet in seconds. And Madam Daeng was back in the scrimmage. But then something unexpected happened. It was as if his opponents had been inflicted with terrible migraines. They held their heads and whined and staggered. Siri understood. They were receiving interference from the circle of shamans. The unification was working.

Siri reached the ladder with no further obstacles. He patted Ugly on the head, removed the amulet from its pack, replaced it around his neck and began to climb. His cloudy old lungs told him to rest after only a few steps. Who was this old invalid? What happened to the school wrestling champion? The boxer? The only boy in his college to win the annual cross-country race barefoot? Why did old age delete the abilities but highlight the memories? By the time he reached the top of the second ladder he was wheezing so loudly the hawks in the surrounding trees called back in reply.

The Sangharaj was walking unsteady laps just two meters above Siri's head. The footsteps gonged on the zinc roof. It was like being beside a kettle drum. Siri couldn't hear his own thoughts. He called out.

"Sangharaj, can you stop walking for a while, so we can talk this through? Ignore those voices in your head. Put aside any suggestions you would never naturally make."

But the *phibob* had transported the mind of the old monk somewhere far from that water tower. Siri would have to antagonize them to break down the barrier they'd put up. He began to recite an old Hmong text he'd learned from a village of women in Xiang Khouang. It was a warning mothers gave their children about the ugly and foul-smelling *phibob* who crept into their bedrooms late at night and ripped off the children's fingers and toes to make necklaces of them. The warning went on for ten verses, growing more and more insulting and disgusting as they progressed.

It was unlikely the Sangharaj would have heard or understood the words, but his body stopped pacing for the first time.

"You're late," he said, or at least the words came from his mouth, but the lips didn't move.

"May I join you up there?" Siri asked.

"I insist," said the mouth of the monk.

Siri climbed the last section of scaffold and stood on the tank, breathing heavily. His introduction caused a loud clunk, as if the tank might cave in at any second. He took a deep breath and looked around. All he could see was a glow from the village lamps and the distant lights of Nam Som reflected against the clouds. He'd expected to be picked out in the beam of a flashlight, but that was not to be. He remembered their arrival when the torch had refused to work.

"Nice place you have here," said Siri.

"You are Yeh Ming," said the voice.

The Sangharaj stood in the center of the tank as immobile as stone. Only his outline was visible against the glow.

"And this is your last night on earth," added the voice. "You'll be with us soon."

"You can't win this," said Siri.

"We have already won," said the voice.

It was then Siri noticed the silence. It was as quiet as the night they'd first arrived. There were no birds, or whispering leaves, or toads or night insects. There was no fighting from below and no singing of "The Person Who Rides the Buffalo."

"We have seven centuries of experience here in Sawan and the best you can do is monkeys?" said Siri.

"Experience of what?" came the voice. Much closer now and no longer from the mouth of the monk. "Of jingling bottle-top tambourines? Of riding wooden benches? Of calling on spirits of entities that never existed? Your little army was a sham, Yeh Ming. Your soldiers were charlatans. It's to no avail, Yeh Ming. Can you hear it? The silence? Your circle of old magicians is quiet. They're all dead, you see? When they saw what we did to their elders, the young ones fled like mice. Too much blood for their tastes perhaps. Do you see the flashlight, Yeh Ming?"

Siri, from principle, had never admitted to anything in his life. He'd never yielded, never confessed, never begged for mercy. But he had to agree things were looking grim up there on the water tower.

"Then what do you suggest?" Siri asked.

"Nothing. You're already lost."

"There is one thing I can do to please you."

"What is that?"

"The super shaman here and I fight to the death. If I win I give you my amulet and you let me go. If I lose you may take the talisman from my dead body. Either way you win plus you get a little blood sport on the way."

There followed an interminable silence.

"Agreed," said the voice at last.

"Splendid," said Siri. "Then let's get it over with."

The knuckles of the Sangharaj cracked as he clenched and unclenched his fists. His torso stood upright and seemed to have shed a decade or two. He really did appear to be invincible. Siri's only hope was to trust. He had to believe the silence only existed in his own head, that the beam of light had been masked only from his eyes. He had to believe the *phibob* were incapable of telling the truth just as Auntie Bpoo—dear, absent Auntie Bpoo—had told him in her poem: *Never trust the ghosts. They have no scruples.* He had to believe that nothing was as it appeared.

The monk raised his fists and seemed to swell with confidence. Siri, still wheezing loudly and exhausted from his earlier battle, crouched with one hand on the metal like a sumo wrestler. He tensed every muscle in his body. He shouted a wordless battle cry, sprang forward and ran at the Sangharaj. The monk was ready for him, and, as Siri's guard was down, he cracked a fist into the doctor's chin. Siri's head rebounded from the blow as if it might come loose from his shoulders. But Siri had expected as much. He had to keep his hands low, so he might get in below the next punches and round his opponent's waist. By the time the second blow came, Siri had already reached his target, and the punch merely glanced his eye. His forward momentum pushed the monk onto his back foot, and his grip prevented the Sangharaj from stepping out of the hold.

Siri didn't stand his ground, he continued to push. The monk flailed at the head against his chest, but Siri didn't let go.

"Siri, what are you doing?" came the familiar voice of the Sangharaj. "It's me. For heaven's sake, you'll kill us both. Please, Siri."

Siri forged ahead until they were at the edge of the tank. Only the monk's toes remained on the metal.

"Help me, Siri," said the monk. "Save me."

But one more shove, and they were both in midair. There it was. The leap of faith.

14

And Now . . . Live at the Morgue

Dtui and her team were awoken by a ferocious banging on the morgue doors.

"We-we-we've been busted," said Mr. Geung.

"Sounds like it," said Nurse Dtui.

She hurried from her sleeping mat to check her patient. Mr. Geung, with the aid of a penknife, had requisitioned the necessary drugs and five liters of blood from the locked supply room. Dtui had removed the blade, repaired a few tears in the stomach wall, cleaned the wound, administered the blood and crossed her fingers. Once the operation was over and the blade lay on its steel tray in a plastic bag, they'd sat beside Phosy, willing him to fight for life. But his vital signs did not normalize. It wasn't until about 3 A.M. that her husband's breathing had become more steady, and she'd chanced a short nap.

Five minutes later came the banging on the door.

"We can fight them off," said Tukta. "We've got knives."

"I think we just keep quiet and pretend we're not here," said Dtui. "If we let them in they'll insist on moving Phosy to a recovery room. That might be more than he can take."

She did wonder why the hospital security man or the administrator didn't open the door with their master keys. And there were no orders to open up, no threats. She walked barefoot to the main door and listened.

It was then she heard a faint, "Siri, Siri, is that you in there?"

The voice was familiar but weak.

"It's Civilai," she said, unlocking the door. She opened it in time to see their old friend keel over and collapse on the steps. Geung carried him effortlessly into the cutting room and laid him on an empty mat.

"Oh, my," said Dtui. "What's happened to you, Uncle?"

"I'm beaten, bruised and bedraggled and my arm's broken in two places," he told her.

A trail of dried blood led from the corner of his mouth and blood stained his shirt and trousers. If possible, he looked more exhausted than Dtui felt. Having reached the morgue, his strength left him. He lifted his good hand, which held a small bunch of car keys. And before he lost consciousness, he said:

"In the car. The Buddha . . . I shot him."

◙ ◙ ◙

For the first time in his later life the Sangharaj woke long after the sun had risen. He was a poor sleeper. He'd come to believe he would witness every hour of daylight until his death. But here he had slept wonderfully and woken with such a clear mind he might have been meditating for a week. His breath had never been so vivid. He felt as if he'd been reborn, launched anew into the world.

But, sadly, not with a fresh body. When he tried to

rise from the wooden flooring, every joint and muscle screamed for him to desist. He was in pain from his feet to his neck. He considered what jungle disease he might have contracted overnight. He'd lived through malaria and dengue and a dozen other ailments that hadn't yet been named. But none had left his head so new and his body so old.

He knew it was a test. To a man who had reached enlightenment, pain should not have been allowed to dominate his feelings. The agony had not asked to be drawn into his body. He was embarrassed to have abducted it and knew he should treat it like a damaged friend who needed his help rather than a vindictive enemy. So he ignored the pleas from his parts and re-taught himself to stand and hobble around the room. It all took some ten minutes. He escorted his vivid breath and his lucid mind into the garden. There, he saw the back of Abbot Rayron meditating on a rock. He was holding a yellow umbrella as he contemplated the carp.

The sun was high in the sky. It was almost midday, but the Sangharaj felt no hunger. He wondered where the old Lao couple might be, perhaps off on one of their adventures. They were a blessing, those two. If anyone could clear the name of Abbot Rayron it was Siri and Daeng. He passed their hut. The door was open. He could see two pairs of feet. It was a peculiar day. Even the Lao had been unable to rouse themselves. He walked on with barely a thought of his pain.

Madam Daeng was next to rise. She too had a clear head and a pained body. She lay awake recalling the water tower and the monk at its summit. She knew the elders of Sawan had joined forces to combat the evil spirits, but . . . from there everything was blank. The pain in her body confused her. She'd fought the demons of rheumatism for long enough, but this was different. It was as if she'd pushed her old body to limits it had forgotten. She wore a neat bandage on her arm, but the wound beneath it stung. Even turning her neck to look at her sleeping husband was an effort.

And what a state he was in. A dry trickle of blood ran from his ear. One eye was black. He lay with his mouth open, and he'd lost another tooth. Was he dead? Her heart held back a beat as she observed his chest. There was no movement. Second heartbeat. Third heartbeat . . . then it rose.

"You idiot!" she shouted and slapped his already battered face.

Despite the rude awakening, Siri's one able eye opened and his mouth curled into a smile.

"Good morning, sweetness," he said.

"I'll give you sweetness," she growled. "I swear, if you do that one more time I'll leave you for a younger man."

"Do what, dear?"

"Pretend you're dead."

"I would never," he said. "I'd either be really dead or not in a position to deny it."

He sat up and she noticed what she'd taken to be a shadow across his chest was, in fact, dried blood.

"Oh," she said.

"Don't panic," he told her, "it's not my blood. I'm sorry. Once I got you and the Sangharaj cleaned up and dressed and into bed I didn't have the strength to take a shower. I lay down for a second to rest and here I still am. I'm not nearly as bad as I probably look."

"Siri, what the hell happened last night?"

"A resounding victory for our team," he said. "Let's get up and find something to eat, and I'll tell you all about it."

"I can't," she said.

"Can't what?"

"Get up."

Siri helped his wife to her feet and slowly to the kitchen. He left her there while he took a long shower. While they ate he walked her through the events of that morning. He'd debated whether to go into detail about her role, but he never lied to his wife. He'd been creative with the facts now and then but never an outright lie.

"You were a monkey," he told her.

She looked into his eyes to see if that was a Siri joke, but his face was straight.

"You know?" she said. "We really do need a camera. These things happen and we don't have any record. What a family album it would be."

"I'm not sure I would have had time to take snaps," he said.

"Was I a good monkey?" she asked.

"One of the best."

"So tell me."

"Well," he said, "always remember there's a very thin membrane between reality, supernature and dreams. So it's never easy to recount what actually happened with any conviction."

"I didn't dream these bruises," she said.

"Perhaps," he said. "But the psychosomatic can be very powerful, so don't dismiss any possibility."

"Is this bandage covering something psychosomatic?"

"No. Ugly bit you."

He told her of his recollection of events up to the duel to the death with the Sangharaj.

"My problem," he said, "was that I was being fed a lot of false information in one form or another. I had to trust that the villagers would not desert Yeh Ming, so I threw us both off the tower. On the way down, all my senses came back to me: the shouts of the rescuers, the flashlight beam, the shaman's song. They had been there all the time, but the *phibob* had blocked them. I can't tell you how satisfying it is to land in a nylon parachute."

"And that was the end?"

"Goodness, no. The battle was on. The *phibob* had lost their hostage, but they continued to fight. Their disciples were breaking free of their trances and falling asleep. The circle of elders had amassed a sizeable following, and they were going from villager to villager evicting the malevolent spirits. Young people were joining the circle, and there was great joy and jubilation when everyone realized the power they wielded. The battle was still raging when we brought you back, but Fortune-teller Doo had seen a future free of *phibob*, so there's nothing to fear. We beat them, Daeng."

The rice porridge in Daeng's spoon was cold now, and she returned it to the bowl.

"I could have married a plumber," she said.

"No, you couldn't have."

She leaned over and kissed her husband's nose. It was the only undamaged spot on his face.

"I don't suppose you solved the mystery of the Buddha murders while all that was going on?" she said.

"Ah, now that," said Siri, "is another story."

He'd forgotten about his lost hours the previous day, or rather he hadn't had a spare second to analyze them. He told his wife about the damned doors and the bathroom where he'd met himself and the vet's waiting room, and the Chinese nurse and Civilai and Phosy with their lizards, and the birthing of the piglet. And they sat either side of their uneaten lunches and pondered.

"I have no idea what Civilai and Inspector Phosy were doing in your dream," said Daeng, "but assuming every-thing else was connected to the murders, perhaps it suggests there's the question of birthright. Do you have a clear image of the vet's face?" Daeng asked.

"Yes," said Siri. "But what good will that do?"

"Peace Corps," she said. "Enthusiastic young people with cameras."

Headman Tham did indeed have a drawer of photographs that had been sent by the Peace Corps desk officer in Bangkok a month after the water tower team had left the village. They were pockmarked and warped, but it didn't take Siri long to spot his vet.

"Why, that's Loong Gan," said the headman.

"I thought so," said Daeng. "That man played a big-ger part in this whole mystery than just being a random victim."

The village was a different place that afternoon. It had become so serene that Ugly joined them on their walk along the shortcut. He was now officially Siri's general, and his untidy walk had become a march. The smiles they met were sincere, and there was a feeling of relief and pride that had not existed a day earlier. Siri's amulet hung almost chilly from his neck. He and Daeng sat in the cadaver hut and drank coconut water with the elders. Aware that every man in the room was a suspect, Siri looked for odd reactions to his questions. They were undoubtedly in the right place for gossip.

"What do you know about Loong Gan's life before he came here?" he asked nobody in particular.

"I remember when he first arrived in the village," said Headman Tham. "They said he'd been a monk at Wat Po in Udon, but most of us have been monks at some point in our lives. It's not always a long-term thing."

"I was in for ten days," said Intermediary Cham.

"I heard he was one of those monks who flit in and out of robes," said Priestess Thewa. "Probably on the run."

"You think he might have been involved in something illegal?" asked Daeng.

"I doubt he was smart enough for larceny or armed robbery," said Thewa, "but he might have been on the run from some irate husband. He certainly had a way with the ladies. He was a fine-looking man. He used to boast about his philandering days. How he'd seduced rich women and been what he called rewarded for his sexual prowess. But of course he didn't phrase it nearly as politely as that."

"Was there a Chinese woman in his life?" asked Siri, remembering his dream.

"There was one married woman he called his money faucet," said Headman Tham.

"She was Chinese, I seem to recall," said Shaman Phi.

"That's right," said Tham. "Fresh off the boat from Shanghai, he used to say. Even though there was no boat from Shanghai."

"He wasn't that fond of the Chinese, so he felt no obligation to be polite when he talked about her," said Shaman Lek.

"And give him a few drinks, and you couldn't shut him

up," said Tham. "He'd go into more detail than anyone wanted to hear. Sexual positions and the like."

"I think we've heard enough," said Daeng, and she stood to leave. Siri joined her. Everyone else got to their feet. One by one they prostrated themselves before Siri *wai*'ing deeply. He blushed.

"Yeh Ming . . ." said Headman Tham.

"I know," said Siri. "You're welcome."

Siri, Daeng and Ugly walked the shortcut to the temple.

"Why didn't you let them gush some more?" asked Daeng. "You know you like it."

"Because you were right," said Siri. "It was as much my ghost hunt as theirs. I used them. But I feel like a curse has been lifted from me."

"Any chance your inner Yeh Ming might step up some-time soon with a word of gratitude?"

"He isn't that sociable."

They walked on hand in hand.

"What's our next move?" asked Daeng.

"The murders?"

"Yes."

"I think we need to go back to Udon Thani. We have a connection now. Abbot Rayron and unreliable Loong Gan were both at Wat Po."

"Not necessarily at the same time," said Daeng.

"But a straw to clutch at nevertheless. At least we'll be able to ascertain whether the old man and Abbot Rayron knew each other before they arrived here in Sawan. Coin-cidences invariably lead to clues, my dear."

When they arrived at the temple they were surprised to see Captain Gumron leaning against his truck, talking to the Sangharaj. Both appeared to be staring at the ground.

"Good afternoon, Captain," said Siri. "Not another murder, I hope."

"Not this time," said the policeman. "A suicide."

The Sangharaj continued to stare at his feet. His eyes were damp.

"Siri," he said, "Abbot Rayron has killed himself."

◙ ◙ ◙

When Dr. Siri retired as the national coroner the morgue had been locked and largely ignored. That was not to say people had stopped dying, just that there was nobody with sufficient interest to discover why. Everyone considered the short, squat building to be deserted. Even with two antique French cars badly parked out front nobody suspected there might be life at the morgue. But the cutting room currently housed three patients—three more than the central post-op ward.

Inspector Phosy had survived for twenty hours, which they all agreed was a good sign. He'd lost a lot of blood, and the transfusion had not gone well. Dtui was afraid the bottle from the blood bank might have been tainted or mislabeled. There was never a way to tell until it was too late. Phosy was running a fever, and it was all she could do to keep his temperature down.

On the sleeping mat beside Phosy's slab lay a man with a shattered shin and a missing foot. He too had lost a lot of blood, most of which was on the backseat of the Renault. If anyone were to poke their head into either of the cars there would be no doubt that a massacre had taken place.

This second patient had responded much better to his blood transfusion, but Dtui had no intention of putting his leg back together. After hearing Civilai's account of his time in Ban Toop, nobody cared too much whether the mechanic lived or not. It was, however, a miracle that he'd survived the journey to Vientiane.

Civilai would heal. Dtui had reset his arm and plastered it. He was eating and very talkative. He'd already held them spellbound with his tales of black magic.

"But why come here?" Dtui asked. "To the morgue, I mean."

"I didn't intend to exactly," said Civilai. "I was on my way to the police station when I got it into my head that I was about to die. I'd been driving all through the night on roads that would have killed a lesser man. I don't know how many sleeping sentry guards I ignored at checkpoints. Any one of them could have shot me. I diverted myself to the hospital. I was on my way to emergency when I saw my old car parked in front of the morgue. I might have even said a little prayer that Siri would be here."

"Sorry to have disappointed you," said Dtui.

"Quite on the contrary," said Civilai. "That old man would come in a distant fourth compared to the ministrations I have received from Dr. Geung, Matron Tukta and Surgeon General Dtui."

Geung and Tukta fell into a laughing fit that spun out of control.

"Dr. Geung," said Geung. "Dr. Geung."

"I've been practicing medicine and performing surgery illegally, Uncle," Dtui reminded him. "I could be arrested any minute."

"Ah, Dtui. Most of the doctors here have studied on

patched up courses the Soviets provided for us dumb people in the third world. I doubt any one of them is legal. You, my dear, are the real thing. A true artist."

"You're sweet," said Dtui. "A born diplomat. But what about you? What are you planning to do about your Satan friend?"

"I'll give him a few more hours till he's fit enough to be bundled roughly back into the car, and I'll complete my journey to police headquarters. Arriving there in a stolen government vehicle with a corpse in the backseat will just make my story all the more fascinating. As you have a senior policeman on your slab I shall not mention my detour here."

"Ugghhh," said Inspector Phosy.

15

A Killer in High Heels

The body of Abbot Rayron lay on the concrete floor of
the cell in which he'd purportedly killed himself. He was
covered in a dirty white sheet. Captain Gumron was reluctant to allow the visitors access to the scene, but as there
was no next of kin they needed an official identification of
the body by a credible witness. The Sangharaj refused to
enter the cell without Siri and Daeng. The chief of Nam
Som police said it was permissible and told the policeman
who'd found the body to cooperate.

The captain peeled back the sheet. The abbot lay facedown. His feet were near the bars of the cell. It was the
type of cage you'd expect to find in a zoo. It had thick vertical bars to the ceiling and two horizontal reinforcements.
There was a door with a padlock, currently unfastened.
Around the monk's neck was a saffron loincloth, the ends
of which lay across his shoulders and down his back like
the scarf of a World War One flying ace.

"He tied himself to the bars about here," said the duty
policeman, pointing to the lower crossbeam about one
and a half meters off the ground. "I discovered the body

at about three this morning. I untied the noose, and he dropped to the floor like he is now."

"You didn't move the body?" asked Siri.

"No, sir, I—"

"This isn't a public inquest," said the captain.

"Do you mind if I turn the body over?" asked the Sangharaj.

"You can't touch him," said the captain.

"If I'm to identify him it would help if I could see him," said the monk.

Captain Gumron reluctantly nodded for the officer to turn over the corpse. They could immediately see the dark bruise down the center of his forehead. His nose was broken.

"Must have happened when his face hit the concrete," said the captain.

The Sangharaj knelt and chanted quietly, not directly toward the body but into the air around it where the abbot's soul might have been waiting for a blessing to continue its journey. Siri worked himself into a position from which he could see the abbot's neck. When the captain was distracted he gestured for the Sangharaj to loosen the scarf. The old monk did so gently as if loosening the collar of someone finding it difficult to breathe.

The captain noticed.

"We'd rather you didn't touch anything, Granddad," he said. "This is police business. We've had enough amateur detectives traipsing all over this case as it is."

Siri hurried Madam Daeng from the building.

"You were quiet in there," she said.

"I was quiet because I didn't want to tell a policeman he didn't know how to do his job."

"You don't think it was suicide?"

"I know it wasn't, if only because suicide is contrary to basic Buddhist values. But from a pathological point of view if you're serious about hanging yourself you'd do it from the top crossbar, not the bottom one. It wouldn't take much to climb up there. And if you're afraid of heights and decide to use the bottom crossbar you'd throw your legs out in front of you. The abbot's feet were close to the vertical bars. And, why make it even more difficult for yourself by tying the knot on the outside? You'd loop the scarf around the bar and tie it in front of you."

"Then what do you think happened?"

"I think somebody came to visit him, grabbed the scarf and smashed his head against the bars—broke his nose. If the policeman was right and the abbot fell on the concrete after he was dead he wouldn't have bled or been bruised. The blow to the head knocked him out, and the killer held him up by the scarf and strangled him to death. The bruising around his neck was horizontal and low, so it wasn't a hanging. The only thing I can't work out is how the killer manipulated the body to be facing away from the bars. Either he was very strong, or he had a key to the padlock."

"Then he'd have to be a policeman," said Daeng.

"Or someone with money or influence who might borrow a key for a few minutes from an impoverished jailer."

"But you think it was the captain, don't you?"

Siri laughed. "Have I become that transparent?" he asked. "I'm not particularly fond of him. He has some issues with the temple, he's certainly disrespectful, and I think he has historical connections with Sawan. But that's not enough to accuse a man of murder. Certainly not three murders."

"Then it's time to gather some new evidence," said Daeng.

"That's my girl."

The first stop was only a few meters away. The jails, temporary courtroom and police station were in the same compound. The guard who watched over them was not a policeman nor would he ever be. He was better dressed than his counterparts in Laos but no more brilliant. He sat on a chair holding a rope that raised or lowered the entrance beam.

"Who has access to the jails?" said Siri, adopting his air of importance.

"Has what?" said the guard.

"Access . . . Who do you let in at night?"

"Nobody," said the guard.

"Not even the police? Prison guards? Cleaners? Meal lady?"

"No."

"Why not?"

"Because I don't work at night."

"All right. Good answer. Who works at night?"

"My cousin Eun. He does six P.M. to six A.M."

"So he could tell me who entered the building last night?"

"Yes."

"Good. So where . . ."

"But so could I."

"Could what?"

"Tell you who came and went last night. He has to report to me at five forty-five A.M. before my shift."

"All right. Then we're getting somewhere. Who had acce—who came in last night?"

"All them people you asked about. They all come. It's a police station, so the police was coming and going. And the court was still going till nine so there were criminals and witnesses and family members."

"And do they have to report to you and Eun?"

"No."

"So anyone could come in?"

"That's right."

"Then what do you do?"

The guard tugged on his rope by way of explanation. Siri squeezed Daeng's arm to tell her the first interview of the day was over.

"Just a minute," she said, and smiled at the guard. "Did your cousin Eun mention anything different or unusual during his shift?" she asked.

"No," he said.

"Okay, thanks," said Daeng and started to walk away.

"Excepting he saw Captain Gumron climbing over the compound wall that night."

"What?" said Daeng.

"I know. Strange, isn't it?"

Siri and Daeng came to heel.

"Was he climbing in or out?" Siri asked.

"Out," said the guard.

"What time?"

"Around nine-thirty. Oh, and the food girl was too pregnant to come so she sent her husband."

"Eun knew him?" asked Siri.

"No. But he said the man knew his wife's name. That's a sort of security check."

"What time was he here?" asked Daeng.

"Six P.M. to six A——"

"The husband!"

"Oh, about eight P.M."

"And he went to the cells alone?"

"Yes."

"Did he have keys?"

"Didn't need 'em. There's a gap under the doors wide enough for a plate."

"And what time did he leave?" asked Daeng.

"Eun didn't see him leave."

"Isn't that unusual?"

"Not really," said the guard. "Eun has two jobs. He drops off from time to time."

"Excellent," said Siri. "I don't suppose we know the name of the pregnant meal lady?"

"Oh, that we do. Her name's Somjit Laoseu. Been coming here since she was a girl."

"Laoseu?" said Daeng. "Why's that name familiar?"

"Father-in-law's the headman out at Sawan," said the guard, "but I doubt you've been there."

As Yuth, the son of Tham, the headman of Sawan, was the owner of the village truck as well as the husband of the meal lady at the Nam Som jail, Siri and Daeng decided it would amount to a conflict of interest to borrow the truck to go to Udon. So they caught the awful bus instead. Even Ugly balked at the thought of it, but rescinded his decision at the last moment and leapt on board.

The Wat Po in Udon was actually called Phothisomphon, but the locals abbreviated the name the way you would that of a dear aunt. Its centerpiece and main attraction was a two-meter Buddha image in the position known as "subduing Mara." They were escorted to the abbot's quarters by a bubbly novice as keen as chili paste.

Abbot Somluang looked around Siri's age and wore bottle-bottom glasses and an enormous hearing aid that predated electricity. He relied on a cane to walk and had on a surgical wrist brace.

As they approached him, Siri whispered to Daeng, "Would you still love me if I . . . ?"

"Not on your life, brother."

The abbot's voice was clear and leathery. "Ah, a young couple come for a wedding appointment," he said.

"So those glasses are just for show?" said Siri.

Daeng elbowed him in the ribs. They *wai*'d the old man, who briefly touched his fingertips together in reply.

"I can hardly see a damned thing," said the monk. "But I have keen instincts, and I can sense great love before me."

"Then you're quite right," said Daeng.

The novice poured them all tea and fanned them with a huge banana leaf as they sat on the rattan furniture on the abbot's balcony. A monkey at the end of a rope swung down from the overhanging tree and did a forward roll on the railing. She earned a sweet biscuit for her troubles. Ugly had no tricks, so he sat and dribbled and got nothing.

"Now, what can I do for you?" asked the abbot.

"We wondered if you remember Rayron Nintana when he was a novice here," asked Siri.

"Ah, yes, young Ray," said the abbot. "I've been hearing all about the goings on in Sawan. Terrible thing."

"What have you heard?" asked Daeng.

"The murders and the desecration and false allegations," said the monk.

"You don't think Rayron was guilty," asked Siri.

"Well that depends," said the abbot.

"Depends on what?" asked Siri.

"What side you're on."

"Your opinion of the murders depends on what side we're on?" asked Daeng.

"My opinion does not alter," said the abbot. "What I tell you depends on what side you're on."

"We're here to find out who really did it," said Daeng.

"Then we're allies," said the abbot. "There is no way on the good earth that man could take a life."

"So you remember him well," said Siri.

"Of course. We arrived as novices within a year of each other."

"You entered late?" said Daeng.

He smiled. He had few teeth.

"No," he said.

"But . . . ?"

"Ray and I are the same age. I know it's hard to believe. You're aware, I'm sure, that different animals age at different rates. I have to assume there was a mix-up at the reincarnation depot and I was born a man with the lifespan of a German shepherd. It happens."

Siri was relieved there was no mention of destiny.

"Were you already here when Abbot Rayron arrived?" asked Daeng.

"No," said the monk. "He came first. He was already the most popular novice. I was a sickly child. That's why my family dropped me off here. The other boys ignored me, probably sensed my weaknesses. But Ray was very kind. We became friends."

"Did he tell you anything about his background?" asked Siri.

"He always talked about his trip here in a car," said the abbot. "It took on magical proportions. We'd make up stories in the dormitory about a boy who was delivered in a chauffeur-driven limousine."

"But nobody could remember anything about the driver?" asked Daeng.

"Ray came back here around 1970. He'd been doing the circuit. Long pilgrimages. Far provinces. Then the Sangha asked him to run a little temple near Nam Som. Nobody else wanted the job. But on his travels he'd nurtured a desire to learn of his roots. He came to see me. There were just the two of us here from the old days, me and mad Boh. We wracked our brains, but we couldn't come up with a single clue. All we knew was the date of Ray's arrival from the novice records, which didn't help at all. Neither did the registration number of the car he arrived in. So Ray left for Sawan none the wiser."

"You what?" said Siri.

"He left none the—"

"Not that. You know the car registration number?"

"Of course. It was a remarkable event. All the boys remembered it. But you can't find a man from the number of his car, can you now?"

"Knock again," said Daeng.

"I'm almost through to the other side of the wood," said Siri.

"She's in," shouted the neighbor who'd directed them there. "Just a bit fixated with her bloody radio."

"And deaf to boot," shouted Daeng.

The sounds of a popular *Look Tung* tune boomed from the little terraced slum. The Lao often said the Thais had just the two control buttons on their devices: off and too loud. In Vientiane Siri often had to endure the latter thundering across the river.

In an instant the radio went from too loud to off.

"Who's there?" came a tarry voice.

"They sent us from the town hall," said Daeng.

"I'm retired," said the woman.

"We know," said Daeng. "But they said you were the motor registration clerk in 1939."

"And for thirty-six years on," said the woman, opening the door. She was a tiny thing in a man's T-shirt that reached her ankles. Her face was powdered thickly, but the cracks showed through.

"We're trying to trace the owner of a car," said Siri.

"Is that so?" said the woman. "And you think I'd memorize every one of the 18,791 vehicles I've registered in my lifetime?"

Something told Siri there was a possibility she had, but this task was easier.

"You might remember this one," said Siri. "In the 1930s they switched from a central registry in Bangkok to provincial branches. As you know, Udon Thani handled the northeast. So in the first couple of years there weren't many cars."

"I know that," she said.

"We were hoping you might remember something about the number," said Daeng.

The old woman was silent. Chewing the inside of her mouth.

"What was the number?" she asked.

"Udon Thani nine," said Siri.

"I thought so," said the woman. "You're with him."

"Who?"

"The old monk."

Old monks were starting to pile up.

"Which old monk?" asked Daeng.

"Boh, the mad one."

"Why do you think we'd be connected with him?" asked Daeng. "We don't even know him."

"Then why are you asking about the same car?"

"He came to see you about Udon Thani nine?" said Siri.

"18,791 vehicles, and I get asked about that same one twice," said the woman. "Bit of a coincidence, don't you think?"

"What did you tell him?"

"You don't know?"

"I tell you we've never met the fellow," said Siri.

"I told him I had no idea," she said.

"Oh," said Siri and Daeng in harmony.

"But I know Udon Thani one was owned by the governor. His son drove it 'cause the governor was afraid of cars. And the son's still around. He owns a nightclub out on Pracha Uthit."

"Yeah, it was just like I told the mad monk," he said.

He was a big chubby man with hair dyed bitumen black and tattoos up to his neck. A line of silver buttons down his cowboy shirt was the only thing stopping his enormous gut from spilling onto his lap. He was sitting at a table in his open-air nightclub auditioning singers. His two henchmen had just manhandled one plump girl off the stage, and they were waiting for the next.

"It was a sort of owners club," he continued. "We were shit-hot in those days. Rich guys with cars. There weren't that many 'in' places to go at night. So when a new venue opened we'd turn up there in our brand-new cars, and there wouldn't even be parking lots. Can you imagine that? I mean, some places still had hitching posts for their ponies. But we'd—sorry." He raised his voice. "Get that next slut out of the toilet in twenty seconds, or she can piss her singing career goodbye!"

Daeng and Siri were at his table sipping the iceless Mekhong Cokes he'd forced on them. It was 3 P.M. It was an open-air restaurant, but Ugly remained outside the entrance. He had a problem with doorways too.

"I mean, we milked it for all it was worth," the chubby man said. "The sluts would come up and admire our engines, try out our leather seats, squeeze our gear levers— if you know what I mean." He winked at Daeng. "So we got to know the other drivers, and I don't mean 'like.' Some of them were pains in the arse. But we were in the money community, you know? You should always be respectful to people with money even if you hate their guts. You never know when you'll need them."

"So you knew the owner of Udon Thani nine?" said Daeng, eager to leave.

"Like I told the mad monk . . ."

The next girl had arrived on the stage. Siri thought she'd probably be beautiful when she grew up.

"Excuse me, Granny," said the chubby man. He stood up and gestured to the girl. "Hitch up your skirt, darling."

"What, sir?" she said.

"Your skirt," he shouted. "Hitch it up. Show me your legs."

She nervously did as she was told.

"More," said the man. He kept saying "more" until the skirt was halfway up her thighs.

"All right," he said. "That's enough. You're hired."

"Do you want me to sing now?" she asked, dropping the hem.

"No, darling," he said. "Come back in a couple of hours and I'll fit you for a costume."

He returned to the table.

"Sorry about that," he said. "No rest for the wicked, eh?"

He clinked his glass against theirs, downed his drink and nodded to the bored waitress for a refill.

"So where was I?" he said. "Right. Udon Thani nine. Like I told the mad monk, Udon Thani nine was owned by the guy who started the Good Health cigarette factory. Of course that was before the Thailand tobacco monopoly robbed everyone blind and took all the businesses. But he had his fingers in other pies. He was a skinny Chinese; Lim was his name. Had a wife from the old country, I believe. She couldn't hardly speak a word of Thai. Marriage arranged by the families. He had a minor wife tucked away somewhere too."

"Do you know where we can find him?" Siri asked.

"Out on the old Ban Chik road behind a big wall," said the chubby man. "It's where all the dead Chinese mandarins end up."

"And the wives?" said Daeng.

"What am I?" he said. "The receptionist to the beyond?" He laughed and quaffed half his drink. "Frankly, I think I've been very cooperative, don't you?"

"Very obliging," said Siri. "Thank you."

The doctor's instincts told him it was time to go.

"You know how you can thank me properly?" said the chubby man. "I mean, for my knowledge and my hospitality."

"No, how?" said Siri, although he knew what was coming next.

"Well, the mad monk fronted up with five thousand baht for the very same information I've provided you with today. He decided it was worth it. I believe one of his fingers might have accidently snapped during the negotiations, but he's still alive today thanks to us. It disturbs me when people get hurt. Especially an elderly couple such as yourselves."

The henchmen were approaching the table. Siri looked at his wife.

"Daeng," he said. "I think the gentleman has been very helpful. I think we should give him what he's asking for."

The chubby man laughed.

"See?" he said. "That's Lao wisdom right there."

"That was five thousand baht?" said Daeng, reaching into her bag.

"Oh, that was the base rate," said the chubby man. "With drinks and entertainment it comes to a round eight thousand."

He motioned for his henchmen to get back to work and laughed again.

"I think this should cover it," said Daeng. She pulled out a very long meat knife. The chubby man was shocked. Once she was sure he'd had a good look Daeng lowered it beneath the tablecloth and pushed the tip against his groin. Siri moved to a seat beside him and put an arm around his shoulder. From the stage it looked like a friendly gathering. In Siri's other hand was his favorite Swiss army knife open to the fish-gutting tool.

"You've probably intimidated a lot of innocent people

with this routine," said Daeng. "Probably as many as my husband and I have killed between us."

The chubby man's eyeballs engorged. Siri used his knife to slice off the top silver button of the man's shirt. He bit it to be sure it was genuine and put it in his own pocket. The chubby man flinched.

"You could call your boys to come and help you," Daeng continued, "but by the time they got here you'd be a eunuch."

"Dorsal artery," said Siri. "Almost impossible to stop the bleeding. It keeps pumping because it thinks you need more blood for your erection. It doesn't realize your penis is on the floor. Strange, that."

Siri cut off another button. The chubby man was sweating like a pig in a bamboo box. A quivering mound of jelly.

"You be careful you don't slice through a nipple in there, darling," said Daeng. "All that fat, you never know what you might accidently carve through."

Siri whispered in the chubby man's ear. "You're going to stand slowly," he said, "and walk with us arm in arm like we're best friends. You're going to take us to where you parked your truck. You strike me as the truck type. You're going to sit behind the wheel and drive us back into town, and then we'll decide whether to let you come back."

"With all your parts," Daeng added.

"Well, that was so much fun," said Daeng. "We should come to Thailand more often."

"And you haven't even seen Bangkok yet," said Siri.

They were driving slowly along a suburban street trying to locate 43E. They were in a stolen truck, but, given the gun and the stash of assorted narcotics they found in the glove box, they doubted the chubby man would be contacting the police. They'd decided to let him out beside the road to walk back to his club. They'd told him the exercise would do him good. If he made it he'd doubtless regroup and come gunning for the old Lao couple, but they figured they had an hour to finish their business.

Udon Thani wasn't Paris, so often the streets would merge into a rice field or a copse of trees. They'd taken a lot of wrong turns, even after the abbot's concise directions.

"Do you think we might go someday?" asked Daeng.

"Bangkok?" said Siri. "Why not? We might even squeeze it into this trip."

"How? We haven't got a lot of spending money."

"Where there's a will, there's a way, dear Daeng."

"There," she said, pointing.

They'd missed the house at 43E on their first circuit because it was too big. They'd looked right through it searching for a hovel, at best a rectangle of bricks with a leaky, corrugated roof. A lifelong monk did not retire to a twilight of luxury. They hadn't expected the two- or three-room bungalow set back from the road with its well-cared-for garden, but the address 43E was stenciled on the telegraph pole directly in front of it.

They walked along the path, ignored by concrete flamingos and pink frogs. Ugly snarled at them.

"Should we go with the 'We know everything' ploy?" asked Daeng.

"It's served us well in the . . . Daeng?"

She stopped. "What?"

"Who do you suppose that is up there?"

Daeng was dazzled by the beautiful sunset, but she

could make out a figure sitting on the spine of the roof with his back to them.

"Monk Boh?" she shouted.

"Shh," said the man.

"If we promise not to talk can we come up?" shouted Siri.

"I suppose," said the man. "Keep to the joists. Don't crack the tiles."

Siri and Daeng climbed the bamboo ladder that leaned against the side of the house. They kept to the joists and sat on either side of mad ex-monk Boh. Together they watched the sun set.

"I know we promised not to talk . . ." said Siri.

"It's fine," said Boh. "The moment's ruined anyway."

Siri was impressed at how much the ex-monk looked like an Asian Woody Allen. Of course very few people in Udon would appreciate the similarity. The pinks and purples of the sky reflected in his glasses.

"It still looks beautiful to me," said Daeng.

"That's because you're not a collector," said Boh.

"You collect sunsets?"

"Yes."

"Where do you keep them?"

Boh tapped the side of his head.

"I wish I could see them," she said.

"I could eat you," said Boh.

He turned to her with no expression on his face. She shuddered.

"You'd be inside me," he said. "Then you could see everything I see, feel my feelings, share my depressions."

There followed an uncomfortable silence.

"She'd only be in there for seventy-two hours," said Siri.

"That is, assuming you minced her. And if you did she'd have no memory of her brief sojourn through your digestive tract."

Boh turned his attention to Siri. "You're not an artist," he said.

"Scientist," said Siri.

"Then, scientist, explain to me in three words what you see there on the horizon."

"Particle refracted light," said Siri. "Your turn."

"Daytime's reluctance to die," said Boh.

Siri thought about it. "Well, technically, that's four words, but I'll give it to you. You win."

"Abbot Somluang sends his best wishes," said Daeng. "But we're here about Abbot Rayron."

"So you're police," said Boh.

"Do we look like—" Siri began but Daeng cut him off.

"Are you expecting us?" she asked.

"Do you like football?" he asked in reply.

"No," she said.

"I'm very fond of it," said Boh. "It's a microcosm of humanity. For example there's a moment when your opponent is running into the penalty area with the ball at his feet and you trip him. The referee has a split second to decide whether contact was made in or outside the area. Nobody's really sure. The referee adjudges that you fouled him outside the box and awards a free kick. You are exonerated. Your team wins the game, but you can never relish the victory because you know deep in your soul that you cheated."

The sun was gone but the sky continued to bleed in its stead.

"We know everything," said Siri.

"Then you can think yourselves lucky you didn't waste fifty years of your life in search of that knowledge," said Boh. "I, on the other hand, know nothing."

"Tell us more about the football," said Daeng.

Boh smiled for the first time. He had brand new teeth. "When it happened, in my mind, I was outside the penalty area. But in reality when I committed my foul I was inside. Only a few centimeters either way, so I thought, 'Who really cares?' I thought I might get away with it, you see?"

"But you didn't?" said Daeng.

"I went to his house," said Boh. "I went to his house expecting him to be dead, old Lim, the Udon Thani nine owner. I thought perhaps I might talk to his legitimate children. It was plain to me what had happened. I'm sure even Abbot Rayron knew deep in his heart: The Chinaman produces a bastard child. The minor wife dies. The father donates the child to the temple and forgets about him. In Thailand it doesn't even count as scandal. The richer you are, the more women you're supposed to impregnate. The courts are bloated with claims from illegitimate offspring haggling over the family estate. And sometimes if there is evidence of the mother being set up in a home with an income the bastard son might win some of the loot.

"My plan was to act as intermediary for Abbot Rayron in his claim for compensation for being discarded. I believed we might be able to settle out of court. Of course Rayron knew nothing about it. He had no idea I was following up on the car registration. You see? I was one step away from being outside the temple, outside the penalty area. I didn't want to die unfulfilled. I wanted the few remaining years to be less . . . disappointing. I'd already picked out my safari shirt and straw golf hat. I wanted to experience all the things I'd supposedly given up but actually had never sampled. But for that I needed money. It occurred to me that through all those years in the robes I had fantasized about wealth; not on a grand scale, just, you know, 'I wish I had fifty baht to buy soap that doesn't bring out my eczema.' That sort of thing. But the doctrine does not distinguish between desire for an ice cream and desire to own the ice cream factory.

"So I went to Lim's house, a big, sprawling mansion of a place up in the hills. And the maids told me he was still alive. I hadn't counted on that. He was on his deathbed but was aware of his surroundings, and he called me into his bedroom. I could have been any old monk paying respects, but it was as if he knew immediately why I was there. He said, 'You were at Wat Po, the temple?' I told him I was. 'You knew my son,' he said. I told him I did and that he was still alive. He sighed then, long and contented. He asked me where his son was and that was my moment. The defining moment of my life of goodness. If I'd told him without conditions I might have been worthy of my calling. My heart might have remained pure for eternity. But then I wouldn't have had a new television or a stereo or a nice Japanese car, would I?

"So I told him I was a poor monk and looked at him. He was shriveled like a dried root under his white sheet, but there were elements of the old businessman still hanging on. He was shrewd. He itemized what he would pay me for proof of the life of his son. How much for a narrative of the monk's journeys around the country. How much for a current address. How much for a photograph. I left with a check to the value of more money than I had ever seen in my life. I was surprised that the bank would even cash it so readily. And I bought my television and stereo and car. I built a house and put flamingos in the garden. I bought a strongbox to put my remaining money in, and I bought women and drank and ate the corpses of dead animals. In two weeks the desire was out of my blood. Was that really all there was to it? Such a disappointment. So every day I sit on my roof and watch the sunset. And when the sky is cloudy and there's nothing to see I sit in front of my unplugged television and I cry."

Siri, Daeng, and Ugly were driving their stolen truck back to Sawan. It was dark, and the road was still awful but the new vehicle had marvelous suspension, so it was a pleasure to drive. Siri had turned over the wheel to Daeng, who had recently learned how to drive in Civilai's old cream-colored Citroën.

"Why do you think the father didn't contact Abbot Ray-ron?" she asked.

"Perhaps the old man died first or perhaps he did make contact," said Siri. "Perhaps Ray just forgot to tell us."

"He's a monk, Siri. He wouldn't lie."

Siri laughed.

"All right, so, if he lied, why?" asked Daeng.

"Perhaps he sought revenge on the father who threw him out. Or perhaps the fault is in us believing the story of a madman who sits on his roof every evening and has a house full of unplugged electrical goods."

"Do you think he'll do what we asked?"

"It's a chance for redemption," said Siri. "An opportunity to spend his ill-gotten wealth on something moral."

Before leaving ex-monk Boh, Siri and Daeng had made a proposal. They'd told him about the mysterious death

of Abbot Rayron while he was in custody. They'd gone on
to the connection with Loong Gan, the second murder
victim from the village. Boh had no recollection of anyone
by that name or description ever having resided at Wat
Po. They talked about his supposed affair with a Chinese
woman and the likelihood of her being Lim's wife. They
agreed they needed to probe deeper into the members of
Rayron's legitimate family. Boh had asked them what he
could do to help.

"You can do some detective work around Udon," Daeng
had told him. "We need to know what became of any children Lim fathered with his Chinese wife, assuming he did.
If the affair wasn't a lie, did Loong Gan and the Chinese
woman produce any children of their own? Was there any
doubt over the parenthood of the legitimate children?
That sort of thing. We need to know how the Chinese
wife and the mistress died. It would help to get the name
of Lim's lawyer and any gossip the domestic staff feel like
giving up."

"And how do you propose I gather such information?"
Boh had asked.

"Spread some of your money around," Siri had said.
"This is Thailand. Money talks here."

Just before leaving, Siri had turned back to Boh and
said, "This might be nothing, but see if 'Than Kritsana
Mukum, Dusit Insurance Company' means anything to
anyone on your travels."

"Where did you get it from?" asked Boh.

"From a dream," said Siri.

The late morning meal the next day was a subdued affair.
Not one to condone yet another misogynistic world

religion, Daeng sat at the table with the Sangharaj and Siri and did not wait for leftovers. The monk did not insist she dine alone. There was not a great deal of conversation. They all thought they'd let the abbot down. He'd asked for help and they'd failed.

"I saw him, you know?" said the Sangharaj.

"Who?" asked Siri.

"Abbot Rayron. The morning he died. He was sitting out there on his favorite slab looking at the fish. It's nice to know he considers this place worth a last visit."

"Are you sure you should be confessing to paranormal sightings?" said Siri.

"To you, Yeh Ming? You of all people know how much magic we enlightened ones have in our arsenal. But the difference is we do not choose to use it. I could levitate right here in front of you both, but I do not aspire to do so."

The monk smiled wryly to himself.

"You should reconsider," said the doctor. "You might need a few circus tricks once you retire."

"Yes, what will you do without the temple?" asked Daeng. "I don't see you playing golf."

"You never really retire from faith," said the Sangharaj. "In fact I think I may stay here for a while. At least until the Sangha sends a replacement for Abbot Rayron. Perhaps the new man will keep me on as a gardener or a fish feeder. I like it here. And, who knows? If I stay on for a while somebody in the village might build up the courage to tell me what happened the other night. Nobody's talking."

"You probably just had a bad dream," said Siri.

The Sangharaj would no doubt hear of his exploits

eventually. Thais were poor at keeping secrets. But for the time being the villagers had agreed to spare the old monk the details of his possession. He was strong as a buffalo, but there was no telling how a man in his eighties might react to such a revelation.

"Not even the worst of my nights has left me bruised the next morning," said the monk.

"You should try sleeping with Madam Daeng," said Siri. "I mean . . ."

"You should stop now, Siri," said Daeng.

"Yes, my love."

"What about you two?" asked the monk. "Home?"

"Not yet," said Siri.

"Why not?"

"Because we're insatiable detectives," said Daeng. "And we'd never be able to sleep if we failed to solve the mysteries of Sawan."

"Plus, I promised my good lady a trip to Bangkok," said Siri.

They heard a distant car engine approaching from the direction of Nam Som.

"Probably the police captain coming to round up all the illegal Lao immigrants," said Siri. "I hear they get fifty baht a head for each one of us they catch outside the refugee camps."

Daeng went to the window.

"Do we know anyone who drives a hearse?" she asked.

It turned out that the vehicle was not a hearse but a Toyota Crown Estate, which many people had compared to a hearse. It was obviously the car of choice for newly rich ex-monks. With the windows down to save the air-conditioning, Boh parked his car outside the temple wall even though there was a fine gravel lot inside. He was dressed in a football jersey—some European club—and flip-flops.

"Mr. Fashion's here," said Daeng.

They went to meet him.

"It's astounding," Boh said, sitting at a concrete picnic table beneath a spreading duck foot tree.

"What is?" asked Daeng.

"What people are prepared to tell you for the sniff of a banknote," said Boh.

"Then you have information?" said Siri, joining him at the table.

"A lot," said Boh. "One contact led to another. I met the staff from old Lim's house and workers from his factory. Met a friend of his mistress. And the police were particularly helpful when you slipped a folded banknote in their palms. Where to start?"

"The beginning," said Daeng.

"First," he said, "there was only one child from the registered marriage of Lim and the Chinese wife: a son named Ananda. That was in the public records at the town hall. According to one of their old nannies he was a bright child but moody. Neither the mother nor the father had much time for him. The father worked all God's hours, and when he wasn't making money he was off at his minor wife's place making whoopee. The mother didn't have much time for the kid either, what with shopping trips to Bangkok, tennis, and . . . get this, one single-story shop house on Nuwong that everyone knew she rented for her lover."

"And you showed them the photograph I left you?" Siri asked.

"It was him sure enough, old Loong Gan—the lover of the Chinese wife. But, according to the neighbors, he wasn't there much. Had other women by all accounts."

"Good job, Boh," said Daeng. "We should hire you for private detective work."

"I confess it did start to get a little stimulating," said Boh. "I was up till midnight, then out again at the crack of dawn. The minor wife was a nightclub singer, and she and Lim had one son together: Rayron. When the boy was eight years old an intruder broke into her apartment, garroted her to death and robbed the place. They never caught him or her, but here's the big news from a policeman who was there at the scene: The boy slept in the same room as his mother. It was impossible he didn't see the intruder and witness the murder."

Boh was far more animated than they'd seen him the previous day. He was almost enthusiastic.

"It would have been dark," said Siri.

"It was, but the intruder lit a lamp in the room when he or she was looking for money. The boy would have looked directly into the killer's face. But when the police questioned him he said he'd seen nothing. He said he wasn't in the room. Even at the temple he claimed to have no recollection at all about what happened that night."

"The trauma probably blanked it out of his memory," said Siri. "It must have been awful."

"Why 'he or she'?" asked Daeng.

"What?"

"Twice you said 'he or she' when talking about the killer."

"Yes," said Boh. "I was getting to that. When they were investigating the crime scene—and don't forget these were the days of clumsy, amateurish police work—they found a strip of material caught on a nail on the window ledge. They concluded it might have come from the clothing of the killer. It had a flower design on it. Possibly from a woman's blouse. And outside the window was a footprint from a high-heeled shoe."

"Ha," said Daeng. "The wronged major wife gets revenge."

"In high-heeled shoes, no less," said Siri.

"The police went to Lim's house to give him the bad news," said Boh, "discreetly, so they thought. But the Chinese wife understood the gist of the conversation, burst into the room and created a scene. The police didn't understand what she said, but it was apparently about the world being a better place without whores. Ironic considering she was having an affair too."

"And she had a rip in her flowery blouse," said Daeng.

"Sadly not," said Boh, "but a lot of people came to that conclusion. The wife was a mad woman, they said. Should have been locked up, they said. Lim was heartbroken. He sent his love child to a temple and was later told by a monk that the boy had died from some disease. He became reclusive, lived in a small room behind the factory. And it was there that people claimed the hatred he felt for his wife grew into a plot to kill her."

"He killed his wife?" said Siri.

"It was three years to the day after the death of his lover. They found the wife facedown in her bowl of corn soup. She'd been poisoned. The cook obviously denied putting anything out of the ordinary into the meal, but during the interrogation she told the police that she'd been shocked earlier that day when she ran into Lim creeping around. Of course it was his house but he rarely went there. He was friendly and told the cook he'd come to pick up some paperwork. Four hours later he was gone and his wife was dead. Again the police had no evidence he was involved, but the next day when the maids were packing up the dead woman's clothes they found a blouse with a strip missing— a flowery pattern."

"Did the police follow up on that?" asked Daeng.

"Any evidence from that earlier murder had been long lost, but the rumors and conclusions lived on in the community. The old man moved back into the house and stayed there alone."

"And one day, you turned up there to tell him his bastard son was alive," said Daeng.

"I admit, learning the husband and wife were both murderers has made me feel much better about my role in this drama," said Boh.

"Any leads from the company name I gave you?" Siri asked.

"I've got somebody looking into it," said Boh.

"What about the will?" said Daeng.

"Ah, the will," said Boh. "I found Lim's lawyer right here in Udon. He refused point-blank to divulge client information about personal wills, but I get the feeling I just didn't offer enough money. I'm still learning the ropes, you see."

"So we don't know about the will," said Daeng.

"Yes, we do," said Boh. "The lawyer's filing clerk was much cheaper and far more sociable. Lim's will was changed on March sixth last year. That was five days after I visited him. Two months before he died."

"Changed in what way?" asked Daeng.

"The name of the beneficiary."

"From?"

"From Ananda, the son by the Chinese wife, to Rayron, the son from his relationship with the singer."

"And there you have it," said Siri.

"Motive," said Daeng.

"And a front-runner for chief suspect," said Siri. "What do we know of the official son?"

"He left the northeast to study in Bangkok when he was thirteen," said Boh. "Came back very rarely as far as I can tell. I think you'd need a real private detective to trace his activities."

"Any photos of him?"

"Not one. The nanny said there used to be photos around the house of Ananda as a child, but they just disappeared. She said the child grew very camera shy as he got older."

"So the trail of the wronged brother has gone cold," said Daeng.

"Almost," said Boh.

"What a man," said Siri. "In less than twenty hours you've gathered more information than the average policeman collects in a year. I have no idea why everybody calls you mad."

Daeng kicked her husband's foot.

"It's a mystery to me, too," said Boh.

"So the trail is not cold," said Daeng.

"Not exactly," said Boh. "The last news the father received about his legitimate son was in a letter from a friend of the family, a police general in Bangkok who said he'd been contacted by young Ananda to provide a reference to accompany his application to enroll in the police academy."

"So Ananda's a policeman," said Daeng.

16

Error of Judgment

"Daeng, there are probably a million policemen in Thailand," said Siri.

They were walking back along the jungle shortcut with Ugly beside them. There was a new happy fairyland atmosphere in the woods now. Even the lost spirits had time to smell the flowers.

"Siri, you know exactly what I'm talking about," said Daeng. "There's only one policeman directly linked with the arrest and killing of Abbot Rayron in custody. He lives within a half-hour drive from the village. He has the same build and Chinese features as the abbot and a crew cut. Why are you defending him?"

"Because you're attacking him enough for the both of us. Once I've whittled our list of suspects down to one, I'll go all out to prove Captain Gumron's guilt."

"Oh, you have a list? I didn't realize. How many men are there on that list, may I ask?"

"Every man in the village," said Siri, "starting with the headman's son."

"Siri, Lim's missing heir was educated to college level.

Brought up in a fine home. The headman's son peels scabs off his knees and eats them."

"Villains go to great lengths to disguise their identities, Daeng. Let's not rush into this. A good detective eliminates suspects one by one until only the culprit remains."

They stopped first at the hut of Yuth, the headman's son, and his wife, Somjit.

"Knock, knock," said Siri as there was no door and nowhere to actually knock.

The young wife waddled to the doorway like a dyspeptic duck. She was huge with child.

"Yeh Ming," she said, "what an honor."

She took his hand in hers and massaged it. She didn't acknowledge Daeng at all.

"Just in the neighborhood," said Siri, retrieving his hand. "Heard you were expecting, and so I decided to stop by to check on your condition."

"Me too," said Daeng.

"That's so kind of you," said Somjit. "But I have Somdet Choepaya, my spirit guide, watching over me. And the coat hangers."

It was often a mystery to Siri how different sects arrived at a security system against bad spirits. This entire hut was surrounded by rusty metal coat hangers intertwining like ivy.

"Well if that works for you I'm delighted," said Siri. "It's just that I heard you weren't well enough to deliver the meals to the prison the other night."

"Oh, right," said Somjit. "I mean, look at me. I don't even fit behind the handlebars anymore. And they were kicking the other night. I think I've got a troupe of dancers in here. I had Yuth drop off the dinners."

"I was wondering . . ." said Daeng.

The girl yanked her gaze from Yeh Ming and noticed Daeng. "Oh, hello, Auntie," she said.

"Quite," said Daeng. "I was wondering why they'd order food from a village twenty kilometers away when they have restaurants and food stalls just a walk from the jail."

"I'm a fine cook," said Somjit.

"Even so. Any profit you'd make would be eaten up in the cost of petrol."

"You're right," she said. "I think it's all down to the kindness of Captain Gumron. I mean, him and Yuth are really close. Yuth does the captain a lot of favors and doesn't ask for payment so the prison concession is the captain's way of saying thank you."

Siri and Daeng and Ugly continued their house calls.

"You're not convinced yet?" said Daeng.

"Getting there," said Siri.

"The captain has an accomplice in the village."

"I know. I also know the girl was lying although I'm not sure what about. One last call and I'm totally on your side. I promise."

Fortune-teller Doo was on his veranda sticking toothpicks in a Barbie doll.

"Hope we aren't disturbing you," said Siri.

Doo looked up. He was one of the few villagers who didn't capitulate when he saw the great Yeh Ming. His goiter seemed to have shrunk since the battle with the *phibob*.

"Never did get the hang of this," said Doo.

"Acupuncture?" said Siri.

"Voodoo."

"Oh, you never know," said Siri. "There might be some blonde fashion model in New York doubled over in pain right this minute."

"I can live in hope," said Doo without understanding. "What do you want?"

"Honesty."

Siri and Daeng stood on either side of his elaborate returning-soul gate.

"That's in short supply around here," said Doo.

"What do you know about Captain Gumron?"

"Why are you asking me?"

"Because you speak your mind."

Doo might have smiled then. It was hard to tell.

"He's got his secrets," he said.

"Like what?"

"Like I've seen him in the village late at night."

"Do you remember when?"

"Clearly. Last time was the night of the old lady's poisoning."

"Why didn't you tell me?"

"'Cause I don't trust you any more than I trust him."

"Did you tell anyone?"

"Any one of them idiots could have been in league with him."

"So why are you telling us now?" asked Daeng.

"The dog," said Doo.

Ugly wagged his tail.

"What about him?" said Siri.

"He tells me you're all right."

◙ ◙ ◙

Inspector Phosy had awoken from his life-saving surgery on the third day. He'd notified his surgeon of his return from the dead by squeezing her buttock as she was trimming his toenails. She'd thrown herself beside him on the slab and cried on his shoulder. She was still crying when he came around for the second time an hour later. After a few days he was well enough to stand and shuffle around. In gratitude, he'd promised to wash the dishes for eternity. It was a job Dtui hated even more than weeding. Reluctantly she'd agreed to drive her husband to police headquarters where he'd made up a fantastic explanation for his disappearance. It involved having been unconscious for three days and waking to find himself under the care of a mysterious surgeon from Cuba.

Phosy had spent the next day putting together the report of his attack. He'd attached a copy of the photograph of his attacker, the man's name, rank and current location, eye-witness accounts from Dtui and the noodle shop staff, a set of fingerprints from the blade which Dtui had bagged before its extraction from his gut, and a copy of the previous report. He'd done all this not because he had faith in the due process of the law but because it was standard procedure. He knew nothing would ever come of it because the case against the ninja had gone as far as it was able. In this system there were no autonomous underling committees. Decisions were made in the nebulous Communist stratosphere, and they could not be debated or overruled.

That was why Dtui set off to blackmail Judge Haeng. She found him after office hours on his way to play boules. He was dressed in a thick flannel tracksuit that failed to make him look sporty. She took him to one side and began by asking after the cat.

"You'd never know she almost died," he said, a smile plastered across his face. "She eats me out of house and home."

"She got a name?"

"Karla."

"After Marx, I assume," said Dtui.

At that point the judge appeared to have remembered his status. He shut down his smile and said, "What do you want?"

She laughed at the man's shift of identity, then calmly reminded him of her stockpile of incriminating data against him. In particular she rather enjoyed refreshing his memory about a letter he'd once written asking for diplomatic immunity from the US consulate in return for certain confidential information. She suggested it would be very nice if he could call in a few favors and secure the release of Noo, the Thai monk. She handed him a copy of Phosy's report and told him she was confident he, of all people, would deliver the goods. She ended with a motto: "A good socialist knows when he's beaten."

But the next day the judge had gone to see her at the restaurant. He'd hit a brick wall, he said. His every inquiry had been thwarted. The matter was far beyond his jurisdiction. His eyes watered when he begged her not to do anything rash with the information she had against him.

"Did you learn anything at all?" she'd asked.

"Only that the arrest was ordered at the highest level," he'd told her. "Your Thai monk must have really been asking for trouble. There were rumors that under an assumed name he was a regular contributor to *Matichon*, the Thai political magazine. He was providing them with anticommunist views and interviews and inside information. Word had it he was a spy and is very likely to be shot."

"None of that is credible," said Dtui. "He's as red as the central committee. That's why he was over here escaping from the military."

"They say he was planted here by them."

"Ridiculous. As far as you know is he still alive?"

"As far as I could ascertain. But there's one more thing. Your Comrade Noo isn't an isolated case. I was able to access the missing persons almanac; it's the list of everyone reported missing since '75. It runs into the hundreds."

"Where did you find that?"

"In the office of the presidential security division. That's where the cases are being investigated."

"You're saying the department that does the kidnapping is the one that's charged with finding them?"

"So it appears."

"And how many have they found?"

"None."

"That's not very surprising. What do you think it would take to get Noo released?"

The judge scratched his chin.

"Frankly?" he said. "A miracle."

◙ ◙ ◙

Comrade Civilai had found more success in dusty Vientiane. He'd delivered his prisoner alive and told his incredible tale. A military unit had immediately been dispatched to Ban Toop to put down the black magic rebellion there. The high priests who hadn't fled across

the river were identified and arrested, and a new administration team was sent in to run the regional office in Pak
Xan. They'd set up rural retraining centers for villages
within a hundred kilometers of Ban Toop. The dark influence had spread far. When they learned the magic circle
had been closed down the locals eventually loosened up.
Beans were spilled. Only the villagers in Ban Toop itself
remained dumb. They had lived in fear for most of their
lives, and a promise of safety from government troops
would not allay those fears. Their recovery would be long
in coming.

Civilai spent several days working on his report for the
Supreme Sangha Council in Bangkok detailing his visits to
the village. It ran to some thirty pages. At breakfast on the
day he'd planned to send it, Madam Nong read through it
to check his spelling.

"It's a page-turner," she said after a long silent read
through. "But you realize you can't send it."

"Why not?" said Civilai. "It's all true."

"Because they'll think it's you who's mad, not the grand
Satan. Nobody will believe a word of it. You've written it
like a film script. They'll think they sent the wrong man
in and find somebody else to interview your Buddha. It
wouldn't be over at all."

Civilai read through it again. He put a clean sheet of
paper in the typewriter and wrote three lines.

"It is the opinion of this independent inquiry that
Mr. Maitreya is not a reincarnation of the Lord Buddha,
and his name should be struck from the Sangha's list of
candidates."

He signed it, put it in an envelope and went out to the
car for a drive to the post office.

◙ ◙ ◙

Boh drove Siri, Daeng and Ugly to Udon Thani in his Toyota, having spent an enjoyable day with the Sangharaj. Before they left, the old Lao monk had invited Boh to come visit anytime. He'd enjoy the company, he said. Boh admitted he was tempted. It was a cold world outside the temple walls. The Sangharaj said his last goodbyes to Siri and Daeng and pulled back only slightly when Daeng gave him an air kiss near his cheek. She knew it was naughty, but she could tell he liked it. Siri's handshake on the other hand was returned strongly and with great emotion. They all knew fate would not be pulling them together again.

On his last night in Sawan the doctor had put together an audacious plan to facilitate Daeng's first trip to Bangkok. Under his arm he carried a brown paper parcel containing the props for his production. At best the couple would have a fine time in the capital, buy a camera and go home to enthrall everyone with their tourism exploits. At worst they'd be put in front of a firing squad and executed.

But first the murders. When the sun rose that morning Siri had still been putting together his copious notes on the circumstantial evidence that pointed to Captain Gumron. At one point he'd looked out the window to see dead Abbot Rayron looking down at the fat carp from the slate slab. Siri had tripped over himself running to the door of their quarters. He had so many questions and so little skill with which to ask them. But it didn't matter because by the time he'd reached the garden the abbot was gone.

Siri had returned to his room and looked down at the handwritten observations. As things stood they were worth nothing at all. He was a foreigner with no legal right to be in the country. His qualifications and experience didn't count here. And he was making an allegation against one of their own. He couldn't walk into a police station, make a statement, hand over his notes and expect a major inquiry. Or any response at all. He couldn't mail it to the Justice Ministry in Bangkok because it would be gobbled up by the machine of bureaucracy.

No. Siri and Daeng had agreed they should identify one honest person with influence who might take on the case for its principle. Siri believed he'd met that person in a small country courtroom in Nam Som.

Boh parked his car in front of the Udon Thani public prosecution department and shared a little more of his dirty money. He returned to the parking lot where Siri, Daeng and Ugly sat under a tree and held up the address with great pride. Twenty minutes later they pulled up in front of the house on a road of neat buildings inside a large government compound.

Siri introduced himself to the prosecutor's wife and her two young children. The prosecutor was in the city and wouldn't be home for another half hour. Siri asked if it would be appropriate to wait. The wife approved. Siri had always imagined a prosecutor's wife to be more stylish. She was attractive enough and could have been glamorous with the right makeup and clothing. Instead she wore her hair tied back severely, had a scrubbed white face and baggy garments. But then again she hadn't been expecting guests.

Boh set off with Daeng and the sleeping Ugly in search of a department store to buy an outfit suitable for Daeng's Bangkok vacation. Rather than enter the house as the wife suggested, Siri thought it would be fun to spend time with the children on their jungle gym in the front yard. Their mother was happy to have a babysitter. Within minutes the age gap had shrunk to a few months and Siri probably had as much fun as the girls. After fifteen minutes they were the best of friends. They led him inside for a cool drink.

"Do you believe in ghosts?" one of the girls asked him.

Siri wondered what the correct response might be to a four-year-old.

"That depends," he said. "Are they nasty ghosts or nice ghosts?"

"Will you stop the ghost stories," called the mother from the kitchen.

The girls ignored her.

"I haven't seen them with my own eyes, but I think they're nice," whispered the younger. "They live in mummy's linen closet."

"Then at least they have somewhere clean to sleep," said Siri.

They thought that was very funny.

"Do you want to say hello?" said the older girl.

"I suppose that would be nice," said Siri.

They took a hand each and led him to the rear of the house past two closed doors.

"This is the family room," said the younger.

It was a dark room with small windows that framed a lush tropical garden. A transistor radio was playing middle-of-the-road Thai ballads. It competed with an old air conditioner that growled as if in pain.

"And that's where they live," said the elder, pointing to a tall varnished white-wood cupboard against the far wall.

"What should I do?" Siri asked.

"See if you can frighten them," said the younger girl.

"Creep up on them," said the elder.

Siri did his sneaky private detective walk toward the cupboard and the girls giggled excitedly.

"One, two . . ." said Siri, and took hold of the cupboard door. "Three," he said, and threw open the door. The girls screamed. Siri jumped back. But the only thing to over-power him was the sweet smell of fresh linen and warm towels. He looked around but the girls were gone. He walked to the sofa and sat down.

"Now everyone's disappeared," he said, which was the cue for the girls to leap out from behind the seat and shout, "Boo!"

Siri feigned a heart attack and collapsed on the sofa. The girls dived on top of him.

"What are you doing back there?" came the mother's angry voice. The girls and Siri sat up properly just as the mother arrived at the doorway. She put her hands on her hips. "Come here this minute," she said, and the girls did as they were told. "Your father will be here at any moment. Get to the bathroom and wash off those nasty smells right away."

The girls ran laughing from the room.

"I'm so sorry," she said.

"No problem at all," said Siri, and meant it.

"I'll get them washed. Make yourself at home."

Siri sat on the sofa with a smile on his face. Little children always made him happy. He would have been a good father, but fate and the Communist Party had denied him the opportunity. He looked around the room: tastefully decorated but nothing of great value. He looked at the linen cupboard. Its door was shut, although he didn't remember closing it. He tried to recall where the ghosts in his own house had lived all those years before. But he couldn't even remember having a house.

Then he heard the voice.

"Can you hear me?"

The words were muffled, a male voice undoubtedly coming from the cupboard. Yet there had been no hiding space inside. How was it possible? He stood and walked toward it.

As he was in Thailand, he asked in Thai, "Who's in there?"

"It's me," shouted the voice. "Can you hear me?"

Siri grabbed the handle and yanked it open. This time there were no sweet-smelling sheets on shelves, only darkness and depth. And as the light of the room flooded into the cupboard, he briefly saw the outline of a man, a short, stocky man, walking away from him. He recognized him immediately.

"Looking for our ghost, are you, Doctor?"

Siri was as shocked by the sound as by the vision. He turned around to see the young prosecutor Suthon, standing behind him. The man smiled and *wai*'d politely. Siri responded with equal respect.

"Your girls have traumatized me with their stories," said Siri.

"Then you'll need a drink," said Suthon. "Hang on there a minute."

The prosecutor left and Siri sat on the sofa. His heart was thumping. He'd wrestled with spirits and vanquished demons, but this was an entirely different dimension. Once again he'd met himself. This was his encounter from that night between the connecting doors. The music. The giggling. The scream. This was what he'd heard. It had happened three weeks earlier, yet here he was reliving it from the other side.

"You strike me as a neat whisky man," said Suthon, handing Siri a generously filled glass. His own drink was its equal. "You look a little pale," he said. "Are you all right?" He sat down opposite Siri on a cane chair.

"Wrestling with the under-fives takes it out of you," said Siri.

"Cheers," said the judge.

"Good luck," said Siri.

They raised their glasses and took a swig. The warmth soothed Siri's troubled heart. Suthon seemed every bit as thirsty for a shot of good whisky as Siri. The doctor wondered how many evenings the man returned home with the weight of doubt on his shoulders. An honest man in his position was doomed to burn out or turn to drink.

"You don't seem surprised to see me here," said Siri.

"I set up my life to avoid surprises," he said. "For example, I encourage our clerks at the public prosecutors department to accept bribes but to inform me as to what they were bribed to do. We all win like that. Today I received a phone call telling me an elderly gentleman was asking for my home address. She told me he'd arrived in an expensive car with a mature couple and a dog in the backseat. I fondly remembered you attending my court with a dog. So I told the clerk to accept nothing less than three thousand baht and to give you the address. Where is the dog, by the way?"

"Clothes shopping," said Siri.

"I'm sure he'll look adorable."

They laughed.

"Why would you let me see you?" Siri asked.

Suthon unfastened his tie and undid the top button of his shirt.

"Can you believe they make us wear these stupid Western clothes in this heat?" he said. "Why did I agree to see you? I'll be honest with you. I heard about the alleged suicide in Nam Som on the day of my return here. Frankly, I don't like it. I don't like anything about it."

"Excuse me if I sound a little cynical," said Siri, "but you do appear to be opening up a little fast to a complete stranger."

Suthon laughed. "You're not a stranger, Dr. Siri," he said. "I know who you are and what you've achieved. I learned most of it the day after you entertained me in my courtroom in Nam Som. We Thais can be most resourceful if we're interested enough."

"And why should I interest you, young man?"

"Because you are what I hope to become. You're brave. You damn the consequences of your actions. You survive against all odds, and you put your all behind even the most hopeless of cases."

"Like Abbot Rayron?"

"Exactly."

"And there I was thinking your embassy in Vientiane was only good for tourist information. Or is your covert data hotline connected directly to the CIA?"

"No need to be paranoid, Doctor. I didn't learn anything negative about you. You have remarkable instincts. You're here because you have information to share with me about the abbot. You chose me because you trust me. So let's stop wasting time and get on with the job. What do you have?"

Siri was pleased with his choice of confidant. The fellow was smart and enthusiastic. In a country where corruption ruled, Suthon would probably be assassinated for his honesty before he reached fifty, but his successes would inspire future generations. Siri read from his report because it was written in Lao and would be slow to plough through for a Thai. Suthon took notes throughout. He asked intelligent questions and offered practical suggestions. Somewhere in the middle of it, the girls came in to say goodnight to their father and to the kind grandfather who had gone in search of their ghost.

"You've done a good job with them," Siri told him when they left.

"I hope so," said Suthon. "It's hard to know what's right. You just have to learn from the mistakes of ignorant parents who let their children raise themselves. You come across them all the time in my line of work."

"I have no argument with you there," said Siri.

They were well down the bottle of scotch when Siri made his summation. They both considered the implications.

"Nothing here," said Siri. "Basically nothing of legal substance."

"I disagree," said Suthon.

"No evidence," said Siri.

Suthon was pacing slowly around the room. He stared at the doctor.

"Siri," he said, "I know you and your wife can't wait around in Udon forever, but I'd like to think I'd be able to call you back to give evidence once we've put a case together."

Siri was delighted. "You're that confident?" he said.

"Absolutely."

"Then it would be a pleasure."

"We'd pay for travel and accommodation, of course," said Suthon.

"Even more pleasurable."

"When's your mad monk driver picking you up?"

"Hard to say," said Siri. "Madam Daeng's shopping in a foreign country that has choices. She can't afford anything, but there's nothing stopping her from trying on everything in the stores. I'm sure they'll be here before dark though."

"Excellent. I promise I'll keep you informed of every eventuality. And rest assured I won't give up until we have that bastard policeman in front of the executioner. That much I can promise you."

Suthon stood.

"Come through to my office," he said, "and I'll give you my business card with some phone and fax numbers on it. I'm sure you'll eventually get a line out of that sorry little country of yours."

Siri staggered a little from the bump of the whisky and walked slowly out into the hall. Either the whisky was a lot stronger than he was used to or the toils of the previous week were catching up with him. He held on to the office door frame and focused. When the room became clear his jaw dropped. He could not believe his eyes. It was not late at night. There were no insects buzzing around a lamp outside the window. There were no dark shadows. But this was the room, the crossover room Siri had entered from the connecting doors.

Suthon was crouched over his desk looking through the drawer.

"I've got one here somewhere," he said. "Lots of cards but never the one you're looking for. Isn't it always the way?"

Siri shuffled unsteadily across the room in search of the door he'd passed through that night. There was none. He leaned against the wall as a wave of fatigue broke over him.

"You probably wouldn't have a card, would you, Coroner?"

Siri felt for a door handle, a hinge, the texture of wood, but there was nothing. He began to slide down the wall like a dollop of cooking lard until he was in a sitting position.

The last thing he heard before he lost consciousness was, ". . . given the shit hole of a country you come from."

"I'm afraid you've missed him," said Suthon. He was standing on the front porch hand in hand with his silent wife.

"He went without us?" said Madam Daeng, still winded from her jog from the car.

"We invited him to stay for supper, but he said he'd troubled us enough already," said the prosecutor. "He seemed to be in a hurry to go somewhere."

"Do you have any idea where?"

"He asked me where the nearest *samlor* taxi stand was. I told him it was on the next block and he headed off. I'm sorry. I didn't think to ask where he was going."

"That's all right," said Daeng. "He's always disappearing. We'll find him. Thank you."

"You're most welcome."

She was about to head back to the car when a thought hit her. "Did he leave you the report?" she asked.

"We went through it together," said the prosecutor. "It's all taken care of. I told the doctor I'd keep you all informed of events."

"That's a relief. Good night, then."

"Good night."

At that moment, to ex-monk Boh's surprise, Ugly leapt from the backseat of the car onto his lap and then through the open window. The dog sprinted past Daeng on the garden path barking wildly. The prosecutor and his wife had barely made it inside the screen door when the hound arrived and butted the mesh with his head. Madam Daeng hurried back, took the dog by the collar and yanked him away.

"I'm so sorry," she said. "He's never done that before."

Ugly continued to bark.

"I have to accept responsibility for that," said the prosecutor. "Our bitch is in heat. Every dog on the street has been queuing at our door for the past week. I really should have had her spayed."

Boh arrived from the car with a length of electrical cord to use as a leash. Ugly was howling. It took the two of them to wrestle the mad dog back to the car. Even as they were driving away, Ugly continued to snarl and drool against the rear window.

Suthon shut the front door, walked past his wife, who stood silently in the reception area with her head bowed, unlocked his office door and went inside. He relocked the door and turned on the light. Siri sat off in one corner on the guest chair. He was gagged with several layers of cellophane tape. His hands were cuffed to the wooden rungs of the chair arms.

"Oh, you're awake," said the prosecutor. "Splendid. I need to talk to you."

He sat on the leather chair behind the desk and started to write.

"I didn't really need to cuff you," he said. "That was just

in case you fell out of the chair. The sedative will eventually work its way through your system, but I doubt you'll have any feeling in your extremities for another nine hours or so. You certainly won't be able to walk. And they warn us about that one last glass for the road, don't they? And do we listen? If I remove the tape do you think you could resist the temptation to shout? I mean, it wouldn't do you any good if you did. The little lady is completely compla-cent, and the neighbors won't hear you because I have air-conditioning in here and thick glass windows."

Siri nodded. The prosecutor took the paper knife from his desk, slit the tape behind Siri's ear and ripped it off. The doctor took four or five heavy breaths.

"Oh, that's right," said the prosecutor, "you have breath-ing problems, don't you? I think I can use that somehow in your untimely death. Running for a bus or something. Nobody will think twice about it. You're old. You should have died a long time ago. Yes. That would have saved me a lot of trouble."

"Congratulations," said Siri. His lips were numb. The words slurred.

"On what?"

"I had no suspicion whatsoever. You weren't even on my list of suspects."

"I know," said Suthon. "That's why I had to see your list. It almost passed inspection, too. Captain Gumron was such a perfect candidate given that you were looking for a policeman. But you see, the Royal Thai Police Acad-emy has graduate courses that allow a bright man such as myself to attain a lofty position. No sooner was I in uni-form blowing a whistle than there I was one step below a high court judge. The land of opportunity."

"What part of my report upset you?" Siri asked.

"That one small item. You mentioned it in passing in your report, and when I questioned you about it you hedged. You said your man was looking into it. Kritsana Mukum, Dusit Insurance Company, Suan Dusit. It was the only clue even vaguely traceable back to me. Where did that come from?"

"I can't tell you," said Siri.

The prosecutor laughed. "You're hardly in a position to refuse."

"Well, if I can't feel my arms and legs, torture isn't going get you very far, is it?"

The prosecutor returned to his desk with a smile on his face. "You really don't care if you die, do you?" he said.

"I've had a good life."

"You do know this is all there is to it, don't you?"

"This what?"

"This earth. This lifetime you're just coming to the end of. You do know there's nothing more to look forward to?"

"Ah, a pure atheist."

"A realist, Siri. Belief is the greatest fault in humanity. You expect a deal from the beyond, from the almighty, from the chosen one. You expect a part two. You get run over by a *tuktuk* on Monday and by Tuesday afternoon you think you'll be sipping a cold beer on a balcony overlooking the gates of whatever heaven you've invested in."

"And where do you think your victims are now?" Siri asked.

"Wherever they're filed or scattered or rendered to ash. Their contribution to earth—if they made one—ended when their hearts stopped beating. The lights went out, the ventilation system shut down and that *being* ceased to be. The story endeth."

"What about your children?"

"What about them?" he snapped.

"Don't they have a right to believe in something?"

"No."

"No? How can you stop them?"

"I can stop them because I am their father. I can stop them the same way you stop your son from smoking or your daughter from dating unsavory boys. You teach them through example. By being a responsible parent."

"Not like your parents."

That reference started a tic in one corner of the prosecutor's mouth. Siri was in no doubt that Suthon was Lim's legitimate son.

"They weren't parents," he said. "I could not be any more unlike them. My children will grow up with a mother and father who are with them whenever they need them. A mother and father who love them and listen to them and tell them the truth. Not false stories about holy ghosts and afterlives and monsters that live in the rafters."

"Your girls have ghosts in the linen cupboard," Siri reminded him.

"It's a game," he shouted, "not a belief. They will never be dragged off to a temple to light candles and stick gold leaf on a dead monk's crotch and listen to the fairy stories about a millionaire who lost his mind and found enlightenment. They won't be sat down in front of an altar to beg forgiveness from ancestors for not refreshing their Coca-Cola once a week. They won't be taken to a concrete tomb to say hello to dead grandma. They won't be locked in their room and bullied into learning the precepts. By the time my children are eight, they'll already know these things are wicked fantasies."

There was silence in the room until Suthon regained his composure.

"Was there a time when you believed?" said Siri.

"It wasn't belief, Siri. It was brainwashing. It was psychological surrogacy. They'd go off and leave me for days. They'd tell me I had nothing to fear because the spirits would watch over me. I was petrified."

"Do you know where they went?" Siri asked. "When they left you alone."

"He had another wife," said Suthon. "I used to follow him after school, wait until he left the factory. They had a house. They'd walk with their son to the park and play ball. They'd hold hands. It was perfect except I wasn't in the picture. Then things started to go well. When the other woman died the boy was sent away. Everything worked out. When the monk came to our house to tell my father the other boy was dead I wanted to embrace him. It was the perfect end to a story. Everything I'd been told about Buddhism had come true. The monk had brought elation and peace to my life. I imagined living like him, wandering from family to family spreading good news.

"My father left home so there was me and the maids and the spirit menagerie. There were only odd visits from her, the Chinese witch. So I followed her instead. That's when I saw my monk again. The monk she'd convinced to lie to my father. Him and her. In the morning he'd dress in his robes and go out to collect alms. In the evening in his flowery shirt they'd drink gin together in open-air restaurants and they'd go to expensive clubs. They'd conspired, of course, even dared show his face in my house.

Might have planned to kill my father for all I know. My old man wouldn't doubt the word of a monk telling him the bastard was dead. More inheritance for the witch and her boyfriend. When she died, the fake monk didn't even come to her funeral. It was all coming apart in my mind. It was a sin, Siri. They taught me what sinning meant, then they gave me practical examples."

Suthon took a bottle and tumblers from the bottom drawer of his desk and poured two full shots of whisky. He drank one and held up the other to Siri.

"No?" he said, then threw back the second.

"You've left out the most exciting part," said Siri.

"And what would that be?" said the prosecutor.

"How you killed the women in your father's life," said Siri.

Suthon's smile had never been so broad.

"Why, you clever little coroner," he said. "How did you work that one out?"

He was already pouring two more glasses.

"Easy really," said Siri. "A lot of people claim to have killed and many more look as if they might, but it takes a rare breed of psychopath to actually do it. Now that I'm pretty certain it was you who killed the villagers in Sawan, it doesn't take genius to imagine you poisoning your mother or climbing through the window of the house of your father's whore. The odds are stacked against two maniacs in the same family."

"I should have killed the little bastard then and there and I wouldn't have had all this hassle," said Suthon. "The whore's son was lying there on the next cot watching me. He was only five years younger than me, eight or so, but he was pathetic there sucking his thumb, crying. He gave me that look—that accusing look—and it stuck with me. Of course he didn't know who I was. I told him that night if he said anything to anyone I'd haunt him for the rest of his life. And it worked. He didn't even have the balls to tell the police. If the investigators had been worth anything at all, I would have been free from both his women that night. I made it look like the Chinese witch had done it, but they didn't even investigate her. So I had to bide my time and kill her on one of my rare visits from Bangkok."

"How did you discover your father had changed the will?" Siri asked.

"His lawyer told my lawyer," said the prosecutor. "One of those safety valves I put in place to avoid surprises."

Siri looked at the young man and sighed. Whatever he had in mind for the doctor was still a secret. Siri could think of no better plan than to keep him talking. Suthon needed no urging on that front.

"It was the final insult," said the prosecutor. "Do you know how much he was worth? Oh, Siri. You could pay back your little Lao national debt three times over with the money that old skinflint had put away. What was he going to do with it? But I didn't want complications. It's the only reason I didn't kill him too. I was patient. He'd die soon enough, I thought. Then I found out he'd decided to give it all to a monk, to some bastard orange cowboy. What a waste."

He finished another glass.

"I was already up here," he said. "I'd arranged a transfer from Bangkok when I heard the old man was on his last legs. Now you have to understand it isn't that easy to get a transfer to a specific location. You usually have to go where they send you. You can't just go into some judge's office and say you'd like to pop up to Udon like he's a travel agent. But there are brokers, and they're usually family members of the judges. It costs a fair bit, but it's worth it. That was my loose end."

He held up an unsealed envelope and took out a check.

"This is the reason you're here, old fellow. This is my final payment to the broker. Before sunlight you'll have told me how you got ahold of this address. As I told you, I'm nothing if not patient."

"Why didn't anyone recognize you when you came back?" Siri asked.

"Because I wasn't an acne-covered teenager anymore."

"But the name?"

"Do you know how easy it is to change your name in this country, Siri? You go along to the district office with your ID card and your new name on a scrap of paper. They type up a new card. You give them fifty baht, and you're somebody else. Then you set fire to the district office, and there's no record of your old name. Amazing Thailand, eh?"

"Why go to all that trouble?" Siri asked. "Why not just hire two thugs on a motorcycle to shoot the abbot?"

The prosecutor brought his second beaker to the sofa opposite the doctor. He was surprisingly steady on his feet despite all the booze.

"That would have been such a wasted opportunity," he said. "You see, I want a province, a fiefdom. I want my father's money, of course, but I need credibility. As a judge—a rich judge—I would very soon become gover-nor. Layer by layer, gold leaf by gold leaf, I would be in a position to dismantle the stronghold of religion in the northeast. Not overnight, I admit, but I could sow doubts through education and common sense. By discrediting the

Sangha and showing the people that all gods are false. By showing them that their lives would be more wholesome, more successful if they gave up their belief in ghosts and believed in themselves. Or, better still, believed in me."

Siri sighed. Now would have been a good time for another drink, but he didn't want to interrupt a maniac in full flow.

"So you made Abbot Rayron your scapegoat," he said.

"I suppose you'd have to call him that," Suthon agreed. "But, as you say, I could have had him exterminated on a dark road in the middle of nowhere. Rural monk. Unknown location. The story would be forgotten in a week. Nobody cares about little deaths in the countryside. But, what if it were something spectacular? He'd be a legend. They all are, the famous serial murderers. You remember the name of the killer but never the victim. This would be Thailand's first international homicidal maniac. The press would give it a catchy name like "The Shaman Slayer": a premeditated executioner killing in the name of the Buddha. Following in His footsteps."

"The mendicant, the corpse, the aged and the sick," said Siri.

"That's it exactly," said Suthon, glowing with pride at his plan. He knocked back his drink and looked in the direction of the desk for the bottle. It was as if he were desperate for drunkenness, but it refused to come.

"It was so well planned"—he smiled—"if I do say so myself. Nam Som was on my circuit schedule once a month. It wasn't so hard to slot things so I'd be there every full moon. The village was only twenty kilometers from town, and there were a hundred places to hide my car. I needed a full moon to be seen, you see. Nobody would be close enough to see my face and a woman's stocking over your hair looks very much like a bald head from a distance.

"The mendicant was a gift. When I heard he was staying at the temple I knew my success was destined. Month by month everything fit together. There was always a body in the cremation hut. There were any number of sick and elderly to choose from. And on my first nocturnal recce of the village I learned a good deal. I learned that your Captain Gumron was knocking off the wife of the headman's son. The cop befriended the husband and sent him off on errands, so he could creep into their hut. He had her deliver meals to the prison so they could screw in his office. I'm certain the baby will resemble Gumron, poor thing."

It occurred to Siri that the prosecutor had never had an opportunity to tell his story. And here he suddenly had a captive and disposable audience. The doctor's only hope was that the man might drink and talk himself into a stupor long enough for the feeling to come back into Siri's legs. The prosecutor returned for his bottle.

"So you didn't go into the village expecting to see Loong Gan?" Siri said.

"Loong . . . ? Oh, that bastard," said Suthon. "No, Siri. No. Not at all. What a discovery. What a coincidence. There he was, the charmer all of a thousand years old still boasting about his conquests, still drunk. The fake monk who'd seduced my mother and lied to my father. Oh, Siri, what a blessing."

"So you sliced him up?"

"Eventually. I had so much fun with him that night. I didn't order an autopsy, but if they'd conducted one they'd have found some vital parts missing, or rather in the wrong places. I'll spare you the details. It was most satisfying and fit the plot so perfectly."

"And the sick woman?"

"She was dying of some disease."

"She was recovering from hepatitis," said Siri. "I treated her."

"Well, you know. Country woman. Unimportant but for her part in the overall pastiche. For perfection it should have been a man. The Buddha didn't seem that concerned about the plight of women."

"You called the press to the court."

"Yes, it was all over the news, wasn't it? After my third hearing of the case I was the cool judge who didn't want to jump to conclusions. I ordered them barred from my courtroom but allowed a press conference later. I knew everyone in the country would be tuned in for the final part in the puzzle. Was Abbot Rayron the fanatic Buddhist serial killer? It would have been so well orchestrated."

"What went wrong?" Siri asked.

"He recognized me," he said, and began to pace again. "You were there with him in court. He asked to speak. I should have said no, but I let him. And he said, 'I apologize for forcing you to make such a difficult choice.'"

"Perhaps he was just being polite."

"He knew who I was, Siri. He recognized me, damn it. He was talking about my choice to kill his mother. His psychological amnesia of that night was suddenly lifted. There in the courtroom he looked at me the same way he had that night in his mother's room. An innocent look that spoke of eternal damnation. That same

I-am-better-than-thou look every religious devotee uses to look down on non-believers."

"He was eight. You were thirteen."

"They instill it in the young. They give them the power."

Siri admitted to himself he was in a dark hole with a nutcase, and there was no way out. It wasn't how he'd hoped to go, but if it was unavoidable he might as well have the taste of good whisky on his lips.

"I could use a drink," he said.

"Oh, where are my manners?" said Suthon.

His steps were more directed than spontaneous but the prosecutor managed to get to the desk, pour two drinks, and bring one to Siri. He held it up to the doctor's lips and poured carefully so that not a drop was spilled. Still leaning over Siri and breathing into his face, Suthon said, "He ruined it all."

"All what?" said Siri.

"The big scandal. The big *Monk Goes Insane* trial with me at the helm. There should have been a good month to build up the tension. Allow debate in the press. Time for the media to lay bare the false image of good clergy. I would have dropped in unfounded accusations that he'd murdered his own whore mother when he was a child. Insinuated there had been no background check on the abbot. That any fool or criminal could become a monk and rise through the ranks. It would have brought out all the laity with their horror stories of bad monks. The whole Buddhist infrastructure would have wobbled.

"But then he recognized me. All he'd have to do was mention my relationship to his mother, and the cameras would turn on me. I'd stop being the wise adjudicator and become a player—a suspect. That couldn't happen. I had to kill him."

"You went to his cell."

"The cell block was in the same compound. My trials had run late. It was dark. Captain Gumron was hiding from his mistress's husband and shared that news as if it were even remotely interesting to me. Nobody questioned me. I often visited the cells to make sure the prisoners didn't die from lack of care. Everyone was asleep. I called to him—the bastard monk. He stepped up to the bars. I said I understood what he'd said in the courtroom. He pretended not to know what I was talking about. I told him I'd like to have a chance to embrace him and beg his forgiveness before I left for Udon. He told me there was nothing to forgive. It was cold in there. Udon nights. He wore a spare sarong as a scarf. I reached in, grabbed it and pulled him hard against the bars. The impact knocked him out, and it was simple enough then to strangle him. Of course I carry a key to the cells. I entered and changed the position of the body to suggest a suicide. You know the rest. You were right. Down to the last detail, you were right about everything. Impressive."

"Thank you."

"That's the story, old man. The only thing that remains . . ."

"Is the insurance company in Bangkok," said Siri.

"Exactly. Then I can let you go."

"To my heaven?"

"To the scene of your accident. After that it's up to you."

"Then why would I even consider telling you?" asked Siri.

"Forty-three E," said Suthon. "I imagine that's where

mad Boh and your wife will be spending the night after not finding you. It's only fifteen minutes from here. Sorry, like I said, I don't leave much to chance. I looked up your monk's address."

Siri could feel a tingle in his nerve endings but no movement in his muscles. He had to attack using the only option available to him.

"Before I tell you," he said, "it might be necessary to change your perception of . . . I don't know . . . everything."

"Siri, I heard about your cabaret at Sawan," said Suthon. "You can sway the feeble minds of farmers with your hocus pocus but both you and I know it's all trickery. I've spent a lifetime exposing your kind. Not once have I been swayed by the chants and fireworks. You're all the same, you shamans and monks and priests. You do your magic tricks and suck people in and then bamboozle them with archaic language. And I don't have time for any of it. So just tell me how you got the name of the broker."

"I saw it here in this office," said Siri. "You wrote the address by hand on an envelope, but you made a mistake in the spelling of Bangkok. I'm not criticizing. It's a hard word to spell in Thai."

The prosecutor smiled and returned to his desk. He looked at the envelope he'd shown Siri earlier and was startled.

"You have remarkable eyesight for such an old man," he said. "Eat a lot of carrots in Laos, do you?"

"Carrots?" said Siri. "It's five meters from here to the desk. And you wrote by hand. I'd need binoculars to see that far."

The prosecutor scribbled out the mistake, ripped the

envelope in half and threw it into the bin. He poured another drink. Everything came together in Siri's mind. It was a remarkable feeling.

"What other tricks do you have for us tonight, great shaman?" Suthon asked. At last he was slurring.

"Well, let me see," said Siri. "Are you missing a hole puncher, by any chance?"

"A what?"

"Come on, you know what a hole puncher is. You've probably been searching for it for weeks. But that's what happens when you don't allow anyone in your office. A cleaner would have found it in a few minutes. It's under your sofa. And don't tell me I have good eyesight. I'd need x-ray vision to see that from here."

Suthon smiled. "Just out of curiosity . . ." he said.

He took his drink to the sofa, got down on his knees and looked beneath it. His expression was one of anger rather than amazement.

"See?" he said, leaning on the seat with one elbow. "These are exactly the tricks that fool farmers."

"You're not a farmer," said Siri, "but you're fooled."

"Magic is a science, Siri. It's learned. If I hadn't had so many drinks I'd be able to work it out."

"There's more," said Siri. "Like the calendar on the post there. I can't see it at all, but I'm certain you didn't get around to ripping off the month of February. There's a picture of the King driving a tractor. You marked the seventh with a tick."

The prosecutor had lost the rosy glow from his cheeks. He glared at Siri, got clumsily to his feet and went to the central pillar of the room.

"How am I doing?" Siri asked. "The curtains are drawn

but if you pull them you'll see a flurry of flying ant activity around the lamp. So it rained recently."

Suthon opened the curtains. The window was alive with insects.

"There'll be more later," said Siri.

"I give up," said Suthon. "How do you do it?"

"Not a trick exactly," said Siri. "I've been here before, you see. I came to your house a couple of times, although then I didn't realize why."

"You could not have come here without my knowledge."

"Well that's just it. I did. The first time I found myself in your linen closet. Must have taken a wrong turn somewhere. I think it was me the children heard."

Suthon put down his glass for the first time and sat on the edge of his desk.

"But I've been here, too," Siri continued. "In this office. Or, you know? The funny thing is I don't think I've been here yet. I think I've been here . . . later. And I'm not sure that's a bad thing because it means I'm alive in the future. I'll probably have to work on the grammar to explain this properly."

"You're doing this inside my head, aren't you?" said Suthon.

"What am I doing, son?"

"Your tricks. The mind games. Your hypnosis. It won't work, you know. I'm stronger than you."

"You're probably right. But at least let me finish. You see? I've made an amazing discovery here. Time isn't linear on the other side. Do you know what I mean?"

The sound of a dog barely distracted the doctor. Distant shouting. Siri continued.

"What I mean is I'm here now, and I've been here

before. But that visit hasn't happened yet. There's no bloodstain on the floor. Your leather chair isn't ripped. There's no broken plaster by the door."

"Yes, this is exactly what you people do," slurred Suthon. "You create doubts, cause confusion, then attack."

"Oh, shut up and listen," said Siri. "The other side thinks that we are the other side and vice versa. When I was over there I thought the other side was a different place. But it wasn't. It was just a different time. Perhaps with some alterations. The door, for example. I enter or shall enter this office from that direction. But there is no door. Isn't that fascinating?"

He looked up to see the prosecutor standing beside his desk holding a pistol.

"And that too," said Siri. "If you shoot me there would be blood here, all over the chair. And there wasn't any. So you don't shoot me here. And as I can't walk you'd have to drag me across to your desk and shoot me there, which wouldn't make any sense at all."

"Stop it," said Suthon, waving his gun.

"So as the blood was by your desk it's more likely you'll shoot yourself or somebody will shoot you."

"I mean it. Shut up."

Siri's green eyes glowed brightly in the light from the overhead fluorescent lamp. His face beamed with happiness. The prosecutor looked at him, bewildered.

"Oh," said Siri. "This is so beautiful. What if somewhere in the future I learn to control these travels? What if I were able to decide where to go and when to arrive? I could come and go through time as I please. It means . . . Oh."

"You're a dead man, Siri," said the prosecutor aiming his pistol at the doctor's head.

"No, son. I've already explained why I'm not. And I think beneath your fear you're as fascinated by all this as I am. I'm a child, and I've just taken my first step. You're a father. You know how that feels."

Suthon began to squeeze the trigger.

"This is the moment," came a voice from across the room.

The prosecutor spun around but there was nobody to his right. Only a blank wall.

"Who was that?" he shouted.

"It was me," said Siri. "Isn't this all just beyond belief? How marvelous."

"Can you hear me?" said the Siri who wasn't yet there.

"Stop it," said the prosecutor.

"Loud and clear," said Siri. "I could use a little help here."

"It's coming," said the wall.

Suthon shot the wall.

Plaster was flung across the room.

"You should control that temper of yours," came a voice from the desk.

Suthon almost jumped out of his skin upon seeing a fat man in a halter top and shorts sitting on his chair. In panic he fired a shot. It could not possibly have missed, but the fat man merely looked disappointed.

"Ouch," said the fat man.

"Is Auntie Bpoo there yet?" asked the wall.

"She's here, but she just got shot," said Siri.

"She'll get over it," said the wall.

The prosecutor staggered backward swinging his gun toward Siri, then the wall, then the transvestite at his desk not knowing who or what to shoot. There was a loud banging at the office door. Suthon shot in that direction but missed by an arm's length.

"Put that away," said Auntie Bpoo. "Or somebody's going to get hurt."

The prosecutor put a second bullet into his chair.

"See? Now I've broken a nail," said Bpoo.

The door was broken off its hinges and Ugly tore through the gap. The prosecutor took a shot at him, but the dog was used to idiots with guns and ducked down behind the metal filing cabinets before re-emerging from behind the desk. He buried his teeth into the prosecutor's ankle. Suthon cried in agony and instinctively shot downward, hitting his own foot and bleeding like a harpooned whale. When they finally got the broken door off its hinges, in rushed Madam Daeng brandishing a knife, two men in uniform and Boh. The prosecutor's wife remained back in the shadows. The scene they witnessed was odd but not as bizarre as it had been a few seconds before. Siri sat handcuffed to a chair, smiling generously. The prosecutor lay unconscious in a pool of blood with a dog chewing on his ankle.

Daeng walked up to him, held her knife at his throat and said, "Not all dogs are obsessed with sex."

17

A Sting in the Tale

Siri put down the phone and frowned.

"What news from Civilai?" Daeng asked.

"Not good," said Siri. "They haven't found Noo yet. We might have to take up the prime minister on his offer."

"We're not scheduled to see him again till Thursday," she reminded him. "I thought we were making our big escape tomorrow. Tomorrow evening's the Supreme—"

"I know. I'll try to get him on the phone. He gave me his private number. I wonder what I'd have to promise him for a favor of this magnitude."

"Noo's a Thai citizen. Our PM wants to keep the Thais happy, and the Thai PM wants to keep you happy temporarily. It might work."

"It's Noo's only chance, especially if he's the spy they say he is. If we're lucky there'll be someone they want to exchange him for."

"You know the prime minister will shoot us if he ever finds out what we're doing."

"It'll be worth it. We've had a nice few days."

"Very nice."

"You got to see your Grand Palace and our Emerald Buddha and float on the river. We've eaten like royalty—albeit early in the day. And everyone's been so polite."

"I know," she said. "It's been marvelous really. But I would like to live long enough to boast about it back home."

"Don't worry. We will."

He picked up the remote and turned on the TV for the eightieth time. The Dusit Thani had all the Thai channels and an in-house movie on a loop with subtitles. There was also a brand new VCR with a stack of films with Thai subtitles. Siri only left the room if he had to. They could not complain about the absence of room service after lunchtime. Nor the fact they'd been dying for a cold beer for three days. But Daeng, a mistress of disguise throughout the revolution, had warned her husband about the dangers of slipping out of character.

"I think . . . Can you turn that thing down a bit?" she said.

Siri lowered the volume.

"Thank you. I think I'll go to see Noo's daughter alone this evening."

"Why?" asked Siri.

"Because it's going to be hard enough for her without all this."

"All this" was Siri and Daeng without hair or eyebrows. It was a saffron robe drying in the bathroom over the king-sized bathtub. "All this" was the fake Sangharaj of Laos and his nun personal secretary defecting to Thailand. It was a guaranteed week of luxury and sightseeing before the formal interviews and the debriefing began. It was Siri and Daeng's greatest scam.

In the temple in Sawan, Siri had not mentioned his far-fetched idea to the Sangharaj, as he'd expected and deserved an angry reproach. But Siri remembered the night he'd seen the Sangharaj digging in the garden. Of course to a man like Siri the temptation of investigating such a strange event had been too much. He'd waited until he was alone that night and discovered what the old monk had buried there. It was himself, or rather it was his old self. In a pouch he found the Sangharaj's citizen identification card, some personal letters and a pair of glasses. He'd returned the letters unread, but kept the ID. He didn't consider it stealing, as he believed it was the monk's intention to bury and forget his old life. Before receiving two thousand boxes of contact lenses of assorted sizes in international aid the Sangharaj had worn glasses. He wore those glasses in the photo on his national ID card and carried them with him for sentimental reasons. It was a poor photo that could have been anybody. And, most importantly, with a shave and a haircut it could have been Siri. Nobody looked too closely at men over seventy. So the old monk had unknowingly donated his ID card to the sting.

Siri and Daeng had waited in Udon long enough to be sure Prosecutor Suthon would be getting his just desserts. Old Boh and Abbot Somluang knew enough devout policemen between them to begin proceedings. The police force was constantly berated by the judiciary for its inefficiency, so it was a delight to turn the tables. A conviction against the prosecutor was looking more certain given the young man's sudden demise. Something had happened to him that night in his office. His mind seemed to have imploded. He'd become a jabbering idiot. The wife he'd selected for her looks and mothering potential had been only too keen to give evidence against him. She told the police what she'd heard through the locked door that night. She'd been terrorized by the man for five years and was glad for her and her daughters to be rid of him.

So with the Udon police in control, Siri and Daeng had phoned the Buddhist council, apologized for getting cold feet and agreed to resume the defection. In order to avoid the snowy-white soldiers they'd made fun of in the Udon bus station they agreed to go directly to the airfield where they were met by air force officers, loaded into a helicopter and whisked off to Don Muang. There had been a look of resignation on Ugly's face as he watched the helicopter take off and soar over the tree line. Not even his great cache of hunting skills would be enough to track his master. But Boh had agreed to keep the dog company until their return.

In Bangkok they were welcomed by the director of the Office of National Buddhism and a delegate from the lower ranks of the royal family, neither of whom had met the Lao Sangharaj. They were temporarily taken aback at the sight of the monk's so-called personal secretary, but . . . Laos . . . what could one say?

They were driven in limousines with a police escort to the Dusit Thani, ensconced in two penthouse suites and spent half an hour with a government official planning their activities for the week. They had no choice but to meet the prime minister the following day but had been able to put off a reunion with the Thai Supreme Patriarch until day four. That was the point where their covers would be blown. The two old patriarchs had met several times.

So their escape was planned for the morning of day four. The military minders—supposedly bodyguards—were stationed by the elevator on the penthouse level, and in the lobby. Nobody was on the fire escape. They counted five men, maybe six. But, really, what were half a dozen Thai soldiers to a couple like this?

"Fancy a Toblerone?" said Daeng, rooting through the fridge.

"I don't know," said Siri. "What's a Toblerone?"

Epilogue 1

They'd been drinking, the boys of the presidential security detail. They liked their booze. They'd spent the night in a hostess club dancing with pretty Lao girls in traditional costumes. It was mostly circle dancing, but at the end of each set there was a slow ballad. In the dim cellar there were a lot of dark shadows for fondling.

The short-haired major staggered out into the parking lot with his mates. They said their goodbyes and Agoon went to his jeep. He was fumbling for his key when a bow-tied waiter from the club limped over to him.

"Sir, sir," he said. "Lucky I caught you. Thank goodness."

Agoon turned to look at him. The waiter was overweight and sweaty and his hair was far too long.

"What do you want?" said Agoon.

"Sir, you left your belongings on the table. You have to be careful in places like this. A lot of dishonest people. Someone might have walked off with your wallet."

"Don't you get it in your head you'll be rewarded for this," said Agoon.

"Oh no, sir," said the waiter. "I just want to do my civic duty."

The waiter held out his hands, and the soldier held out his. He looked up briefly into the waiter's face, but he recognized him too late. He hadn't seen Phosy since the night he'd stuck him with a blade. He heard the click and felt the warm metal around his wrist. He was suddenly aware of the unusual weight at the end of the chain. The hand grenade had been welded to the last link of the single handcuff. The inspector held up the pin, smiled and jogged calmly away raising his wig like a hat as he went.

The soldier yanked at the cuff, pulled frantically at the chain. He cursed and spat, but his final five seconds on earth passed remarkably quickly.

Epilogue 2

"I don't care if I-I-I don't ever see another noodle," said Mr. Geung.

"Madam Daeng will be here tomorrow," said Tukta. "You can go back to entertaining customers."

"I can't wait. I can do my new d-d-dance."

He demonstrated it and made her laugh. He loved making her laugh. They were cleaning up after the evening session. As usual they'd had a full house and there'd been no rest. Dtui was upstairs counting the money. The evening silence was disturbed by the growl of a jeep. The sound of a vehicle had come to signal trouble in Vientiane. Geung and Tukta stared at each other, willing the jeep to pass by, but it slowed down in front of the noodle shop. They heard the sound of a thump like a sack of turnips falling off a truck, and then the jeep roared off.

"Don't go," said Tukta. "It's a bomb."

But Mr. Geung was already at the shop shutter looking out into the darkness. All he could see was an outline drawn by the glow from the upstairs window.

"What was that?" said Dtui, running down the stairs.

"It's a bomb," said Tukta.

"It's a person," said Geung, and he walked out into the street.

Dtui followed. The crumpled body was ungainly, limbs disorganized like an octopus out of water.

"It's Comrade Noo," said Mr. Geung. "The monk."

Dtui felt for a pulse.

"He's alive," she said. "He's alive."

Continue reading for a preview from the next
Dr. Siri Paiboun Mystery

The Rat Catchers' Olympics

CHAPTER ONE
March 1980 – The Bald Eagles Have Landed

There were occasional relaxed periods of what the Lao called *sabai*. The weather was comfortable, the markets had fresh food and the children played in the road with no danger of being hit by vehicles. Nothing moved fast enough to cause injuries. Everything seemed to be so peaceful and casual you'd forget there was another layer— the echelon of the impossible. You didn't experience it until you attempted to rock the boat. It might take you so long to obtain a *laissez passer* to visit an ailing aunt in another province that she'd have gone up in smoke long before you arrived. Your name on a housing list was more prone to retreat than to advance as the names of those of influence were slotted in above you. And a stay in a hospital was as likely to kill you as to cure you.

Then there was one more stratum that was unfathomable. It was so dark and sinister you'd never make any sense of it. There needed to be nothing more than the perception of antisocialist activity. It was a nether world where neighbors disappeared, where trusted members of the Party were ousted as traitors, where the paranoid ruled. Comrade Noo the Thai forest monk had been enticed into that twilight zone from which few returned. He'd vanished for two weeks. Not the supernatural vanishing that had recently hounded Dr. Siri Paiboun—more a bureaucratic disappearance, like a file or a record lost in the system. A misplaced person for whom nobody was accountable.

Most agreed that Thai Comrade Noo was primarily a conservationist, a man who would bury himself up to his neck to stop a bulldozer destroying national parkland. Others saw him as a journalist reporting on the abuse of monks in a socialist state. The Lao authorities might have seen him merely as an illegal immigrant or a troublemaker or a religious zealot. You'd never know because the administrative line was ignorance.

"No. Never heard of him."

And it made no difference what he'd actually done because he was perceived to be an enemy of the state so even the story of his life was irrelevant. The Party had its bloodhounds. It was their duty to drag in trophies to justify their existence. Noo had headed off on his bicycle one day only to be kidnapped by some military thugs. There was no announcement, no trial, no trace of him. They'd gobbled him up as they did anyone who dared defy the overlords. But mysteriously they'd spat him out. None of his friends and supporters who'd gathered around him in that small concrete room knew why he'd been released. It was unprecedented. He'd quite obviously been beaten and had horrific injuries from being thrown from a truck. But he was still unconscious so the details of his detention remained wrapped inside him. For three days he'd teetered on the edge, bones not setting, wounds not healing, deep in a coma. But if he were to die, Comrade Noo would not have been forgotten like the many before him. He was admired and loved and it could only have been the will of his supporters that kept him alive.

Nurse Dtui was there with him. She was the one who'd found his pulse that night he was thrown from a truck in front of Madam Daeng's noodle shop. Mr. Geung was there. His physical and mental strengths often overshadowed his Down syndrome limitations. He was the one who'd carried the broken body of the monk to the upstairs mattress. His partner, Tukta was there, she too a member of the secret club of those with Down syndrome. She was the one who'd ridden the noodle shop bicycle to Mahosot Hospital and returned with dressings and ointments and morphine although nobody knew how she had achieved this feat without money. She refused to say.

Nurse Dtui had done her best but she wasn't a doctor. There were forty qualified doctors at Mahosot, none of whom she trusted. The one she really needed was Dr. Siri himself, the country's last coroner.

"So, where is he?" asked Gongjai, the reformed prostitute.

"Still in Thailand, as far as we know," said old Inthanet, the puppet master.

"He'd know what to do if he was here," said Gongjai.

There followed a silence as dense as river clay.

"Dtui kn-kn-knows what to do," said Mr. Geung.

"I know," said Gongjai. "I'm sorry, I didn't mean . . ."

"It's all right," said Dtui. "I wish he was here, too."

They were assembled in the front bedroom of Siri's government-allocated house just a short walk from the

That Luang monument. It was a building that housed
far too many characters to commit them all to memory.
Even the doctor lost count and muddled the names.
The inhabitants had been collected from the uncharita-
ble streets and ideological gutters of the city. They were
characters who didn't fit the system. There was Crazy
Rajhid, the homeless Indian who'd spoken only three
times in the past four years. There was Inthanet's portly
fiancée, Jit, who had fled to the city to escape a farming
cooperative that was starving her family. There were the
young, the elderly, the brilliant and the insane. Joining
them in the circle around the patient this evening were
two monks who'd turned up one day without explaining
how they'd heard of Comrade Noo's plight.

Nurse Dtui's little daughter, Malee, was asleep in a
hand-made cradle. Her father, Phosy, often attended these
candle-lit vigils, but tonight he was off investigating a case.
The senior police inspector found himself working odd
hours.

Also missing from the group was Siri's best friend,
Comrade Civilai, the ex-politburo member. He'd taken
it upon himself to drive his old Citroën to Wattay Airport
to meet every flight from Bangkok on the off-chance Dr.
Siri and his wife, Madam Daeng, might alight from one of
the Lao Aviation DC3s. As a retired senior Party member,
Civilai had been allowed to stand on the tarmac beside the
ground controller, whose signals were generally ignored by
the Russian pilots.

The March nights were balmy, still carrying the weight
of the hot season days but fresh and breathable. On this
particular evening Civilai sweated as he watched the 3:40
P.M. scheduled flight arrive from Don Muang. It was after

eight. The porter wheeled the steps to the exit, climbed to the top and banged on the door. He then ran back down the steps and dragged the stair unit away from the fuselage so the stewardess could open the door. Civilai was ever bemused by the inefficiencies he saw around him every day.

A number of elderly, dark-suited men were first down. They were met by small delegations that whisked them off to waiting Zil limousines. They were followed by foreign-looking gentlemen in unfashionable clothes, men Civilai took to be Eastern European "experts." Technically, an expert was somebody who knew more than the Lao, which, Civilai conceded, included most of the civilized world. He watched the Soviets and East Germans and Poles, a smattering of Cubans and one or two Vietnamese advisers walk across the tarmac to the dilapidated terminal. They'd been shopping in Bangkok and proudly carried their duty-free goods for all to see. Even inside Laos these were good shopping days for the few people with money to spend. The Thai borders were currently open, the markets were full, consumer goods were available. But the locals knew this cross-border romance would not last for long so they had to stock up while they could.

Just as Civilai was about to head back into the terminal the last passengers stepped out of the aircraft. They were an odd-looking couple. They stood at the top of the steps and waved royally at nobody in particular. They blew kisses willy-nilly. They were dressed like golfers in loud slacks and even noisier polo shirts. But the oddest thing about them was the fact they were as hairless as boiled eggs. Dr. Siri's thick white mane and bushy eyebrows were gone. Madam Daeng was equally naked above the neck. Both seemed unconcerned about their looks. When they saw Civilai their smiles beamed.

Civilai approached them at a seventy-five-year-old trot and they descended with an equally mature enthusiasm. They hugged and kissed messily.

"*Bonsoir, mon copain,*" said Siri.

"I told him you'd be here to meet us," said Daeng.

"I never doubted it," said Siri.

"You both look even more bizarre than I remember you," said Civilai, breaking free from the embrace.

"And why not?" said Siri. "We have avoided a firing squad by a nipple and a half. We are back in our beloved Laos."

"And we bring souvenirs," said Daeng, handing him a bar of chocolate.

"How's Noo?" Siri asked.

"No better than I told you in our last phone call," said Civilai. "But still alive. I was worried when I didn't hear from you again."

"We got a little tied up," said Siri. "In fact the Thais placed a sort of discreet bounty on our heads. They didn't exactly put wanted posters up in post offices or in the newspapers but they did alert the scouts and the military checkpoints. Of course the land crossings were on alert."

"Flying was the safest way to get here," said Daeng.

"Does one no longer need passports for international air travel?" Civilai asked.

"That's a long story that needs a drink to be told properly," said Daeng.

"But it's true, we're lacking certain documents so it would be better if we didn't attempt to clear immigration," said Siri.

"Our passports are not exactly our own," said Daeng.

They were walking away from the terminal in the direction of the VIP gate. A security guard in a uniform that was too small for him called out, "Hey, Comrade. This way." He pointed toward the terminal. Civilai ignored him. Two porters were wheeling the baggage on a trolley whose wheels were diametrically opposed. It would be several days before the passengers could claim their bags.

"I hope you don't have any checked luggage," said Civilai.

The old couple patted their shoulder bags and smiled. At the VIP gate they didn't even bother to speak to the guard. Civilai glared disdainfully and the sentry opened the door a crack. Arrogance was a badge of authority in Laos.

In five minutes they were in the car and headed for That Luang. Civilai produced a bottle of Chardonnay and a corkscrew from the glove box.

"Well, it appears the borders are open again," said Daeng.

"We old politicians get first crack at the imports," said Civilai. "It was a present from the Thai coup leader's family cellars to our politburo. Wine isn't to the old boys' taste so they gave me a crate of the stuff. I'm afraid it isn't chilled."

They toasted their return.

"And I believe I've earned a story," said Civilai.

"Too right," said Siri. "And it all began, as you know, with us paddling across the river in a PVC rowing boat. So we didn't exactly clear Thai immigration on the way in. We did a little bit of business in Udon."

"Funny business," said Daeng.

"I'm telling the story," said Siri.

"Sorry, darling."

"Daeng had always wanted to visit Bangkok," Siri continued.

"It had been a dream of mine since I was a little girl," said Daeng. "But our budget was a little low."

"In fact we didn't have any money," said Siri.

"So my husband had the idea to impersonate the Supreme Patriarch of Laos and go to Bangkok on an official state visit."

Civilai inadvertently veered to the wrong side of the road in surprise. It didn't matter because his was the only vehicle at the time.

"You didn't!" he said.

"Yes, we did," said Daeng. "They were expecting the actual Supreme Patriarch and we sort of stepped in on his behalf. We knew he wouldn't be turning up. I was Siri's personal secretary-nun. Hence the haircut."

"They bought that?" said Civilai.

"It's amazing what you can get away with if you slot into people's expectations," said Siri.

"So I got my sightseeing tour," said Daeng. "And we were put up at the Dusit Thani and given the best treatment."

"And chocolate," said Siri.

Coming from anyone else, Civilai would have labeled such a claim ridiculous. But this was Siri and Daeng and they didn't follow any human rules.

"Wait," said Civilai, "this didn't have any bearing on Noo's unexpected release from custody by any chance?"

"Hard to say," said Daeng.

"We'd like to think so," said Siri. "We did ask a favor from the junta's own prime minister."

"You met the prime minister?" said Civilai, swerving again.

"Of course," said Siri. "I was the Supreme Patriarch. He wanted me to defect and make public my anti-socialist feelings. As you know, the Thai military are a little threatened by the thought of communism."

"You are insane, the pair of you," said Civilai, but he couldn't hold back his delight.

"*Merci*," said Siri.

"Didn't they even check your ID?"

"When Margaret Thatcher steps down from a jet do you see anyone rush up to check her passport?" said Siri.

"Surely someone would have noticed your face didn't match."

"Civilai, if you donned saffron robes and glasses they'd have given you the same reception. Most men over seventy look alike."

"You could have been killed if they caught you out."

"What a lovely way to go," said Daeng.

"We didn't get out a minute too soon," said Siri. "That phone call to you was our last official act. We were due to keep an appointment with the Thai Supreme Patriarch and he'd met our guy a few times. So we had to flee the scene. We borrowed clothes from a golfing Japanese couple in the suite below ours without their knowledge, evaded the security detail watching us and blended into Bangkok street life."

"We discovered Khao San," said Daeng. "Even the oddest-looking backpacker fits in there. We found a kindly but dishonest Chinese gentleman who was able to provide us Lao passports in twenty-four hours. He charged an absolute fortune."

"Which we didn't have," said Siri.

"So we broke into his office late that night and stole our

passports and enough money for the flight," said Daeng.
"He wasn't likely to complain to the police."

"And here we are," said Siri.

"Bravo," said Civilai.

Comrade Noo looked awful but Siri's prognosis was
positive.

"Everything seems to be in working order," he said. "I
couldn't have done anything Dtui didn't."

The household clapped.

"So why doesn't he wake up?" asked young Mee.

The girl lived there with her mother and younger
brother and several other squatters. It was hard to keep
count. Siri and Daeng had turned their government allotted residence into something of a hostel for the homeless
and helpless. It was a functioning commune embedded
deep in a non-functioning communist state. Siri and
Daeng themselves lived above their noodle shop.

"It's called a trauma," said Siri. "Sometimes, something
so horrible happens that your mind can't take it anymore.
It shuts up shop and puts a 'closed' sign in the window.
Comrade Noo is in there and his parts are recovering very
slowly but his mind isn't ready to come out. I can't imagine
what they did to him but he needs time every bit as much
as he needs medicine."

Over some eleven bottles of Lao rice whisky and endless
plates of pork *lahp* and spicy salad, the residents listened
to Siri and Daeng's amazing adventures in Thailand. All
the couple left out were tales of possession and séances
and running battles with malevolent spirits, even though
they were true. Just as there were bureaucratic layers of
impossibility, so there were supernatural dimensions that

rational educated people in the West would never believe to exist.

The average Lao, brought up in a small community, had no doubts that there were spirits. They sought advice from them. They asked for forgiveness. Even the business people in the capital erected spirit houses to placate the ghosts. Many claimed to have seen the phantoms but few would have had the type of relationship Dr. Siri had developed. Despite his scientific training, Siri had been forced to concede that there were spirits. He would have preferred it to be otherwise but he was undeniably possessed by a thousand-year-old shaman by the name of Yeh Ming. The old Hmong had never made direct contact with Siri but had been a magnet for a menagerie of ghosts that had passed in and out of the doctor's life. This science-versus-supernatural dichotomy had fascinated and confounded him in equal measure.

Only recently had Siri learned the fundamentals of communication with the dead. Portents had shown that he would someday gain control over his innate abilities. But he was seventy-five—a few months off seventy-six—living in a population that barely made it past fifty. He was starting to wonder whether being dead would be such a bad thing. It would certainly simplify matters. What better way to communicate with spirits than to become one?

In the meantime, his only functioning spirit guide was a boisterous transvestite fortune-teller by the name of Bpoo. They didn't get along. She was sarcastic and rude and even though she saw the future she kept it to herself. She was forever criticizing the doctor for his slow progress as a medium.

Of late, Siri's social circle had changed somewhat. He

spent more time with shamans and healers. During an audience with a witch in the north, for example, he'd made a dubious deal that affected both himself and Daeng. The woman produced elixirs that substituted one condition for another; the witch had replaced Madam Daeng's chronic rheumatism with a tail. This was an exchange Daeng was delighted with; Siri had no complaints. In fact he found her new appendage somewhat erotic.

The witch's solution to Siri's problem, however—that of his inability to talk to spirits—was a little more complicated. And as a result of her elixir he had started to disappear from time to time. He found himself in places created in his own mind. Daeng would turn over in bed to find a warm but empty place beside her. Yet lately, when he was no longer in the same dimension as his wife, he had discovered portals to the other side. He learned that those who resided there believed that the other side was where Siri had come from. All very confusing even to the doctor and not at all helpful when it came to his hobby. Dr. Siri was in fact a most competent amateur detective and as such one should imagine that seeing spirit signs everywhere would be an invaluable asset. Yet only once had he been able to interpret their significance before the case's resolution. Invariably he was left to his own devices to solve mysteries in the old fashioned traditions of his hero, Inspector Maigret.

Other Titles in the Soho Crime Series

FRANCINE MATHEWS
(Nantucket)
Death in the Off-Season
Death in Rough Water
Death in a Mood Indigo
Death in a Cold Hard Light
Death on Nantucket
Death on Tuckernuck

SEICHŌ MATSUMOTO
(Japan)
Inspector Imanishi Investigates

MAGDALEN NABB
(Italy)
Death of an Englishman
Death of a Dutchman
Death in Springtime
Death in Autumn
The Marshal and the Murderer
The Marshal and the Madwoman
The Marshal's Own Case
The Marshal Makes His Report
The Marshal at the Villa Torrini
Property of Blood
Some Bitter Taste
The Innocent
Vita Nuova
The Monster of Florence

FUMINORI NAKAMURA
(Japan)
The Thief
Evil and the Mask
Last Winter, We Parted
The Kingdom
The Boy in the Earth
Cult X

STUART NEVILLE
(Northern Ireland)
The Ghosts of Belfast
Collusion
Stolen Souls
The Final Silence
Those We Left Behind
So Say the Fallen
The Traveller & Other Stories

(Dublin)
Ratlines

REBECCA PAWEL
(1930s Spain)
Death of a Nationalist
Law of Return
The Watcher in the Pine
The Summer Snow

KWEI QUARTEY
(Ghana)
Murder at Cape Three Points
Gold of Our Fathers
Death by His Grace
The Missing American
Sleep Well, My Lady

QIU XIAOLONG
(China)
Death of a Red Heroine
A Loyal Character Dancer
When Red Is Black

JAMES SALLIS
(New Orleans)
The Long-Legged Fly
Moth
Black Hornet
Eye of the Cricket
Bluebottle
Ghost of a Flea

Sarah Jane

JOHN STRALEY
(Sitka, Alaska)
The Woman Who Married a Bear
The Curious Eat Themselves
The Music of What Happens
Death and the Language
of Happiness
The Angels Will Not Care
Cold Water Burning
Baby's First Felony

(Cold Storage, Alaska)
The Big Both Ways
Cold Storage, Alaska
What Is Time to a Pig?

AKIMITSU TAKAGI
(Japan)
The Tattoo Murder Case
Honeymoon to Nowhere

AKIMITSU TAKAGI CONT.
The Informer

HELENE TURSTEN
(Sweden)
Detective Inspector Huss
The Torso
The Glass Devil
Night Rounds
The Golden Calf
The Fire Dance
The Beige Man
The Treacherous Net
Who Watcheth
Protected by the Shadows

Hunting Game
Winter Grave
Snowdrift

An Elderly Lady Is Up
to No Good

ILARIA TUTI
(Italy)
Flowers over the Inferno
The Sleeping Nymph

JANWILLEM VAN DE WETERING
(Holland)
Outsider in Amsterdam
Tumbleweed
The Corpse on the Dike
Death of a Hawker
The Japanese Corpse
The Blond Baboon
The Maine Massacre
The Mind-Murders
The Streetbird
The Rattle-Rat
Hard Rain
Just a Corpse at Twilight
Hollow-Eyed Angel
The Perfidious Parrot
The Sergeant's Cat:
Collected Stories

JACQUELINE WINSPEAR
(1920s England)
Maisie Dobbs
Birds of a Feather